HER CAPRICE

Keira Dominguez

www.BOROUGHSPUBLISHINGGROUP.com

HER CAPRICE
Copyright © 2019 KEIRA DOMINGUEZ

ISBN 978-1-948029-67-4

For The Uncrushable Debbie West

4

ACKNOWLEDGMENTS

I would like to thank the Klickitat Writers – Christine Sandgren, Afton Nelson and Marianne Monson – for pounding the table and shouting, "It's a romance! Where is the romance?!", when I needed them to. I would also like to thank an army of beta readers, particularly Mandy Dominguez, Kylene Grell, Amanda Wanner and Donna Lessard, for going over every line and giving me priceless feedback. Finally, I offer my deepest gratitude to my husband Nathan, who, like LeBron, is the greatest of all time.

HER CAPRICE

Chapter One

"She's ready," Mama stated, and the two young women fell to work at once. One of them stretched a measuring tape between the points of Beatrice's shoulders and the other wrote the numbers down in a slim black book.

Scratch went the pencil as the women took more measurements—bust, neck, the length of her back, the span between her neck and her heels, hips, waist—until the page titled "Miss Beatrice Thornton, April 18, 1812" was filled.

They left as quickly as they came, and Mama busied herself sorting the pile of parcels into a more correct order, her nervous energy making her daughters as silent as a graveyard. Penny shot Beatrice a cross look. "Liar," she mouthed.

Beatrice ignored it, longing to reach for the woollen shawl she'd discarded with her dress. She was sick of freezing on the fitting room platform in a thin shift. She was sick of pretending that chartreuse was her favourite colour. She was sick of her little sister calling her a liar because of it.

She would be far sicker by the Season's end.

Beatrice took a deep breath. She was in London, and in the hallowed shop of Madame Durand, no less. There was magic here—possibilities unfolding with every tinkle of the bell over the front door—and she felt an unformed prayer press against her lips, conflicting with the dutiful course she had decided upon. If a miracle could come to pass, then surely—*surely*—it would be at the hand of Madame Durand.

Beatrice wanted such small miracles. A closet full of lovely things to liven her time in London and friends to attend lectures and parties with. To be free of Mama standing quite so close, to dance with a young man… Her lips twisted and she finished her list with things as likely to happen: to part the Red Sea and turn water into wine.

She ought to be long past hoping for miracles.

A shiver went through her and she wished again for her shawl. Thankfully, the proprietess did not keep them waiting.

"Madame. I wish to—" Mama began, commanding in her elegant walking dress. Her honey-blonde hair, threaded lightly with grey, was neatly tucked under a scrap of lace. Not even the smallest whiff of rural Dorset clung to her hem.

But Madame clicked her tongue and held up an imperious hand.

"No. I will need a moment," she said, in a light Gallic accent. Mama made her displeasure evident by using excessively good posture. Madame ignored it, turning to study Beatrice.

Beatrice wanted to shift on nervous feet but made herself stand, tense and frozen. She wasn't used to scrutiny. Nobody ever looked at her. Not the neighbours who hardly took note of the part she played as the colourless, sickly Thornton girl. Not her parents who took her compliance for granted. Not even herself. When she wasn't really looking, it was much easier to ignore the fact that her life had become as constraining as a too-tight shoe.

Beatrice gave her head a tiny shake. This restiveness would disappear in the hurricane of activity that would soon pluck them up.

Madame walked slowly around the platform and began, her assistant scribbling in her book as she spoke. "Tall for a girl. Nice figure. Nothing serious we have to hide...." Beatrice found her hand picked up and turned over. "Good hands, slim wrists"—the dressmaker twitched up her shift a couple of inches—"and ankles." Madame looked square into Beatrice's face. "Green eyes—leaf green. Light brown hair, like a, like a..." Her hand whirled in the air for a moment and then she snapped her fingers. "...camel."

Beatrice's eyes crinkled at the image, sudden laughter lighting her face.

"A sense of humour, too. A pity your hair could not decide whether to be blonde or brunette. Is it long?" she asked, and Beatrice nodded.

"Older than our usual debutantes...." Her voice contained a faint question.

"Twenty," Beatrice replied, determined not to sound apologetic.

Madame's eyebrow flicked up and Mama explained, "We were in mourning for two years. Her grandfather and then her aunt."

"A whole year for an aunt?"

Beatrice darted her eyes to Mama, who only lifted her chin.

"My condolences, of course." Madame dipped her chin. "But it makes it easier since there is no puppy fat to manage. Not a raving beauty, but we can make a good deal of your daughter. Better than has been made."

She turned disgusted eyes to the hook holding the old blue gown Beatrice had come in. Beatrice was surprised at the protective feeling she had for the thing.

"Madame—" Mama broke in.

Madame paid no attention. "But at least the colour was correct." She half-turned her head, calling out to the assistant, "Blues and greens for her—small patterns are acceptable. Soft whites, like cream on the top of a fresh pail of milk—"

Beatrice could not stop the word when it came on a delighted breath of sound. "Yes."

Mama's eyes shot daggers and she gave her head a tiny, furious shake. Beatrice blushed hot and swallowed her words.

"Rich pinks. No light yellow. No brown. It would ruin her." Madame clapped her hands, almost conjuring the dresses out of thin air, and Beatrice felt her heart beat like an ocean in her chest.

"Madame," Mama called, not quite shouting. "A word, if you please."

Madame Durand turned with exaggerated patience and raised her eyebrow again, communicating the right mixture of inquiry and rudeness that her people had mastered.

Madame dismissed her assistant and Mama sent Penny to the front of the shop to select a few of her own things. As her little sister left, Beatrice envied the jonquil muslin that graced her girlish figure. It had all the hallmarks of Mama's excellent taste, and made her look exactly what she was, fresh and fourteen.

"What is it you wish to say, ma'am?" Madame Durand asked. Beatrice felt a flush crawl over her skin and began an earnest prayer that Mama, for all her authority, would not be able to bend the formidable dressmaker to her will.

Into the silence, Mama dropped a small conversational pebble that sank and rippled out in waves. "We wish to hire you on a limited basis."

Madame's superior eyebrow crept higher. "Limited? The people who can afford me do not do so for my limited service."

"Thorntons pay their bills on time," Mama scoffed, looking grander than Beatrice had ever seen her. "Though we want your service to be limited, I am prepared to pay the full sum."

That got Madame's attention. Mama pulled a sheaf of papers from her reticule, handing them over to the Frenchwoman.

Madame leafed through them, moving her lips over the lines as she read, shuffling them back and forth as a sharp, vertical line formed between her brows. "Your own designs?" she asked politely, the promise of payment, no doubt, colouring her tone. "They are not—" She pulled one of the papers loose and stabbed at it with a finger. "This is most unorthodox. I do not know what they are doing in Dorset, but if it is this, it is a wonder they are still breeding."

Money would only go so far with Madame.

The famous dressmaker moved her arms wide, hardly encompassing her disapproval. "No flounces or trim anywhere, and that the neck is to be cut—cut nowhere at all. Has Miss Thornton become a leper that one should shroud her so fully?" She smacked the pages with the back of her hand.

Beatrice dreaded these gowns, never mind the lies she told Penny. But this was what Mama—what she, herself, had planned. While the dressmaker became more voluble, Beatrice forced herself to stand silent.

"And this. You have written that it should be made in a colour you've named 'old jellied salmon.' The mind reels. The stomach revolts."

Mama turned with rebuking calmness to the table behind her. "I anticipated your difficulty in finding what I wished. I took the liberty of shopping for fabrics at Grafton's before coming."

Madame glowered at the pile. "If they carry rotting salmon silk, my estimation of that establishment will plummet like a rock."

It did plummet like a rock.

Mama unfurled the salmon silk and the boiled yellow velvet and a brown muslin stripe that Mama insisted should be cut width-wise, and many other less awful fabrics whose only sin was that they were not flattering to her daughter in the least.

Beatrice looked longingly at the faded blue cotton dress. Had she really hated it only last week? She remembered that it felt tired and drab and made her blend into the walls, but now she imagined herself pulling it down and banging past her mother and a shocked

Madame. She would charge through the door with the bell jangling after her and sprint into the street with it, pinning it closed as she went.

She looked away and swallowed, repeating the litany which had borne her though the last six months. *The British Museum and the Royal Gallery... and Astley's Amphitheatre... and Gunter's ices, and all the books I could want from Hatchard's.*

"Show me the next outrage," Madame instructed, dropping the brown muslin stripe. Mama continued unwrapping parcels, not finished until an entire wardrobe's worth of horrors lay on the table looking as discordant as the contents of a rag-man's cart.

Madame fell into a chair and leaned against the table, her head in her hands. "We shall have to call a priest to bless this room when you go. Those horrors are surely proof that *le bon Dieu* did not create everything. I will not lay those at His door." She scrubbed her face and slapped her hands on her thighs, coming to a decision. "I cannot do it. I won't."

Le bon Dieu, was this a reprieve? Beatrice wanted to throw her arms about Madame's neck and weep. For *how* could the monstrosities be made if no one would make them?

"Let me speak plainly. Those fabrics are ruinous, Mrs Thornton," Madame stated. "Do you *want* her Season to be a failure?"

Silence reigned in the tiny fitting room and Beatrice made sure not to look Mama in the face. Madame had actually spoken the words aloud, but she didn't know—couldn't possibly—that a failed Season was exactly what she was planning. She and Mama and Papa.

Mama gathered her composure. "I will not accept your refusal, Madame," she sniffed.

Madame pinched the bridge of her nose. "This is not how it was with your eldest daughter"—she snapped her fingers several times, searching for the name—"Miss Deborah. No expense was spared in that case. Her clothes were some of my best."

Mama's lips thinned.

"You stayed in Dorset, if I remember," Madame said, her look shrewd. "And left the whole of it to her godmother. Perhaps you should—"

"You do not need to involve yourself in my personal arrangements, Madame."

"I agree. I do not need to involve myself at all. You could hire a rough needlewoman mending sails down at the docks to execute those...." Madame left the rest unsaid and gave the shudder that Beatrice had been holding.

Mama held up a firm hand. "Throughout London, your establishment is famous for discretion. Gossip is said to come in these doors but does not come out. It is a rare quality, and one I will pay handsomely for."

Madame's eyes narrowed. "How handsomely?"

Beatrice stared hard at her toes.

The number Mama named made Madame suck in her breath and still her mouth. A curt nod and the bargain was struck. Beatrice's lip shook before she captured it between her teeth. Why be upset now? She had known this day was coming for a long time.

Mama smoothed her hair and Madame smiled a tight, sour smile. The fittings proceeded in the regular fashion—if one ignored that Madame sounded like an angry bull, breathing in furious gusts. The assistants, when they joined the room, fluttered nervously at the sight of the fabrics and gave one another speaking looks over Madame's bent head.

Standing as still as could be, Beatrice swallowed. Madame had been her last bulwark. It was going to unfold just as Mama said, and she went hot and cold at the thought. However, she was in *London*. Beatrice became pliant, letting her arms be raised and then lowered as the women manipulated the fabric on her body.

Gunter's. Hatchard's. Astley's. The British Museum.... She blew the sting of tears away with slow and steady breaths as she was turned this way and that.

While taking the last fitting for a walking dress in the hated chartreuse, Penny entered again, settling onto the chair.

"Looser, Madame," Mama instructed, repeating a phrase that had become a litany. "More fullness in the bust and sleeve."

Madame glared. "You should go to the fabric emporium and throw a bolt over her shoulder, my lady. Maybe tie a rope around her waist." She waved and Mama, possibly feeling her luck running out, subsided to a spot near the wall.

Penny's mouth dropped open. "Ooh, it's dreadful."

Beatrice blushed, but was quick with an answer. "No, it isn't. I'm sure Mama knows what would suit me best."

Simple. Plausible. Beatrice almost believed it herself, which, as Mama had instructed, was the best way to tell a lie.

She danced a little farther out on a limb. "I've been buried so long at Thorndene that I can hardly be expected to know the fashions."

The words jostled against the careful fiction Beatrice had been constructing, threatening to topple it. Seven years in Dorset and still Beatrice kept copies of *La Belle Assemblee* squirreled away among more worthy periodicals at her bedside. Beatrice stifled a sigh. If those fashionable pages could know what she was doing, the paper would curl up and burst into flame.

It took every ounce of willpower to smile and say, "It will look different when the needlewomen begin." Madame, her mouth full of pins, snorted.

Penny blinked. "But I got such beautiful things. Why—"

"Penelope." Mama snapped, managing to threaten the loss of Penny's Hatchard's subscription and to send her back to Dorset without even saying the words.

Madame smiled and stirred the pot. "This one has taste, huh?"

She secured a pin under Beatrice's arm and said to Mama, "If you would care to finish Miss Penelope's order, you may do so now. I have only a few more minutes with this. The mademoiselles," she nodded to her assistants, "will attend you in the shop."

When the door clicked shut, Madame pinched Beatrice on the arm. "Ouch," she yelped, rubbing the spot and casting a wounded look at the dressmaker.

"Listen, girl. I am being paid enough to be *profoundly* incurious. You are trying to smile for your sister and trying to smile for your mother. A girl should smile a little for herself, *non*?"

Beatrice stared, her eyes like saucers.

Madame leaned close. "Not one of these dresses will suit you. I am sorry, but your Mama is a genius in her own way." She spread her hands. "Her taste is terrible, but her money is good. When you can, use a scarf—a pretty scarf in blue or green—or a hat that frames you." She spread her fingers across the crown of her head indicating the type of hat. "A gentleman, despite what pains we take, won't notice the horrors of the dress if you give him something else to look at."

Beatrice nodded and then her eyes were caught by her figure in the looking glass. She had none of Deborah's vivid colouring to carry off such a shade. Her quiet looks were well and truly eclipsed by the difficult green.

Madame followed her eyes. "Heaven knows how you will manage to make a match. I will light a candle for you, *mon petit*."

Beatrice's smile faded as Madame departed. A hundred such candles would do her no good. Scores of girls would be descending on London for the Season, all of them looking about for a husband, and each of their mothers would be as anxious to make them good marriages as the girls were themselves.

But Beatrice's mother was praying for failure. Marriage, as Beatrice had been told from the time she was thirteen, was not for her.

In the coming weeks, they must navigate the Season as quietly as possible and enjoy the pleasures of London. Mama had told her she was lucky not to have any other distractions. Beatrice blew a clean breath and shook her head. Mama was right.

But alone now, Beatrice allowed the voice at the back of her mind to speak.

Liar.

Chapter Two

Beatrice swallowed past a sudden lump in her throat as she watched a vision in pale blue and gold thread make her way up her godmother's grand stairway. It would be easier for her to leap across the English Channel than to bridge the gulf that lay between that gown and her own.

She gripped the handle of her fan as Mama's eyes roved over her person. What did she see? Hair bristling with hairpins. A face made sallow next to the uncompromising whiteness of the dress. A figure hidden by yards of unnecessary fabric. Mama ran proprietary hands along a seam and pulled out a loose thread, adjusting the neckline of Beatrice's gown.

"Best get it over with at once," Mama said, confronting the stairs like Saint George addressing the dragon. Beatrice felt a giggle bubble to the surface. This was ridiculous.

"What?" Mama snapped, as brittle as kindling.

"Nothing," Beatrice replied, tucking her smiles away. They would not be needed tonight. "We have nothing to fear. I'm well practiced at failure."

That put a pucker across Mama's smooth brow. "Tonight will be a great success if everyone decides that you are not worth knowing. See that you don't encourage—"

"I will be a ghost," Beatrice assured, careful not to crush the ivory fan. It would be a pity to damage it. The fan, at least, was beautiful.

But as they gained the top of the steps, the fan slipped from her fingers to dance at the end of its silken ribbon. Beatrice stood with her mouth slightly agape. Before this moment, she'd rather righteously talked herself out of having her head turned by London glitter—told herself she would be wise. *Fool.* Mama had never allowed her the excitements of even a country assembly and she was now hit with a wave of sensation—hundreds of shining candles reflecting from every surface, sweet perfume filling her nose, glinting jewels around every neck sparkling ostentatiously.

Thank heavens the steps of the dance were easy to follow. They ought to be—she'd learned them along with Deborah. But practicing the figures of a cotillion in Thorndene's empty ballroom with Penny banging out the music on the pianoforte or in a tiny drawing room with the carpets rolled back, partnering some elderly gentleman Mama deemed safe as he steered her into the tea table…. This was something else altogether.

Beatrice watched as an elegant young couple circled one another.

She began to sway ever so slightly, the heaviness of her gown swishing against her ankles until she felt Mama's eyes on her. She stilled at once and felt the warm flame of her own curiosity and humour snuff out like a candle pinched between wetted fingers. She didn't belong here. It had been stupid to think Mama could merely bring her to London and there wouldn't be a cost.

She was in London now. People would notice her—see how dreadful she looked, speak with her, and decide that she was as dull and lifeless as this wretched gown on her back.

She shifted on her toes, heat rushing to her cheeks, poised for flight.

Mama must have felt it because she held Beatrice's elbow fast and said in a strangled voice, "Oh Lord, here comes your godmother."

***

With a passion soul deep, Captain Henry Gracechurch wished to crawl into bed. One that didn't fold up, roll up, or rock to and fro with the waves. He blinked slowly and ran a gloved finger around his collar, looking for a clock. *Five after eleven.* Hours too early to leave.

"Speak of the devil," a drawling voice at his elbow muttered, and Henry turned to see a tall, black-haired man, slightly older than himself. "Brave Harry Gracechurch back from the wars."

The voice called him "Harry" like a schoolboy coaxing another off to mischief—as indeed the voice had done over and over.

"Fox," he exclaimed. "Good to see you." His hand clasped his cousin's and they clapped each other on the shoulders in a violent greeting that ended as Henry flicked the folds of Fox's cravat. "Such elegance you've achieved, cousin. I hate to damage it."

"Not all of us wish to broadcast that we are honest, upright, and out of funds," Fox answered, leaning back as he looked Henry over. "Particularly since I am none of those things. But where have you come from? I thought you were in Spain, hoping to get your head blasted off for King and country." Fox lifted two glasses of wine from a passing footman and handed one over to Henry.

"I was, but three weeks past. I've been travelling flat out." He'd been desperate to leave the past behind him, desperate to return to all that was secure and familiar.

"I doubt you will find England a tolerable reward for all that exertion."

Henry's face was impassive but he could feel the tight, tired drag around his eyes. Spain, with its starving peasants shattered by war, was even less tolerable. "Well, I'm not on leave. I brought the dispatches from Badajoz."

"Did you?" Fox asked, his look quickening. "Are you one of Wellington's precious couriers? This is famous—a ripe apple dropping in my hand. Tell me everything."

Henry nodded and took a drink from his glass, willing his hand to relax around the stem of it. Fox could have no idea of what "everything" entailed. And Henry would be shaking when he finished the telling. "It's bound to be in the papers tomorrow or the next day, I expect."

"Yes, but what's the point of meeting a relation—fresh from the front—if I can't hear the latest news from Spain before anyone else?"

"Is that why you are so pleased to see me?" Henry asked with a light smile, but he turned back to watch the dancers. "For news? Well, you'll know that Badajoz is taken." Henry tossed back the rest of his wine. "At great cost."

He didn't want to talk about the battle—or all the battles before it—so someone could show it off for its novelty, like a new snuffbox or team of horses. It was the last thing Henry wished to do—arrange a table-top battle for a crowd, lining up cutlery and dishes to represent his fallen brothers-in-arms.

"Do you think Wellington will press further inland right away or hold the line?" Fox asked.

This time Henry's smile was real. "I remember when all you talked of was drinking, wenching, or gambling. What category does that question fall under, do you suppose?"

"Dredging up my bad old days, indeed, Harry. It's gambling, I should think. Is Wellington much of a gambler?"

"No more than I am."

Fox looked into his glass as though the wine were sour. "Temperate as a Methodist."

Henry ignored that. One had to with Fox. Petty insults were his mother tongue.

"Wellington doesn't gamble at war. It's not gambling if you know you're going to win."

Fox waved a servant over to take their glasses, and as he did so, a gentleman—a towering figure—bowed himself in front of Henry.

"Captain Gracechurch?" The man had a black armband and Henry knew, almost before he opened his mouth, what he would say. Henry pushed his fatigue aside and felt his collar lift away from his throat as he straightened, readying himself for the question when it came.

"My boy was William Jameson, Third Division. He fell at Ciudad Rodrigo. Our hostess said you might have known him?" he asked, hopeful. "A big, yellow-haired boy with shoulders—" The man spread his hands in front of him as wide as his own.

"I did," Henry replied, scraping around in his memory for something—anything to give the father, like alms to a blind man. He spoke without hesitation of the little he knew of the lad's regimental honours, then added, "They would call him Snuff. He made noises—"

"In his sleep." The man smiled, his expression telling Henry better than words that he knew the sound. Perhaps Lieutenant Jameson had made that noise as a boy—had made it in his mother's arms, even. It stuck in his throat, that thought, threatening to unman him even here in the middle of a party.

Dogs, kicked and beaten, knew enough to find a quiet place to curl up and lick their wounds. Henry glanced to the dance floor, seeing faces flushed with wine and laughter. He hadn't the sense of a dog.

"Do you know Sir Neil?" Fox asked Henry when the old giant had bowed himself away. Fox's gaze followed the man across the ballroom. Henry shook his head. "He works with Lord Liverpool—something to do with the war. You can introduce me the next time you meet. His is a valuable acquaintance."

Fox's eyes stayed pinned to the man's back. "Are you getting a lot of that—mothers weeping into your neckcloth, fathers coming to ask after their dead? You ought to prepare something." Fox placed his hand over his breast. "'He was slain with his sword raised, charging into the teeth of the dread host.' Carried away on the wings of angel maidens, or some such. Think how much more thrilling that would sound."

Fox had never been fired with youthful idealism, but he would not have said such a thing when they were boys. The man he'd become—with his sharp white neck cloth, his smooth black hair, and his voice that measured and judged—would need to have common decency explained to him. Henry opened his mouth to do so.

"Will you look at that?" Fox laughed, lifting his chin and nodding at the dance floor.

Henry turned and took it in. *Poor thing.* He didn't give himself time to think before tearing off after her.

***

Beatrice stared dumbstruck at Lord Knowlton's back.

Lady Sherbourne, her godmama, had introduced them, hissing behind her fan, "The only son of an old duke. Nothing like jumping in with both feet." And then she had carted Mama off to the card room, leaving Beatrice to get on as best she could.

Lord Knowlton, in turn, had given Beatrice a look like she was a crate of dry goods dropped at the delivery door.

Now, after a truly dreadful dance, he wasn't even giving her that. Instead, without so much as a bow, he was chasing after a girl whose tiny bodice had been performing heroic, if ultimately futile, work in aid of public decency.

Beatrice looked after him, furrowing her brow, the shock of his rudeness rooting her in place. So little was demanded of the clod—light conversation, a few observations on the weather this time of year and, finally, after they'd both decided they would rather die than be paired off again, he would escort her from the floor and they'd declare it the nicest half-hour either of them had ever spent.

But, no. The slithering reptile was completely gone. She stared after him in bewildered outrage until the sound of the room changed. No music for the moment and no sound of footsteps walking on and off the floor, only a low chatter ebbing away.

Beatrice looked around, the hairs on her arms standing up. She was suddenly alive to the fact that she was the only person conspicuously still on the vast ballroom floor—almost in the centre. She ground her teeth, incandescent with fear and rage, as her face went a telltale red.

How dare London be such a crushing disappointment? How dare it serve up a man who was no better than a... a...? There were no names she could think of that would not be an insult to idiots, vermin, and bastards.

Heads were beginning to swing toward her and Beatrice felt her cheeks turn white, leached of colour. Should she walk backward until she could melt into the crowd or pretend to answer a wave across the room and dash off purposefully? Flying out of the room was hardly possible. The back of her neck prickled and she could feel eyes sweeping around the ballroom, stopping on her lone figure.

If Mama and Papa had allowed her even one visit to the local assembly, she might not be so utterly at sea. Still, Mama would charge to her rescue, if only she could be found. Beatrice stretched her neck and raised herself onto her tiptoes, ready to fabricate an acquaintance over near the tea board—the shame of it making her eyes burn. *Blast that man.*

In the dreadful silence, she heard a scuffing sound and turned to watch as a soldier in a scarlet uniform broke past the wall of bystanders. He walked toward her, his steps unnaturally loud in the silence. "Thank you for waiting for me," he called, his voice amused but apologetic, and loud enough to carry to the edge of the floor. "I've been looking forward to this set all evening."

He bowed over her hand and whispered a command: "Chin up. Smile like you're happy to see me."

Beatrice squeezed this stranger's fingers, feeling an immediate lightness. Her breath broke as she exhaled, but she was proud of her control. Her lips arranged themselves into the proper shape.

"Good show," he commended, and the praise warmed her. "Captain Gracechurch, at your service. Your name, miss?"

"Thornton." All this was offered with set, smiling expressions. Their eyes darted around the room as though they were spies in the middle of enemy territory, waiting for encoded messages or a hail of bullets.

"Do you want me to turn an ankle or go into a swoon?" she asked as couples began forming the set, filling the space around them like a flood of water. He looked confused. "To leave the dance floor," she explained. "It's quite all right now. You've saved me from the worst of it and no one will care if we have to leave. I was taught how to fake an excellent headache."

"Along with drawing and embroidery?" He stood, looking down at her, the warm brown of his eyes dancing with humour. "You're not thinking of abandoning me here, are you?"

Her smile was real this time, though hesitant. She didn't speak with men—not unless one counted her father or the old rector down in Morton's Cross. And Captain Gracechurch didn't look a thing like the rector. Too young, too strong. Several locks of dark hair curled boyishly around his ears and there was a jagged little scar on the side of his chin, white against the weathered brown of his skin. Perhaps he went about beating sense into only sons of old dukes all the time.

"You don't have to do this," she said, her voice husky.

He lifted one hand and bowed over it as the opening strains of the dance began. "I'm going to get myself talked about if you don't take pity on me."

A less pitiable creature could not be imagined. Still, her eyes shifted to the card room doors. Mama might walk through them at any moment. The familiar fear kept her frozen in place as another, foreign emotion seemed to push her right between the shoulder blades. She couldn't remember wanting anything as badly as she wanted to dance with Captain Gracechurch now.

"Come," he encouraged, his voice inviting.

She looked down at his hand holding hers. What could be the harm in it? Beatrice took a giddy breath, cognizant of a warm flicker of excitement underneath her ribs, and allowed him to draw her into the figures of the dance.

Was it excitement or mortification that made her movements so stilted and clumsy? "Pardon," she murmured when she trod on his toes a second time. "I'm not well-practiced at this. You should let me—"

"Oh no you don't," he scoffed, his voice soft and his mouth tilting up on one side in a way she found beguiling. "I rescued you. You owe me."

"Owe?" Her eyes flashed with amused outrage at the word and she forgot her mother's instructions—to lower her head and whisper and flatten her personality so that there was nothing to see. "You carried yourself here, Captain. I did not drag you by the heels. If you insist on this dance, it serves you right if I crush your foot." She snorted. "Owe."

He answered with a grin and she noticed that her dancing was smooth now, unexceptional. He'd provoked her on purpose.

At length he said, "I hope you do not take Knowlton's shabby manners to heart, Miss Thornton. It was kind of him to spell out so clearly that he is not the man for you. Think of the progress we have made in London already, weeding one out."

She laughed outright, drawing the eyes of the nearer dancers. "We? Are we allies fighting a common cause?" she asked, relief and amusement carrying her far beyond the boundary Mama had marked out. She flushed, wishing to call the words back. He'd simply misspoken, and she'd made a reply which sounded, even to her untrained ears, unmistakably flirtatious—all while wearing this ridiculous dress. She held her breath for his set down.

"It wouldn't do to march into battle alone, miss," he stated, missing his cue to draw away from her, a chance-met stranger. "We would do well to form an alliance in the event Lord Knowlton is carried away by another benevolent fit and wishes to teach you more of his character."

"He will not get the chance."

His voice was hushed. "Good show, Miss Thornton," he murmured, turning her about in the dance, his head inclined to hers. She felt him touching—pressing—into the space she always afforded herself and tensed for a moment. No. It would be quite all right. She looked like a dowd—and helpless too. There was no fear he would follow her up. Still, for the first time, she appreciated why Mama disliked dancing so much.

As awareness of him lit every nerve, she rushed to fill the silence. "Now, Captain, we must discover how I may be of service to you." His look was questioning. "In your search for a wife, of course. Shall I draw up a list of acquaintances? Eavesdrop on conversations in the retiring room? Perhaps if I knew your list of requirements."

"There are other reasons to come up to London besides marriage," he chuckled.

"No. Really?" she asked, open-eyed and incredulous, a little too surprised to be believed.

He clutched his heart. "A direct hit, Miss Thornton. I should not have assumed that was your aim in coming to Town. Allow me to repent. What, may I ask, brings you to London?"

Drat. The satisfaction of scoring off him was short-lived. It had been a sweet little challenge to trip him up, to catch him in the snare of his own presumptions. She was the one caught now. The figures of the dance parted them and she searched for something true she could tell him.

"Parliament," she replied, when they came together again. "My father and I subscribe to the Parliamentary journals and follow the speeches closely. Being in London alongside these political figures, at the same time these issues are debated, will be incredibly interesting."

He cleared his throat. "A worthy occupation."

Her eyes widened, but would he see the laughter in them? "A terrible thing to say. 'Worthy occupation.'"

"Do I betray my disinterest?"

"Acute disinterest. Flooding the room, getting all over my slippers."

A dimple made a deep tuck in his cheek. "The soldiery are the subject of debates, but don't often have a voice in them."

"How wonderful to discover a gentleman who understands how the ladies feel," she answered, having no compunction for closing a trap he all but walked into.

"Dear Miss Thornton," he grinned. "You do have a knack of knocking a fellow back on his heels." Though he looked as though he enjoyed the exercise.

She certainly did. Beatrice took a long, clandestine look at the back of his neck as he turned—red regimentals banding a strong, brown column. Had she ever felt so satisfied in company before?

No.

Why not?

This was not Mama's voice in her head, but her own. The question hovered on the edge of Beatrice's mind as they moved in time with the music, hands catching hold of one another. She found an answer. Mama hadn't gotten to him first.

Mama had a way of preparing people for her least favourite offspring. She would say her daughter was a girl who wasn't well, was shy, self-effacing, hardly bothered with her own appearance, and preferred her own company. People found it easy to see what they had been told and with Mama's heavy words weighing Beatrice down they'd fill any gaps like a winter blanket.

The captain, however, knew nothing of the sort. Beatrice danced on light feet, enjoying the weightlessness of his lack of expectations. Of course it gave her pleasure.

The answer was a clean one. Clouding the issue was the way her eyes lingered on him when she thought he wasn't looking.

"When you aren't reading political broadsheets and Parliamentary periodicals, Miss Thornton, what else will you do to fill your time in Town?"

"Nothing so virtuous, I assure you. I plan to do lots of shopping while we are here."

She felt his eyes flick over her gown and wanted to cross her arms over her bodice. Again, she had so easily walked onto ground which seemed to crumble beneath her feet. He was much too easy to talk to.

"And what brings you here?" she asked, turning his attention. "Your regiment?"

"My regiment is in Spain, Miss Thornton," he stated, using her name as correctly as any distant acquaintance. Still, he somehow made her feel as warm as a cat in a patch of sunlight. "I am selling out." A shadow crossed his face and he banished it with visible effort—at least, it was visible to her. His smile was forced, his voice hearty. "And that's enough talk of the war in a ballroom."

Manners dictated that she pretended she'd seen no moment of gravity and unease—and she did it, smiling with blank brightness as he turned the topic. But he'd let her see himself for that brief moment, and she heard, in her mind, the groaning and creaking of a ship when the great square sails caught the wind, snapping them taut, and changing its course. She had liked what she saw.

"The music has gone, Miss Thornton," he noted, shaking her from her reverie. "If we don't make our bows now, you'll be stranded out here with me."

"A fate worse than death," she smiled, sinking before him.

He reached for her hand, guiding her to a chair as if she were made of Dresden china.

Beatrice looked down at their hands. She was wearing long white gloves that Mama had not bothered to ruin, and she took pathetic little satisfaction in her graceful arm and elegant fingers. He was wearing short gloves, exposing the cords of his wrist as he turned his hand back to hold hers. They were not touching at all really. The thought made her frown.

"You're quite happy to be left without your mother?" he asked, seeing her to a chair.

He could not know how much. "Quite." She looked up at him, worrying her lower lip, her tone suddenly sober. "You must know that I am in your debt. I wasn't sure what to do. May I thank you for—"

He shook his head. "Miss Thornton," he said, "it was the nicest half hour I've spent in years. Don't you dare thank me. Not for that."

Then he ran a gloved hand over his face. Why hadn't she noticed before? The poor man looked as though he'd been up for days and it was only the starch of his scarlet uniform holding him upright. Still, he was smiling, lending her courage if she needed it. Faced with such a man, she must rise to meet his challenge.

He looked around, surveying the crowd, and finally sat at her side, the delicate cane chair creaking with his weight. "I'll keep you company until your next partner comes, if I may."

Could he see the pulse beating at the base of her neck? "Oh," she breathed. "How kind." She began twisting the spines of her fan. There would be no partner coming, and, suddenly, she had an image of their grey and dusty selves, waiting in this spot until the house fell down around their ears.

Her lips twitched. Mama would be here long before then, snatching Beatrice up and running her as fast and as far from the personable young man at her side as she could get. With the feeling that the last sands were tumbling down the hourglass, Beatrice glanced around the room.

"Tell me, is this the usual kind of party?" It was uninspired, as questions went, but she'd never had reason to store up half an hour's conversation with a man who wasn't the rector. And, though something of an expert, Beatrice was not prepared to hold forth on the subject of leaky church roofs.

"Are you so new to London?" he asked.

"The Thornton household is quite fresh from the country. My hands still smell of turnips."

"Then let me tell you that this is a good deal better than the crowded rooms and thin wine of most balls. Lady Sherbourne is a noted hostess, and her invitations are highly sought after. So, you must have much more to recommend you than turnips."

"Turnips are not to be patronized, sir." The smile on her lips faded as she looked past him—Mama, lending an ear to the lady at her side but sweeping her eyes across the ballroom.

A metallic shiver bolted through Beatrice's limbs at the thought of being caught like this. She might as well be caught in a passionate clinch in the darkened garden for all the distinction Mama would make.

There was only one thing to be done. Beatrice moved her foot over the hem of a lace-trimmed petticoat and stood, pleased to hear the sound of ripping material.

An escape made possible.

***

The retiring room was empty. Beatrice twirled around the door and, leaning against it, pressed her palms flat on the panels.

Breathe. She would need to compose herself before she flew right up to the ceiling in sheer delight. Catching a glance at herself in the mirror, she laughed. The reflection sparkled with the energy of a summer storm.

But the longer she held her own gaze, the more her smile faded. When she put hesitant fingers to her hair, it hurt to touch, each strand scraped into a tight bun and bruised at the root. No ribbons. No curls. No lover's flowers. The dull silk of her dress hung from her frame, bunching in odd places. The ragged petticoat trailed on the floor. She pinned that up at once and then, reaching behind her, she gathered up several loose inches of the lifeless bodice, pulling it into a closer fit.

But she couldn't go back out there with her hand twisted up behind her all night. She dropped the fabric, letting it fall into shapelessness again.

The price of a London Season had seemed small when Mama had put the matter before her. She might do and see all she liked as long as she excited nobody's interest. But her mind returned to the captain. She could not seem to help it. But she would not see him again, called a voice from the back of her mind that was persistent and sounded remarkably like Mama.

Pressing her fingers around her scalp, Beatrice relaxed the knot of hair at the back. It was silly to have one's head turned by the first man who showed an interest.

Her mind was a wheel bowling along the ground, slowing at that word, circling around it. *Interest.*

It might have easily been pity, she thought, her stomach twisting. Pity was a perfectly fine emotion to feel for a lame dog, but if that's what the captain felt... *How horrible.*

Then again, it might be simple courtesy. So... pity, or manners, or masculine interest? Beatrice sent a dark look to the ceiling. If she had gone about in society at all, she might know. But here she was, twenty years old, and still as unsure as her little sister.

The voice in the back of her mind grew louder and more commanding. It didn't matter what the captain felt—couldn't possibly ever matter. It whispered into her ears, holding her by the wrist, though she wished to wriggle away and shrink away from it. Captain Gracechurch was not for her.

Drawing a stiff breath, she looked up, blinking. This feeling, as insubstantial as a cobweb floating in the breeze—this liking—it was stupid to make so much of it. It mustn't be allowed to take root.

Still, she thought, tugging off a glove and wandering over to the window, it was a shock to discover how much it mattered. Reaching out to touch a window pane, she drew little figures in the condensation covering the glass. A church. A churchyard. Some nursery birds and fat clouds. She looked at her hand, grimy from the window and rubbed the grit between her fingers.

Wasn't she a dutiful daughter, ready to heed her parents' wishes? She'd never had reason to doubt it, but now she wondered.

She began to draw the sail of a ship and halted, her finger hovering an inch from the glass. Scrubbing furiously, she wiped the drawing away and leaned over, cupping her hands around her eyes to block the light. She jerked back, took one ragged breath and sprinted to the door.

***

She found her mother in the card room.

"Mama," she called quietly, her tone as even as she could make it. Strangers' gazes looked her over and made their devastating assessments before darting off to catch the interested faces of others, but Mama rose with elegant slowness and came aside a little way.

"What is it?" she whispered, leaning her head forward as she reached to adjust the ribbon on Beatrice's fan.

"Fog—covering the garden and mews," Beatrice said, catching her breath in tiny gulps. "I could hardly make out the house next door. It's what Papa said I should watch for. If we don't leave at once—"

"They won't let us leave," Mama finished, her voice tight. She held Beatrice by the elbows for a moment and her face took on an expression more at home on a battlefield. "I'll call for the coach, you collect the wraps." She looked to the windows. "Quickly."

Beatrice did not need to be told twice. She sped through the crowd, sliding sideways between fashionable people who had never been jostled in their lives. Her pace was checked again and again until she began to wish she had a cudgel to beat them back.

An opening.

Darting through it, she banged into a scarlet coat. She stepped away, muttering a hasty, "Pardon," when her elbow was caught in a soft grip. She yanked it away.

"Excuse me—"

Beatrice looked up. Captain Gracechurch.

Her urgency was not great enough to wholly murder the common—utterly common—wish to forget Mama entirely. But she could not. "I beg your pardon, Captain. I might have flattened you," she admitted wryly, already leaning away, her feet poised for flight.

He gave a low chuckle. "You offer me such singular entertainments."

A breath of a laugh escaped, but she prepared her lie, hating it. She'd uttered hundreds of lies in her life, thousands, but this little one felt forced from her throat. "My mother has a headache and I must collect our things." She looked over her shoulder. "Is everyone in Mayfair crushed into this one room?"

"Allow me," he said, offering an arm. Keeping her clasped to his side, he reached forward, carving a way through the crowd. Her pace was quickened now, though she could feel him push and bump people aside. He broke through into the hall and she followed after him, colliding into his broad back. She stepped quickly away, putting a hand to her neck where she felt the colour start to climb.

"In there." She pointed to the cloakroom. Better to ignore this feeling—as if her stomach were a spinning toy on the end of a string, rolling up with a jolt.

"Thank you for your assistance, Captain," she credited him as he handed her the wraps.

"May I see you to your coach?" he asked.

Yes.

"No," she laughed, trying for lightness. Heaven knew what would happen if he saw the fog. Bar the door, probably. Beatrice gave a shadow of a grand curtsey. "You have done your duty."

He bowed low, echoing her mock formality. "I thought we understood each other, Miss Thornton. It was my pleasure."

"Captain," she said, beginning to walk away but looking over her shoulder to where he stood. Her eyes reproved him, but her cheek curved in a smile. "You really must learn to accept my thanks with graciousness."

"I will endeavour to improve, Miss Thornton." He smiled and tilted his head to one side. "You may school me further at our next meeting. You don't have far to travel, do you?"

His question seemed to ask more than it did, and she hesitated as a war raged in her chest. *Disappear, Beatrice. Say as little as possible. Don't encourage him.* "St. James's Square."

Enough of that, she scolded herself, dashing down the staircase to where her mother waited. Mama wasted no time, plucking her cloak from Beatrice's arms, sweeping it around her shoulders and ushering Beatrice out the door with a quiet, "Come away."

As the coach pulled from the curb, Beatrice watched the dazzling light streaming from the house grow diffuse, devoured by the night and fog.

Chapter Three

"Always the hero," Fox stated, appearing from the ballroom as Henry trained his eyes down the hall where Miss Thornton had disappeared. "But it's caddish to give a girl hopes, Harry. Particularly such a dull-looking mouse."

Henry's jaw set. It hadn't been like that. Meeting Miss Thornton had been more like finding a brother-soldier, someone whose warm laughter and ready wit had plucked him out of the madness of Spain and put his feet down on the soil of England. For a few brief minutes, she'd made him feel that he was not wholly alien here.

In the face of that, the fashion of her dress was totally irrelevant.

Henry followed Fox into the ballroom again and they watched the dancers until Henry put the back of his hand to his mouth, yawning. When Miss Thornton left, all his energy had seemed to go with her, and the weariness that was a massive wave he'd been outrunning since Spain was finally going to break.

"You should be in bed," Fox noted, stifling his own yawn. He raised his voice over the violins and noise of the party. "Speaking of which…. Where—?"

The music came to an uneven halt and the long lines of dancers froze like grappling statues. "Dear guests—" A voice rang out from a tiny woman at the dais. Lady Sherbourne. "I had hoped for an exciting party, but did not dare pray for something so memorable. London has brought out one of its finest fogs for us."

Talk rumbled through the room.

"That's torn it," muttered a man to Henry's right. "Can't leave now. I'm for the library sofa. Every man for himself."

Gentlemen closest to the garden doors swung them wide, displaying a thick wall of fog that rolled through the crowd like a malevolent guest, arriving late and sending dangerous greetings left and right.

Henry's heart skittered to a stop. How long had it been since Miss Thornton left? A quarter of an hour? More? The answer made him sick. It was too late to chase after them.

Lady Sherbourne's voice rang on. "I hope no one is fool enough to leave. As you can see, it is impassable and dangerous. But if everyone will exercise a little patience and continue the party, I shall manage to put everyone up comfortably." She paused, bursting with mischief. "With only seven or eight to a bed." A wave of laughter rippled through the room, and Lady Sherbourne bid the orchestra strike up once more.

Henry managed his way to the nearest door and stalked a few steps into the cool night air. The fog met him, pressing in on all sides. "The devil take it," he muttered, his voice muted by the thickness of it.

Miss Thornton was no fool. If the fog closed in on them, she would find refuge, no matter her mother's condition. He looked into the night, hardly seeing past his own arm. *She had to.*

"Why such a bother?" asked Fox, strolling from the door. "A chair in a drawing room is still better than anything you had in Spain, I wager. Or are your lodgings close enough to chance a walk?"

"These *are* my lodgings," Henry stated, jerking his head over his shoulder at the house.

"What? With Lady Sherbourne?"

"She *is* my godmother."

"Ah, yes," Fox acknowledged, leaning against the stonework of the great house. "Your respectable connection. Well, aside from me." He clapped Henry on the shoulder. "You won't get a bed now. Is it important?"

It felt silly to say yes.

"Desperately."

"You could always come home with me. Leave a note for your godmama in the hall—"

"How shall I address it?" Henry asked, half laughing. "To: Lady Sherbourne, Who I Hope Will Not Wring My Neck?"

"That's it. I'll put you up for the night—no, for the duration of your stay in London—and be glad of some company," Fox offered, looking, in the dim light, like the motherless boy he had once been—large-eyed and lonely and in need of having his face wiped clean.

"We'll walk it. Not so much danger there. I know the way like the back of my hand, and you'll be tucked up in bed in half an hour."

Henry looked over his shoulder at the impenetrable cloud and turned back to Fox with a tired grin. "Lead on."

An hour later, they were still wandering out in the fog like fish in an endless ocean, occasional landmarks guiding them home.

"I think we're—" Fox missed a step, stumbling blindly into the road, cursing as he slammed against the cobblestones. "Ow," he grunted, more outraged than hurt.

"You know your way like the back of your hand," Henry jibed, knocking Fox with his knuckles until Fox could find his hand in the dark.

Fox hit out at it first before he allowed Henry to pull him to his feet.

"Where do you think we are?" Henry asked, stuffing his gloves inside his coat and doing the buttons up again. He felt his way onto the sidewalk and found the metal railings in front of a townhouse wet with mist, picking out each feature more plainly with his bare hand.

"Bury Street? It won't be long now if we are. But, by thunder, we should have been home half an hour ago." The fog had been much worse than either of them had supposed. Some time back they'd stumbled over the shattered remains of a hackney carriage, splintered wood littering the road in each direction. The harnesses were cut, the horses were gone, and it was anybody's guess what had become of the driver.

Fox turned to go up the street, but before he had gone five steps, a clattering roar sounded behind them. Henry shoved Fox hard against the railing, ready to leap over it. A coach skidded onto the curb where Fox had been standing, striking sparks from the wheeled rims, missing them by inches. It slid off again with a slam, lumbering on like an elephant crashing through a forest.

For a moment the only sound was laboured breathing, and then Fox's hands came up, loosening Henry's stranglehold on his coat. They watched the smudgy lanterns on the coach sway and jounce through the fog.

Fox laughed, but Henry took a long drag of air. He could feel his heart hammering in his chest, and it took a moment for his body to remember he was not in the smoking hills of Badajoz. "We've got to get out of here," he said.

"Ten more minutes," Fox promised, leading off.

The wild sounds of the night held few terrors for Henry. He could hear no dying men begging for water or calling for their mothers, no evil-minded scavengers fleeced the dead. But thoughts of Miss Thornton returned to him over and over. She and her mother could yet be out in this. The idea made his stomach clench. Even on foot, he was in danger. Any horse would be floundering on these cobblestones. Riding in a coach would be suicide. Heaven help that they'd had the sense to stop somewhere and take refuge.

"Uppercross," Fox called, several minutes later, stepping into the street. "Bury jogs up to meet it and—yes," he said, feeling along a brick wall and railings that must have been familiar in some way. "Mine is third house down on the left. Number thirty-two."

Still, they had to pick their way until Fox rapped against his own door, loud enough to wake the dead. "Join me for a drink?" he asked.

The door swung wide and Fox pulled off his gloves, handing them to a waiting footman. His cravat was loose where Henry had mangled it, but otherwise he looked as though he were returning from an afternoon stroll. "You can explain the whole peninsula strategy by rearranging my bottles of liquor. I even have Madeira."

Henry leaned against the newel post, his smile flickering in and out. "Bed. I'm all in."

"As you like," Fox replied, giving him a mocking salute.

The manservant showed Henry up two long flights of stairs and into a spacious room overlooking the street, setting a taper to a well-laid fire before bowing himself out. The bed was a miracle.

Henry shrugged out of his coat, tossed it over the back of a chair, and pushed his braces off his shoulders, letting them dangle at his sides. Unbuttoning the loose shirt, he pulled it over his head in a quick motion. Firelight picked up the irregular skin across his chest and back. Old scars and new ones weaved together.

There was a bottle on a table before the fire and he uncorked it, ignoring the cut-glass tumbler, and took a swallow. French. Too good to be anything else—smuggled no doubt. Henry was too tired even to be angry with his cousin and took another pull. He pulled off his boots and slid between the snug sheets. His body relaxed muscle by muscle. As he watched the fire, the flames blurred in the grate and blackened. Would the nightmares come again with their sounds of battle and smell of death?

But Miss Thornton's laughing face waited for him behind his eyelids. She was not going to let him walk gently into the arms of sleep, and his foggy brain wondered at it. It was the sight of her standing there on the dance floor, that sweaty pig Knowlton trotting off. He'd registered the plain terror he'd seen in her eyes, understanding it at once. He'd bathed in that emotion for years. There had been no thought of ignoring it.

Now she crept into his mind like a stray kitten, winding around his heels and begging to be picked up. She might yet be out there in the fog.

He drew the blanket over his shoulder and furrowed his brow. He wanted to sleep, blast it, but his mind had taken hold of the thought, and he was not the master over it.

Go to sleep, Gracechurch, he told himself sternly. *The woman is safe.*

Chapter Four

Beatrice flew across her mother's lap, striking her head with an awful crack. As the coach reared drunkenly on two wheels, creaking and straining at the breathless apex, her legs buckled beneath her. *We're going.* She sucked her lips tight before the vehicle slammed upright again. The crash knocked Beatrice onto her backside and then to the floor. In the silence that followed, Mama groaned.

The carriage was still rocking, and Beatrice cried out, dazed, "John. Are you there? Are you still on the box?"

Mama spread her arms from one wall of the carriage to the other as Beatrice climbed back into her seat. "Murderin' pillock," John shouted as the other vehicle careened on. Hot words volleyed back, filling the night air.

"Coachman," Beatrice cried again, clutching her head to keep it from spinning. Shouting hurt, and her voice drifted into nothing.

"Yes, miss," he said from the box, his voice muffled by the panel that divided them. The relief of it made her heart jump in her throat. "Almost lost my seat. The half-wit tore off again but 'e only scraped up our paint pretty bad, I guess." The coach jerked forward several paces and Beatrice's heart jumped down her throat before John had control again.

Her head was beginning to throb. If they'd lost the coachman in the dark, with no driver and panicked horses—she swallowed, biting back tears.

"I'll set here for a bit, miss," John called. "The horses were that rattled."

Not only the horses. Beatrice put a gentle hand to her hairline, finding no blood but a vicious knot beginning to form. She hunted for her hairpins and made a molehill of them on her lap. Her tortured hair unfurled down her back and she thrust her fingers in at the roots, rubbing her scalp, taking care to avoid the swelling bump.

"Piccadilly," Mama said.

"What?" asked Beatrice.

"We were going east on Piccadilly and only have to look out for Duke Street." The stunned and wide-eyed woman of three minutes ago was banished. "When John recovers his nerves, we will have him wheel about and walk the length of it again. The fool was going too fast to see it."

Beatrice blinked. There was not a prayer they were on Piccadilly. She would stake her life on it, hoping she wouldn't have to. Taking a shaky breath, she began, "Do you hear other coaches? If it were Piccadilly, there would be more—"

"If? Of course it's Piccadilly. I know exactly where we are. It's this fool coachman who keeps turning us in circles."

Fool? Of the three of them, John deserved that epithet the least. He had somehow managed to keep them going, slow and steady, even when animals shot into their path and keening shrieks rang across the stones, upsetting horses and locking wheels. They owed him their lives.

"Do you remember Piccadilly feeling so narrow?" Beatrice asked, coming at the point sideways like a street urchin picking a pocket. "You know London better than I do."

Mama scooped up the pins in Beatrice's lap and dumped them into her reticule. "It's Piccadilly." *And that's that.*

Though Mama was often officious, being driven around in unknown streets for almost three hours seemed to lend her confident air a brittle quality. She was wrong about where they were—terribly and ruinously wrong, but she sounded as she always did. Correct.

"If the stupid coachman will do as I say, we will be home in moments. I'm going to tell the man to carry on," Mama stated, raising her hand to knock on the sliding panel above Beatrice's head.

How it had happened, she could not afterward say, but Beatrice's hand shot out, holding Mama's wrist in a firm grip, her knuckles inches from the panel. Mama's eyes went wide and then blazed, promising to rain fire and brimstone over her daughter's head. "Beatrice."

"Don't do that. We're not on Piccadilly," Beatrice informed her mother, shedding the passive uncertainty she'd been schooled to use for years now. "And we cannot afford to be wrong. It is not our lives alone that you risk, but John's too. Do you really know where we are?" she asked, pointing to the window.

The coach lamps penetrated mere inches into the thick gloom. The coachman let out a soft, singing call to the horses who responded by stamping hooves on the rough stones, communicating their unease with a shake of the lines. "Whoooooa. Whoa, there."

"We must do something," Mama insisted.

"We must do the *right* thing," Beatrice replied, letting go of Mama and turning to the window.

"What are you doing?" Mama asked as Beatrice, suffocating with helplessness, worked at the clasp and lowered the glass.

"I want to listen." She leaned her head out, the mist wetting her face like a cloud of steam rising from an opened pot, and listened against the dense, sooty cloud. Strange sounds echoed across the city. She heard the slow rumble of carriage wheels, terrified and muffled shouts bouncing in from every direction, and screams of horses plunging against walls and obstacles. But she could not hear any sounds near them. A street or two away, at closest, she thought. She strained her ears, needing to be sure.

There was the anxious nickering of the horses, but otherwise not so much as a footfall. This was going to take courage.

Captain Gracechurch's image was suddenly before her, warm and sure. He held his hand out with a smile that invited her to be brave. *Chin up.* Beatrice wanted to do as her Mama told her. It would be nicer, and easier. But she was in peril and it was no time to cower and hide. Beatrice raised the window with a snap. "I'm going to need you to get up, Mama," she stated, unused to issuing commands.

Mama gave way and slid across to the other seat with a mulish thump. "What do you think you can do that hasn't been done?"

"The carriage was almost splintered to bits and the horses are ready to bolt." Beatrice knelt and tilted up the seat. "I'm getting the rope. It must be fifty feet long at least, don't you think?"

"Yes, but—"

Beatrice hauled out a length of stout hemp rope, too heavy to lift out in one neat bundle, reaching her arm back and forth again and again until she came to the end. "You're going to hold onto this." Beatrice put the rough rope, kept in the carriage in case of accident or emergency, in her mother's hands. "Don't let go of me."

Mama dropped the rope as though it were fire. "What do you mean to do?"

Beatrice mined a thin vein of courage and met her mother's eyes squarely and unflinchingly. "I'm not going to wander into the fog and knock on any doors, if that is what you are thinking." Two gentlewomen alone in the fog would be pressed to take shelter, made to accept the sort of hospitality they had fled from.

"What do you mean to do?" she repeated.

Beatrice began to knot the rope around her own waist, threading the ends inside and out, pulling at it. "I'm going to find out where we are." She looked up to the ceiling of the coach; her mother's face, already pale, went ashen.

"What can you be thinking? You can't." Mama's voice was low but intense.

"I can, Mother, and it's necessary. I will be quick."

"Your sisters, Beatrice. What if you are discovered? What of them?"

Beatrice's hands went still. Her head was bent over the knots. It was cruel to use that argument at such a time. *What of you and me, Mama?*

"The fog is too thick, and there is no one on the street." That would have to do for an answer. "I will take a few moments, but I can't stay here hoping not to be killed." If she stood firm, Mama would make the best of a bad job. She was good at that.

Beatrice pressed again. "We *must* know where we're going." She left her mother to weigh the choices and returned to securing herself.

Another moment later, hands reached out to brush hers away. "Let me," Mama said, giving the knot a rough pull, jerking Beatrice forward an inch, and nodded. Then Mama reached her hand to Beatrice's cheek and pressed lips to her other in a quick salute. But the softness didn't last long. "If I don't have you back in two minutes, I'm going to wrench you down. Careful, girl, and don't be seen."

Beatrice turned the handle of the door and leaned out, looking to where she could see the shadowed form of the coachman. "John, my mother wants you to stay still a few more moments while we get our bearings. We might see something. A minute or two more."

"Yes, miss," he said, faithful but anxious. "The horses are restless. 'Tis a good part of town, I think. We might look for a door. Try knocking on it. No one would—"

"No, John. Mama won't rest until we are home, as we shall be in minutes, I am sure. Let us stay where we are for a moment."

"Yes, miss." She could tell he was not pleased.

Beatrice waited until he turned back to the horses, talking softly to them in the darkness. She stepped to the street, careful not to rock the carriage as she left it. Mama pushed the rope to the cobbles and clasped the end in both her hands, her heart in her eyes.

Beatrice began to walk backward slowly, orienting herself in a line, as near as she could tell, from the head of the horses to the coachman to the coach itself. Within moments she was swallowed in the deep ocean of fog and soot, the substance settling on her skin, invading her lungs. Not until the only thing she could see was the rope snaking into the gloom did her feet leave the cobblestones.

She began to rise.

Chapter Five

Beatrice slipped her moorings, cleaving up into the deep cloud, no longer fighting the urge to lift, but free to follow it. *Linens caught in the breeze. Dust motes floating in sunlight. Skirts whirling in a dance.* She fed her "rising" with thoughts of weightlessness, straining with focus, until she broke through the thick mist into the bright moonlight of the night sky like a fish splashing out of a silent pond.

A quicksilver bolt of exhilaration went through her, and for several deep breaths the wide bowl of the starry sky arched above her, open and limitless. How far could she go? She felt the temptation to keep feeding her power the way a footman might shovel coal into a roaring fire. The feeling was deliciously sweet.

Fog drifted around her, shifting in feathery patches, and she came back to herself, scanning the horizon for landmarks. There was not much to be seen this high over the city. The chimney pots dotting every rooftop disappeared to her right. Could it be the river? A park? Her eyes narrowed on the distance ahead where a grey dome rose from the fog. St. Paul's. They were well west of it.

Movement caught her eye and she gasped with relief. A standard flying atop a townhouse. "Garish," Papa had harrumphed when he drove her out this morning. It hung limp now, pushed around the flagpole in the desultory air. Her eyes followed the chimney pots home, finding the topmost branches of the ancient maple tree that stood in the centre of St. James's Square exactly where she expected it to be. They were close.

"Beatrice." The shout came from below and she grabbed the rope tied about her waist and shook it once—hard. *Coming.* She dared not linger, but as she descended she stretched her neck to see the last of the star-flecked sky. The fog was close and private, holding a fascination all its own as it veiled her, but loud voices carried up from the street.

"Don't say you let her walk into the fog, mistress. The master. What will he do?" John wailed. "I must follow that rope. It'll mean my job, Mrs Thornton."

Urgency lit her insides, but Beatrice could not speed her descent. Hurtling toward the unseen street at breakneck speed would be asking for a broken ankle.

"You will not," Mama commanded. "Stay as you are. I'll follow the rope."

Beatrice ignored the panic in Mama's tone and concentrated on thoughts that would carry her steadily down. *A casket of gold ingots. A hod of bricks...* Weakness was stealing through her limbs and the rope was dragging at her. She fought the urge to plummet.

"I'm here, Beatrice," Mama's soft voice came through the night. The sound couldn't have carried more than a few feet. "Speak to me."

"Here," Beatrice replied, starting to shiver, her legs and arms growing feeble.

A hand wrapped around the hem of her skirts and guided her the last few feet until she was down. When slippers met stone, Beatrice sagged against her mother who asked, "Where are we?"

"Three streets more. Up this street and a little south should do it. Does Coachman—?"

"Suspect you rose in midair? Nonsense."

A long creak sounded, and they froze together.

"Who's there?" Mama shouted, wariness in her voice. "John?"

He called back, his voice reassuringly distant. Beatrice felt Mama's air leave her lungs in a great gust.

"Come," Mama ordered. "He thinks you went knocking on a door, and that I was fool enough to let you. That's the tale you must spin."

A bare ten minutes later found Beatrice deposited in a deep chair and curled up in a tight ball, shaking violently before the library fire. The flames could have been stained glass for all that they warmed her. Mama's hands chafed her arms, but for several minutes Beatrice was hardly aware of anything more than how cold she was, how tired, and how heavy her body felt. But she'd done it—risen above the fog, and saved them. The memory, what she could catch hold of and examine, was a wonder.

"Sit up," Mama instructed, tugging off her own cloak and adding the warm weight of it to Beatrice's legs before settling into the chair opposite her.

Beatrice struggled upright and looked at her hands, pressing them flat on her lap to stop the tremors. Papa knelt before her and took up her palms, curling them around a hot cup of tea. "Drink," he urged, not taking his gaze off her. "You won't like it cold."

Ignoring the delicate scrolling handle, she tipped the cup to her mouth like a child, feeling the hot liquid travel the length of her throat. She grimaced and frowned into the cup, finding a thick milky sludge settling into the bottom. Sugar. There was a small mountain of it. Enough to make the hollows behind her jaw tingle. But she could feel it working, sending strength to sapped limbs, keeping her teeth from chattering, lending her energy to think again.

Papa gave a short, satisfied grunt and brought a simple wooden chair over to the fire. He talked to fill the silence, Beatrice thought, though each of them must know there would be a reckoning.

"When we saw that a fog was rolling up from the river, I knew you would have to leave the party. I aged ten years tonight," he said, taking Mama's hand and kissing it fiercely, not yielding it back to her but keeping it pressed between his large ones.

Beatrice turned her face to the fire, envying Mama the comfort of a husband. Strange. Had she ever envied her that before? Too tired to think, she rested her cheek against the arm of the chair, hardly able to keep her head balanced on her neck.

Mama moved suddenly, her skirts swishing between the chairs. Beatrice closed her eyes, then Mama was pressing a hot, damp napkin to her forehead. "I'd forgotten your head. I wrapped the tea leaves in this. Hold it there a bit."

"What happened to her head?" Papa asked leaning over.

"We had a small accident," Mama muttered, brushing him aside when the topic was anything to do with Beatrice. "Nothing to bother about."

But this time Papa declined to be put off. His voice was low and intense. "Sarah, she looks like she's been throttled half to death." An exaggeration surely, Beatrice thought, catching a dim look at herself in a mirror as a rivulet of cold tea rolled down her cheek.

"It's nothing, Charles. We made it home, safe and sound."

"This is 'safe and sound'?" he growled.

"The carriage was hit," Beatrice mumbled. It was hard to talk. This is what came of getting out of practice. "I think the paint's scratched."

"I don't care about the paint."

Beatrice lifted the poultice before plonking it on again. "That's when I got this. I'm sorry, but we were so frightened. I used my—" How could she say "curse" when it had saved them? The words they had always employed to describe it seemed wrong now, and she wrinkled her brow before remembering it would hurt. She held her hand out and it still shook like a leaf on the edge of winter. "You can see that I rose. Right above the fog," she informed him, sitting up again and straightening her spine with a bit of ridiculous dignity.

Papa sat, straining the joints on the little wooden chair, and reached a hand to her knee, taking such care. He started to speak. Stopped. Began again. "Thirteen years old and as light as thistledown. My thistledown girl, I called you. You shook then too."

His thistledown girl. Papa was forever trying to put the best face on things, but Beatrice felt her heart drop and a tiny seed of shame take root. *More accurate to call it a thistledown curse.* How long were they going to take care of her?

"Was it an accident? The rising?" he asked, his effort at understanding making it worse. "Did some kind of fright send you up?"

She shook her head. "No, I decided—"

"To disobey your mother," Mama cut in, scowling into her tea.

While saving our lives.

"Do you feel better?" Papa asked, breaking across the undercurrents.

"I think so. Tired though. I haven't risen on purpose in—" *Never.* "I don't do it often, you know." But she smiled as she said it.

Papa reached to chuck her gently on the cheek with the back of his hand. "You should be tucked up in your bed, honeybee."

Mama voice was a hard staccato. "Bed? No. We have to decide if we have to leave London."

"Leave?" said Papa.

"If she was seen…"

"She was seen?" Papa blanched under his beard.

"No." Beatrice raised her voice, though it sounded small and fragile still. "I wasn't seen."

"Sure of that?" Mama asked, tapping a silver spoon against the rim of her cup one, two, three, five times, until Papa reached an arm out to still her.

"The fog was much too thick," Beatrice explained.

Papa looked to Mama. "Was it?"

"It was thick," Mama allowed, her face an irritated mask. "She decided *on her own* to rise up, displaying a wilfulness I did not condone." Mama snuffed through her nose and turned to Papa. "But, with all these people living on top of each other, is it difficult to think she might have been seen? And what about that noise we heard?"

"Sounds were bouncing in from all directions, Mama. It could have been a window three streets away," Beatrice answered, sorting that noise into the most convenient, innocuous pigeonhole. "And we saw no one."

"Should I be prepared to stake Penny's future on it? What of Deborah and her husband? She's expecting a child in the fall. What about your father's future? Mine?"

Mine.

Beatrice tipped her head back against the chair, surprised to meet Aunt Martha's eyes as she smiled down from the portrait hanging over the mantel. There had been the old magic in her too. This curse of rising that ran with a sort of vicious randomness through the Thorntons.

Her aunt's serene and youthful expression, so foreign to the paper-thin, rigidly controlled woman Beatrice had known, made her say emphatically, "No one saw me. I'm sure of it." She turned to Papa, her best hope for a reprieve. "Truly, Papa. We have nothing to fear for my sisters."

Her father expelled a shaking breath and nodded.

Mama, however, was a kindled flame. "You're quick to dismiss my worries. Do you think the gentlefolk you mixed with tonight will cast a tolerant eye on your curse? What of the bloodline that carries it?"

A muscle in Papa's cheek flinched. But Mama swept on, pinning Beatrice with her gaze.

"You want me to be content to watch you be thrown into an asylum with the raving insane until you ran mad yourself? Or imprisoned like a criminal? Maybe they will resurrect the old-fashioned practice and burn you as a witch," Mama choked out, her voice tight and high-strung. "Your sisters…"

"My sisters are safe," Beatrice ventured, weak with unshed tears, inexpressibly tired. "They don't have this—"

"What mob will stop long enough to make that distinction?"

"Enough," Papa commanded. "Enough."

Beatrice slumped back in her chair.

This was the first real row she'd ever had with her parents. All this for rising. Such a stupid thing.

It would be different if she could fly, winging over the fields and treetops, setting off from London and not wetting her slippers until she stepped down in Dorset. That might be a power worth suffering privations over. But this? She could only travel upward, and, unless somehow buffeted about, she would return in precisely the same spot. But the cost of it was high. She had no friends, not really. Even her sisters had to be lied to and held at an arm's distance. And her future…. That was already decided. She would never go beyond London, and would drop back at Thorndene in precisely the same spot.

And the rising left her so weak. She drew her brows together in concentration. It hadn't always done so, not when she'd done it every day. Beatrice lifted the sodden cloth from her head and dropped it with a squelching sound into a tray. She'd been younger then.

Mama turned to Papa. "You have always left these decisions to me."

His look was grim and his arms were folded over his chest. "Look at our daughter, Sarah, and tell me that wasn't a mistake."

"I have done the best—"

"But I have not," he answered, his voice quiet, inflexible. "It's my 'bloodline' as you called it."

"Charles."

"So it is proper that I should involve myself. Together we can decide how to keep our girl safe," Papa said, angling his head around Mama to see Beatrice better. She held perfectly still as the room seemed to sway for a moment. This was a change, indeed.

Mama snorted and sat back, her thumb running along her lower lip. "It would be safer to go home to Dorset. There are too many people in Town. The risks of discovery are much higher." Beatrice's breath stopped. "But three days in London won't stop the tongues from wagging in the village. If anything, it will be worse."

Beatrice rubbed her face. Not for the first time, her future hung in mid-air. She watched the pattern on the old chair blur before her eyes, knowing that once she left London, she would never be back. It would be too risky.

She was lucky to have come at all. Mama had put it off until the gossip in the village had reached even her ears. *A whole year of mourning for an aunt, and a second year of it. Would the Thorntons never get that second girl—the sickly one who seemed to stay so close to home—fired off?*

Beatrice glanced up again to Aunt Martha's portrait and stated with resolution, "There is no reason to leave London."

Papa's eyebrows went up, but he gave her a smile. "Our girl knows the risks better than we do, Sarah," he offered. "She has as much right to decide as anybody. So long as she is sure she was not seen…"

Here was the time to speak, to confess any doubts, and hash out any uncertainty. Beatrice clamped her lips together.

Papa's gavel fell. "We stay. For now."

Mama set her teeth as she collected the cups and clattered them onto the tray. "I hate this pretence, acting as though I'm a half-wit to dress her like that."

Beatrice was too exhausted to guard her tongue. "It must gall to pretend to be something you are not."

"That's enough, Beatrice." Papa's voice was surprised and stern, as if he'd been bitten by a well-loved puppy. Beatrice couldn't chance a look at Mama, feeling instantly ashamed of herself. "Off to bed."

Beatrice stood, leaning along the chair backs as she made her way from the room, her steps not quite steady. As she reached the door, she turned to see her parents settled together in the chair, Papa's hand running gently between Mama's shoulders, his voice low and soothing. Then, leaving, Beatrice glanced up again at Aunt Martha.

That poor lady, stuffed into a forgotten corner of Dorset to moulder like a piece of fly-specked lace. Her life had been uneventful, and safe. She had been a faithful daughter, in time a doting aunt. She had kept pugs.

Beatrice made a disgusted sound as she turned up the stairs. She didn't like pugs.

She blinked at her own bitterness. It had been easy to love her aunt. Why, now, was the thought of her life so untenable?

The answer sucked the air from her lungs. *Because they expect you to live it.*

Had her aunt never been tempted to kick over the traces and run a little wild?

Finally within her room, Beatrice discarded her dress, thwacking it on the ground for good measure before repenting and draping it on the back of a chair.

She had run a little wild tonight, she thought, donning a nightgown and combing light fingers through her hair. Plucking a length of white ribbon from the bureau, she wound it around her finger. She'd danced with a dashing captain and forgotten the wisdom of Mama's plan. She'd been a little daring. Cupping her hand around the candle flame, she blew it out, considering Captain Gracechurch.

It was unlikely they would meet again. Godmama's gathering had been too small and intimate for Mama's liking. She would prefer a Season of overstuffed balls, of being crushed in a room with so many people that Beatrice could disappear. And the captain.... Her insides slid a little sideways until she took hold of herself. He was not here for the Season. Why, tomorrow he might leave for Spain. She bumped into a brick wall beyond which lay his Christian name and the location of his home, and whether he had any sisters, or had learned to speak Spanish.

It would be wise to leave such a wall alone. It would be unwise to drag a ladder over and climb it.

Beatrice flipped back the covers and slid between the sheets. She found the small loop in the bottom sheet. It was quick work to thread the ribbon through the loop and lay down in the middle of it, wrapping the ribbon around her waist and tying it off firmly. What an unholy row it would have caused in Grosvenor Square if she'd been caught floating in the air at dawn—the panic and outcry that would follow.

She settled into the soft down and pulled her covers up to her chin, thinking muddled thoughts.

Fatigue tugged one of them loose.

She didn't need ladders to see over brick walls, she knew how to rise.

Chapter Six

The ribbon cut into her waist, digging through the heavy folds of her nightgown. Beatrice blinked her eyes open, shocked to find herself floating—straining—against her tether.

Throwing the blankets off, she concentrated her thoughts on heavy things, such as the sound of thick mud hurled against the side of a barn. The sight of a tree bough loaded with snow before it crashed to the ground. The china closet, groaning under the weight of a table setting for fifty people.

If she could focus, pushing away the fright, she would drop. Panic and reason tangled until, finally, she felt the soft mattress against her back and legs. She ripped at the ribbon, rolling away from it and scrambling off the bed, her lungs gulping great draughts of air.

Sometimes she floated in her sleep, but never like this. Never with this intensity.

Her eyes stared at the bed, trying to make sense of it. The sword that hung above her head had swayed, and she should run down the hall and tell her mother so she could make a discreet mark with a red pencil in her calendar. Red for rising.

Yes. She should do that.

But Beatrice could not make herself move. She stood with bare feet, feeling the boards with her toes. The grain of the wood was solid and firm. Mama didn't need any more excuses to send them packing for Dorset. The slightest thing would do it, and this was *so* slight. What did it amount to? She woke pulling against the ribbons instead of gently bobbing. Nothing different, only a matter of degree.

Beatrice walked a few paces back and forth on the rug, feeling the weight of herself, and made up her mind. She would tell only if Mama asked.

With that firm resolution in mind, she went downstairs, prepared to face her family. Penny pounced as soon as she crossed the threshold of the breakfast room. "I can't believe you're alive after last night."

"Oh, the fog wasn't—"

"If it had been me in that dress, I would have expired on the spot," Penny waxed, pointing her fork at Beatrice.

"Penelope Victoria," Mama warned.

A warning Penny disregarded. "You would do better to wear that," she said, indicating the faded blue gown, which suited Beatrice in a quiet way. She had been allowed to keep her old things to wear around the family. It didn't matter what she looked like while she took her breakfast.

"To a ball? It's a morning dress and three years old," Beatrice noted, happy to stand ankle-deep in the steady stream of her little sister's chatter. Cheery sun slanted through the windows of the small breakfast room, though Mama was scowling at it. How dared the sky be blue and brilliant, as though nothing had happened.

Mama went back to dragging her finger down the newsprint columns, discarding *The London Times, The London Gazette,* and all other sister publications in turn. Papa plucked up each jettisoned page, shuffling them to rights and depositing them in an orderly stack next to his plate.

"At least it fits," Penny muttered. "I would be surprised if anyone looked at you twice in that tent."

Beatrice's cheeks pinked at the memory of the gentleman who had looked at her twice, though there had not been much pleasing to see.

"You should let me choose your clothes from now on if you insist on making such a hash of it."

"Oh, should I?" Beatrice scrunched her nose and stuck her tongue out behind her hand.

"Decorum, Beatrice," Mama cautioned, having not looked up from her task. How did she do that?

Harrison, the butler, gave a loud rap on the door and entered carrying a tray filled with more toast and jam, as well as the morning's letters, which he set at Mama's plate. A posy of deep purple violets, bright gold in each centre, he placed next to Beatrice.

"Not for me," she said, holding them out again.

The old man nodded to the table. "They came with a card, miss."

Beatrice felt her mother's finger pause on the page. Papa flicked a corner of *The Times* down and looked over it. Penny leaned across the table. Flowers? Flowers for Beatrice? Small wonder. Time seemed to skip to a stop in the small breakfast parlour. She picked up the card, her eyes scanning the name. Captain Henry R. S. Gracechurch. Henry. His name was Henry. Her face warmed as she traced fingers over the scrolling letters and felt the crease where he had folded down the corner. Hand delivered. *St. James's Square*, she had told him. And he'd remembered.

Flipping it over she read a message scribbled in pencil. "For Miss Thornton who took pity on me." She smiled.

"From that man you danced with," Mama stated, turning the question into a declaration.

Beatrice slipped the card into her lap and nodded, her heart thudding against her ribs. "It doesn't mean anything."

"Of course it doesn't. It's the done thing when you've danced with a girl to send her a posy. And violets are nothing to fuss about."

"Why?" asked Penny.

Why? Beatrice laid a soft hand on the velvet petals.

"Because they can be purchased from any flower monger in Chelsea for a ha'penny. If a man wants to signal his attentions, he would send orchids or rosebuds."

Mama handed the last paper over to Papa and dipped a white napkin into a dish of water, scrubbing the black ink off her finger. "But it was a polite gesture by Lord—what was his name? Something-or-other. Rowland? Knowlton," she queried and Beatrice's eyes shuttered. Of course. He *was* the man her mother had known she had danced with.

For once, Mama's habit of conversing with people like a millstone grinding wheat into fine flour served Beatrice well. "Past time you were off to your lessons, Penelope," Mama instructed, sending Penny away with a look. "Try to learn something of civilization."

Penny waltzed out with her nose in the air, though the appearance of exaggerated elegance was spoiled when she swiped a piece of toast from the rack on her way. The door clicked closed and Papa leaned forward. "Well?"

Mama barely paused. "*The Gazette* had something. An old lady reported seeing a ghostly apparition flying through the fog last night." Beatrice's breath stopped and she put her knife down. "Hampstead."

Beatrice exhaled and Papa flicked his paper back up, speaking from behind it. "Miles away. We may all go on with our business as usual."

"Which is...?" asked Mama, picking up her letters and tapping them on the table.

"The club. I ran out on Lord Liverpool last night when they announced the fog. I should apologize. You?"

"I had Harrison talk to the footman yesterday."

"George? What's the fellow done?"

"He keeps entering rooms without knocking."

"They're public rooms, my love."

"Unacceptable," Mama stated, leafing through her correspondence. "George was warned. But if it happens again, I'll need to hire—" She stopped, letter in hand, flipping it over with a furrow on her brow. She picked up the narrow bone-handled knife and sliced through it, shaking the letter out and reading it at a glance. "Oh. That woman," she scoffed, handing the letter over to Beatrice.

'Dear Sarah,
  I am home at any hour today to receive your apologies.
  Affectionately,
  Emily Sherbourne'

Godmama was not inviting them to attend her this morning. She was commanding it.

***

Godmama, though tiny, looked as magnificent as a queen. Sitting silent and straight, she only needed a dais and a sceptre to complete the terrifying effect. Beatrice, who had spent the whole morning watching her mother pace holes in the carpet, felt a giggle welling up.

Lady Sherbourne gestured for them to be seated, and after a long, awkward silence said, as though to herself, "I hardly know whether to order the tea things to be brought. Do the dead take tea, Jarvis?"

The footman at the door must have been used to such treatment for he stood there unmoving.

Lady Sherbourne continued her strange monologue. "Does one communicate with ghosts by tapping on the table three times or whistling?" Beatrice was all anticipation. "I never learned to whistle." It was a crushing disappointment.

Mama looked like she might be grinding her teeth. "I'm afraid we didn't get to say our goodbyes last night," she offered, words sneaking past pursed lips. "I had a terrible headache, but you will be pleased to know we arrived home with little bother."

"Will I?" Godmama asked, looking put out. "You ought not to have made it at all. I should, by rights, be selecting black ribbons to trim my gowns and settling in for a miserable season of mourning. That fog was treacherous."

Mama's mouth tightened even further. "We must have threaded the worst pockets. I'm sure we were a good deal more comfortable than your guests."

Godmama threw her hands up and crashed them into her lap like a child having a fit. "Everyone was a good deal more comfortable than me. The *whole* bed to myself and there I was, tossing and turning in it. I might as well have slept six to a bed with the kitchen staff. You had me worried sick."

"In that case," Mama said deferentially, seeing that Lady Sherbourne would extract what she wanted or continue digging this well indefinitely, "we are quite sorry to have added to your discomfort."

Lady Sherbourne waited, expecting Mama to go further. Perhaps to prostrate herself on the carpet, but when she did not, Godmama gave a gusty snort and called for tea.

"The horde left me as soon as the dawn broke. I daresay, some ladies remembered that sunlight is not so kind as candlelight. They will be irritated to learn that you made your way home with so little trouble."

Beatrice fixed a blank, pleasant smile on her face, hoping that her hair, arranged loosely for once to hide the magnificent goose egg, was doing its job. Mama picked a speck of invisible fuzz from her skirts.

Godmama filled the silence. "We did not have time, before you scampered off into the Black Jaws of Death last night, to discuss Beatrice's future. Her ball—when is it? May is best, though June—"

Mama broke in, saying, "Beatrice's health had been so delicate last winter that we did not plan—"

"*That* was clear enough from her clothes last night, and this morning. Did every warehouse in London burn to the ground? Has every needlewoman within fifty miles gone blind? Have *you*?" Godmama accused, tipping an open palm to Beatrice in her curdled-white muslin gown and dust-coloured spencer in a way that made Beatrice wish to apologize for coming outdoors this way. Godmama closed her hand and took a sip of tea, setting it down again with extreme care. "Though, I notice you are looking as lovely as ever, Sarah."

"We do not feel we can hold a ball for Beatrice at this time." Mama's prepared remarks were tiny rocks striking a massive boulder.

"Marvellous." Godmama beamed and Beatrice felt a mixture of thrilling adventure and certain doom. "It's decided. You'll leave the whole thing to me."

Mama turned purple. "I would thank you, my lady—" she began, only to have Lady Sherbourne cut her off.

"You're welcome, my love. Between us we can get this girl fired off." Godmama gave Beatrice a look of grim assessment. "Though I do not know what you can be thinking, Sarah. Deborah was not given such shabby treatment."

Beatrice watched as her mother closed her eyes for the briefest moment. It was wrong to enjoy this so much. "Due to her health, we are going slowly."

"Go any slower and she will be in the grave before she is at the altar. If the whole thing is too much for you, you ought to have sent her to me as you sent Deborah. Her season was a triumph, and, if you had let me drop a hint or two about her fortune, I'm sure we might have nabbed the heir to old Norwich."

"And instead she nabbed our neighbour Michael, who would have taken her without a shilling," Beatrice commented, bundling away the topic. Nabbing the heir to "old Norwich" held no attractions even if Mama had been of a mind to do it.

"Is she increasing? When will she present you grandbabies?" asked Lady Sherbourne, and Mama fell on the change of subject with relief.

"Yes," she started. "In the fall. She expects—"

"My lady," intoned the footman at the door. "Captain Gracechurch."

Beatrice caught her breath, sure she could not have heard correctly.

"Henry," smiled Lady Sherbourne, her voice swinging high with delight. "This is just the thing." She bounced a little on her seat and smiled at Beatrice as if she had magicked him out of thin air. "Show him in."

Captain Gracechurch. His name was like dandelion fluff brushing up her neck, tickling the back of her ears. She wanted desperately to be wearing something flattering—even a faded blue morning gown. For a moment, she wished her curse would dissolve her into a puddle of water or make her disappear into a puff of smoke, but there were other, more enchanting feelings flying around in her chest. She'd been hoping for this, though telling herself it was impossible all the time. She was meeting him again, and somehow she knew that in the sober light of day, he would not fail to come up to expectations.

The sound of his footsteps reached the top of the stairs. This was the end of hiding him. Mama would find out about the dance and the violets and she would see how Beatrice could not prevent herself from smiling when he looked at her. But surely it was better to be hanged for a sheep than a lamb. She sat up straight and raised her chin. She was going to make the most of this.

She thought her memories were accurate, but as he walked through the door, she was struck anew by the bright scarlet of his regimentals and the way he walked as though he were eager to get where he was going. His eyes were brown, like rich Ceylon cinnamon sticks.

Lady Sherbourne cleared her throat. "Do ghosts get hungry?"

Oh, Godmama.

"Oh, Godmama," he teased, bending to kiss her papery cheek and presenting her with a small nosegay. "You aren't going to pretend I've died again, are you?"

The laugh, until now suppressed, bubbled up and spilled over Beatrice's lips, and Mama reached over to hold her arm. Did Mama think she was going to fly away?

Captain Gracechurch unbent and looked to where Beatrice sat with her mother. "Good morning," he said, surprise and pleasure blending in equal parts in his expression.

"Good morning."

Mama snatched up her reticule and shawl and put a hand to Beatrice's back, ready to tip her out of her seat. "We are going."

"Sit down, Sarah. You've hardly touched your tea." Lady Sherbourne brought the flowers to her nose as Mama sat on a thin sliver of the sofa. "You always know what I like, Henry. Let me make you known to Mrs Thornton and her daughter."

"Ma'am," he murmured deferentially, bowing over Mama's hand. "I am delighted to find you made your way home safely. Once I realized that you and Miss Thornton had gone home in the fog, I worried a good deal."

Mama whipped her hand away. "Unnecessary," she stated. Her look was an icy dagger and the captain should have, by rights, been bleeding at her feet.

As he straightened, his attention fastened onto Beatrice and she felt herself go warm. "Miss Thornton needs no introduction. Our encounter was unforgettable."

Beatrice would pay a price, but for once Mama could go hang. The sides of the captain's eyes crinkled in well-used lines. Beatrice had nothing to improve her appearance except her smile, so she turned it on him now.

"Thank you for the violets. They are my favourite flower." They certainly were now. Mama's indrawn breath was sharp, but she ignored it. "You chanced the fog last night? You might've been crushed."

"And by something less delightful than the charming young woman who almost bowled me over in the ballroom," he answered.

Her look was one of concern. "Oh dear. You've made a pun."

He grinned. "What a rotten girl you are."

She grinned back.

"Rotten? Nothing of the sort," interrupted Lady Sherbourne. "I only make the best people my godchildren."

Captain Gracechurch turned to glance at the old woman, puzzled.

"You've called my goddaughter rotten, Henry. Apologize."

Beatrice dared a glance at Mama, who looked at Beatrice like she was a three-headed changeling switched by a demon king.

"Only if she wants me to." The captain's eyebrows rose in a question and Beatrice tugged her hand out of his clasp. Drat conventions. If he forgot to let it go, it should have been no business of hers.

"I'll call him 'wretched' in return and we'll consider it a draw."

Godmama was content. She poured out tea and handed cups around.

"How many godchildren do you have, Godmama?" he asked, settling himself on the chair nearest Beatrice. "Will I discover scores of them?"

"Only you and the Thornton girls. I suppose you would have met long ago if you had not been so determined to let Napoleon murder you. The Thorntons have no excuses. They've preferred to plant themselves in the countryside like a row of turnips." Beatrice coughed back a laugh and met the captain's dancing eyes. They both darted a quick gaze to her hands.

"My lady, what nonsense," Mama began. "We should leave you with your guest."

"Now who is talking nonsense, Sarah? I mean to speak to you about this Season," she asserted, serving around wedges of dark, rich spice cake and pushing one into Mama's hands. "Henry, take Beatrice to the window. This will bore her."

It most certainly would not. Mama and Lady Sherbourne were like armies squaring off in battle. But, for once Beatrice was happy to be steered aside. The captain and the cake and the close window seat could beat those two generals any time.

"We must do something, Sarah." Godmama's voice carried even so far.

Captain Gracechurch leaned over to Beatrice and whispered, for her ears alone, "I am thankful to see you looking well." He looked at her more closely, his eyes suddenly widening. Then he reached careful fingers toward her forehead before recalling himself, his hand hovering an inch from the bruise on her forehead. "Not so well. Do you owe that to your coach ride?"

Beatrice put a self-conscious hand to her head. Would he never see her at her best? An early morning inspection had shown the area to be an angry blur of blue, purple, green and yellow. "I attempted to argue politics with a coach door," she stated in mock outrage. "The dratted thing was intractable."

"They usually are," he said, smiling slowly, exactly the way she liked. "They never see reason as you hope they will." His expression settled into more serious lines. "It must have hurt terribly, Miss Thornton, but I hate to think of how much worse it could have been. I was so relieved to find that you'd arrived safely home. Your footman must have thought he had a madman at the door this morning. Did nobody warn you about the fog? It can be deadly."

She took care with her answer. "There are so many rules in Town that are a matter of life and death. Never dance more than twice with the same gentleman. Always wear spotless white for one's first Season. Strive to imitate, as best as possible, a statue from antiquity—be cool, well-formed and have nothing to say."

That got a laugh and she allowed herself to join him, burbling the rest. "In the face of all that, it's a small wonder no one ever got around to warning us about the fog."

A well-bred squabble from the sofa became loud enough to intrude. "There is no need for it, my lady. I am perfectly capable—"

"I see no evidence of that," Godmama countered.

Beatrice blushed and turned again to meet the captain's intent stare. He returned to his cake, a soft smile playing against his lips.

"We will be leaving soon," Mama called, not as absorbed in her own conversation as Beatrice hoped she would be.

"Your mother will have none of me," the captain grinned, his voice a husky whisper that seemed to encompass the window seat in heavy curtains. "It must be the regimentals. Uniforms make mothers anxious."

They made maidens anxious too. Though Morton's Cross had weathered several encampments of soldiers without her becoming the least bit overset.

He finished off his cake and pressed a thumb onto his plate, picking up the last of the crumbs and nibbling at them like a small boy until he looked up to see her watching.

"My nanny would have pinched my hand for that," he admitted. "Terrible manners. I'm hardly fit for company anymore."

"Last night you told me that you had returned from Spain. How long have you been back?" Beatrice asked, even as she could feel her mother's eyes on her.

The captain tensed but said evenly, "I rode into Town yesterday."

"From Plymouth?" she asked incredulously.

"Yes, from Badajoz."

Her eyes widened. The whole of London was tense with anticipation after the first bulletin had sped from the coast. Papa had stood with the crowds at Whitehall yesterday, jostling about with the mob as they waited for news.

Captain Gracechurch used his fork to trace a pattern on the plate. His knuckles showed white where he gripped the utensil.

Beatrice quietly turned the topic. "No wonder you clean your plate so quickly," she noted. "I imagine there is little spice cake in Spain."

He laughed, she thought in relief, earning him another scowl from Mama. "You imagine correctly, Miss Thornton."

She nodded, feeling helpless. "I hope you are able to tell me about it sometime, Captain." It was plainly put, and his face met hers squarely.

He was silent for a long moment as her heart beat in her ears. "Will you come on a ride with me?"

Her colour rose as she considered the cost. He could not know what he was asking of her.

The time stretched and he said, self-deprecation in his smile, "I am beginning to wonder if my regimentals have lost some of their old power. They always seemed to do the trick before."

Her brow arched delicately, she roused to answer him back. "I'm sure there never was a *before*."

She glanced over at her mother, still pitched in combat. Mama was not the sort to lock Beatrice in her bedroom on a ration of bread and water for a week. She'd simply appeal to her own rightness—knowing that Beatrice would do the safe and proper thing. But Mama wasn't always right. Last night those once-clear waters had become muddy.

"Yes," Beatrice replied at length. She nodded more affirmatively and he smiled. "Yes. That would be nice." Nice. Such a tepid word. It wouldn't be nice. It would be earth-shattering.

"Tomorrow?"

There was another hesitation. Heaven above. Wasn't she going to ask Mama? Consult with her better judgment?

Was Beatrice really going to do it?

"Yes."

Chapter Seven

When Henry turned up the shallow steps of Fox's townhouse, a figure strode past him, knocking into his shoulder.

"Pardon," the man muttered as he spun around, his thick burr so low it was hardly audible. He put a quick hand to the brim of his hat in apology and jogged on.

Henry knocked Fox's boot aside with his own and took the deep chair opposite him as he asked, "Who was that character?" The library's heavy curtains obscured the late-afternoon sun. "Spotted neckcloth, bolted from the house a moment ago?"

Fox lifted his head from where it rested on the rich leather. "Did you talk to him?"

"There was no time for it."

Fox leaned back again. "A business acquaintance. He should know to use the tradesman's entrance."

Henry saw a book in Fox's hand. An actual book. "You're reading *Debrett's Peerage*? Is that what nobles do when we little people aren't looking?"

Fox put a finger in the volume, already filled with scraps of paper sticking from the top, to mark his place. "You've ruined my whole day, Harry. I was waiting to see you at breakfast, but you had already gone."

"I was visiting some old haunts," he said, omitting that he'd chosen a posy of violets for a girl—the first such flowers he'd bought in more than four years. He had spared himself the expense of delivery, and assured himself of her safety, by delivering them to St. James's Square.

"Walking is common, Harry."

"I'm common, Fox. Your mother was the one who married the title and the lands and the hereditary honours. My mother had the good sense to wed a simple 'mister.' I do as I please."

"I've a stable of horses I insist you make yourself free with. Where did you go this morning?"

"I had some calls to make."

"So soon? The ladies must have missed Captain Gracechurch." Fox laughed.

"Any women I knew four years ago are married now." Mothers, even.

"Plenty of scope for amusement there too."

Henry's reply was as stiff as the gold braid on his coat. "I was with my godmother taking tea."

Fox looked like he might vomit on his boots. "I hope you're in the will," he drawled, picking up *Debrett's* again. Henry's eyes strayed to the side table on which lay a well-thumbed social directory. Fox was sitting in a whole room of histories, biographies, theological discourses—even novels if he wanted amusement. What was so engrossing about a list of dusty old peerages?

"I went to Whitehall too." Henry folded his arms, leaned back in his chair, extended his legs, and looked down at himself. Army, as far as the eye could see. Starch and brass, ready for a parade review.

"Whitehall?" Fox asked. "You turned in your dispatches, Harry. What more could Wellington want? What was in them?"

Henry's neck prickled and then he laughed at himself. If there was anyone safe to speak freely with, it was Fox. Hadn't they been born only miles apart? Hadn't they been terrified together that first year at Eton? But the habit of war—of imagining everyone was after his neck—was not easily laid aside.

"No, no, let me guess," Fox went on when Henry didn't speak. "Wellington asks for a fleet of elephants to charge over the Pyrenees?" When this didn't receive any answer but a smile, Fox shook his head. "No? Then, a thousand of our best opera dancers to distract French forces." Henry didn't respond. "Not that either? In that case, I will simply have to keep guessing until you tell me."

"Feeding them—the elephants or the opera dancers—would be the difficulty. There's little enough food to go around. But I didn't crack the official seals. If I had, Liverpool would see me court martialled. The dispatches will be published tomorrow, anyway." Not for a moment did he betray the fact that they had been dictated by his own hand.

Fox arched his back and stretched, his eyelashes drooping lazily against his cheeks. "Aren't you the least curious? You were holding Wellington's strategy, laid bare."

"Nothing so consequential. One of them was my letter resigning my commission."

Fox slapped the book onto the table. "Great smokes. Army-mad Harry Gracechurch selling out? Why ever for? Is Spain a lost cause?" Fox leaned forward, wanting, Henry supposed, to be comforting in his way.

"Wellington doesn't let anything stand in his way," Henry shared, shaking his head. It was the vaguest generality, but one which was true nonetheless.

"I can admire that," Fox replied, a lazy hand reaching for a bottle of brandy and tilting it at Henry who shook his head. "The man had the terrible luck of being born Irish. A fourth son? Should, by rights, be scraping out a living as a music master. But he got a viscountcy for Talavera," Fox noted, staring deep into the bottle and lifting it slightly by the lip again and again, turning it counter-clockwise on the small table at his side. "Then an earldom for Ciudad Rodrigo." Another turn as Fox clicked his teeth together. "There's no telling how high he may go. The King might make him God before we're through." He tipped the bottle to his lips and took a swallow. "How quickly fortunes rise in war."

Henry's eyes were hard as glass. *Fortunes rose?* Men died, shovelled like coal into unmarked graves. Thousands of them. Lined up in row after row after row until, walking down it, you went almost mad thinking of the wives and children and mothers and sweethearts at home, waiting to hear the news. Waiting for the dispatches. Sheaves of paper with the names written on them—the ink running like blood.

Henry's eyes bored into the ceiling and he breathed in and out as Fox went on with what was only nonsense, after all. Ignorant nonsense. Henry must get a handle on himself.

"I should have followed you off to war. I wouldn't be consigned to be a piddling baron my whole life."

That, at least, was laughable. Henry summoned a grin. "Only a poor baron. The most pitiful creature in all England. Do you *know* how few barons there are?"

"Eighty-seven. Existent," Fox answered without hesitation.

"You've counted?"

"And plenty of those are lesser titles. Half the barons you meet are in line for something better when their fathers die."

Henry snorted and reached for the bottle of brandy and took a swallow—his tongue pressing against his teeth as his throat burned.

"I would think they would dread it," Henry said, continuing when Fox looked puzzled. "Fathers dying." He sat up and set the bottle on the table again. "My father broke his foot in January. He did not ask me to resign, but...," Henry left off. Something as *quaint* as a longing for hearth and kin had no place for Fox.

Henry doubted Fox even remembered his parents, they had been dead so long. He'd been packed off to London and raised by some aunts on the Fox side. His other family, Gracechurch cousins, had only received duty-visits once or twice a year. Fox said it gave him a certain flexibility. Maybe it did, but Henry, overrun with family, could never think of Fox without pity. If his mother had survived the fever, she might have kept him from the habit he sometimes had of treating people as a mess to be wiped up with a soiled cloth, dangling from the end of two pinched fingers.

"Oh, I say," Fox called, not really saying anything. "Are you going home straight away?"

"No. Nothing so urgent. He is on the mend, but slowing down. Anyway, Whitehall wants to pick me clean—make sure I take nothing back to Sussex but my bones. I am looking tomorrow for more permanent lodgings."

"Bosh. You'll stay here. Even if you won't tell me anything about your business." He went on with a note of wounded pride in his voice. "Do you treat everyone like a black-hearted spy?"

"It's all dreadfully dull." Henry dropped his voice so it contained a bit of regimental, white-whiskered bluster. *"Captain, what are the billet requirements for such-and-such regiment? Are the mules going lame hauling such-and-such provisions?* All like that for hours and hours while a secretary scribbles a report if I so much as sneeze."

"And what do you tell them? About the mules."

"The truth."

Fox collapsed back into his chair. "You're really determined not to give me the slightest morsel of information. If I were one of those beggars outside a church, you would sweep past without dropping a sou."

"I would hardly have French money rattling in my pockets."

Fox blew a laughing breath. "A plain, English farthing then. Come, didn't your good night's sleep mean anything to you?"

Henry was tempted to relent. To tell him that Wellington was stretched painfully thin. That the slaughter at Badajoz had sparked an undisciplined rage in the great man and it was just as well the enemy did not know. This, along with other important truths about the war, was a bottle stoppered up inside of Henry and he wished he could tell somebody.

But Fox would not understand.

"You know," Henry began, pivoting to something more banal, less wearing, "I didn't sleep that well. There was shouting from the street and I could swear one of your servants was running through the house, pulling doors open and shut. Terrible racket."

Fox raised a finger. "That was me. I ran out to see what was what, but the coach had moved along before I could offer a refuge."

"That was good of you."

"I can feel your low expectations emanating from your seat, Harry. I am sorry the doors hadn't been oiled, though," Fox stated, all trace of amusement gone. "You can be sure heads will roll down in the servant's quarters."

"Not on my account," Henry insisted, hoping that Fox's mood would not sustain itself long enough to deliver the promised punishment.

Even now, Fox ironed away his black looks and gave an easy smile. "Any plans tonight? We could have dinner at my club. The Secretary of the Navy comes most days, but he never wants to talk to anyone not in uniform."

"Excellent. My social calendar is filling up."

"Oh? Military connections?"

"I'm taking Lady Sherbourne's goddaughter for a ride in the park tomorrow," Henry replied, surprised to find how much he wanted to talk about Beatrice.

There had been that moment at his godmother's. *I hope you are able to tell me about it sometime, Captain.* A straightforward remark, but it told him she was not only capable of bright flashes of wit and teasing turns of phrase. If he were of a mind to talk, she would listen.

"You had *better* be in the will," Fox asserted. "Goddaughters are always dire, and plain as buttered peas."

Buttered peas couldn't smile like Beatrice did. "It's the young woman I danced with last night. Miss Thornton."

"Thornton?" Fox picked up the social directory and rolled it into a tight scroll. His thumbnail flicked the pages where they fanned out.

"Miss *Beatrice* Thornton?"

Chapter Eight

Papa filled the uneasy silence with snippets of the morning papers being read aloud. "There's something here about the Royal Horse Artillery," he said, moving along when there was no encouragement. "And a dog who can bark out 'Lambeth' and count to five. Then there's a hot air balloon exhibition in Hackney next week...." His hopeful eyes darted between Mama and Beatrice.

She poured milk and stirred her tea, her mind far away. She took a sip and smiled into her cup where no one would see. The captain would be crossing their threshold this morning.

Papa cleared his throat and continued, "'Captain Henry Gracechurch,'"

Beatrice sat up, her teacup clattering onto the saucer.

"'...Aide-de-camp of General, the Earl of Wellington, arrived two afternoons ago at this Office, bringing dispatches, addressed by his Lordship to the Earl of Liverpool, of which the following are extracts.'" He looked up. "Do you want me to go on?"

"Do," Beatrice urged, half commanding, her fingers itching to tear the paper from his hands.

"'The river *Agueda* was not fordable, the fire continued during the fourth and fifth.'" Papa pressed forward, humming and mumbling his way between bits of coherency. "'I determined to attack the place that night... the French scrambled to protect the walls of the old fort, letting loose volleys of musket and cannon fire. British infantry poured through the gaps in breached outer walls, but soon the dead and wounded grew to such a number as to become insurmountable.'"

An echo of Shakespeare came to her and she shivered. *Close the wall up with our English dead.* The captain could so easily have been one of them.

Papa was still running on. "'Despite the obstinate resistance of the enemy, the castle was carried. This dispatch will be delivered to your Lordship by Captain Gracechurch,' etcetera, etcetera," Papa finished, folding the paper and laying it by his plate with a smack. "How about that?"

Beatrice dropped several inches back into her chair and chewed her lip. "The account is somewhat… graphic."

Papa snorted. "That was a bare sketch. They are not likely to print the worst of it in a newspaper," he stated, making her more anxious still. He then picked up *The Gazette*, whose thick black headline blared *Storming of Badajoz*. His gaze jumped back and forth down the column and he began to summarize. "The ship carrying the dispatches almost foundered in the Bay of Biscay."

Beatrice's stomach lurched as she tried not to imagine Henry lost at sea. *Henry*. It felt unsafe to think of him that way in front of Mama, though her mother could not rifle through her mind as easily as she could through a purse. Still, Beatrice cast her eyes down where they could not betray her thoughts.

"Then he rode all the way from Plymouth with the colours of Badajoz flying over his coach. You know, I should like to meet him," Papa said, caught up in the story.

He looked up then and encountered Mama's expression. "What is it?" he asked, puzzlement writ across his face. He picked up a snowy napkin. "Have I got something—?"

"Captain Gracechurch," Mama huffed, slicing open a letter, leaving a jagged tear. Her mouth opened and closed several times before she went on. "Beatrice has an appointment to ride with him this morning."

Papa slapped the table. "Capital. He's coming here, you say? What sort of…?" He trailed off, finding in his wife's countenance an unwelcoming harbour.

Mama lifted her chin at Penny, busy buttering a roll, and then she looked directly at Beatrice. There was no softness, entreaty or persuasion in her face, only certainty that Beatrice's small rebellion would be a temporary aberration, quickly solved and swept neatly into the rubbish bin.

Beatrice pushed her plate aside and stood. "Yes, Papa. I accepted a perfectly ordinary invitation to ride in the park. Now, if you'll excuse me, I must get ready." Then she went from the room, every line of her back stiff with defiance.

What was so unreasonable about driving with a gentleman? Young ladies danced and spoke and laughed with men every day of the Season and it need not be anything serious and lasting. She coughed away the lump in her throat. There was a new and dark corner of hurt inside herself when she thought of the captain, and she was not brave enough yet to examine it closely.

Casting open the doors of her clothes press, she gave a long, defeated breath. She had to find something to wear. There was nothing of what she wanted. Still, her eyes roamed over the dispiriting choices until she unpegged a walking gown the colour of day-old porridge, slipping it on and doing up the tapes as tightly as she could. Spinning on her toes, she assessed how well the fabric skimmed her figure. This gown fit her better than most, relying on its lumpish colour to put men off. If Beatrice imagined, she could think of it as an amber overskirt with a fresh cream trim.

Now for the hat.

Beatrice stood on her tiptoes and reached for the box, brushing it with her fingertips. She grunted and reached higher, but still the dratted thing didn't move.

This is silly. Nothing was out of her reach. Why was she pretending it was?

Leaning her head around the door she checked the room and tapped her fingertips on the wood, recalling an image of herself in the library, curled up on a chair, weak and shaking. Helpless. That image had haunted her these past days, making her sick with shame. She had done that to herself, letting her power become as useless as a rusted tool, abandoned in the field.

But rising had been useful the other night. She looked to the hatbox and heard a memory of a blacksmith's hammer striking across a ploughman's blade, making it sharp, bright. Rust could be shaken off. It should be.

Beatrice brushed her palms against her skirts, filling her mind with lemon drops, tufts of sheep's wool doing cartwheels on the lawn, soap bubbles carried on the summer air, and felt her slippers lift from the rug. A mere foot or two, but it felt heavenly to rise, to uncoil the spring that kept her earthbound. She let herself enjoy the feeling for a moment, turning in a slow, elegant pivot like a figure in a music box. Not too much time. Not at first. She must be fit for the captain when he came.

Beatrice reached for the hatbox and found herself in the wrong spot. *Bother.* She pulled herself along the top of the wardrobe, feeling the powdery thickness of the undusted wood, until she could lift the box from a stack.

Bang went the door and Beatrice forced herself down in a panic, landing on the carpet in a crumpled heap, the hatbox tumbling after her.

"What were you jumping for?" Penny asked, her braids dangling down as she leaned over.

"You are supposed to knock," Beatrice scowled, feeling the ebb of panic as it washed away. All that fuss and she had forgotten to lock the door. *Idiot.*

"That's a stupid rule. I didn't startle you off a chair, did I?" Penny asked, offering Beatrice a hand up while looking around.

Beatrice brushed out her skirts and Penny picked up the hatbox, opening the lid and flopping backward on the bed as though mortally wounded from enemy fire. Within was a high poke bonnet trimmed in an orange-y red ribbon and purple plumes, which would do nothing for Beatrice's green eyes.

"Oh, Beatrice. No. I forbid it. You cannot go on your first—" She sputtered for a moment. "—your first *everything*, looking like… No."

Beatrice plucked the hat away and turned to the mirror, perching the bonnet upon her head. Her hair was nice, she thought, but not vivid. Not golden or brunette or raven or auburn. Merely a nice light brown. The garish colours of the trim made it look muddy. She strangled off a frown and got on with it. "Such dramatics. It's a hat." She laughed, tying the vermilion ribbons under her chin.

Penny leapt at her and, in a swift motion, pulled the ribbon loose, lifting the hat from Beatrice's head. She dashed to the fireplace and threw the bonnet into the flames. "And good riddance," she cried, her young voice low and intense.

Silence reigned for a few seconds and then Beatrice drew a breath, wrinkling her nose against the pungent smell of feathers crisping. How long had she wanted to do that? To take the contents of the clothes press and tip them into a heap and light a bonfire. The correct thing to do would be to take another hat down. Violent pink and plodding brown or limp and orange all over.

Instead, Beatrice threw open the window sash, letting in a fresh breeze. She picked up her gloves and swatted her sister's arm. Nerve carried her on. "You owe me a hat."

***

Beatrice found Papa waiting in the salon, far from his usual confines in the library, reading the Parliamentary report. When he saw her, he patted the seat next to him. She sat and for a long minute there was only the gentle swish of paper, until he said, "This unpleasantness…."

Beatrice felt the leaden weight of guilt. She'd been unforgivably rude to Mama. "Papa, I—"

"Do you suppose the wreckers believe they can dis-invent the machines?"

The words crowding her throat cannoned to a halt. Her eyebrows shot up. "You're speaking of the weavers' riots in Yorkshire?"

"What else?" He tilted the newspaper in her direction as she blinked. Papa wasn't going to rake her over the coals about the ride after all. He could call her foolhardy and reckless. Uncaring. And the rebuke would sting as Mama's had not, because his scolds were temperate and rare.

Beatrice looked to the clock, grinding its way to eleven, and ran a tongue along dry lips.

"He's not late," Papa noted, his gaze back on the paper, a smile playing over his face.

The jangle of curricle and horses, followed closely by a knock on the door, made her sit up. A man had come for her and the air had left her lungs.

"Compose yourself," Mama scolded as she walked sedately into the room, the first words she'd uttered to Beatrice since the withering "You'll ruin us all" of yesterday.

Beatrice looked down at her hands crossed in her lap. She might feel like a herd of cattle was stampeding around her insides, but there was nothing in her manner to cavil at.

Beatrice made a mental tally mark against Mama only to have the entire thing obliterated by the sight of Captain Gracechurch on the threshold. The cattle in her stomach stopped their frantic run, standing tense and nosing, waiting for the slightest thing to send them off again.

He bowed over Mama's hand first. "It's a pleasure to meet you again." He proffered a sunny bouquet.

"Primroses," she said dryly, and lay them aside at once. "How… seasonal."

Beatrice sucked in her lip, ready to apologize for the slight, but Papa got there first. He shook the captain's hand with both of his own. "You're one of Wellington's aides, I hear. A wonderful man. The stories you must have."

"It's a pleasure to meet someone who shares my enthusiasm for him." The captain smiled.

Papa nodded and even his whiskers were trembling in anticipation. "Is it true what was reported in the paper?" he asked, pulling a folded sheet of newsprint he happened to have from his coat pocket.

Mama coughed slightly and Papa took the hint, though not without giving her a frown. "Another time, perhaps," he deferred, tucking the paper back where it came from. The captain cast his eyes on Beatrice.

"The horses are fresh," he said. "We shouldn't keep them waiting."

"I'll get my hat," Beatrice replied, dashing to pluck it from the hall table. She perched it on her head, giving it a dashing angle as she tied the soft, rose ribbons under her chin. Her eyes met her reflection in the mirror. *Almost perfect*, she thought, bouncing on her toes. When he looked at her, the captain's admiration was unqualified.

"That's your sister's hat," Mama burst out, breaking the slim silver thread that seemed to stretch between Beatrice and Henry.

Beatrice nodded, her smile tight. "Mine has gone missing. Penny was good enough to lend me hers."

Mama's mouth pursed, but Papa ducked under the brim of the hat to give Beatrice a quick salute on the cheek. "Have some fun," he whispered, and scooted her out the door.

The captain helped Beatrice into the carriage and leaped up to the seat next to her. She arranged her skirts, and they were off, moving away from the dark cloud of Mama's disapproval.

Traffic was light for several blocks, and he began to talk. "Miss Thornton. Have I somehow managed to...?" His firm hands handled the reins as he groped for words. "Your mother seems—what are you laughing for?"

"You made her acquaintance yesterday. I'm trying to work out what you think you could have done."

"Nothing except ask you to ride out with me. Was that it?"

She wrinkled her nose in amusement. "That would be silly," she teased, so careful with her words.

He was looking at her again when a front wheel dipped into a large pothole in the road, sending her sliding across the seat. He caught her with one arm around her waist, looking down into her face for a moment as their breaths, quick and short, mingled. "I ought to take more care with you," he said, putting her back where she had been and withdrawing the arm that held her fast.

"Mmmm," she murmured, her heart racing, not trusting herself to speak. As she took hold of herself, her eyes scanned the cobbles below for pits and ruts, her mind cursing the men who had laid them so well.

Beatrice steadied her breathing and held tight to the curricle seat. She had spent all morning insisting to herself that she could ride out with a man without anything untoward happening, and she shouldn't now be thinking of casting herself into his lap at the first opportunity.

As they navigated the park, watching the butterflies of Society stop every yard or two to greet a new acquaintance, they laughed together at the notion of taking in the fresh air amidst such a dense crowd. He asked, "You've been to Hyde Park before?"

"Not for many years. When I was a girl we used to come up to Town every spring and I would take riding lessons from an old horse-dealer." She raised her arm, pointing across him, and turned her face to find him near. She pulled her hand back and retrieved a few important inches of space. "Nearer the west end."

"But not since?"

"No, we've not come to London for some time."

His eyes held a question. This was her cue to rehearse Mama's story about how she had been sickly—how she still was. How it confined her to the country, and made her a poor friend and a difficult companion. Her heartbeat drummed in her ears.

Some deep, cracking boom shattered around the lies like a massive oak falling in a wood, splitting the atmosphere, as cannon fire blasted over the river. Papa's "something" about the Royal Horse Artillery and official celebrations over the battle won came to mind. In front of them, a great flock of birds took flight, their wings beating the air as another boom followed. And another. And another. And another.

Beatrice turned to smile at the captain and found him ramrod straight, his face hard, his eyes unseeing. His hands were fists, threaded through with reins.

All about them, horses rolled their necks and shook their harnesses. But when the last echo of cannon fire faded, activity around them became brisk again. It seemed to be shaken off at once. Carriages sped onward, hats were raised, voices mingled merrily, and still the captain sat on, as still as stone, his jaw clenched.

She waited for several moments, sensing the crowd behind them bunch around the curricle, feeling curious eyes begin to rest on him the way they had once rested on her. He'd rescued her then.

Beatrice reached over and took the reins from his hand, loosening his tight grasp with a firm one of her own. She gave a sharp, unladylike whistle and then gave the near-side horse a light flick on the rump, ignoring the heads that turned to watch.

"I'm not good at this," she apologised, her voice as gentle as when she talked to a startled mare. She drove them up the carriageway until there was a break in the traffic and, steering to the side, she brought the team to a halt. "I taxed my father for months before he agreed to teach me."

At her side, she felt a breath leave Henry. Poor man was shaking, ragged. He wiped a hand across his mouth and they sat on until the breeze played up. He straightened again, his tongue running along his lower lip. "It was the cannons. I was never so afraid in Spain, but…." He swallowed and shrugged. "Fear is settling its accounts, I think, demanding payment now that the danger is over." Henry took another breath and pushed his hands through his hair. "Better now than when I faced the guns."

That was, no doubt, true. But it offered little comfort for what he had suffered. "Has it passed?"

"For now. The old soldiers say it eases in time. I don't expect to hear artillery when I am returned to Sussex," he said, trying to smile and failing "Miss Thornton, you must think—" His eyes were on his hands. They lay splayed on his legs.

"There is nothing I *must* think, Captain," she stated, shading her eyes and gazing into the distance, giving him room to collect himself. "I confess a passionate interest in your middle name, however. Or do you have several, as befits a proper Englishman?"

He regarded her for a moment before his lips curled into a smile. Then he nodded. "Only two. Robin and St. John." She looked him over critically, as a doctor might, but encountered an intensity in his expression that reminded her that Captain Gracechurch was not a helpless patient.

His eyes glanced up. "I like your hat," he added as the wind picked up and stirred the streaming ribbons of her bonnet between them, dancing them over his shoulder to caress the long column of neck under his ear.

Penny would never get it back now.

Beatrice had to say something. The coolness with which she had taken command of the carriage was gone, burning away like dew under a morning sun. "Mere plain chip straw, pleated grosgrain edging, and three silk rosebuds for trim." Oh heavens, she thought, wishing she could clap hands over her mouth. "It's nothing special, really." *Stop talking. Stop.*

Henry placed his hands over hers and she quit breathing. "Miss Thornton." That scar on his chin was only inches away. "If I may have the reins?" She blinked and her cheeks burned as she tugged her hands from his. He threaded the leather straps between nimble fingers.

They were once again swept up in the stream of carriages and horses. "Thank you for that," he murmured, eyes on the path.

She shook her head, though she could not look up. It was easier to forget how dangerous this attraction was when they were simply laughing together. But their conversation, which seemed so often to sparkle like the sun on a shallow stream, only had to flow into still pools of deep water for her to remember. She liked him too well.

She shied away from examining it too closely. "Everyone is looking so fine," she noted, glancing around because she had to look at something that wasn't him. "I'm not used to so much splendour. It's impressive that they manage it, day after day."

"It's easy enough when one has the money," he said, smoothly following her lead.

She dared a look at him and glanced away again, pushing her words in the space between them, worried that it was already growing too late for prudence. "That one," she tilted her chin, "has more money than sense."

"The fellow in the liverish waistcoat?"

"Heavens." She gave a low whistle, too vulgar for Town. But the captain didn't seem to mind. "That *is* eye-catching. No, I meant the woman in the orange landau. The one with the ostrich plumes jutting out every which way." The matron rode by in splendid style looking for all the world like some lost mate of a brightly-plumed tropical bird. The woman gave them a vague smile as she passed and turned her face to the sun, her multi-hued plumes bouncing and bobbing as she went on her way.

Beatrice broke into a grin. "I take it back. I take it all back. You know, I rather envy her."

"Do you really want a hat like that?" he asked, a little horrified.

"Well, no. But I'm not joking. Her hat is not to my taste, but it is to hers and she is wearing exactly what she pleases. Imagine being someone who doesn't care a rap what anybody thinks and has the courage to be themselves."

"It's a rare quality."

"My little sister is that sort of person."

The captain's eyes roamed over Penny's hat and rested on Beatrice's face, taking his time at it.

"I already told you I like the hat. She has good taste."

"That's Mama's taste, mostly. Penny expresses herself in other ways, but one always feels that she is offering a kind of royal dispensation in allowing our mother to take such extreme care over her appearance. Mama gets so anxious if we don't look 'just so.'"

Beatrice remembered her gown and, suddenly she felt a flush rush to her cheeks. Lord. He'd got her talking again and she'd stepped up to her neck into trouble. Too late to say that Mama had no taste or didn't care what any of them wore. What reason would he come up with to account for her gown, whose color in this light, she decided, was more like oily three-day-old gruel than plain porridge. He was going to say something about it, she was sure.

"I should like to meet your little sister. I hope you'll allow me the pleasure soon."

Beatrice bent her head, intent on creating the straightest seams her gloves could achieve.

Her hopes for this outing had been modest. To draw a small circle of independence around herself that Mama could not fail to notice. To collect some memories—lovely ones of her time in London. To admire some gold braid on broad shoulders. She had not considered that Captain Gracechurch might want to call again.

She was ready with her prepared speech. *I have a wasting disease.*

But the idea of him wishing to visit her again was like a will-o'-wisp—dangerous, tempting her to explore. "I'll have Penny keep her ears scrubbed for when you happen to pass our door."

"You may depend on it." He smiled, snapping the horses into a brisk trot.

The pleasure of his promise won out over the worry of what Mama might say. A social call was nothing. A gentleman might call on a young lady any day of the week and it wouldn't have to mean anything. Beatrice was still on safe ground, even if she seemed to be flying over it in a breathless rush.

"Captain, I—"

"Henry." A female voice cut through the noise of the park and Beatrice, along with half the Social world, twisted her head around to look.

The captain performed a tricky bit of driving and pulled the carriage nearer to a stand of trees. Half-crouching out of his seat, he searched the crowd. "That baggage," he muttered.

Baggage. What should have been an insult was said with too much affection to lend it any sting. To her surprise, Beatrice found herself praying. The existence of a young lady with the right to call him by his Christian name was a setback, unless, by some miracle, it was one of his sisters dropping in from Sussex. Or a cousin. She prayed, never more fervently, *Please let it be an ugly cousin.*

A glossy yellow high-perch phaeton pulled to a smooth stop next to them and the baggage—a tiny thing with hair the colour of midnight and the sort of face that invited one to imagine wood nymphs—jumped to her feet.

Beatrice looked heavenward, accusing.

Henry slid an arm along the back of the carriage seat, encompassing Beatrice as he leaned over. "Meg, you nit, sit down or you're going to cause the horses to bolt. Can't you go anywhere without frightening the birds out of the trees?"

Nit. No tone could make that loverlike. Beatrice reminded herself to say a thankful prayer tonight and relaxed a little until feeling Henry's hand brush across the middle of her back made her sit up again.

The nymph plopped to her seat, a wholly human grin crossing her face. "When did you turn into such an old woman?" she asked, rearranging her skirts.

"Miss Thornton, may I introduce you to Miss Margaret Summers, the worst hunting companion a fellow ever had?"

"Quite true," Miss Summers nodded her head in greeting, but her eyes darted between Henry and Beatrice, speculative and amused.

The girl's escort had his boot propped lazily on the footboard, his smooth black hair brushed back, close against his head. His astonishing sky-blue eyes hadn't stopped looking at Beatrice since they pulled up. She wriggled a little in her seat.

The introduction Beatrice expected was not made, however, because Miss Summers was charging on like a brigade of light infantry. "When did you get back from the continent? I saw your family less than... let me see...." She had a look of concentration on her face. "Right before I came down to Town, I believe, and I got here in the middle of March. Your mother has been magnificent, Henry, running the estate. Have you been home?"

"Slow down, Meg. You run too fast. I've not yet been home. I will be here a few weeks more, I should think." Beatrice's heart cannoned into her side. A few weeks, that was all. And most of them would be occupied some other way with people who would have a greater claim on his time than a chance-met girl. She would be lucky to get a house call and another ride before he was gone forever.

Henry continued. "I'm surprised to see you in London. I didn't know they allowed grubby urchins into ballrooms."

Did he have eyes? The girl was a goddess.

"Grubby and relegated to holding your tatty," Miss Summers coughed, the picture of innocence, "and empty game bag, as I recall," she teased. "I was nineteen, last September. Grandfather banished me to my aunt to see if she can make anything of me. She calls me 'beastly child' at every meal." Beatrice smiled despite herself.

"You deserve it?" he asked.

She looked slightly wicked. "Of course." Beatrice could feel the girl's eyes sweep over her—over her dress—and wanted to shrink in her seat. But, however undisciplined Miss Summers's actions, the girl hadn't a hint of guile. When she smiled, Beatrice could not help but smile back.

"You must forgive me, Miss Thornton, for being impertinent," she apologised. "But it's best you know what I am from the outset."

"Outset of what?" the man beside her roused himself to ask.

"Our friendship," Beatrice replied, bristling at his tone. Her words surprised herself and earned a look of touching gratitude from the goddess. "'Begin as you mean to go on.' Isn't that what nannies say?"

Henry touched her arm and, again, awareness tickled down her wrist and up to her shoulder. "Miss Thornton, I've neglected to introduce you to my cousin, Lord Fox. He grew up alongside Meg's family and mine."

"Charmed, Miss Thornton," Lord Fox breathed, brushing the air with a salute. "Enjoying the air of London?"

"In the park? Yes. It's a lovely day." His gaze crawled over her as they continued to exchange banalities. It was because of her frock, of course. Lord Fox could hardly be expected to look past it. No one could.

The captain does.

The thought, coming in on the heels of the other, was as good as a Christmas present. Better, even.

Finally, Henry touched her arm and said they must be off. She looked back at him and nodded brightly, and he bridged the short distance between them with a smile.

Despite Mama's best efforts to render her invisible, this man saw her.

Chapter Nine

The bedsheets were damp when Henry woke, twisted around his body like a strangling rope. He shoved them roughly off and sat, head in hands, on the side of the bed as his breathing slowed. The moon lit the room with a dim glow.

He'd had it again—the same nightmare. Always the same. Howling wind, rain lashing him in the face as he struggled through sticky mud to crest a hill. Hell unfolded itself before his eyes. He jerked and flinched against the cacophony of exploding mines, artillery, and hand grenades as they shot from the walls of Badajoz, each burst sending earth and bodies skyward. Across the hills the air was thick with burning. The black smoke roared up to heaven.

Then, with the peculiar logic of dreams, he would find himself in the hot centre of the battle, grapeshot pinging past his ears, hand gripping sabre or pistol—God knew he could not hold them now without sweats—fighting up the ladders, tangling in them, until the vicious swipe of a blade crossed his ribs.

Henry put a clammy hand to his side and fell back on his pillows, feeling the puckered skin along the scar where it interrupted the planes of muscle. The sword had cut him in Talavera. Years ago. The wound had long since healed, but the memories chased him, tumbling over themselves in their haste to eat away at his peace.

He closed his eyes. *Peace.* He breathed in and out, repeating the word.

Beatrice was there again. Behind his eyelids when he closed them. And she was always grinning. He grinned too and felt his skin cool. He flexed his fingers against his chest and sensed, again, her small hands easing the reins from his yesterday and taking command when he'd lost all ability to move. How calm she had been. He had waited for some show of distaste or recoil, some indication that she thought him damaged or unmanly—things he couldn't help but think of himself at times—but it never came.

He lay like that for a long while, chest rising and falling, and let the feeling she brought wash over him as he fell asleep.

In the morning he felt foolish. He always did. Sunlight had a way of turning ugly memories and dark nightmares into a cheap village pantomime that should hardly have the power to scare an old woman. Nothing so dramatic as demons haunted his dreams, he told himself. Nothing so unearthly as an angel guarded his sleep.

But later, as he crossed St. James's Park on his way to Whitehall, he realized she was with him still, waiting on the edge of his consciousness. Not offering him peace, now, but disturbing it. He allowed that bringing her to bed had given him the first decent night's sleep in weeks, but it was time to put Miss Beatrice Thornton firmly in her place.

Like a servant organizing a dusty attic, he hauled a crate to the front of his mind, labelled all over with one word: ally. It was a clean word, a word that would get him home in several weeks unencumbered and ready to plunge into the management of his father's estate.

But how to get her to go in the box? And, once there, how could he get her to stay?

"It's the wrong time for this," he muttered, picking up a switch and swiping at the grass where the lawn grew woolly and wild.

"The wrong time for what?" asked a voice, and he didn't need to turn around to know whose it was. That voice had been in his head for days.

"Miss Thornton," he acknowledged, turning toward her with a hearty smile, determined to meet her as… how had he thought of her once? As a brother-soldier.

"Captain Gracechurch," she replied, with clear eyes and a mouth that hovered on the edge of a laugh. A blue shawl draped from her elbows and the plain green of her morning gown matched the fading bruise along her hairline. The dress was years old by the look of it, and, though it tugged against her figure in interesting ways, he oughtn't be attracted at all.

He oughtn't be. But he was.

"What brings you to the park this fine morning?" she asked.

When he didn't answer, she raised a sable brow. "Have you brought your china mug and shilling for a cup of milk?" She pointed to where the small herd of dairy cows mobbed under a spreading tree near a milling queue of nursery maids and their charges.

"Only a walk," he answered, his eyes returning to her smiling ones. "May I tempt you to join me?"

She gave him a long, considering look and answered, "You may."

A footman, trailing after her, dropped back and she slipped her hand around the curve of Henry's arm. "I enjoyed our ride yesterday." A warm pink brushed across her cheeks.

"You were kind to my friend," he said in a tone he never would have used with a subaltern. "Miss Summers, I mean. I appreciate anyone who is kind to her."

Her brows knit. "That must encompass a good many people. She has happy manners." Her fingers worked against his sleeve and she looked down before meeting his eyes again. "I envy how comfortable some people are in society. What could—"

"I thought you must know about the affair," he stated, reddening.

"Know what?"

Damn.

"Meg's sister Isabelle ran away in spectacular fashion during her Season—it must be five years now—the summer before I left for Spain. It ripped right through London all the way to our little market town on the coast. Society is cruel enough to vent its spleen on Meg."

Henry waited for Miss Thornton's prim statement, polite and consoling, but closing off any future connection. He found himself hoping for better.

Her eyes followed the course of a swimming duck as white teeth plucked her lower lip. He watched, tense and waiting. "She has little hope of a respectable match, then. Respectability is such a narrow road," she noted, her voice bitter and resigned as though she had run afoul of the boundaries of it herself. "And she wasn't even the one who stepped off it."

Dragonflies darted and zipped, barely making shadows on the water.

When Miss Thornton spoke again, her voice had all the finality of a picnic blanket being shaken out. "Well, I want no part of it. She's not an unexploded keg of powder."

Henry looked away, swinging his switch and lopping off dandelion heads. It was either attack the grass or kiss the girl, as the sudden strength of the feeling took him by surprise.

"Your thoughts do you credit, Miss Thornton," he said, to which she waved an irritated hand. "Though there is nothing to be done about it."

Her lips became a hard, implacable line and she reminded him, in that moment, of a fierce and taciturn old sergeant he'd served with in Spain. That ought to have put paid to his wayward thoughts, but it didn't.

"If Miss Summers wants my friendship, that's what she has."

He turned with her and walked up the path, grinning in the direction of St. Paul's where she could not see it. He had known, somehow, that she would answer him as she had. "It would mean much to Meg, and I hope the cost is not too dear."

"Cost?"

"If you should find yourself invited to fewer parties, Meg wouldn't be happy if she felt she were spoiling your chance at a successful Season. And your mother, of course, wouldn't like it either."

Beatrice gave a short laugh, though he couldn't see what was so funny. "Captain," she scolded, the smile still clinging to her lips, "you're going to have to make up your mind that I want to stand alongside Meg. We are in this together, you and I."

"We?" he asked, missing a step, pulling her to a halt.

She gave him another long look, which scrubbed away all thoughts of Sussex and returning home. "We are allies, are we not?"

Henry felt the sudden, wrecking confusion of a whirlwind and gave a soft, contented sigh. Love. It was love. Never mind how impossible it was or how fast it had happened. Love had found war-mad Henry Gracechurch.

His surrender was swift and sweet.

Chapter Ten

The stately landau rolled through well-kept neighbourhoods until it reached a section of Town that had never been fashionable. Beatrice blew a gust of air through her teeth, feeling like Queen Charlotte being carted around on a royal processional.

"Are you looking forward to it, my girls?" Papa asked from his backward-facing seat. Penny sat at his side, a large hamper resting between them.

"I get chills thinking of it. A real hot air balloon rising into the clouds," Penny gushed, looking deliciously afraid. "Don't you, Bea?"

"I'm not so frightened." Beatrice shrugged, cocking her head. "Being up so high would be a thrill, I imagine."

Mama gave a strangled exclamation and put in, her colour high, "What has Cook sent, I wonder? Be a dear, Penelope, and take a look."

"Cold chicken, sharp cheese, and ginger beer," Penny recited as she pawed through the contents of the hamper. Mama sent Beatrice a look that said there was to be no more of that.

"The spectacle will be most diverting," Mama murmured, her words for Beatrice's ears only.

"Diverting from what?" Beatrice asked, her voice low. The family had driven miles into the country for church on Sunday. Astley's on Monday. Gunter's on Tuesday. The Tower menagerie on Wednesday. A long trip to Hampton Court Palace yesterday. They had popped in to see Lady Sherbourne twice, but not during a fashionable visiting hour, and not, Beatrice had noticed, with any prior warning. "We have had so many diversions."

Mama's glance narrowed. "Sometimes I think you are not at all happy to be in Town again."

"These things amused me when I was twelve."

"You said it would be strange if we did not get out more," Mama replied. "See more of London. I remember the very words." Hot words spoken when Beatrice had merely wanted a simple ride in the park with a gentleman. And now Mama was twisting them around.

Beatrice clamped her lips. She could pick a fight with her mother for these transparent attempts to keep her from seeing the captain, but that wasn't the source of this cramped, snappish mood to which she was waving the white flag and throwing open the gates this morning. For all her machinations, Mama had no power to keep the captain from knocking on the door of Number Six and leaving his card.

And he hadn't.

"I'm going to have a day at home tomorrow," Beatrice stated. She forced her voice to be cool and pleasant. Though what good staying at home might accomplish, she did not know. After that chance meeting in the park, rambling along the edge of the pond, she had been sure the captain meant to seek out her company. She'd even allowed herself a few self-important reflections on the wisdom of encouraging his attention. All unnecessary.

The press of traffic thickened as they pushed on towards Hackney, and when finally they arrived at a broad green field, they found it already teeming with people. Papa coaxed the landau into a choice position on the eastern edge of the meadow, slipping a whole guinea into the hands of a labourer, whose family melted away from their spot, astonished by their good luck.

Beatrice lifted her face to the sun. A few wayward curls had escaped her hat to dance against her forehead. She shoved them back into her bonnet and hopped out of the carriage, pulling her sister after her. "We're off to see the balloon," she said, not waiting for permission. Mama would not dare call after them.

They raced breathless and laughing through the press of people, halting at intervals to watch no less than three Punch and Judy shows and jugglers of varying ability vying for small coins the crowd was ready to part with. Meat pasties, hot buns, ribbons of every colour tied on the ends of poles, bought by the high and low-born alike as a thick mass of people snaked around the base of a gentle green hill.

"Will you look at it." Penny stood with her mouth half open when they stopped to rest. She pointed to the balloon. "It's the best thing that's ever been invented."

"Better than the printing press?"

"I'm going closer," Penny replied, tossing a handful of raisins into her mouth and dusting her gloves before racing up to join a group of young boys making a nuisance of themselves near the anchoring ropes.

Beatrice was left alone to take in the whole scene. It was familiar to her, in a way. She had seen illustrations of balloons before, studied them closely from books and newspapers. The flying machine could do what she did, and yet there were reasons for it, purposes, a whole science, explanations of the mechanics.

"It's magical," a deep voice intoned at her side. She looked up to find Henry standing next to her as if he had always been there. Beatrice felt the solid ground she stood on almost melt away.

Quarry stone, the involuntary thought flitted through her mind, and she blinked, feeling herself grow heavy and pressed more firmly into the grass. That was strange. It was not as though she had been about to float away at the mere sight of him in the middle of a bustling London crowd. What a silly thing to think. She shook her head and met his eyes.

There was the usual delight she felt each time she saw him that sent her insides spinning, but it was tempered by the knowledge that he had not called. It was the merest chance that brought him here.

"It's not magic," she retorted, swallowing deeply. Six days since she'd last seen him. He had no right to look like he hadn't been wasting away. Drat. "It's hydrogen. The gas is produced when sulphuric acid is poured over scrap iron. How did you happen across me in this crowd?" she asked, thankful for the cool morning air, which would be a plausible reason for her pink cheeks.

"Magic," he asserted, offering her an arm, which she took. He did not lead her anywhere but stood, gazing up at the activity on the rise. "Have you been busy these past days?"

Busy? She felt the shame of returning home each afternoon, her eyes hungry for some sign that he had come. "This and that," she answered, hoping with all her heart that her tone conveyed a calendar too full for waiting and longing.

He looked down at her. "You've not been at home," he stated.

It wasn't a question. The damp ground at the bottom of the hill began to seep through her slippers, but she would not move for anything. "No. My mother had a sudden enthusiasm to see everything in Town. I am not sure the carriage horses can take much more. You?"

"I passed your door, hoping that—"

"You called?" The surprise of it made her yelp.

"I said I would."

Beatrice looked up at him. "You left no sign," she stated while feeling great relief. Forgetting to leave a card—it was endearing, though it had cost her the enjoyment of racing through the maze at Hampton Court, of savouring the ice at Gunter's.

His head cocked to the side and his brows came down. "But I—" And then his lips shut into a firm line.

Beatrice waited for him to finish and then, finally, when it was clear he would say no more, the wheels in her mind began to turn. She looked up the hill again to where the balloonist had given Penny a small parcel, some silk fabric full of hydrogen. Her sister let it go and, as it drifted up and up, it moved in easy state, tossed lightly by sudden currents of wind. The crowd let out a great cheer, and in that clamour, Beatrice whispered, "You did leave a card, didn't you?"

"Yes."

Penny waved to her as she dashed down the hill and away toward the carriage.

Beatrice lowered her brows. She might have missed the card in her meticulous search of the entry hall, when she had turned each paper over and over, upending the tray and running her fingers along the back of the table, and then closely questioned the townhouse staff. It would not be so amazing if she lost— "Just the one?"

"One each time I visited."

"Each? What do you mean? How many times was it?" she asked, her words tripping over themselves.

His look was keen. "Seven," he answered and then his mouth lifted. "I'm almost out of cards."

She answered quickly. "But it's been six days."

"Exactly six? Has it?" he asked, his eyes narrowing like a cat on the trail of a limping mouse. "How clever you are to know the precise number. I came twice on Wednesday."

Beatrice put a hand to her pelisse, fastening and unfastening the button. Seven cards. Seven messages scrawled on the back. Seven times he had come. Seven times. She couldn't let the number go. A girl might have her head turned by a thing like that.

Henry didn't say another word, and merely waited for her to work it out—though the way his eyes studied her face wasn't helping her concentration at all. It set her blood to warming and her mind to wondering if the world really would come crashing to an end if she leaned up on her tiptoes and kissed him on those firm lips. But the cards.... She dragged her attention back and took a long, clean breath. Seven *missing* cards.

Mama.

Beatrice's lips trembled. Elation and anger running together like water coursing through a millrace. "I must have... misplaced... I must..." She looked up, running her tongue along her lips, only to encounter his calm expression. He deserved better than an antiseptic lie. "I didn't see a single one of them, sir." She smiled though it felt a grimace. The enormity of Mama's insult to this man, to this war hero, was shocking. "I must apologize."

He shook his head. "No."

"You won't come again," she continued, too angry to feel the full weight of sorrow. That would come later. "It wouldn't be quite the thing. Would it?"

"Knowing how your family feels, I ought to take myself off as soon as may be," he replied, unmoving. He was looking down at her, the light wind picking up feathers of his hair and tossing them.

That was it, then. It would be humiliating to beg him to stay. But what did it matter? The captain would be lost to her, be it if he disappeared now or a month from now. So why not snip the thread, tie off the knot, and roll up her work?

What did they have, really? A dance, a ride, some conversation. However, no matter how she tried, she could not get the proper total from her calculations. It ought to add up to nothing. But when she thought of not seeing him again, she felt the same sort of nervous restlessness in her stomach and limbs that she used to feel about heights, once.

"Aren't you going?" she asked, when he didn't move. She glanced up again and caught her breath at his look.

"I'll go when you tell me to go," he answered, and then they were an island, small and isolated, in the swelling sea of people about them. Silence stretched, and she could say nothing, but held his gaze so unwaveringly that the corner of his smile began to lift in that slow way.

"Harry," came a shout and the captain turned, frowning. His hand reached to cover hers where it curled around his elbow. It was his cousin, his ill-timed cousin, riding up on a grey stallion. Behind, he led another horse, black with a blaze of white down its nose.

"I had no idea where you ran off to," Lord Fox said, dismounting. "Won't you agree, Miss Thornton, that the army does nothing for a fellow's manners?"

"Why is it that I have yet to hear you approve of anything or anyone, sir?" she asked, wanting to kick at something and finding him the nearest target.

"I certainly approve of you, miss," he retorted, sketching an elegant bow.

"Unjust," the captain stated, turning to his horse. "At least *you* approve of me. Isn't that right, Ceph?" he said, rubbing his hand down the muzzle.

"Ceph?" asked Beatrice, laughing. "That can't be short for Bucephalus, can it?" A dull red stole up the back of Henry's neck. "Alexander the Great's horse. Captain, haven't you any humility at all?"

"Don't blame me for it. Fox won't give his horses any comfortable names. No Bess or Dobbin for him."

"I'm not a farmer, Harry." Lord Fox looked anything but in his elegant riding clothes. His well-cut gloves would never have held something so common as a spade.

"Does this handsome fellow have a millstone to live up to as well, sir?" Beatrice asked, trying to be easy with Henry's cousin. Her eyes skimmed the grey flanks and the neat Arabian ankles of his lordship's mount. His taste was impeccable, anyway.

"He's called Marengo," Lord Fox answered, and her brows flew up. The weight of Henry's gaze settled on her.

"Napoleon is an unusual association to cultivate at present," she asserted.

"Greatness interests me," he replied.

"You mean infamy," she taunted.

"You sound like my cousin." He shrugged. She could not imagine Henry shrugging like that. He would argue his position or make some clever remark, and not name his mount for the most notorious warhorse in Europe.

"The balloon is almost ready to lift, Miss Thornton," Henry put in, approval in his expression. "Do you wish us to leave you to return to your family?" The question was ripe with all they had spoken of earlier. It was no good telling herself what she ought to do. The knowledge of what Mama would wish was before her. It was always before her. Beatrice should bob him a curtsey and turn on her heel. It would be right to do so. It would be wise.

I'll go when you tell me to go. She could hear herself take in a long breath.

"Ungallant, Harry," Lord Fox chided. "Leaving a lady to make her way alone. See what I mean about those manners, Miss Thornton?"

She smiled at Henry's cousin. He had his uses.

Then she looked up at Henry. "Let's practice them now."

Chapter Eleven

Henry's mortal enemy was unpacking a picnic hamper and handing around bottles of ginger beer. But when Mrs Thornton looked up and saw Beatrice walking to the family carriage, her hand tucked into the crook of Henry's arm, Mrs Thornton's mouth pursed up as though she had sucked on a lemon. Too late for surprise attacks. The dread host had spotted his advance.

It was a pity. The woman might have been as beautiful as her daughter if only—No, Henry corrected himself, glancing down at Miss Thornton's freckled nose. Not as beautiful as that. Miss Thornton's hat framed a face with arched brows and a determined chin. The ribbon, tied under her ear, traced a line along her neck that he longed to explore. Her frock was regrettably the colour of an over-boiled egg yolk. Love could not make him blind to that.

"Good morning, Mrs Thornton, Mr Thornton." Henry's hand tipped his hat. He helped Beatrice into the carriage and he watched every sway of her skirts until she settled herself, feeling fifteen again.

"You remember Captain Gracechurch?" she asked her parents. "He found me in the crowd and was good enough to escort me back." *Found me in the crowd.* Henry's mouth twisted. He'd bribed her butler for her location, raced Fox through his breakfast and across Town, and hunted through the crowd, looking for a needle in a haystack. Henry hated crowds.

"This gentleman," she said, nodding, "is the captain's cousin, Lord Fox."

Lord Fox. Hearing her speak his cousin's name felt ominous. His cousin's title had never bothered him before. If anything, the effect of it on people had amused him. But there was nothing funny about it now, not with Mrs Thornton setting herself square in the middle of the path that led to her daughter. Would she let a lord through where she had blocked the way of a mere captain?

Henry watched Mrs Thornton's face, waiting for signs of warmth and welcome to break across it. Instead, she surprised him. "I thank you for returning my daughter," she stated, a note of finality in her voice.

Fox ignored the dismissal. "Thornton." He pinched the bridge of his nose and looked up. "I'm trying to remember my *Debrett's*. Wasn't there a Thornton... married a Purefoy?" he asked.

Mrs Thornton blinked but leaned forward, plucking up two sandwiches, handing them across Beatrice and over to Fox with a napkin. "How delightful. I was a Purefoy. Are you a connection?"

Fox absently handed one of the sandwiches over to Henry and walked around the carriage to carry on his conversation at closer quarters. "None at all, ma'am. I read the peerage to put me to sleep."

Mrs Thornton gave a trilling laugh and Henry looked at Beatrice in wonder. Was that all it took? An interest in family trees and a lack of interest her daughter?

Beatrice's smiling eyes crinkled along with her nose. For her sake, he would pore over pages of material written about every Gracechurch down through the Norman Conquest. Heaven knew his mother would love him for it. But he could not ignore Beatrice. That was impossible.

"Have you ever seen such a majestic sphere?" Fox asked Mrs Thornton, pointing to the balloon.

Henry heard Mr Thornton's snort, followed by Beatrice's own more delicate one.

"Heaven preserve us from poets," Mr Thornton muttered under his breath.

"It looks like a bed warming pan," Henry jibed, earning him a grin from Beatrice's more affable parent.

"An overstuffed reticule," Beatrice's father offered.

"Pig bladder," a young lady added, all but hidden tucked away on the other side of the carriage.

"Am I meeting Miss Penelope?" Henry asked, looking into a face that was much like her older sister's.

She made a sound of disgust. "Miss Penny. And only if Bea has told you nice things."

"I know that you lend hats." He smiled and caught a guilty look sneaking across her face.

She glanced away. "Will he be killed, do you think?" she asked, making them all blink at her sudden turn. "The balloonist?"

Beatrice recovered first. "What a gruesome imagination you have, Pen. I hardly think that will happen," she said, looking toward the hill.

Mr Thornton leaned forward, his eyes alight. "What a weapon that might be in battle. Rising above the host. Spying. Firing from above. The military uses could be incalculable."

"I can only agree," Fox sniffed, though he had shown no sign he had been listening.

"They can't steer it," Henry explained, as they watched the balloon, still anchored with tethers, gently bobbing twenty or thirty feet high in the slight wind. The whole of their company was listening now. "Once this one is untethered, it might wind up anywhere. Maidstone or Hastings, or the muddy Thames estuary."

The crowd erupted into shouts as the great silken machine slipped its fetters as gracefully as a bird. The balloonist waved his hat from the basket and the carriages that intended to follow his progress began to fight their way out of the meadow. Henry looked to Beatrice. Her eyes traced the path of the balloon, but her form was still as the figurehead of a ship, her profile etched against the blue sky.

"But if they get the steering mechanism sorted?" Mr Thornton asked. Henry pulled his gaze from Beatrice. If he could not be in the good graces of both of her parents, he could certainly be in the good graces of one.

"Napoleon tried using a balloon corps to map battlefields. But filling them with gas, tethering them safely, the time it takes to get them in the air and safely back… Well, you can see how long it took this morning." He spread his hands. "Logistics are the very devil."

"Wasn't the incomparable Wellington willing to find a solution to that?" Fox asked, slipping a vial of poison into his words. Henry wondered if he even knew he was doing it.

"*General* Wellington never consulted with *Captain* Gracechurch," he replied. "Anyway, a man in one of those would be a sitting duck to enemy fire. Exposed and defenceless."

"Alone," whispered Beatrice, claiming his attention. The word was as cold as a snowflake.

Fox leaned forward. "But think of what it must be like, Miss Thornton. To feel the air press in from every side. To watch the ground fall away until everything is reduced to the size of an ant. To shed the fearful creatures we are and lift higher and higher."

More poetry. But Henry saw that Beatrice was looking at his cousin with her eyes wide and her mouth slightly agape.

It was that look that led Henry into error. "I am hoping we might find time this week for an excursion, Miss Thornton." Henry rushed his fences. He saw at once that it was a mistake. Mrs Thornton was prepared for a direct attack.

"What with the demands of the Season, my daughter has quite a full schedule for the foreseeable future, Captain. Perhaps someone else is in need of an escort."

So that's how it was to be. Mrs Thornton was back to playing the scaly backed dragon, breathing fire down the neck of any man who tried to steal her golden horde.

"I'm sure I will not want for company," Henry stated, sounding offhand. He turned to Fox. "As a matter of fact, I've press-ganged Miss Summers to come out with me on Monday," he said, baiting his trap. Waiting... waiting.

Mrs Thornton gave an exaggerated sigh and clicked her tongue several times against her teeth. "And that's the one day next week that Beatrice is unengaged," she said, a whisper-thin veneer of regret lacing her words. "I fear your paths are never destined to cross."

"Pity." He held her eyes. "Fox?"

"Mmm?"

"Won't you come with us—Meg and me?"

"As a gooseberry? No. I thank you."

"Then bring along a companion. I'm sure *someone is in need of an escort.*" Mrs Thornton's eyes became slits. *Hurry up, Fox.*

Fox's look narrowed. "Miss Thornton. You don't have plans. Come and make up a fourth? My cousin won't—"

"Yes," Beatrice answered quickly, beaming at Fox. "As my mother said, I had nothing whatsoever planned."

Chapter Twelve

Mama was still upset and had been for days. Even when her face took on the form of pleasant repose, there was a storm cloud roiling behind her eyes. Beatrice knew she should lay her cards on the table and state as plainly as she could that as long as the captain cared to issue invitations, she would accept them. But then Mama would start again, beating out her litany until Beatrice felt like a vibrating piano string struck ceaselessly by the hammer.

Now Mama was venting her wrath at Papa. Beatrice slowed her breathing and pressed her ear against the panelled wall at the back of the hall cupboard to hear the voices that carried through the wood.

"I didn't think I married a fool, Charles." Mama's clipped steps could be heard pacing up and down the length of the library.

"Nor have you," Papa replied. His voice was softer, projecting his habitual calm.

"Oh? In spite of the dangers, you're encouraging the boy—"

"Not a boy, madam."

"You're encouraging him to pursue our daughter, a girl who can never be his." Beatrice felt the words fill the dark, constricted stillness of the cupboard. "You're being a *fool*," Mama accused, and there was a long silence.

Beatrice shifted her arm within the cramped space, letting the blood flow again through that limb, and felt the crinkle of paper in her hand. Deborah's latest letter wherein she charged Beatrice not to take the first offer of marriage that was made to her. She begged her to take pity on the swathes of gentlemen who threw themselves at her feet. She pleaded for details of dances and dresses. *'Dearest, as I grow ever closer to the size of a house, you must have fun enough for the both of us.'*

Fun enough. Wedged inside a tight closet with her face shoved up against the panelling, reduced to spying.

"If she never tastes freedom, how can we expect her to ever settle down?" Papa entreated, his voice weary.

Settle. Even Papa spoke of her eventual resignation to Dorset. A life filled with pugs and newspapers.

She hated the thought, more now than before.

"I've begged her to remember her sisters. I talked about it until there is nothing more to say. I might as well be speaking to a brick wall."

"She is careful of them already."

"Then why does she insist on these risks? It is not in her nature to be so headstrong," Mama asserted, her voice querulous.

"Are we so sure of her nature?" Papa asked.

There was no response to that, and, after a long pause, Papa suggested, "You could be kinder to him."

Mama gave a long, ragged sigh. "It's kindness to run him off. Have you seen how he looks at her?" Beatrice pressed her ear harder against the wall, straining to hear an answer that Papa didn't speak.

Mama continued. "Then what choice do I have?"

"You were more than civil to his cousin."

"That one doesn't care tuppence for Beatrice. I am not kept up nights worrying about Lord Fox. The least you could do is support me on the matter of the other one."

"Captain Gracechurch," Papa said, pulling the rug from Mama's evasions. "I don't know that I can support you. We brought Beatrice to London, and we can't treat her like a prisoner."

"I don't know why not. Your sister—"

"Let's leave Martha out of it." There was sharpness now in Papa's tone. "Let the poor woman rest."

"No one held her in as much affection as I did. She was my constant companion and she loved being with us at Thorndene."

Beatrice exhaled sharply. Aunt Martha, the contented pattern-card of virtue, had been shoved under her nose as an example from the time she was thirteen.

"How can you really believe that?" Papa asked. Beatrice's brows shot up and she leaned so close to the wall that her ear was almost fused to the wood. "After the curate?"

Mama's voice rose suddenly and dropped equally as fast. "He was no match for her in any case. Not with her money. It was a shocking presumption that he asked her, and at their age."

"Little more than forty. And he loved her. A man needs no more permission than that to chance the question, whatever his circumstances. It was the greatest act of evil I ever did to drive him off."

"At the time you agreed."

"At the time. Yes. I was persuaded, or wanted to be, that she was better off at Thorndene without her penniless curate and his motherless children." Papa's next words were hardly audible. "Lord help me."

Beatrice bit the back of her hand, staunching the tide of tears.

Mama was unbowed. "A tiny vicarage with seven people. She could never have kept her secret there. It would have ruined us all."

The room grew still and silent and seemed to fold around the tiny cupboard in the hall, suspending them in time.

"We'll never know. We never gave them a chance."

"But—"

"Enough." Papa's voice was firm. "Beatrice knows the risks."

"You cannot tell me not to worry. It would take so little to open us up to—"

"Villagers with pitchforks?" There was a smile in Papa's tone when he answered her. "How did you keep from calling in the magistrate when you found our daughter could rise? And from running as far and as fast as you could from the mad Thorntons?"

"You were as frightened as I was, Charles. You had no idea of such a thing running in the family until Martha explained. And we had been married fifteen years," she said, sounding as tired as Papa. "I loved you too much."

Beatrice retreated to her bedroom when her parents moved on, too near tears to linger over all that she had heard. Lord Fox would be collecting her for their outing with Henry and Meg in an hour, and if she let loose now she would be unfit for company.

She flipped through a dog-eared copy of *Ackermann's Repository*, forcing herself to think of other things, when her finger arrested over an illustration of a young lady in a modish gown. Her hair was swept up in loose waves and braids and was coiled in an easy knot. The whole of it was secured by a ribbon criss-crossing over the crown of her head.

Beatrice ran to her dressing table, pulling pins from her tight bun and scattering her brushes. "Penny," she called.

***

Beatrice took a quick peek at her reflection in the hall mirror. Her hair looked well. Penny's willing hands had got the approximation of the illustration right. Here was hoping it wouldn't tumble down in company.

Walking into the drawing room, she found Mama arranging the tea things. Her eyes flicked over Beatrice's hair and her mouth took on the shape of a yardstick.

The sofa being no refuge, Beatrice turned and joined her father and Lord Fox near the window. "It would be a service if I could seek your counsel now and again," Lord Fox said, and Beatrice lifted her brow.

"Lord Fox is interested in our corner of Dorset," Papa informed her, running amused eyes over her hair. "He is asking after properties. Do you think Oak Lodge might suit him?"

The house was situated about three miles from Thorndene. An easy ride on a clear day. Henry might visit him there.

"It's charming it has a bluebell wood and a clear southern prospect. A delightful spot, quite private. You are looking to relocate, sir?" Beatrice asked. Her eyes narrowed on the cut of his coat. Dorset tailors could not produce cloth so fine, fits so exact.

The corners of Lord Fox's mouth turned up, though his eyes were empty blue sky. "I have been searching for a bolt-hole. Dorset has such good roads that I would find it easy work to travel up to London as it suits me." At the clatter of an arriving carriage, he turned to look out the window. "It's Harry and Meg."

Beatrice's hand made it to her neck before she pulled it back, wishing for a mirror.

When she saw the new style, Meg could only shout, "Beatrice," before dashing across the room. "I'll have to kidnap your lady's maid. Your hair is a triumph." She turned Beatrice this way and that, beaming with delight.

The weather had been wretched yesterday and Meg had come to keep her company while Mama and Penny were out. For so long, Beatrice had kept herself from people, forming friendships that might soften the constraints which bound her to home or involve her in invitations she would have to decline. Even her sisters had been held at a slight distance. But Meg seemed to bash through her reserve and Beatrice felt herself warm to such a friendship, like a flower turning its face to the sun.

Now Beatrice felt herself blushing and dipped her head, eyelashes fanning across hot cheeks. "My little sister gave my hair a try. The whole of it will be ruined as soon as I put my hat on."

"Let her breathe, Meg," Henry scolded, following her at a more reasonable pace. His eyes rested on Beatrice and she grew fidgety. "I once grew a moustache," he told her. "As I struggled to get it just so, my only wish was that the fellows would stop talking about it."

Beatrice's lips twitched as she tried to picture it.

"And you are to stop imagining it on my face," he laughed. "It was a misguided experiment. So my only comment is that you look lovely. As you always do."

"May I offer you a refreshment before you get on your way?" Mama asked, steaming away beneath the cordiality.

Ten minutes of tea and conversation had Mama relaxing, and giving way to relief that Meg was so beautiful and so at ease with the gentlemen. *"This diamond,"* Beatrice could almost hear Mama thinking, *"would soak up every drop of attention."* She might almost approve of this friendship.

Almost.

Mama put down her teacup and smiled, carried away in admiration. "That is a beautiful material, Miss Summers." Mama gestured to the rich strawberry sarcenet in Meg's gown.

Meg flicked an unmistakable look at Beatrice's frock. "I have the name of an excellent dressmaker, ma'am, if you are in need of one. Her rates are not too dear."

Beatrice almost choked on her sandwich and it wasn't long before Mama tipped them out on the pavement. Beatrice accepted Lord Fox's hand as he helped her into his phaeton. Meg joined the captain in his and the vehicles were brought alongside each other. "Where are we going?" Beatrice asked.

"Not far. It's a surprise," Henry answered, and then he looked past her to Lord Fox. "Follow me." And he was away, bowling down the street with Meg, whose hands, as she sat at his side, never ceased moving. Laughter carried back to Beatrice, and as she glanced over at Lord Fox she tried, without any luck, to withhold comparisons.

The drive was not long, however, and they pulled up outside Westminster. "You get Meg, Fox?" Henry asked, not waiting for an answer, but jumping down and striding around to assist Beatrice.

Beatrice looked to Henry. Her eyes held a question.

"You told me," he began, reaching up, his hands sliding neatly around her waist as she held his shoulders. They lingered like that for a moment that bordered on dangerous ground, skirting the edges of propriety until he lifted her from the carriage and set her on her feet. "You told me weeks ago that you read the Parliamentary report. Have you been to any speeches?"

Her voice was uncertain. "Ladies are not allowed in the Strangers' Gallery."

Meg and Lord Fox joined them and Henry shuttered his eyes, making his expression more general. "I discovered that there is a place for the ladies." She felt a bubble of excitement as he pulled two tickets from his coat and pressed them into her hand. "I had to hound an MP for those, so don't lose them."

Fox looked over her shoulder at the two scraps of paper and then at Henry. "Is *that* what all those letters were about?" he asked. Henry gave him a sharp look, but Lord Fox's next words ambled along like a parson walking down a lane on a Sunday evening. "I wondered if you might stand for Parliament one day. Hopes dashed, Harry. You've no ambition."

The gentlemen escorted them to the separate gallery, a tight little room directly over the ventilator in the roof of St. Stephen's Chapel.

Henry's face when he saw it was horrified. "I didn't know."

"It will be fine," she assured him, touching a light hand to the gold braid on his uniform. "Go find your seats. I'll send you a message when we're ready to leave."

Lord Fox was already halfway down the stairs and Meg was leaning forward to gauge the view. Henry looked past Beatrice's shoulder at the tiny room, frowning.

Henry looked most put out. "What commotion do they think ladies will cause, I wonder."

"Swooning?" Beatrice guessed. "I would promise not to swoon." She winked up at him.

Henry caught up her hand between them and pressed a kiss to her gloved fingertips before retreating. Beatrice bit her lip, taking a few lighter-than-air breaths.

That hadn't been a polite kiss of fingers that curved over his hand. Even in her limited interactions, she'd received more than her share of those. A man couldn't leave a room without bowing over a lady's hand and dropping a kiss. It meant no more than the tip of a hat or help descending from a carriage.

This kiss had been an inch or two off from that bloodless social convention. He had turned her palm, and pressed his lips against the pads of her fingers. An inch or two, she told herself. It was nothing. Nevertheless, her heart beat loudly in her ears when she hurried to join her friend.

There was refuge in pointing out MPs and officers of the Crown to Meg as Beatrice's gaze skimmed the room. A trickle of perspiration beaded under her stays and she fanned herself with her reticule, looking down on the MPs with envy. Surely the air down there moved. Surely that room was not on the surface of the sun. There wasn't space for even ten women up here.

Peering below again at the proceedings, she found that the sound, at least, was excellent.

"This room is an outrage," hissed Meg.

"Shhhh." Beatrice leaned closer to the edge.

"Really," Meg whispered. "I begin to understand the Gunpowder Plot."

"Meg."

Sound must have carried down as well as up because several heads turned to cast looks of white-bearded disapproval at the ceiling.

That quieted Meg, but it did not silence her. As they heard a long speech calling for a select committee on the subject of the Catholic claims, and a short one about the Luddite riots, Meg whispered asides all the while. And then a man with a slight frame and full features stood. The Speaker recognized Mr Wilberforce. Beatrice turned to Meg and said, as she might have to Penny, "Shut up, do."

Meg smiled, drawing an X on her mouth with her finger, and leaned in to listen to the speech. Mr Wilberforce's words rose up, filling the small room with unbearable darkness.

"A number of unfortunate African slaves, men, women, and children, had been discovered hidden on board a vessel professedly laden with cattle. These wretched beings had been induced to conceal themselves and to abstain almost from breathing, by the master of the vessel."

Meg squeezed Beatrice's hand, her chin tight. And so she remained for the duration of the address. When it was concluded, they collected their things and descended the stairs. Cool spring air met them as they came down the steps and Beatrice summoned a page to deliver a message to the gentlemen.

"Did you enjoy it?" Henry asked, joining the ladies out of doors. He took her hand and tucked it in his arm. He led the small party toward the entrance to the park. "That room...."

Beatrice smiled up at him. "Nothing you could have chosen would have pleased me half so well. Meg was—"

"I was heroic," Meg spoke up, veering from the path and turning toward the coolness of the lake. "I'll even go further to admit that I was riveted by Mr Wilberforce."

"Were you?" Lord Fox asked, walking at her side. "But he's a scrubby little man. What did he mean, banging on about slavery? What does he imagine he can *do* about it?"

Beatrice hitched to a stop and the others turned to look at her. "He imagined he could outlaw the trading of slaves, and he did. He imagines that he will, one day, abolish the practice of slavery altogether, and he will."

"Not with that neckcloth," Lord Fox drawled, scooping up a handful of gravel and lobbing small rocks into the pond.

"Is that why you take such care with your linen?" Henry asked, eyeing the snowy folds of his cousin's cravat. "To meet your appointment with destiny, properly clad?"

Lord Fox batted his hand away and Henry laughed. "Mr Wilberforce has managed things that even Wellington has not. That is greatness."

"Great men do not look like half-boiled shrimp," Lord Fox insisted.

"Perhaps you are right," Beatrice began, speaking slowly so the man could understand each word. "They spring to life fully formed, cast in bronze on a rampant horse, sword at the ready, and perched atop a granite column."

Meg giggled and Henry grinned. Lord Fox's only rebuttal was a bow. He turned up the path toward Westminster with Meg on his arm, the shadow of leaves running in a river of pattern over his back.

Henry and Beatrice followed, some silent, mutual consent slowing their footsteps. Then he stopped altogether. She glanced back to find his eyes on her and heard an echo of her mother's voice. *Have you seen how he looks at her?* Warm, intense, interested. No wonder Mama was worried.

"Shall we get a little lost?" he asked.

It was on the tip of her tongue to say no. She ought to say no. *I'm already lost.* But she only nodded, lifting the hem of her skirt a little and stepping off the path.

"I like it here," he told her, as they left the well-trod trail behind. "It's quiet, and not so much like London. No crowds, no city."

It was hardly wild here. There was no London park really, but the bushes were overgrown, and the sun hardly penetrated the trees. The faint clatter of carriages seemed far away.

"You dislike the city?" she asked, following with her hand in his. How right it felt. Still, she wished to peel their gloves off and feel his war-battered callouses against her palm.

"I do." He paused then, choosing his words like he was assembling them one letter at a time. "But I can't seem to leave."

He drew to a halt, giving her another one of those looks that Mama would disapprove of. "I haven't told this to anyone, not Fox, or Meg, or any of the officers at Whitehall turning me inside out. This happens when I think of Spain." He tore the glove from his shaking hand and lifted it before her eyes.

Beatrice held tightly to herself, tamping down the longing to wrap her arms around him, to hold him close and absorb what she could of this. His mouth was set, tight at the edges. He had never told anyone. Lord, how could he bear it?

Then Henry took a shuddering breath. "The noise of Town doesn't let up. And all I hear are camp followers, warhorses, and rolling artillery wagons." He tugged the glove on again, performing the action with extreme control. "Only the strongest feelings could induce me to stay."

"Then why…" she began, a line between her brows, then trailed off. His look was unmistakable. He stayed for her. That's what he brought her here to say. She felt the weight of it. Felt the lightness.

"Miss Thornton, I used my wits to have your company today, but seeing you more often is difficult."

She gave a nervous, husky laugh. "I do not wish you to overtax yourself, Captain," she teased, and regretted it at once. It was not the time for raillery.

But she was afraid of him in this mood. Afraid of herself too. Afraid that she had not yet answered a question that would rush her forward, matching his pace: How far could this go?

He swallowed thickly but offered her his arm. He was going to allow her this slight retreat, though she could see the cost of laying his feelings bare only to pack them up again. They began to walk back to the others and Beatrice allowed herself to be led, uncertainty making her silent. Soon they gained the safety of the path again.

He smiled and his arm bumped her out of her stride as his tone attempted to match her teasing words. "If I knew your social calendar, it would be a simple matter to see you again."

Her answer was prompt. She could give him that much. "We're staying in tonight. Lady Stemple's rout on Tuesday. Let's see, Wednesday is a lecture at the Geographical Association. Thursday is a musicale. I hate musicales. Papa is driving us out to some races at the weekend. A Venetian Breakfast on Monday. Does that satisfy?" she asked.

They stepped from the shade of the plane trees into the bright sun, but his look was far warmer. "I think you must know it does not," he replied, surprising her with the truth. "But it will do for now."

Chapter Thirteen

Beatrice dropped her pen onto the writing desk and reached to tease the curtains back. Thunder drummed through a dark sky and clouds dripped an obstinate rain, the kind that would carry on for hours. Growing puddles were fast becoming spreading ponds in the square. She cast the curtains from her hand.

Her letter for Deborah was long overdue. Beatrice picked up her pen again and began to scratch out, '...*The subject of the lecture was The Flora of Bohemia, Moravia, and Silesia and, I assure you, it was not as deadly dull as it sounds.*'

Henry had been there.

Her lips turned up as she looked down at the page. Papa had escorted her and Mama to a row of cane chairs and Henry had whipped up to her side almost as soon as she had taken her seat as if he had been watching for her. His knee had brushed hers as he leaned over to greet her parents.

"You're interested in plants?" Mama asked, holding the program.

"Not at all, ma'am," he had answered, seating himself on Beatrice's right as Papa choked on a laugh.

Beatrice started, caught in her reverie, and a fat blob of ink rolled from the tip of her pen, splashing onto the paper. She let out an exclamation, sanding the spot and shaking the excess off.

Mama lifted her head from where she sat plying her needle, her eyes searching. "I thought you would have so much to talk about after the lecture."

Beatrice aimed a mechanical look at the set of Meissen shepherdesses on the mantel above Mama's head. "I'm a bit tired."

"Are you feeling well?"

"I am fine." She clipped Mama's concern off at the bud. For pity's sake, when Mama was her age she had been a wife and a mother. Beatrice could be trusted to look after herself. "I ought to retire early."

Mama's look was wounded and reproachful before she cast her eyes down at her lap, pulling the needle in and out through the worked fabric.

Beatrice set her lips. There had been a time when she would run to Mama, go down on her knees and say anything, lies, to erase that expression. She'd always done so before. Years of peace and serenity rode on the back of such gestures, putting off the day when their feelings would boil over, allowing them both to pretend that they never would.

Beatrice steeled her heart and collected the half-written letter, striding through the doorway before she was tempted to apologize for too much. Once in her room she went to her desk, smoothing two letters, the one Deborah had written and the one she was writing in answer. Her eyes skimmed over her sister's loose, florid scrawl.

'I am perishing for want of information. Do, dearest, save an earl for Penny, or a duke if one can be spared...'

Beatrice smiled. She would be happy to spare the dukes and the sons of dukes and every earl in the kingdom if that's what Penny wanted. They were safe from Beatrice. Whether a certain officer should also count himself safe was a matter that tagged along after her every thought.

Beatrice dipped her quill, tapping it on the lip of the inkwell. Her response was light. *The peers would like me well enough if knowledge of my fortune was more general. If I fail to arouse any interest on my own merits, I will scatter the ground with pound notes as I walk into a ballroom, tucking a few into my bodice for good measure.*

When she was finished, she folded the papers, daubed red wax across the envelope, and sat back, tapping the letter on the desk. Thunder rumbled, uneven and rough over the house, and Beatrice's diffuse thoughts hardened.

Throwing off her shawl, she walked to the window and loosened the curtains. They fell straight to the ground and she shook them closed, retrieving several long, sharp hat pins and poking them through the rich brocade fabric in several places.

It was dim now, so she went to the hearth, lighting a taper and guiding the flame to a candlestick. Once the light caught, she waved the taper out as the smoke curled and rose.

Then she went to the wardrobe and pulled a gown from a hook, rolling it into a long, loose twist and stuffing it against the crack at the bottom of the door. She dropped to her knees as she looked along the length of it, checking for chinks of light.

Reaching up, she jiggled the door handle and then sprang to her feet, pulling a chair from the dressing table to the door. She tipped the chair in one deft movement and wedged the back under the door handle. Then she retrieved two pillows from the bed and piled them on the chair, high enough to cover the keyhole.

There.

Through daily practice, she was getting stronger and more competent at rising. Confident that she could keep her activities secret she thought as she stepped to the centre of the floor. The giddy, swimming feeling in her stomach thickened and she felt herself lift from the carpet.

It was so easy now. She didn't need to think of things lighter than air. She need only remember Captain Gracechurch's conversation today, his low voice teasing her about the superior merits of Sussex, near Pevensey, where sun-yellow daffodils splashed against the mellow grey stone of his home, and the sea air tumbled over the rolling fields. There had been longing in his face when he said that it was past the time for daffodils now.

Up she went.

Five minutes she allowed herself, poised midway between the floor and ceiling. Her breathing slowed and the tense coil in her stomach unwound. Perhaps Mama thought that if she kept Beatrice from rising, she'd somehow unlearn how to do it. Beatrice's eyes fluttered closed. Easier for a fish to forget how to swim. In the air was where Beatrice was born anew, nurtured as easily as the wild hibiscus flowers in Bohemia. But Mama could hardly speak of it, her words full of euphemisms and half-finished sentences.

Have you done any... by accident?

Is it any worse in the morning?

Any changes?

Everything had changed. Beatrice smiled. She was half in love.

Not halfway, Beatrice. All the way.

It had taken so little time, but nothing could go back to how it had been when she had agreed that Invisible Dorset Spinsterhood was the best course of action. That if jolly Aunt Martha could stick it out so happily, so too could jolly Aunt Beatrice.

Rubbish.

Beatrice turned in place, feeling the internal axis that anchored her.

Could she lift something? She'd used to be able to. Her eyes blinked open and she saw the small table by the bed. *Go to it*, she thought, trying to push herself through the air. *Hummingbirds and cricket balls, and schoolboys running with a poached trout.* She scooped her hands through the air a little and laughed. She wasn't a flyer. She wasn't going to become one now. Moving across the air seemed to be no part of her power.

She set herself down on the floor and went to the table, lifting the solid marble-topped piece. It was a simple matter to rise with it, though she bore the weight on her arms and it grew difficult to hold. There was something she could do about how heavy it was. The memory of it fluttered on the edge of her vision, begging for attention.

Could she do it?

Aunt Martha had spoken of it only once in a whispered story about a few long-dead Thorntons, who stared down from stiff paintings in the gallery with silks and lace and powdered wigs hiding their secrets.

Her secret.

"My grandfather used to think of pouring," Aunt Martha had told Beatrice. "Glasses of lemonade, that sort of thing, and then the rising seemed to shift to the thing he was touching. Oh, but you mustn't try," Aunt Martha had said, faithfully discharging her duty to teach Beatrice to stay grounded. "You mustn't."

She must. Beatrice brushed her mind clear of clutter and thought of treacle slowly spilling from a pitcher and of water coursing from a pump. Nothing.

The table was becoming a burden, so she tried again, this time adding the thoughts that fuelled her lightness—hot air balloons, rising smoke… Henry. There. She could feel it. Gathering energy, and then prickles moving up her back and over her shoulders. The sensation continued down her arms, warming her fingertips until the heat seemed to dissipate. She gasped when it went.

The table was not weightless in her arms, but it became lighter, easier to hold. Then came a sound. She froze. Were those footsteps? Mama come to take her to task? A maid? Her eyes went to the door, checking all her safeguards. She heard a murmur of voices and her sister nearby.

"But I left it in her room."

Beatrice's eyes darted to her bed where Penny's book, *True Adventures of a Lady Botanist,* lay on the coverlet.

"Come away, Penny." Mama's voice was sharp, coming from the stairs. "Beatrice is resting."

No. Not resting, she thought as the voices receded and she set the table back on the ground. Beatrice walked to the centre of the room and rose once more. She set herself the last exercise. Travelling slowly to the ceiling, she descended, stopping every eighteen inches, or so, smiling at the scale of the images her mind had to grab hold of to come down. *St. Mark's Cathedral. Forty elephants. A wagonload of Sussex mud. Whoops.* Her descent checked, she snatched the thought of something else. *A wagonload of Scottish peat.* She was down.

She dropped on the edge of the bed and put her head against the post, breathing in and out, a little laboured, but she felt satisfaction in her weariness.

By and by, Beatrice lifted her head and went about setting the room to rights, returning to the desk when she was finished. Seven years ago, she had been a helpless thirteen-year-old girl, frightened half out of her wits, terrified of herself. A year later she had been clumsy, spending all her energies on self-control and staying rooted in place. And then she'd mastered it.

Beatrice's mind leafed through memories.

Five years of rigid control, bar the odd floatation before waking, which no one had ever actually seen her do. There was less chance of it now that Beatrice had shortened her sleeping ribbons almost to the down mattress. And such was Mama's training that the staff found it unthinkable to walk in unannounced.

Beatrice took out a fresh piece of paper. She pushed aside Deborah's letter and the words in it that read: *'Bring me back a brother I can love, Bea. A sturdy one who will bear up under the strain of my delight.'*

Could it be done? That was the question that followed after her these days, nipping after her heels as she went from one elegant party to another. Could she maintain secrecy and safety alongside having a family of her own? Mama's answer had always been no—a no as large as Westminster Cathedral and equally as immovable. But Beatrice had never worked out the question for herself and, indeed, had never had reason to do so.

Now she had a reason. Why shouldn't she try?

She began to write out a list comprising every accommodation her mother had instituted at Thorndene for her comfort and secrecy—special bedlinen, a private room, knocking at every entrance, no personal maid, incurious and loyal staff, and the suggestion of illness. She made another column, blushing furiously but determined to be thorough, of the expectations of marriage. Sharing intimacies, bearing children, living all the time with someone... the words flowed quickly from her pen. They had been in her head disregarded and ignored for so long that they broke on the page like water from a burst dam.

By the end of it, the length of each list was astonishing. Could they be reconciled? She began to strike lines though the items under "Henry" that would not present problems if she ran her own establishment as strictly her mother did.

If he wished to court her, he would have to accept these terms. That she would wish to maintain her own chambers, have complete discretion as to the hiring of household staff, and there would be a centre of privacy she expected at all times. Her marriage would look nothing like Mama and Papa's, she thought, feeling her heart chip against the hard edge of that reality.

Soon, the paper was filled with hash marks. But there was one word that left her pen hovering over the page.

Children.

She picked the paper up, willing herself to find a way. She looked over her shoulder to the window. Still raining.

She looked at the paper again.

Children.

Any one of them might rise.

What would Henry do if he found out?

Beatrice leaned on her elbows, trying to work it out, feeling as constricted as she had been in that cupboard, listening to her parents till this same ground. Then she sat up, her heart beating away in her throat. Mama hadn't run from the mad Thorntons. After years of marriage, she'd thrown her lot in with Papa, taking on the responsibility of making a place for Beatrice to be protected and safe. Why?

Mama's voice echoed in her ears, devoted and sweet.

I loved you too much.

It made her sick to think that Henry would never find out about her. But if, at some far-off future time, he did… there would be years and years of marriage between them. Years of loving him.

Beatrice struck a tentative line through the word and wondered if he could ever love her that much.

Chapter Fourteen

The wax seals crumbled and broke off in Henry's hands and the pages of his letters gaped open so wide that he could read the text within.

"You can thank my upstairs maid," Fox muttered, lifting his own ill-used stack of correspondence and flinging it on the table. "Put a heavy basin of water right on them, ground the seals to bits. My apologies, of course. I've turned her off."

"I wish you hadn't," Henry replied, pushing the wax fragments into a mound on the table.

"It's already done."

Henry frowned. Dismissed without a certificate of character.

"You've weighed me and found me wanting," his cousin said, though he didn't sound particularly wounded by the judgment.

Henry tried to make him see. "What honest housekeeper will take a chance on a girl with no references?"

"I am not in the habit of suffering inferior service, Harry."

"Mercy would cost you so little."

Fox picked up his teacup and took a drink. "But it would cost me."

Henry looked at the mess of papers. An invitation from an invalided brother-officer living in Lambeth, another summons to Whitehall to look over requisition orders, and a letter from his mother.

He saved his mother's letter for last and walked to the window, leaning against the casing to read:

'My dear Son,
    You are to put your mind at rest. I long to see you but am overjoyed to have you back on English soil...'

Henry exhaled. But squirreled between Mother's forgiveness and further information about Father's injury was a pointed question.

'Dearest, can you feel how I want to ask what keeps you in Town?'

Henry had written lightly of Beatrice, though could not bring himself to express his hopes so plainly, but perhaps the dry expression he had settled on—*business of a personal nature*—had said more than he thought.

Mother did not demand answers, but instead turned the subject to their family writing of Laura's confinement, the new curacy for Susan's husband, and how Esther and the others fared at home.

Finally, in a postscript she wrote, *'The cows from the home farm have been calving. Three bull calves and eight heifers. I feel I've won the pools. The estate can afford to splash out a little, though there is no claim on the money as yet.'*

Henry grinned, folding the letter away. Heifer calves. Mother guessed what his business might be.

And that solved one problem. His mind had been turning over the question of how to bring a bride home—a dowerless bride. He smiled again as he looked down at the pages. A bride with one hat to her name.

"What are you up to today?" Fox asked, wiping his mouth and pushing his chair from the table. "Lord Liverpool's offices?"

Henry shook his head. "Lady Sherbourne is having something she calls a Venetian Breakfast. I need some fresh air."

***

Henry stood at the top of the stone steps, looking across the bright young ladies dotting the lawn in their pinks and blues, each indistinguishable from the next. It took no longer than a moment to tell that the one he wanted wasn't here yet.

He found his godmother seated on a stone bench set under an oak tree, commanding a good view of her party, and he went to her. She sent her companion away with a wave and held her face up to receive Henry's kiss. "Why don't you go home, young man?" She patted the bench next to her. "It's been weeks and you are still in your uniform."

Henry seated himself. "The Army is going to squeeze every drop of information from me until I am wrung out and they can toss the hollow rind into the street," he replied, his eyes straying to the broad steps. Beatrice could not arrive any other way.

"Oh, stuff," Godmama grumped, drawing her shawl around her. "They are as good as done with you and have been for more than a week. So says Lord Liverpool. It's something else."

"Liverpool?" Henry's brows arched. "Are your sources so good? You would have made an excellent spy, Godmama."

"Do not distract me, young man. Four years gone and no great rush to return home. I pity your mother."

"That, she would not thank you for, ma'am," he said. "Only this week I wrote asking if my mother could spare me a while longer, and she assured me that she could."

"Lies," Godmama scolded, though full of good humour.

"My mother has told me father is doing well. His leg is healing, if he will only stay off it long enough, and she would approve the business which keeps me—"

Henry pulled himself up short and cleared his throat, watching as Lady Sherbourne's eyes narrowed with a predatory gleam. Blast.

"Planting season seemed to go well. I expect," he trailed off, leading the red herring across the field.

Godmama gave a slight smile. "This 'business' must be something essential to keep you from home, lingering in Town these many weeks. A place you have expressed no particular love for in all the years I have known you." Her gaze pinned him. "Well." The word dropped like a lead shot, pinging the ground.

In the silence that followed, Henry could hear the gravel scraping under his boot.

"You were such an honest little boy." A backhanded compliment if he ever heard one.

Henry expelled a breath. His hopes were as fragile as a yellowed manuscript that might crumble into dust at the first ray of sunlight. "What do you know?"

"I know you have been seen on several occasions in the company of my goddaughter and another young lady. A curious bit of news, I thought, since Sarah—"

"Mrs Thornton wishes to see me roasted over a spit."

Godmama sighed. "I had thought that a match between you two would serve, Henry." Her small hands, spotted with age, pressed his. "But, for reasons known only to herself, Sarah wanted to cut your heart out when you came for tea. You did get on well enough with Beatrice, though she hardly looked—" Lady Sherbourne became red-faced for a moment and then ploughed on. "Well, I am sorry it has not sorted itself out."

"You have no reason to be sorry," he assured her, unable to keep the grin from his face. Love made him sound like an arrogant young buck, though nothing had been spoken of, nor settled.

"Henry," she exclaimed, bouncing a little. "Do you mean...? Oh, how lovely."

"Not lovely yet, Godmama. Beatrice" —he said her name aloud and Lady Sherbourne made her fingertips prance against each other—"has given me reason to hope. But Mrs Thornton has not budged an inch." He must dampen the old woman's runaway enthusiasm. She would call for the banns before the day was out if he did not take care.

What would be so wrong with that? His own thoughts had already carried him far past that point. The wedding could be before the harvest, if it could be managed, when the summer was high and hot, and the great barn waited in repose for the din and dust of threshing.

"We haven't spoken of it," he admitted, but there was no uncertainty. "It's too soon."

"Nothing would please me more." Godmama patted his hand. "Your family is... in straits." Her hand sketched a half-apologetic little motion in the air that seemed to describe the lower fields prone to flooding and the window casements that yielded only after persistent coaxing. "While the Thorntons have more money than they know what to do with, and little of it is entailed. If I had conjured a bride for your needs, I could not have done better."

Henry meant to turn her aside, but he was arrested by one word. "Money? What do you mean?"

She considered for a moment. "What do you mean, 'What do I mean?' They could rebuild the London house in gold brick and not miss it."

Henry sat up. Godmama must be mistaken. The Thorntons lived plainly, never showing any sign that they had that sort of money.

That thought was a rope, slipping through his fingers. He had but to grab it and hold on, and all would be well.

"Sarah Thornton has been such a disappointing adult." Godmama arranged her shawl more satisfactorily, muttering, "Burying herself in Dorset, hiding away from Society, towing along a daughter dressed in the drabbest—I mean, Beatrice *is* lovely...." She caught Henry's frown. "Those clothes, though. You are to be commended for cultivating loverly feelings, but goodness me, you had little cloth to cut that pattern out with."

Yes. There was the matter of the clothes. Lady Sherbourne must be mistaken over the money. Why would a woman clothe her daughter in dresses that looked like castoffs from a charity bin if she could afford better? His mind turned over the question.

"Vanity," Godmother pronounced, taking up her fan and tapping it on her chin. "You know, Sarah was the Toast of London during her come out. Attention is a dose of opium to some people. I wouldn't have thought it of her, but what else can it be?"

The answer, when it came, seemed to slam into him with all the force of a charging horse, knocking him from his feet. Henry smiled, though it cost him. "There's a simpler explanation, Godmama, and one which reflects better on your friend's judgment."

"I would like to hear it," she instructed, nodding to a passer-by.

Henry wasn't blind. When he had thought about it, he presumed the family was scraping together enough money for a Season and doing the best they could with the cheapest clothes that could be bought. He'd imagined that his offer—he swallowed now, a dull red climbing his neck—of a comfortable home in Sussex filled to excess with family, a life of linens that needed careful mending and gardens that needed tending, and trips to London if the harvest was good, might answer.

"Do they raise cattle?" he asked, though it felt like an entire house was sitting on his chest.

She nodded. "Not primarily."

"How many head do you suppose...?" His mouth went dry. How much would put her out of his orbit? A few hundred?

"Thousands, I should think. If you add up all his estates together."

Henry looked up into the criss-crossing branches of the oak tree and picked his words carefully. "By choosing such a wardrobe, Mrs

Thornton could be protecting her daughter from the attentions of fortune hunters."

Lady Sherbourne looked blankly back at him.

He spelled it more clearly. "That's what she thinks I am."

Godmother's mouth fell open, but Henry knew he was right. He could feel it. Soon, she would realize it too.

Henry leaned forward, resting his arms on his knees, and felt the pages of his mother's letter crinkling inside the breast of his coat. All that excitement over a few heifer calves. What a fool he'd been. He had never wanted a fistfight more in his life.

Lady Sherbourne snorted. "My godson. A fortune hunter." Another snort. "The idea."

Godmother's outrage matched his mood but did nothing to alleviate it. Henry was proud that his laugh was not bitter. "Isn't that what you suggested? That I could raise my family's circumstance with a tactical marriage? Isn't that fortune hunting?"

"What a horrid way to put it. Simply because I noticed the advantages doesn't mean I think you did."

"What mother would believe that?" Henry asked, feeling the acridness of disappointment billow and spread within him. He stood and bowed. "I think it would be best if I left. You may give my regards to the Thorntons."

"You aren't—" She checked and turned her head. "You may give them yourself, if you are brave enough for it."

Henry followed her gaze. Mr and Mrs Thornton picked their way across the grass and Beatrice trailed in their wake on the expensive, elegant arm of his cousin. Hang the man. What was he doing here? And hang him for looking so ornamental.

Mrs Thornton wasn't chasing Fox away like a goose honking and snapping at a stray dog. No, that treatment was reserved for a man who'd spent four years being shot at for his countrymen's sake.

Lady Sherbourne interrupted his dark thoughts, whispering from behind her fan. "You should decide soon if you're too high-minded to make yourself, that girl, and your aged godmother happy, Henry. Some other man might not be so insulted by her fortune."

The Thornton party passed several yards away without taking any notice of the figures seated on the bench beneath the shadow of the spreading oak tree. However, as Beatrice and Fox came level with them, Beatrice looked over, her face peeking around that hat of hers. Fox was talking, but Beatrice kept her eyes fastened on Henry and smiled, her eyes laughing, telling him without words that she thought her companion tedious, inviting Henry to share the joke. She turned her head back to look at Fox as they followed her parents and walked on.

Blast and hell. That smile. It went through him like a cannonball.

He could not meet her smile with one of his own. Not now.

"Excuse me, ma'am," he said to his godmother.

Godmama had been watching him and her look was pleased. "Don't let me detain you from your mission, Henry." She nodded in the direction of Beatrice and her parents.

He turned on his heel and left.

***

Hours later, Henry climbed up the staircase of Fox's townhouse, his face flecked with mud. His uniform would have to be brushed out, washed, and pressed. He ran a tired hand through his hair.

"You're back." Fox came from Henry's room, turning quickly away from the door. "I was looking to see if you were home. Where have you been?"

Henry began unbuttoning his coat, three and four buttons at a time. "Middlesex, I expect." He brushed past Fox. "I gave Ceph his head."

Fox caught his arm. "Then I'm surprised you didn't end up in Northumberland with a broken neck. That horse is half wild. Have you not heard the news, then?" Fox asked.

Grab me one more time, Henry thought, surprised he still felt so much like brawling. He shook his arm loose. "No."

"The prime minister was shot. Killed, not twenty steps from where we stood with the ladies last week." Fox's eyes were bright. "The man who did it was caught and confessed."

"Is he French? Is it something to do with the war?" Henry asked.

"It appears not." Fox stood on the stairs, half up, half down. "I thought I saw you at your godmother's today, but then you disappeared, no doubt chasing a skirt or two. The crop was unusually good."

Henry's mouth twisted. "I don't have your talent for picking up every handkerchief that's dropped in my path. My heart must be a stubborn organ, meant to be given only once." He swallowed. "I saw that you had come. You were with the Thorntons."

Fox smiled and, again, Henry longed to put a fist through his face. "I'm buying a property near their Dorset estate. They have been good enough to invite me several times to their home to discuss the particulars."

Henry's answer was mechanical. "Kind of them."

Fox's smile grew bored, his eyelids heavy. "Not kind. I have a title and a fortune. They hope I will marry their daughter."

Chapter Fifteen

The day after His Majesty's government hanged Mr John Bellingham for the crime of murder, Beatrice told herself that she still had every reason to hope that she was still being courted. It was natural that the pace of London's social calendar should grind to a halt during this upsetting week. Natural that few people had come calling.

Since the prime minister's assassination, hostesses were cancelling anything livelier than a card party, and no one had dared to announce an engagement in *The Times*. Still, no one could raise an eyebrow to Captain Gracechurch spending half an hour of stilted conversation perched on the edge of her mother's settee.

Beatrice chewed on her thumb. Probably the man was unusually sensitive to the national mood.

She turned the page of the newspaper with eyes that danced from headline to headline, unable to focus on any. *Perceval Widow Leaves London, Murderer's Clothes Auctioned, Spies Suspected at Whitehall*. A noise rose from the back of her throat and she crumpled the paper into a ball, tossing it on the floor.

"Upset?" a soft, prowling voice came from the door. She scrambled to her feet and made herself look welcoming. Lord Fox.

Beatrice lifted her neck and searched the hall past his shoulder. He bowed and for a moment she allowed disappointment to cloud her face. "Your cousin is not with you?"

"That black thundercloud? No, he is visiting every corporal he ever mustered with before he returns home." Lord Fox brushed his hands, shaking off the topic. "Your footman has seen so much of me this week. He did not protest when I said I would show myself up and I don't know whether to be relieved or cast down that he did not suspect me of seduction." She was expected to smile at that and she barely managed it.

"The footman will be retrieving my mother from the garden presently, I am sure," she said, leading Fox to the settee.

"Shame," he muttered, and his voice was a soft willow branch brushing down her arm. "I came from my solicitor's office. He had me sign the deed to the property your father was good enough to recommend. I am here to proffer my thanks."

"How kind. He will be pleased to see you," she answered, feeling like she was reading from a list of suitable remarks, ticking off boxes. She shook her head. This was Henry's cousin. She must make a push. "It's rather mad to purchase a place without even seeing it."

He trained his azure eyes on her. "Don't you think I can be carried away on a tide of feeling?" he asked. "Moved by passion?"

Something in his look made her shift in her seat and glance around for her mother. "You might pay a price for it. Many do."

"Such as?" He followed up, and Beatrice, who had only been talking to fill the silence, cast around for an example.

"Meg. Her sister."

Lord Fox's lip curled. "Yes. Meg does pay. But her sister Isabelle, Lady Ainsley, was never carried away in her life. She was always a calculating creature."

Beatrice dropped her gaze, but Lord Fox returned to perfect command. "There are so many attractions of Oak Lodge. For instance, the way you spoke of the bluebell wood."

"I?"

"You called it delightful and private." He leaned forward and she was too bewildered to move. "It was enough."

"Lord Fox." His hold on her was broken as Mama swept in bearing blooms from the garden. "How delightful."

He stood and made an elaborate bow. "Not half so delightful as seeing you, ma'am."

Beatrice leaned down and rolled her eyes at the carpet, picking up the crumpled newspaper and smoothing it out on her lap.

When they had exchanged honey-saturated pleasantries, Mama turned to pour the tea and Lord Fox put his hand out, touching a corner of the wrinkled paper. "Has the news distressed you?"

Not quite. She had been in anguish that Society was so ordered that she, a woman, could do nothing about the fact that the captain had not come to call.

She tossed the papers onto a side table. "The news has been far too full of such a vile, little coward."

"Coward?" Lord Fox's brows flew up in genuine surprise. "He wasn't that. I would say that Mr Bellingham—"

"Prime Minister Perceval's murderer," Beatrice interrupted.

Lord Fox gave a rather Gallic shrug. "The man was not a coward. It took bravery to do what he did, to wait for his chance, follow through even when he knew what it would mean. Despite his station, despite his being a merchant, in a moment, he changed the course of history. We'll remember his name forever."

Beatrice cocked a sceptical brow. "Over a financial grievance, he changed the course of Mr Perceval's poor family. But history?" She shook her head. "We will have another prime minister in due course. The government continues."

"It will be Lord Liverpool, most likely. Does that please you?"

"What do you mean?"

"Only that his attitude on the slave trade, for instance..."

Beatrice darted a tongue along her bottom lip. "Lord Liverpool has spoken in support of the trade in the past, but—"

"I know. Wilberforce, your Sainted Prawn, got it outlawed. But his speech in the House of Commons was an acknowledgement that it still goes on, beyond the reach of government to stop it. How much more will it flourish when we have a prime minister who looks the other way?"

Beatrice fell silent.

"Thousands of lives, Miss Thornton. Mr Bellingham held them all in the palm of his hand. Wilberforce was at his cause for years, an unknown MP. It was the merchant, through great daring and unsurpassed courage, who wielded his power in the blink of an eye."

"You sound admiring."

"Beatrice, honestly," Mama scolded. "Such manners."

Lord Fox waved his hand. "Miss Thornton honours me with her candour," he said, that smile of his playing across his lips.

He likes to win. The thought came unbidden, and there was no reason it should so disconcert her so.

***

The next morning, Mama slapped *The Times of London* onto the breakfast table. "No less a personage than Lord Knowlton, heir to a dukedom, announced his engagement to"—Mama paused and brought the page close to her eyes—"The Honourable Louisa Carstairs."

Beatrice remembered the gorgeous girl in the tiny dress. It was Lord Knowlton's pursuit of her that had plunged Beatrice into this mess.

Mama continued. "I expect that now the whole Society will feel itself bound by duty to resume throwing parties, and it's only been two days since…" Her voice dropped to a whisper. "…the hanging."

Papa winked. "Can't let assassins think that they've scored a hit."

Penny laughed outright. "It's been quieter than Thorndene," she groused. "And nothing ever happens there."

"Has London polished you too brightly for your old home, girl?" Papa asked, kissing the top of her head. "We'll be back before long."

Mama's head was bent, but she murmured, "A week or two. We must get through Lady Sherbourne's ball."

"'Get through'?" Penny's brow wrinkled. "Why do you say that?"

Papa swatted her on the backside. "Go to your lessons. I'll take you to Gunter's if you finish them in good time."

She was off in a flash.

Mama turned and looked at Beatrice. Her expression held none of the frustration of the last weeks. Instead, she looked at her daughter like she was a beggar-child outside St. Paul's.

"Beatrice," she began, her fingers tiny mallets, hammering the table in unison. "Sometime, we should choose a dress for the ball."

Mama had not been able to stem the tide of Lady Sherbourne's officious generosity, but she had persuaded Godmama that Beatrice's health would be compromised by standing in a receiving line, greeting people as the guest of honour. Godmama had bowed to that stricture, but missing the party altogether was out of the question.

"Not today," Beatrice replied, scooting out of her chair and out of the room, her pace careful until she rounded the door. Then she swiped at the inoffensive potted plant in the hall with the flat of her hand, leaving the fronds bouncing behind her. Mama might feel sorry for Beatrice, but it could not be denied that Mama's problems would disappear if the captain stayed away.

Bah.

Beatrice snatched Penny's old hat from the wardrobe and rammed it on her head. She would take herself off to Meg's this morning.

She enlisted a footman to escort her in the light chaise and within half an hour, Beatrice was set down before a solid grey stone townhouse in Berkeley Square. "The inflexible one that looks as though it's scolding its neighbours," Meg had once said of the house. But, as a nod to practicality, she had also mentioned the house number.

Beatrice gave a quick rap of the knocker, stepping back and smoothing down her skirts. Her social visits back home were to old ladies who darned socks to pass the time. But she needed help and there was simply no one else.

"Thank heavens you are here," Meg near gushed when Beatrice was shown in. She pushed a grey cat from her legs, set down the novel she was reading, and strode across the room. "I've not seen anyone for days."

Beatrice felt a flicker of hope. Maybe Henry…

"Except Henry. And he is in a bear of a mood."

Beatrice's small spark of hope extinguished. She sank to the couch and put her hands to her head, rubbing at her temples.

"Bea…" Meg's voice was close and confused. "Whatever has happened?"

"The captain." Beatrice closed her eyes and swallowed her longing to wail. She took a long, clean breath and when she sat up she tried to appear poised again. "Forgive me." She sniffed and her voice became brisk. "The sun is warm. I—my family expected a visit from him. He hasn't come."

The cat jumped onto Meg's lap and her hand pushed into the fur behind its ears. "I am sure he never meant to neglect you."

Beatrice smiled. She could not bear to see the same pity on her mother's face appear on Meg's as well. "Yes. It's been only little more than a week." *Who was counting?* "But I worried that something had happened."

"A week?" Meg's shriek stopped the cat's low, rumbling purr. "He's been moping around here like some dour-faced clerk when he ought to have been… I'll kick him, that's what. Right in the shins."

Beatrice's composure broke. Bless Meg. "I don't know what's happened. I've seen and heard nothing of him and I had thought—" She stopped herself.

"Thought that he was moments from declaring himself. I know," Meg waved her hand. "Nice young ladies don't finish sentences like that. But I'm not so nice." She threw an arm over Beatrice's shoulders. "Well, what are we going to do about it?"

We. Beatrice felt as though she'd been drowning and was now plucked out of the ocean and dumped onto the safety of a boat deck.

Beatrice swallowed. "Meg, I wondered... I wondered if you could help me... with my clothes."

A roguish smile cocked the corner of Meg's mouth and she took Beatrice by the hands. "I thought you would never ask." She sighed, giving their hands a tiny shake.

"Now," Meg said, picking up her book, flexing it in her hands and doing violence to the bindings. "We don't have much time. The Army releases him this week and then he is sure to go home. Let me be indelicate. Is money an object?"

"None whatsoever."

"We'll go to Madame Durand," Meg stated, casting the book aside like a gauntlet flung to the ground.

***

Even at this early hour, the dressmaker's shop was doing bustling trade. Meg had wandered off, intent on investigating the wall of small drawers to one side of the shop, pulling each one out and pawing through the trimming and buttons found within. Beatrice busied herself with the fashion plates, flipping pages and pages of them until she found one that arrested her hand. She drew a finger along the severe lines, tracing the mannish cut. In sapphire blue this might...

Someone came directly behind her, looking over her shoulder. "Excellent. But as you are so young, I would suggest a hem with one row of gathers."

Beatrice could see it. She smiled. "Yes, that's exactly what it needs," she agreed, turning to find herself being appraised by the chic figure dressed entirely in black.

"My assistant tells me you have something of an emergency," Madame said, her eyes travelling the length of Beatrice's figure, taking in the ill-fitting yellow sarcenet. "And that you are a hopeless case."

Beatrice's smile faltered.

Then Madame looked to where Beatrice's hand rested on the open page of the magazine and then travelled the length of her limp grey gown. "Even in that abomination, I don't think that you are hopeless."

Reaching into her reticule, Beatrice brought out a thick roll of banknotes. Almost every pound of pin money she had saved. Such a large sum hardly dented by her few purchases in London. New gloves, books, petticoat linen, and such.

"Won't you take me in hand, Madame?" Meg wandered over to stand at her side. "I know you could fashion me something a good deal nicer than what Mama ordered."

Madame frowned. "Nice? I am not some peasant needlewoman. I don't make nice clothes. But your mama was not particularly interested in my opinions."

Beatrice considered the stakes. *Captain Gracechurch.* She pressed on. "I haven't come here to please Mama, but to please myself. Think of the triumph it will be to turn the plainest girl in five Seasons into something of a beauty. I wager you can."

Madame regarded her for a long moment and then clapped her hands sharply, causing Meg to jump in her slippers. An attendant was at Madame's side at once and she said to the girl, "The ball gown. An immediate fitting. Though," she looked at Beatrice's figure with a professional eye. "It won't need more than a few stitches." She waved the woman away and turned to Beatrice.

"You are in luck. I have something you can take with you today which did nothing for the original buyer, as I told her it would not. But it could have been made for you." Madame tucked the roll of banknotes into a capacious pocket and slid out a sketchbook. The woman muttered in her slightly accented English as she lifted the droopy muslin of Beatrice's dress. "She ought to have known better."

"I cannot believe you bargained," Beatrice said, watching for the chaise as she idly plucked a taut string which made a happy thwack as it snapped against the dress box. "I could well have afforded it."

Meg grinned. "The price was outrageous. Anyway, it was her mistake for saying it had been made for someone else. She was lucky to have you take it off her hands."

Inside the box, swathed in layers of tissue paper was a soft white ball gown in a cut that accentuated, Madame explained, the excellence of Beatrice's figure. She had let the dressmaker's explanations wash over her. She did not care about balance and contrast and Greek inspiration. She did not know anything more than that the gown turned her into something really worth looking at.

Three more dresses would follow in the next few days. Dresses in azure blue, tart lavender, and soft rose. Still more would follow in the weeks to come, no matter if the only people she wore them for were the servants at Thorndene. Whatever the future held, she would not go back to being invisible.

The dress in the box was so lovely that perhaps Captain Gracechurch would fall irrevocably in love with her. She snapped the twine again. It was an awful lot to ask of a length of silk.

Meg touched her on the elbow as the chaise pulled up outside the dress shop and Beatrice handed the parcel to the Thorntons' footman George, lifting her skirts to step into the carriage.

"Oh, it's Henry and Fox," Meg whispered conspiratorially, clutching at Beatrice's sleeve. "Henry," Meg's shout rang across the cobbles.

At the sound of his name, Beatrice glanced up, meeting the eyes of Captain Gracechurch where he stood across the street. The space between them crowded with unspoken questions. *Where have you been? Why haven't you come?* He glanced away.

She caught her breath. He hardly looked like himself at all. There was no laugh hovering on the corners of his lips. No restlessness to be at her side.

He made a curious movement and she thought he would press on, not acknowledging them, but he remained standing poised on the opposite sidewalk.

She went hot and cold as her eyes darted to the box. It seemed ostentatious and loud, broadcasting her hopeless efforts to attach a man who looked, she could not deny it, like he wished himself in China. What remonstrances she would get from her mother for its contents. But it had been worth it when she had thought she was being courted. Look at him now.

It was Lord Fox who grabbed Henry by the arm, marching him over.

"Meg," Henry greeted, when they bridged the distance, his face tight and drawn. "I didn't see you."

Meg snorted and dipped the barest curtsey. "We've been out shopping, Beatrice and I. Spent every last cent she had. You won't even know her when we're done."

Oh Meg. Beatrice curled her toes into her slippers as Henry nodded in her direction, his eyes hardly making it within two feet of her face. Perhaps the pavement would be good enough to open itself up and swallow her.

Beatrice felt his eyes wander over to the footman. "Do you need help?" he asked, and the look he swung to Meg was intent. "Or did her every cent buy only one box?"

"Only the one," Meg answered, and Beatrice watched his shoulders relax. "The others will come later." Meg grinned and put her arm through Beatrice's, holding it close. "Bea is going to be buried under the deluge."

Beatrice became aware that the captain grew rigid, his back ramrod straight, face carved in granite. She shrank from the cold remoteness of his look. "Lord Fox." She turned to the only port she had in this storm.

"Miss Thornton," he answered.

Lord Fox was laughing at her, but at least he was willing to look her in the face. "My lord, I hope we will see you at Lady Sherbourne's ball on Saturday." Lord Fox moved closer, cutting her off from Henry. For once she thanked heaven for it.

"Now that I know you're to be there, I will be sure to accept the invitation. I hope you will reserve two dances for me."

She set her lips and nodded. It wasn't what she wanted. None of this was.

Meg broke in. "You'll be there too, Henry. You must be."

Twenty minutes ago, Beatrice had been desperate for him to come. Now? If he wished to be in China, she wouldn't stop him from going.

Captain Gracechurch looked up the street. "I expect to be home by then, Meg."

"They have spared you this long. A day or two more cannot matter. Besides," she told him while tucking her arm into Beatrice's. "It's your godmama's ball. You will have to give your judgment on Miss Thornton's new appearance."

"Meg," Beatrice almost pleaded, hoping to put a stop to it. Nodding to the gentlemen, she turned Meg to the carriage, holding on to dignity as tightly as she was to her friend's arm.

Let Henry stare off toward Brighton until doomsday if he liked, she thought, accepting George's hand. She was not going to stand there like an object of charity.

"Yes," Henry stated, arresting her foot on the carriage step. His gaze was still firmly fixed in the direction of Brighton. "I'll come."

Chapter Sixteen

Henry tugged at his coat and scowled. It was all the crack, the tailor had said. Dark blue superfine—a double row of dull brass buttons over a white waistcoat with a cravat tied under the moderately high points of his collar. Nothing ostentatious, quiet and well made. He looked like everyone else in the ballroom, if a little more severe— and they didn't look stupid. Ergo, *he* did not look stupid.

He felt stupid.

Fox handed him a drink. "Your godmother keeps sending you dark looks, Harry. Probably wonders if you'll ruin the party with your scowls."

Henry turned a smile to Lady Sherbourne where she received her guests in regal splendour. She nodded her be-turbaned head in a gesture that seemed to offer conditional forgiveness, in the event that he behaved.

Henry turned and took in his cousin's appearance. In stark contrast to himself, Fox looked like he'd made his entrance to the world wearing elegant evening clothes. "What are we doing here, Fox?" he asked. The room was suffocating. The cravat was suffocating. The thought of seeing Beatrice again took the breath from his lungs.

"You're here because you don't know how to disappoint Meg."

No. The thought went through him, as sharp as the point of a sabre. *I can't stay away from Beatrice.* Still, he asked, "So why are *you* here?"

Fox lifted his glass, tossing back the contents. "A ball is the best place to find a wife."

Henry's brows lifted. "A wife? I did not know you were on the hunt."

Fox laughed. "More hunted than hunting."

Henry's mouth twisted. If he'd been the one with a title and a fortune… "I'm sure that happens to you frequently."

Fox tipped his glass in acknowledgement, a gesture that stoked Henry's desire to tip it from his hand and plant him a facer. The accident of birth and privilege wasn't Fox's fault. Henry should remember that. Instead, he allowed himself to turn a knife, tipping his head at a passing couple.

The young woman was Miss Carstairs, on the arm of Lord Knowlton, a man whose expression was a walking announcement of his mental vacuity. "Some ladies are beyond even your touch, cousin," Henry asserted, resorting to words he would never have uttered at another time. "To win the prize of the Season, you'd have had to be more than—what was it you called yourself? A 'piddling baron.' You'd have to be heir to a dukedom."

Fox's smile bared his teeth. "You're lucky, Harry, never having to worry over titles. But I'm sure Miss Thornton will take me as I am."

Miss Thornton. Henry's chest was tight. Fox had never been interested in Beatrice.

"You've shown no sign."

"Haven't I? The compliments I've paid to her mother, buying that dumpy house in Dorset. Anyway, she's an heiress." Henry could feel Fox shrug. "And there is the succession to think of. I might do worse."

Fox swiped another glass of champagne from a passing footman, but Henry stood there, prodding at the sore spot like a man with a toothache, touching the source of his pain again and again with the tip of his tongue.

He hardly registered the chatter and music of the party until he saw Meg wading through the crowd.

"Oh," said Meg, reaching them at last. "Oh, this is perfect, Henry." She ran light fingers down his sleeve and looked him over, turning him this way and that, approving everything. "You're a lovely butterfly, Henry. You really are. We'll stand you next to Beatrice and compare."

"Is she here?" The words from Henry's thoughts came out of Fox's mouth.

"No," Meg answered, glancing over at Fox. "I am sure they are not. She was so funny about her clothes, but I told her that there was no need to get so worked up about a dress. Ah." She gave a little squeal and pulled on Henry's arm.

He knew who he would see before he turned his head. It would be Beatrice. It would be better for his sanity if he didn't look, if he travelled without deviation forward out of the room and climbed over the garden wall, trampled the shrubbery, and walked straight to Sussex, never looking back the whole way.

He should do that. But he wouldn't. He was an addict craving his draught.

He braced himself and turned.

His first impression was that Meg was dead wrong. There was an exceptionally good reason to get so worked up about a dress. Henry hadn't known Beatrice's precise shape, and it had grown less important over these weeks. But what had been conjecture and guesswork in the early days of their acquaintance resolved itself in fizzing certainty.

A voice reached him through the thoughts that crowded his mind. "She worried it would make people stare, as indeed it has. The room is agog, Henry," Meg said sharply, and she jerked his arm. He blinked.

If Beatrice had been out of his reach before, how much more so was she now? He cursed the dress clinging to her figure.

Meg closed the gap, grasping Beatrice by the hands and leaning forward to kiss her cheek. "You are so perfect, I want to scratch your eyes out."

Beatrice laughed, as in command of herself as his self-possession was slipping. "They should put you in charge of troop morale, Meg. Napoleon would be routed by summer's end."

Then Henry saw the blood beating in a vein at her neck and the way her mouth tightened on one side, the flush on her skin. She was as nervous in her new clothes as he was. He breathed more easily. She was still herself.

"Isn't she beautiful?" Meg asked, like a conjuror at a fair.

Henry's tongue stuck in his mouth.

Fox, however, bowed. "A vision. Aphrodite rising from the waves. A goddess."

Beatrice's low laugh rolled through Henry, shaking his control like a hard wind might rattle a window. "Rather more fully clad than that, I hope."

"Henry?" Meg looked at him expectantly.

"Meg, stop," Beatrice protested, turning her face away. "I'm not a prize pig."

She didn't want his compliments? They could not match Fox's effusions. Henry ought to say nothing. Words forced their way out of him. "You look very well." He dammed up the flow before they could flood the ballroom. *Enchanting. Bewitching. Captivating. I love you.*

Meg shook her head, disappointed in his terse reply. Then she turned to Beatrice. "Now what do you think of Henry?" she asked. "He's had his own transformation."

"Oh, I am sure he would not want me to..." Beatrice began, looking down and untwisting an uncooperative ribbon on her fan. But Meg would not leave her be and, finally, Beatrice's green gaze swung to his.

He endured her look, reminding himself not to fidget or adjust these thin clothes that felt so alien still. She took her time before saying, "You've been discharged?"

He nodded and tried to make a light thing of it. "I'm no longer entitled to come to a ball trussed up as tightly as a Christmas goose."

She glanced to a cluster of officers nearby enjoying an easy camaraderie. "You feel neither fish nor fowl nor good red herring."

He swallowed. She understood. "I'll become a fish by and by."

She did not meet his eyes, but her voice dropped low enough so that only he heard her reply. "You won't."

Meg broke in. "Well, I think he looks quite well. Dashing, despite himself."

Beatrice laughed suddenly and caught his eye. Henry grinned. He'd meant to be austere, uncaring, not butter in her hand. But, as quickly as it had come, her smile snuffed out and she turned from him again. It was better that she should.

Fox bowed over her hand. "I hear the music striking up, Miss Thornton. I believe this is my dance." Meg's attention was claimed as well, and Henry was left staring after Beatrice. Foolish to make a spectacle of himself. He pushed his way to a less crowded corner of the room, where he stood rooted to the spot, his arms crossed over his chest, watching.

"Your cousin," a voice at his side probed, bumping his elbow with a champagne glass and proffering it. Mr Thornton. The man took a sip of his own drink and bid Henry to do the same as they watched the couple. "What sort of man is he?"

"Fox?" Henry asked, never dragging his attention away from Beatrice. "He went to Eton and then—"

Mr. Thornton waved his hand. "Know all that. Succeeded to his title young, orphaned, went to the same schools everyone else seemed to. You aren't the sort to think that tells me anything about him, are you?" His brow furrowed.

Henry shook his head. Battle was a great leveller. He'd seen men with the best bloodlines freeze in terror at the first sound of a flintlock cracking against the pan. And he'd seen farm-born privates charge the enemy without ammunition. It hadn't mattered who any of them had gone to school with. "No."

"Didn't think so. You didn't strike me as that sort of man." Mr Thornton gestured at the dancers with his glass. "But what sort is that?"

Brash among fellow men. Ruthless to anyone he deemed inferior. Indifferent to Beatrice. Things that were impossible to say. There was a long pause and finally Henry allowed, "Weston cuts his coats."

Mr Thornton barked a laugh, "And that tells me nothing. My wife has been drowning him with tea by the gallon. We haven't seen *you* in some time." His voice was affable and easy but his eyes pinned Henry in place. "Not even to bribe the footman."

A deep flush rose up Henry's neck as Mr Thornton went on. "Not a thing happens in my house that I don't find out sooner or later."

"Sir," Henry said. "I—"

Mr Thornton waved his hand again, dispersing mists of masculine embarrassment. "My wife's footman from our courting days is probably sitting on a mountain of small change somewhere, living like a lord."

Henry cleared his throat. There was one thing to clear up before Mr Thornton said something he would regret.

"I haven't a mountain of small change. Enough for my needs certainly, but—" He cleared his throat. "Lady Sherbourne is my godmother, but you should not suppose...."

"That you have two guineas to rub together?"

Henry nodded.

"I did not. But I can't think why it would matter to me, or to anyone in my household, come to that." Mr Thornton rocked on his heels.

Henry must be more plain. "Sir, your wife doesn't approve of me."

"My wife and I will sort ourselves out. Beatrice too, I expect." He wandered away then, whistling between his teeth, leaving Henry alone with his thoughts.

When the set was over, Fox made his way to Henry. "She's a triumph, though half of it is the surprise of having low expectations overturned. She was besieged almost as soon as the music stopped. It's well that I already have a lead on the others," he stated, gesturing toward a thick knot of gentlemen. "I won't waste it. She's quite the most desirable woman in the room."

Henry grunted. She had been that even before the dress. "You sound like you're appraising the points of a horse before purchase. 'Smooth gait. Fifty pounds cash. Delivery on Saturday.'"

Fox gave a little tsk. "Saturday would be hasty," he replied. "But I will have her. The mother likes me. Miss Thornton, herself, doesn't hang around my neck and would be a biddable creature if I tuck her away near her family and supply her with newspapers. Won't you congratulate me?"

Fox's words sent Henry cutting through the crowd. Fox was going to marry her, was he? Going to do it bloodlessly, dispassionately. Hide her away in his country home. Put her on a shelf to collect dust.

And here he had been, Henry thought as he pushed his way onward, wringing his hands about his dignity, about the ignominy of appearing to be a fortune hunter.

He pulled up before the tight circle of men surrounding the woman he'd come for and adjusted his gloves.

Damn dignity.

Chapter Seventeen

Henry had been hovering on the edge of her vision all night, irritating her eyes like a speck of dust she couldn't rub out. But now Beatrice could see him making his way across the ballroom and the mote was turning into a beam. Her breathing quickened and she turned to a gentleman who had just compared her to a Bengali sunset. He was young, all knobs and elbows, and would have to do. "Do you dance even better than you pour out nonsense?"

It was skirting the line—quite close to an open invitation—but Henry would be upon her in moments.

"Much better, miss," the affable Mr Gordon answered as he offered his arm. The other gentlemen in the circle grumbled amiably but cleared a path. Beatrice took his elbow and sailed past the thwarted form of Henry Gracechurch.

The surge of triumph lasted until she took her place in the set, looking across the floor to Mr Gordon, who was, no matter how she squinted, nothing like Henry. "You've been to India?" she asked him.

"In books," he replied, and then he went on, reciting their contents, seemingly by memory. Good. It would allow her to think— to consider the ruins of her life, she thought with a cold plunge into self-pity.

The dress hadn't helped at all, though it had turned more heads than in the whole of her life. Maybe it had even turned Henry's. That had been the gown's purpose, to dazzle him past the point of reason and bring him around to her. Was that why he was, even now, standing on the edge of the floor, his eyes following her like a prowling tiger?

She'd had such high hopes for the dress from the moment she slipped the whisper-soft material over her head. It was of silk, and when she had seen herself in the mirror, with the ruby pendant Papa had given her on her eighteenth birthday clasped around her neck and her curls woven through with a silver ribbon, she was overcome. She'd spread the overskirt—as thin as a spider's web and hung all about with swinging teardrop pearls—and dipped into a curtsey, the white silk of her gown pooling out on the floor.

"My word," Papa had breathed when he saw her walk into the library clad in Madame Durand's breath-taking work. "You look wonderful." He'd patted his waistcoat as though searching for a watch or a snuffbox. "My word." He'd walked to her and kissed her lightly on the forehead. "I'm not going to disarrange anything, am I?"

Beatrice had shaken her head, her nervous gaze avoiding her mother's chair.

"Come," Papa had coaxed, holding out his arm. "Have a drink and tell me if I should increase your allowance."

Beatrice had smiled and let out a breath she hadn't known she was holding. Maybe this wouldn't be painful, she'd thought. Maybe it wouldn't be a shock. Maybe they had come to see the necessity of all this as she, step by step, had come to see it. She'd opened her mouth to speak.

"Are you mad?" There it was. The accusation had burst from her mother's mouth like a flow of lava, spreading over Beatrice and trapping her like an insect.

"Darling," Papa had urged. "Don't be hasty."

"*Hasty*?" Mama's voice had risen and broke into a hush. "Hasty? Seven years of our lives, Charles. She's about to throw all our hard work away for a dress. And her sisters…" She took a ragged, incredulous breath.

"If you will be so good as to speak to *me* about my future." Beatrice had allowed herself to speak up even though she had been covering a deep well of hurt—fathoms deep.

Mama's eyes had widened and Beatrice had taken the opening. "I do quite a lot of thinking about my sisters." Her lips crimped, pulling to one side. She swallowed. "How their days rush them forward into lives that might take as many turns as a labyrinth. Deborah left Thorndene. She became a wife, a mother." Beatrice faltered at that and rushed on. "My own life stretches before me, straight down a road that only narrows as it goes. I wanted to step off it, if for a Season."

"You can't dance off into the forest and expect to return to the path as you were." Mama had been scathing.

Beatrice's smile had been tight. "No. You are right." Beatrice had raised her eyes to the painting of her aunt. "I thought I would come to feel as she had. As you told me she had. I thought that I would be content without—"

"—parties and dresses." Mama had flung her words down.

Beatrice had taken a steady breath. "A husband. A home. Children."

"Children?" Mama had seized on that. "Bosh. You've not shown the slightest interest."

"Can you think why?" Beatrice had asked, a fist twisting against her breast, grinding like a millstone.

Mama had turned her face away.

Beatrice had let the silence reign for a long moment. "Do you want to know what I think about husbands?"

"Stop, Beatrice. That wasn't part of the bargain." Mama's voice had been hard and fervent.

"A bad bargain struck when I was thirteen. I cannot live this way."

"You will ruin our lives."

Beatrice sucked her breath between her teeth and then sank, perching heavily on the arm of the chair.

"We've had enough of that," Papa had finally spoken, his voice soft. "This talk of ruin. Martha didn't ruin my life." He tapped the fireplace fender with his booted foot, staring down with unfocused eyes.

"Because she did as she was told," Mama had stated, near tears.

"Perhaps," he'd answered. "But it's certain that I ruined hers. Our father treated me like the treasure of his household and he treated her like the packing straw, fit only for protecting me, for absorbing the hard knocks. For throwing away." He shook his head. "Beatrice, what is it you're after?"

She'd had time enough to think. The words left her mouth without another second of thought. "I want to marry."

"That soldier," Mama had accused.

Beatrice had been well past the point of being reticent. She spoke nothing of her doubts, of his absence. "If he will have me."

"If he will have you," Mama had muttered. "The greatest heiress in Dorset. And what will he do when he discovers your curse?"

Curse. Mama had wielded the word like a cudgel. "He won't. If you have taught me anything, Mama, I certainly know how to keep my taint"—Papa gave a muffled exclamation—"hidden from my loved ones. You've taught me the art of ordering my household to keep my privacy. Deb and Penny have lived under the same roof as I for these many years and have not found me out."

"A sister is not a husband."

Beatrice had felt the red rush to her cheeks, but she was not a young girl, she'd reminded herself, to be overset by the thought of intimacies. "In that, we agree," she'd answered. "A sister is no substitute. No matter how much I love my sisters, their husbands will have first claim on their affections. Their children could never be mine."

Beatrice had sighed. It didn't have to be like this—knives drawn. She rushed to Mama's chair, the seed pearls on her overskirt beating onto the wooden floor as she sank to her knees. "I do not rise on accident. Don't you see? I never have. The only danger is before I wake. If I guard my privacy in those hours, no one will ever have to know. I will take such care, Mama."

Mama had refused to meet Beatrice eye to eye. "I am not persuaded," she'd stated, her voice clipped.

Beatrice had sat back on her heels. "You don't have to be. Mama, I am a grown woman."

From the mantel had come a quiet, "Hear, hear."

Mama had stood and pulled the long white gloves from her arms, slapping them onto her seat, almost in Beatrice's face. "I refuse to take her out like that." And then she'd slammed out the door, rattling the whole house as she did so.

Papa had looked down at his boots and rumpled coat. "I'm in no state to take you, Beatrice."

Beatrice had no more cards to play tonight. The dress could go back into the clothes press. She clambered to her feet and turned a brave face to his.

"But if you'll allow me twenty minutes, I think I could do you credit."

God bless Papa. He had done it in fifteen.

All Beatrice's hopes had come with her to Godmama's party, pinned to the train of this dashed dress. She could see her mistake now. If the reason that Henry was back was because she appeared as bright as a silver shilling, her heart would break. She ground her teeth, hardly able to make sense of herself. She wanted Henry—desperately. But it turned out she was not silly enough to want him on those terms.

She sent a smile to Mr Gordon, who had done nothing to earn her scowls, and he shepherded her back to her seat. Gentlemen pressed in on her again. Men who had never given her a second look all these long weeks.

They were her shield now, preventing her from finding a corner and having a good howl. A young hussar offered her a piece of cake, but her hand arrested, startled by the arrival of navy blue superfine.

"I've come for our dance," Henry stated, looking better in civilian clothes than any man had a right. He didn't elbow any of the gentlemen away. He didn't need to. His voice cut through them and they were already shifting from foot to foot. They would be driven off in another moment like chickens before the wheels of a coach.

Beatrice straightened her back and thanked heavens for the dress now. It lent her the courage to raise her chin and sit as placid as a pond, unmoved by his gruffness.

She took her time standing and said, her voice dripping with treacle, "You must forgive me. You went out of my mind. I completely forgot you asked."

Henry's eyes were blade sharp as a hearty guffaw sounded from the circle. The shot had gone home.

Still, when he offered his arm, she took it and walked with him to their places at the top of the line. As she stood opposite him, thoughts swam through her head. She caught hold of one.

"Aren't you, too, going to tell me my appearance is much improved?" she asked, cynicism in her voice, her gaze everywhere but on his face.

"Is that what they've been saying?" he answered, looking back at the knot of men. Her gaze traced the line where his hair met his collar where it curled up invitingly behind his ear. She schooled her gaze away when he turned back to her again. "I credited them with more brains than that."

"It was mannerless," she agreed, her brow lifting in unaccustomed bitterness.

He shook his head. "It was untrue."

She executed a turn, feeling the weight of her skirts brush against him. "I did not think you would lie to me, sir. I know what I looked like."

"And what was that?"

Why was he challenging her? She answered him plainly. "A brown mouse."

"'Brown' I will allow. I never saw so many shades of brown. And orange. And shocking green."

He ran a tongue along his lip before he spoke again. "You may have changed your dress, but you did not change yourself." His eyes were warm and his words were low. "And you are beautiful. To me, you have always been so. Beatrice."

She drew in a sharp breath at her name on his lips and they stopped, dead still, though dancers brushed past them. Then he swallowed hard and took her by the elbow.

"What are you doing?" she asked, as he broke the set. His gaze swept across the room and he steered her through a small crush of people. She saw the set reform as they moved away.

"Where are we going?"

Air pushed past his teeth, not even a whistle. It was the sound she used to check her horse, Blackberry, from kicking up a fuss. "We're taking some air," he informed her, letting go of her elbow and turning so that he faced the dance floor, looking as nonchalant as possible. But his coat was stretched over his shirtfront and his hands were tucked behind his back, as he intently unfastened the latch of the tall, glassed doors.

Snick. He pulled the door open and reached for her.

"Quickly," he urged, under his breath. She went through in a flash, and he followed her.

At once they were enveloped in the dark night, lit only by stars and the blazing candlelight from the ballroom, which slanted across the terrace where they were… alone. Henry did not linger there, but traced his fingers down her arm, picking up her hand as he went. He drew her into the deep shadows and the air, swirling and cool from its journey across the lawn, pressed them into an alcove.

Was she still angry with him? She couldn't think with him standing so close, with the velvet seclusion of the night wrapping around them. What explanation did he have for avoiding her this week? Yes, she was still angry. Or should be. *She should be.* She held the thought like a shield.

"Thank you for your consideration, but I was not overwarm," she murmured, backing away from him, feeling the rough brick of the old building catch at her skirt. It gave her a few inches of breathing space, no more.

"No?" he answered. He stepped so near that if he crossed his arms over his chest, he would brush her. "I was."

She reached up, her fingers searching for a wayward strand of hair she might tuck away, her feet shifting against the steadiness of his gaze.

"And we have things to discuss," he added, sounding, in the darkness, as implacable as the wall at her back.

Her breath was a laugh, and weak as watery tea. "The ballroom is the most proper place to have such discussions."

"Haven't we had enough of these games?" he asked.

"I have no notion of what you mean," she replied, feeling her cheeks blaze hot. Beatrice retreated a fraction and pressed herself against the brick yet further, as though, by wishing, they might absorb her.

He made a noise from the back of his throat, low and aggravated. "I have not seen you for far too long."

Beatrice blinked. *How dare he.* At once, the blood in her veins was a lighted fuse and she left the safety of the stonework, lifting her eyes to clash with his. "You would have run away to Sussex with no word to me if Meg and I hadn't chanced upon you the other day. Can you deny it?"

He crossed his arms and the fabric of his sleeve brushed against her, sending a tingling through her fingers. Still she could not read his face. "I don't deny it. I wouldn't be here if Meg had not forced my hand."

It was true. She sucked in another tight breath. Each one seemed to make her body heavier and heavier. However he rated her attractions, they had not been enough to keep him. "I wish you well on your journey." She turned her head and his arm shot out, pressing the flat of his palm against the building.

Henry leaned forward until his voice was only inches from her ear, soft, like a penitent at his confession.

"I have nothing. Nothing to my name except a heart that will love you until it beats out its last. It is a poor bargain." She took a breaking breath at that. "Your hand for my heart, but I will never give you reason to regret it. Love—" The word sent a shiver through her. "Do not make me give you up. I cannot. Tell me there is some hope for me. Somehow I'll make your family believe I care nothing for your fortune."

Fortune? What did he know of her fortune? She pressed a hand over her abdomen. Had he found out? Her breath came in tiny gasps as realization broke over her head.

Mama had tried to hide Beatrice away in plain sight, clothing her in gowns that repelled the eye and swallowed her up. That had been the main aim. But Mama had also taken into consideration the fact that the Thornton wealth would be an attraction. Few men of means would look about for a wife in poor circumstances, a wife whose clothes appeared to be castoffs. The knowledge of her fortune would draw the wealthy and the unscrupulous, and Mama had been wise to disguise the enormity of it.

How unfortunate then that Beatrice's choice would be a man of honour and modest means. Her dowry would drive such a man off at once. It should have driven Henry off.

But Henry had not known.

"You had no idea," she began, hardly daring to believe it.

"Not until Godmother told me what a fine thing it would be if I—if we—made an alliance. She sat there ripping apart my hopes as easily as tissue paper, and I understood then that I would be classed as a fortune hunter."

Her voice was a whisper, hardly louder than the beat of her heart. It was agony to speak. "The money—"

"I know, I know, I know." He repeated himself like the rasp of a gate, hastening to close. "I thought it mattered. Maybe it still does and I should not be presuming—"

She wrapped a hand around his wrist. "The money is nothing. Not if—" She swallowed, her throat dry. There would be no turning back, no pretending that what lay between them was as ephemeral as a fog on the meadow. "Not if you love me... as I love you."

She felt his stillness carry through her fingers and up her arm. Finally, she raised her gaze and when it met his she heard her own soft gasp. Nothing more divided her from Henry, no obstacles or impediments remained to be navigated. This distance between them—what was left of it—could be closed as easily as walking over a stile.

And Henry meant to close it. Bringing a hand to the curve of her waist, his eyes searched hers for an objection, and finding none, slid it further, pressing his palm into the small of her back and pulling her close. Even through his glove and the silk of her dress, her skin warmed to his touch. Beatrice raised her slippered feet onto tiptoes and touched the curl of hair behind his ear, drawing him forward, her hands giving expression to her heart.

The last moments had blasted away her uncertainties. Henry dipped his head and her eyelashes dropped, feathering against her cheeks. Blood roared in her veins. He was a breath away.

A sound, hardly louder than the scrape of a match, shocked her into awareness, making her eyes fly open. "Henry," she whispered, against his lips. When he didn't lift his head she put a hand to his shirtfront, feeling the pounding of his heart. "Someone's here."

Chapter Eighteen

Beatrice wished her words unsaid as Henry squeezed his eyes shut, his hand balling into a fist against her back. His fierce curse was blown away by the soft breeze, and his hands that had held her close now dropped away, leaving her to steady herself against the rough wall.

Henry ran shaking fingers through his hair, looking like he'd been planted a facer, and though neither of them were in any condition to confront a stranger, she was more used to wearing a mask than he was. Taking a long, shaking breath, she straightened herself and brushed the back of his hand as she went past him, swift as the beat of a bird's wing.

When she saw the figure that had interrupted them, standing with his hands resting on the stone balustrade like the captain of a ship sailing into the green lawn, her first impulse was to push him off the terrace. The man deserved to break his neck in the shrubbery for wandering where he was unwanted.

Then he turned, his shoes scraping at a bit of gravel, and her eyes widened.

"Lord Fox. There you are," Beatrice greeted, clenching her hands. Her voice was over-bright and she made an adjustment, dropping her tone, slowing down. "Have you come to claim your dance?" She skirted into the garish light and gathered up the ragged edges of control. How much had he seen of them, embracing in the shadows?

"I thought I'd seen you slip out, but convinced myself that my eyes were playing tricks on me. Do I find you dallying in the moonlight, Miss Thornton?" Lord Fox asked. His tone was amused and she felt her stomach twist with protectiveness. His laughter was a desecration, as though he had stolen into a church, smashing the holy relics.

He looked past her to where Henry stood, face and figure cloaked in darkness. "I did not think my cousin would—"

"Dally?" Beatrice was proud of her laugh. Emotions she didn't know what to do with had her by the throat even yet. "Catching a breath of cool air, more like. The ballroom was an oven. Never fear, though. Captain Gracechurch has been terrified we would be found out and wished to scoot me inside again."

"Harry is the wrong man."

Beatrice's eyebrows shot up. *Of all the insufferable...*

"I had better be the one to take you inside again," he said, and she let out a little huff of air. It hadn't been quite the insult she was preparing for. Lord Fox offered his arm, and she placed her hand on it. Looking deep into the shadows, he said, "It's just like you to waste the moonlight, Cousin." Lord Fox glanced down at Beatrice, giving her a wolfish smile as though she were a sheep to be devoured. "Harry always was a slow top where the fair sex was concerned."

Beatrice smiled. The man could not have seen them if he could say such a thing. Still, she made no attempt to contradict him.

Lord Fox stroked her hand, which rested in the crook of his arm. "Yes, better to come with me. Walking out with a peer will do you more credit than harm, no matter what the prattle says. A half-pay officer however...." All things concerned, it was best not to cause talk, but she hated Fox for that—for making Henry sound like nothing at all. Lord Fox seemed to have an unerring knack for pointing out ugly truths.

She took another deep breath, her limbs still slack and shaking from Henry's embrace. What would have happened to her if he'd had more time?

Heat climbed her cheeks and Beatrice flicked open the fan dangling from her wrist, waving it across her face. Someday soon, she decided, she would make sure he had all the time he needed.

She followed Lord Fox, but checked her step before the doors, looking back to where Henry stood still as ice. "Don't forget our next dance, Captain. The one before supper?" she called. Henry bowed, the gleam of a silver pin in his neckcloth winking out at them.

If only Lord Fox had been a minute later she would know, for certain, what had been decided. Was she affianced? Beatrice pawed through the words they had exchanged. No. Not quite. But she was on the point of it.

She wished to shake Lord Fox's hand from her arm and run back to Henry, longing to settle it at once. *Settle.* The dry, business-like term was wholly inadequate to describe the way Henry would mark the event.

"What has put the roses into your cheeks, Miss Thornton?" Lord Fox asked as he stepped through the doorway, past ladies whose eyebrows raised and whose heads dipped toward one another, hiding their gossip behind snowy white gloves. *See the Thornton girl out to catch herself a title.*

"It's so warm." She coughed into her hand, covering her smile.

They took their place on the floor. "Then, perhaps, you wish for another turn on the terrace. Though, I warn you, I am not one to let a good moon go to waste."

Beatrice gave a tiny shake of her head and then forced a laugh, one that kept him at a distance. "I am sure you are not. Your cousin, though, cured me of wishing to step outside with anyone else." That was nothing but the truth. "Proprieties," she added.

"He has always been good at following the rules."

"That sounds as though you weren't. Were you the one in scrapes and he the one quick to tattle?"

"Worse," Lord Fox admitted, giving her a lopsided grin that she liked much better than his more conventional ones. "He'd neither tattle nor scold. Merely go his own way," he explained, his fingers walking across the air.

Lord Fox's tone was so full of remembered injury that she smiled. "How trying."

"I couldn't even be properly mad at him."

She laughed then, feeling her tight-coiled emotions seize on this release.

"Are you quite sure you won't come out to the terrace with me?" Lord Fox asked, training his eyes on her face.

"You ought not to go around issuing those invitations, my lord. Some lady will take you up and then where will you be?"

"Caught in a parson's mousetrap," he replied, his eyes narrowing. She wanted to laugh again, though this time there was a nervous energy that seemed to spring up between them. That intense expression looked like that of a cheap fortune-teller, trying to mesmerize a naive young girl out of her pence.

"I did not see your mother here," he noted, when she gave no rejoinder.

"Mmmm?" Beatrice answered. Her eyes followed Henry as he slipped in from the garden, melting into the party so slowly that he hardly seemed to be moving at all.

"Your mother," repeated Lord Fox.

"Pardon me," she shook her head. "No, she wasn't feeling well." Henry's colour was high, but nothing that could not be chalked down to the heat of the room.

"Have you heard the gossip?" Lord Fox asked, following her gaze over his shoulder. He frowned. "One of you unmarried misses became engaged yesterday and it's overset several ladies. They speak of nothing else."

"Oh?" she murmured, watching as Henry planted himself by a column, crossing his arms over his solid chest. It was only the truth, she thought, reaching a hand to her neck. Her fingertips had told her how solid he was, not ten minutes ago.

"…throwing herself away," declared Lord Fox, and she felt her attention jerk back to him.

Beatrice blinked. "Excuse me. Who is throwing herself away?"

"Lady Carissa. Bedford's daughter. Certainly she could do better than a knight."

"Throwing herself away?" Perhaps it was because she, herself, was so close to happiness that Beatrice felt a sudden desire to take up the cudgels and do battle for the lady and the man of her choice. "If she loves him…"

"That can hardly be the only consideration."

"Can't it? Why should her heart have no say in the matter?"

"Not *no* say. The esteem of a husband for his wife is desirable," he said too offhanded for Beatrice's taste.

Esteem. She recalled Henry's hand around her waist, his warm breath above her lips. The colour climbed up her cheeks again. Perhaps exploring Lord Fox's philosophies on the state of matrimony would douse the betraying blush. "Then what are the proper elements of a good match?"

"Brace yourself, Miss Thornton," he cautioned with a mischievous grin she almost liked. Was this the face he showed his cousin? "I'm going to speak the truth. Ready?" She nodded. "Breeding, wealth, distance—"

"Distance? Between a couple?"

"I mean that exactly."

Beatrice's tongue got the better of her sense. "Maidens are forever being warned about that distance closing too precipitously." She reddened and cleared her throat. Better to practice prudence. "Your list contradicts the wisdom of the church. Countless homilies entreat a married pair to be one, to leave behind father and mother and become one flesh."

"But I deal in practicalities."

Beatrice let out a tiny snort he couldn't possibly hear.

He continued. "Have you ever felt like you wanted to be alone? That, no matter how dear your loved ones were, you couldn't bear them for one more minute?" He spoke as he had that day the balloon rose, saying words that she thought but could never say aloud. How often had she crept past Mama's sitting room at Thorndene, desperate for her own company? How often had she had to account for every moment?

Lord Fox's voice was as careful as a tightrope walker. "A person ought to have room to do as they wish, to have a retreat from the prying of others."

"Prying?" She shook her head. "Even from his wife?" Papa would never have used such a word to describe the world he shared with Mama.

"Yes, Miss Thornton. Even from his wife. No one should break down the doors of your holy temples without invitation. Even in a marriage, there must be privacy. Distance."

And that's a load of old trot. The distance he spoke of wasn't a private sitting room, a circle of personal friends, or the ability to think one's own thoughts. That was normal enough. Healthy. No, Lord Fox's distance was of withholding one's self. Of not caring what the other did. Of looking the other way. Of not having even the right to ask.

Who wanted a life like that?

Anxiously, her teeth pulled at her lower lip. Was that what Henry would think when she accepted his proposal? Would she sit him down and tell him not to be too curious about her, too interested? Would she explain quite calmly that doors between them would remain locked unless she opened them? Would she be able to persuade him she wished to hold something of herself back? Especially when she didn't want to.

She had known, when she first started down this road, that it was what must be done. But that blurry event in the future was hurtling closer and closer, each detail picked out more sharply. And it was beginning to look a little ugly.

How unfair it was for her to turn her nose up at Lord Fox and his ideas of marriage. When it came to it, she would lay out her case to Henry and ask him for distance. Could she make it sound better than Lord Fox's sensible, unromantic approach? Moreover, would Henry accept it?

The worry made her eyebrows draw down. If it had been Lord Fox doing the proposing, he would agree to her demands with a shrug, never bothering to discover what was behind them. His heart would not be involved. But Henry... he loved her. And he had made a career of laying siege to strongholds.

Beatrice gave an aggravated sigh. Dash Lord Fox and his theories. She would have to take care that Henry would have as much of herself as she could safely give him. Though there were things she must conceal, he would not know it. He could not.

Unspoken was her worry that his love only went so far.

Lord Fox cleared his throat, waiting for her reply and Beatrice smoothed her brow, asking, "Wouldn't forgoing marriage altogether be the best way for you to ensure you had all the distance you required, my lord?"

"A novel idea," he chuckled. "But there must be someone to tend the cottage and the chickens when I'm gone."

"Chickens?" She cast disbelieving eyes heavenward, but there was a smile in them. "You mean the heir to the barony and title. I understand that those things make bachelors fretful. But a lady often has no such considerations. Why should she settle for esteem when she might have more?"

"An apt word, Miss Thornton. *Might*. Who would wish to stake their happiness on such a word? I prefer certainties."

"There are no certainties in life, my lord. But I am listening. What is more certain than love?"

His answer was swift, as though he had given it thought. "Protection. The sort of protection a woman could only get by allying herself to a respected name and an elevated rank."

"Protection? From what, do you imagine? These aren't the oozing alleyways of Covent Garden."

"And not every danger is a knife at the purse strings. My ancestors are found in the pages of five hundred years of English history, Miss Thornton. Members of Society wishing to hurl any manner of abuse at my baroness would need to think hard before assaulting that breastwork. *Lady* Fox would be untouchable."

Untouchable. And unloved by her husband. Beatrice felt a tide of pity for the future Lady Fox. "It's a transaction, then? Your heir for her protection? You sound like a vegetable monger haggling over a load of cabbages."

He gave a sad sort of smile then, which made her feel she had stepped beyond the bounds. Her warm heart wanted to apologize, but he would not thank her for seeing his weakness.

"I suppose so. But it is better to know, going into the agreement, what one expects out of it. Terrible to be in the market for cabbages and come away with carrots. With me, a lady would know exactly what she was getting." His eyes never left her face. "Have I shocked you?"

She gave him a polite, if uncertain, smile. "Of course not."

"I can see I have," he said, sketching a bow as the music concluded. He straightened and held her hand in both of his own, neither playing the outrageous schoolboy or the bored peer. His voice dropped. "I do wish you will remember all I have said."

A frisson of surprise went through her. Was he, in this strange way, angling for her hand? She looked again to where Henry stood, his eyes lit with a banked fire, sending silent messages flying across the ballroom.

"Perhaps I am too late, already," his lordship murmured, his glance encompassing Henry and herself.

It was too late. The captain had stormed the defences, taken the city and captured the standard already.

Lord Fox handed her off to a gentleman more interested in Madame Durand's craftsmanship than in herself, and she allowed herself to drift along in the current, going from partner to partner, her eyes straying to the clock as often as they did to Henry. Her thoughts were a witch's brew of doubt and elation.

Finally, the supper dance was called. Beatrice stood perfectly still as Henry pantomimed a war whoop and cleaved through the crowd, pushing his way to her side.

"Miss Thornton," he said, bowing over her hand when he broke through at last, covering his pleasure with a layer of formality.

"Captain Gracechurch," she sent him an arch look, sinking into a deep curtsey. "Has the time come so soon?"

"Time is my enemy," he stated, offering his hand. The strings, lively and bright, struck up in an old-fashioned Scotch reel. She would be breathless when it finished, but it suited her mood.

She curled her fingers over his palm and followed him to their place, looking up at him. "Have you not enjoyed the ball?"

"Two dances, Beatrice—Miss Thornton," he corrected, glancing quickly around, his voice dropping, "is hardly enough." His thumb brushed across the back of her glove, too slow and methodical for chance. She felt the blush bloom on her cheeks.

Which of them would be sensible? Ducking into a garden for the second time would— Her mind lost its way for a long moment, the blush rolling over her neck, the longing for privacy lancing through her. She shook her head, not wanting to clear her mind but having to. *Collect yourself, Beatrice.*

Her breath was short and her question, when she asked it, told him where her mind had been. "Why were you so silent out there with your cousin?" she asked.

"I wondered how you could speak. I could not. Fox would have heard how it was with me." There was a long pause and then he spoke again, his voice rough. "I cannot wait." Henry's hand tightened over her own. "Tomorrow. Tomorrow I will come to your father and ask for his permission to pay my addresses. Do I have your consent?"

Her heart beat in time with the music. "You have it," she breathed. "Papa is 'at home' each Thursday. You could not have picked a better day for him to receive you." She grinned. Then she skipped to the centre of the set, raising her forearm to the other ladies in the circle, hitching her skirts to make room for the steps and turning around the middle like a starburst. Somewhere, a man let out an untamed cry and another answered the call. The old dance had made them all country-folk—passionate and plain dealing—lifting the heavy mantle of elegance.

The star pattern broke apart and she returned to Henry. He caught her, spinning her to his side, and once more their hands joined, and clung. Feathers of hair, unbound now, brushed across her neck.

"Meg is going to be insufferable," he murmured, leaning down to her cheek, the mint on his breath filling her nose. "She'll think she arranged the whole thing."

"Didn't she?" Beatrice asked, baiting him. It was delicious to watch him rise to it, to use power she didn't know she had. "You said you would never have come tonight without her."

He could not resist the enticement. Henry's eyes gleamed. "No one else was out there begging me to stop your mouth with a kiss, you impudent girl." Her stomach tightened at his look. He was as dangerous to her self-possession in a navy coat as he had been in a scarlet officer's uniform.

"You had better develop a taste for impudence," she countered.

He threw his head back and laughed, the sound lost against the fervour of music and dance.

This was as close as they might be for days. Tomorrow she would promise herself to him. In weeks—no more, she vowed—she would be his wife. That there were things she must keep from him was the only dark cloud and even that seemed too small and too far away to trouble the sunny skies. Beatrice gave herself up to the joy of it, feeling tremulous in her bones, and a fire in her veins.

Henry twirled her around, his exultance matching hers. "You're as light as thistledown in my arms," he said as her slippers left the ground.

She laughed. Thistledown was too heavy for how she felt. She was air. Light. Sky.

Thistledown.

Her skin suddenly tingled with awareness. At first, with the indistinct feeling of wrongness, then with a breathless terror as she waited to feel her toes touch the smooth wood of Godmama's ballroom.

She wasn't coming down.

Lord. Sick with fear, she forced herself down, fast. Weight, like thousands of stones, pressed on her, sending her stumbling onto the floorboards, crushing her into the ground until she could hardly breathe. Darkness crawled up her vision, blacking out the room and the candles and Henry's face leaning over her own. Panic tore through every sinew, stuffing her ears and gagging her mouth so that when she heard a whimper, it sounded like an animal caught in a snare hundreds of yards away. Not like her voice at all.

Somehow she had risen under sharp eyes in a well-lit room, stripped of the control she had pinned all her hopes on. Mama had taught her to discipline her power or be at its mercy. Taught her that if she could not master herself, it would be done for her. Half-remembered words pierced her like arrows, frightening her more now than when she was a girl of thirteen.

Anchored. Bound. Hidden.

She had more to lose now than she had then.

Beatrice felt tears trail down her cheeks as her dreams—dreams that belonged to the light—seemed to groan and crash in an explosion of spark and ash.

Chapter Nineteen

Confusion clouded Henry's eyes. Beatrice's cheeks were as white as chalk. Dancers, in a widening eddy, slowed and made room for him as he bent over her, holding her wrist. "Beatrice," he whispered. In another moment she would sit up and brush herself off.

In another moment.

In another—

His stomach tightened in a familiar way, but he had no sabre at his side, no enemy to charge.

Then a shuddering breath came from her lips and he didn't wait, scooping her up. *Beatrice, damn it, open your eyes.* A rush of anxious dowagers settled in his path, clucking over him.

"Oh, Captain."

"Simply overheated," he assured them, not pausing his step, the authority of his voice wrapping itself around his own panic like a fortified wall. *Open your eyes.*

How long was too long to be unconscious? One minute? Two? Should he have collected a container of smelling salts? Some of the women in the ballroom looked like they didn't leave the house without a whole apothecary case stuffed into a purse.

The hallway was quiet. What did he know of the business? Beatrice hadn't fainted from a bullet wound or powder burn. His rough field doctoring was no good here. Maybe it *was* better to get one of the ladies. He began to turn and then looked down to find Beatrice blinking up at him, silent and staring. "There you are." He let out his breath, the relief washing over him like a wave. All would be well. "Love…"

The hazy confusion in her expression burned off and she turned her face to his coat as her shoulders began to shake beneath his arm. Reaction. "What is this?" he crooned, lifting her closer. "No. No need for tears. You fainted and—"

"Henry," Meg called, skidding into the hall and raising her skirts to run the length of it.

Here was help. "She's going to be fine. But find me somewhere to lay her down. Somewhere quiet."

Meg shot past him, opening several doors before waving him through one at the end of the house. She pointed with a fluttering hand. "The sofa," she called, bustling around with a lighted taper, touching it to several candles. "Well?" she prompted when he continued to stand there, holding his burden tight against his chest, unwilling to let Beatrice go.

"Henry," Meg near shouted. He came back to himself with a start and laid Beatrice down.

The first thing she did was curl away from them. Her knees were drawn up and her shoulder became a shield against who knew what.

Him?

Don't be stupid. Whatever it was making her weep had nothing to do with him. It couldn't.

"Are you in pain, love?" he asked and heard Meg's indrawn breath. It wasn't the time to explain his easy endearment. "Should we call for a doctor?"

Beatrice shook her head. In that moment he could see the skin across her chin puckering and he crouched beside her, reaching a gentle hand to brush the hair from her temple.

Beatrice flinched away, as though he'd grazed her with a scalding iron, and scrambled to sit upright, rocking him back on his heels. "Don't touch me," she cried, her face pallid and tracked with falling tears. The shock robbed him of words. *Don't touch me.*

Meg snorted, putting an arm about Beatrice who stiffened and then leaned against her. Evidently, Meg was exempt from inspiring the—alarm? Was that the right word?—that he, himself, had caused.

"What did you do?" Meg mouthed up at him. In this moment she was a fierce, raven-haired Valkyrie.

Nothing.

"Papa," Beatrice gasped, her teeth clenching. Her free hand clutched the arm of the sofa as though it were an open boat in rough seas. "Get my father."

Meg gave him a look. *Go.*

"Meg," he challenged.

She shook her head. "We've scandal enough. *You* get her father," she insisted, stabbing at him with her finger.

The words were unwelcome, but Meg was correct. He'd carried a woman through a crowded room, looking like a lovesick boy. But, what did he have to fear from the gossips? Would they try to force them into marriage? Could they manage it faster than he could do it himself? They were welcome to try.

This week should see them betrothed. The next month would see them married. *Betrothed then married.* He kept those thoughts close like dogs on a lead, barking and snarling after other, darker thoughts, which must be kept at bay.

Henry raked a hand through his hair as he tried to settle his mind. It was a faint, nothing more. Probably she really *had* become overheated. He thought a moment longer—long enough for a question to bubble up, shattering his easy answers. If the faint was nothing, why was her reaction to it so out of proportion?

Meg pointed to the door and Henry took his orders, speeding down the hall, only to find Mr Thornton almost upon him.

"Gracechurch, there you are. What's this I hear about Beatrice?" he asked as Henry doubled back, leading the way. A note of incredulity entered his voice. "She hasn't *really* fainted, has she?"

"Yes, sir, for a few moments," he answered, his eyes dark. Henry's hand went to the door. "She's having some reaction to it."

"*Beatrice?*" He sounded like he might expect it of anyone else at the party before his own daughter. Let the man see for himself. They found Beatrice staring into the empty fire grate while Meg sat at her side, speaking in a low, steady stream. Meg looked to them as they entered and she shook her head, giving a puzzled shrug.

"The captain tells me you are not feeling yourself." Her father's voice was easy and light. He knelt at his daughter's feet and Meg got up to pour out a glass of water, which she handed to Mr Thornton. "Thank you." He took the glass, delivering it to Beatrice by putting her free hand under the tumbler. "Funny how much heavier cut crystal is than tin. Imagine carrying a whole crate of them. Heavy," he said, speaking in a slow, soothing voice. "So heavy."

Beatrice nodded and then let out a thread of a cry. Mr Thornton leaned forward, touching his forehead to hers, breathing in and out as father and child. After a long moment Beatrice straightened, giving a sniff as Meg scooped the glass from her grasp.

"Papa, I am not quite well." Simple enough on the face of it, but his love's hands, Henry saw, were in fists, white-knuckled fists, crushing the delicate skirt.

Was it a simple matter of illness?

"Miss Thornton," Henry called. Only Beatrice did not turn her gaze to him. "I'm not sure you will remember it. You were dancing one moment and in a faint the next. I wondered if you'd turned your ankle."

There were no assurances about her memory, no gratitude for his part in delivering her through the crowd, no rush to tell him that she hadn't been injured at all.

The silence that followed seemed full of words that might be said. But there were none. Instead, Beatrice's eyes were trained on her father's cravat as Henry waited for her to acknowledge him. In that pause, his heart began to pound like a hammer. Bang. Crack. It was hard to escape now, this feeling that something was quite wrong.

"If I could have my girl to myself for a moment?" Mr Thornton asked, all affability. His tone should have reassured Henry—told him he was a fool for this worry that gnawed him from the inside.

Meg grabbed him by the arm as she went and pulled him from the room. She closed the door almost in his face and he put a probing finger to the keyhole, the seam of his glove flicking the opening. It wouldn't be honourable to stoop down and put his ear to the door. Yet he felt himself beginning to do so when Meg pulled at him again, tugging him down the hall. "What did you do?"

"Did she say anything?"

"You're not listening," Meg snapped, twitching his sleeve. "Beatrice is—" Meg wet her lips. "—upset. It's about you, I know it. What have you done?"

His lips twisted into a shadow of a smile. "Your second sight tell you that?"

"Don't laugh at me," she scolded, serious.

"Does she seem ill to you?" Henry asked, training his eyes on the door handle.

The door swung back six or seven inches and Mr Thornton—grave and stern—said, blocking the view to his daughter, "We want to leave without upsetting the party. Miss Summers, if you will be so good as to collect her cloak? Gracechurch, if you will call for the carriage to be brought around."

"I can carry her," Henry told Beatrice's father, fingertips touching the wood door, wishing for once that he was the sort of man who would push his way in. "She's no weight at all and I—"

"You've done more than enough." Mr Thornton's eyes softened. "And I'm grateful. But, Beatrice should be on her feet. The carriage, if you please."

Henry was dismissed.

It took no time to perform his errand and he raced back around to the entrance hall. Henry meant to see them as they passed, as though doing so would sort everything out in his head. A tall, gilded mirror took up one wall and he observed himself for a long moment. Except for his clothes, which he would have to accustom himself to, he looked like his usual self. Nothing to repel.

It was his expression, falling into deep, brooding lines better suited to a poet that made him wonder. The uncustomary harsh look should have no place on a night such as this. Beatrice had promised to welcome his addresses. He ought to be over the moon that she was his as he was hers.

But his was not the face of a man who was as sure of that as he would like to be. If possible, his expression was blacker still than the one he'd worn as he dressed for this wretched party.

Henry rubbed the back of his neck and took a clean breath. Maybe he was wrong about imagining some calamity. It seemed foolish here, in the entry hall of his godmother's townhouse, to think that the foundation he and Beatrice had laid out there on the terrace would dare blow away like a mound of dust.

Better to imagine Beatrice's reaction might simply mean that she was embarrassed to fall to the floor in a dead faint. Or felt compromised when he'd embraced her so publicly. Yes, he thought, grasping onto that explanation. Society was cruel, quick to make even the most innocent actions appear sordid. Perhaps she hadn't meant to sound so hard when she'd flinched away from his hand.

Words seemed to drip through him like candle wax.

Could.

Possibly.

Almost.

Almost could he convince himself that he'd misread the situation. Almost, but not quite. Still, Beatrice could banish all this confusion with a single look.

He heard the slow but steady tread of Mr Thornton and Beatrice as they came through the hall from the servants' stairs. Mr Thornton's arm seemed less to be propping her up than holding her down and Henry frowned. It would be better if they'd let him carry her. Beatrice looked like she could hardly walk.

Her free hand strayed to every piece of furniture and chair rail. She ran her fingers along each, lingering along and under them. She need only to look at him. Flash a ghost of a smile that told him all his plans and hopes could keep multiplying.

He waited for it as they drew level.

Waited.

Waited.

Felt the blood in his head and his heart beat like a roaring river. "Is there anything I can do?" he asked, only to see the sinews of Beatrice's neck tighten, her chin draw so slightly away from him.

"No, no." It was Mr Thornton who answered, not pausing as they made their way to the door. Beatrice hadn't taken her eyes from the floor. His voice was still maintaining the fiction that all was well, ordinary even. "I dare say it's all these late nights catching up on us."

It was Mr Thornton's friendliness that kept him at arm's length, thrusting Henry away as surely as a cut.

Their shoes made scratching sounds as they made their way down the steps. A footman swung the carriage door wide and Mr Thornton handed his daughter up. She managed it easily enough, Henry thought, and she took hold of the strap hanging from the window and tucked the fingers of her other hand under the bench, looking as though their carriage was poised for a cross country flight instead of a quarter hour's drive on well-paved streets.

Her father scrambled up beside her and the door was shut. Still Henry did not move. *Look at me*, he thought, as though by thinking it, she would grant his wish.

Why would she not face him?

"Can I call on you tomorrow to reassure myself that Miss Thornton is well?" How inadequate these words were. How idiotic. His pride was gone. *Why doesn't she turn?*

Mr Thornton gave him a pitying look and then told him, "I'm never home on Thursdays. In fact, the whole household has plans. Another time, perhaps." He banged the woodwork twice with the flat of his hand. The carriage jerked forward.

Beatrice was gone.

Chapter Twenty

Papa sent the yawning footman off to his bed and removed his hat, scratching his forehead. "You can't expect me to lie to your mother, honeybee." That old endearment reminded her who was the parent and who the child. "The bare fact of you rising, against your will, is the last thing that should be kept from her."

Beatrice put her hand on the newel post and tapped it with her palm, drumming it over and over again, her face turned up to the darkness of the upper stairwell. "I never asked that you lie, Papa," she said, her voice under tight rein. "I only—" She gathered her skirts in one hand and lifted her foot to the tread. "I know what she'll do."

"Then you know more than I."

"I have to be the one to choose what's to be done. You see that?" she asked, knowing herself to be cornered. There was only one choice she *could* make—to take the long, west road to Dorset. Home. Whether Mama dragged her there or she chose to run, in the end it would be the same. But—and here Beatrice could feel herself preparing for the years ahead—the hard-won right to make decisions for herself must never be ceded back to Mama.

Papa looked grave but nodded and Beatrice began to move forward. Then his voice called, "What of Captain Gracechurch?"

She stopped, her back rigid, brittle, her arm mooring her to the bannister, her form too still. *What of Henry?* She closed her eyes against the image of his face, hurt and confused, only to find it burned against her eyelids.

What of Henry? Her spirit shrank from the question. Not yet. The wave that threatened to break over her head must be held off until she gained the refuge of her room or she would disgrace herself on the stairs.

Beatrice shook her head and swept on.

***

The noise that woke Beatrice was a perfunctory knock and the squeaking swing of the door. Late-morning sun striped through the curtains and she tensed, feeling around for the bed, gasping in relief. She was still on it.

"Tip over your barrow, Bea. I want every detail." Penny sprawled across the foot of the bed, smiling and uncomplicated. "Let's hear how you caused a riot and were danced off your feet."

"What?" Beatrice asked, as she tugged at her ribbons, struggling to sit up.

"That gorgeous dress, Bea. You looked so good. Heavens." Penny peered at her face. "Now you look dreadful. Didn't you get a scrap of sleep?"

Yes. Somehow. She had dropped off when the tears ran dry and in spite of the scouring pain that had reached into every part of her. After enough time, pain all over felt like numbness.

Beatrice sank back onto her pillow and took stock of her condition.

The heartache. Yes. Still there, sharp and frightening in these first moments of awareness. It couldn't be ignored. She tried to anyway.

The rising. She could not test it now and didn't want to, in any case. She'd never hated it in this way before, but now it was as abhorrent as a festering boil. If it were possible to lance it clean, she would wield the knife herself.

The tears. *Oh lord.* They had replenished themselves overnight. "Get off, Penny," Beatrice told her sister, her foot pushing at her sister through the eiderdown. "Let me be."

"Hmm," Penny sniffed, scooting onto her feet. She tossed a packet over her shoulder that landed on the bed. "A fine thanks I get for delivering your mail."

Letters. Beatrice snatched them up, her mouth going dry.

"Two beaux," Penny informed with glee, hanging onto the bedpost, her brows waggling. If she hoped for a gossip, she was going to catch cold. "That's one more than yesterday."

"Not now," Beatrice insisted.

Penny's forehead wrinkled and Beatrice pushed her pain and confusion aside long enough to soothe her sister. "Later," she told her gently. It was the best she could do.

Penny accepted the crumb. She jutted her pugnacious chin into the shadows by the bed and, crooking her little finger, hooked it around Beatrice's. "Only because you look so grotty."

When Penny was gone, Beatrice slid the first letter open. It was Henry's hand. A thousand thoughts poured themselves from her mind before she even shook open the page.

'Dear Miss Thornton,' he began, quite correctly. *'I came at first light hoping to hear some news of you, but your effective footman tells me nothing. He is a tall fellow and is breathing down my neck as I dash this off. Dearest,'* he wrote, and she bit into her lip, *'I will call this afternoon and pray you are recovered enough to see me. Yours,'* it finished, *'Henry.'*

She could not do it. She could never do it. There was no hope now of following that carefully constructed plan of hers. At the heart of it had been control and secrecy, and a rock-solid knowledge of what she was capable of coupled with an equally fierce determination to keep that from Henry. Now, neither of those things were sure foundations. She'd known it from the moment she touched down again last night after those hectic, joyous moments he'd held her.

She shook her head. Near impossible to think that any future with Henry would not have more of the same. Not each day, of course. Mama and Papa were proof that marriage comprised a good deal of more earthbound goings on, such as sick children, mud-stuck carriages, and burned beef. But were they not also proof that a lightning spark of happiness might strike even while one pushed lumps of gravy around one's plate?

Damn. *Damn, damn, damn,* Beatrice wished for brothers who might have taught her to swear properly. There was no way out. Not unless.... It was possible that her feelings for Henry would fade enough that he became a stolid, phlegmatic companion, as unexciting to be around as his cousin. She considered that for a long moment and then let out a short, bitter laugh. Henry wasn't an old dog, fit for lying in front of the hearth. He was a man who made her fly.

So that was that.

Beatrice slid her feet to the carpet, scrunching her cheeks against the tightness of dried tears. Mama would have to be told today. The house would be packed up. She would return to Dorset. Silent tears slid down her cheeks. Maiden aunthood beckoned like a ghostly Aunt Martha patting her hand on the sofa, making room.

Beatrice tossed the unopened letter onto her dressing table and tilted the mirror. A wan girl looked back at her with a face burned out like a candle stump. Nothing of the goddess she had been last night.

Instead of repairing the ravages done by weeping, she slid open the second letter. Her eyes darted across the page as she read the scrawling, sloppy hand.

'What would happen if the captain saw your trick? How fast would he run?'

Beatrice's breath stopped in her chest, but she forced herself to keep reading.

'Do you know what they do to the unnatural? Can you imagine a cell in Bedlam? Would you prefer a cage in the circus? How thrilling would it be to see this curiosity. What will become of young Penelope? What of Deborah?'

Beatrice let out a choking sound and turned the page over, looking for a signature. Who wrote this? How dare this monster know those names.

'Will she have to beg the church to baptize her child? Can you imagine the uproar?'

The author's terrifying giddiness hauled her further into a dark, hellish pit.

'Do you think your mother would die of shame? How strong is your father? He has no title, no rank to hide behind. His money won't protect you from being dragged like a demon into the light. Can you trust your neighbours? Do you imagine they would be kind? What if I told them you can fly?'

The words almost trailed off the page, but down in the bottom corner where the black ink sputtered and flicked over the paper, there was yet another question. Was it meant to be helpful?

'Where can you turn for help?'

Chapter Twenty-One

Beatrice dragged a shaking arm across her mouth and pulled a heavy cloth over the basin. Perspiration trickled between her shoulder blades. Lord, what she must look like now. But the retching seemed to have passed, leaving her clammy and weak. Her stomach, at least, had accepted the fact that forcing up its contents could not purge the terror of that letter.

Staggering to her feet, she went to the dressing table where it lay, as innocent looking as a list of items to be bought, or things to be done. *Pick it up.* It wouldn't bite her, but every word dripped poison.

When Mama had woven her nightmares, this had been the stuff of them—tales of bad men with evil designs who were able to destroy their family as easily as they might tear the wings off a butterfly. But maintaining the fever pitch of vigilance and fear had been impossible. Over time, Mama's nightmares had seemed overwrought and silly.

Pick it up.

Beatrice scooped the letter off the table, and her eyes skimmed it again. He—for it looked like a man's hand—wasn't only menacing her with exposure. That would have been bad enough, but she had imagined dramatic details a thousand times of having things hushed up, being sent away from her family, moving again and again if her secret was discovered. Taking another name and inventing another story.

This, however, was worse. The author cut them all down, her dearest loved ones, and burned the stubble black.

Because of her.

Beatrice put fists on her hips and lifted her head, pulling the air through her narrowed lips, fighting off another trip to the basin. She must think. They were words, only words, she reminded herself, pressing the paper flat against the table.

She read the text aloud, whispering as softly as a broom brushing the floor. He had found out about her, and had taken the time to discover what he could about her family. That much was plain. Not only the names of her sisters, but Deborah's condition too. Godmama was the only one in London who knew about that.

He'd hunted Deborah down in Morton's Cross, and had watched her sister, or had sent some nasty spy to do it, every day noting her increasing form. An ice-cold dagger ripped through Beatrice at the thought. How had someone discovered her secret?

She closed her eyes tight and remembered the night of the fog. Her mind riffled through detail after detail until she came to that little sound, a creak of metal on metal. It could have been a door or a window. Strange at the time, but it had been lost to her memory amid all the other sensations of that terrible journey.

A bitter laugh burst from her. How proud she had been that she'd saved their lives.

Another dashed tear slipped down her cheek and she scrubbed it away, squaring her shoulders and searching the letter again.

There were no demands, no requests for money. There was only unbalanced glee as he listed out how easily he could ruin her and those she loved.

Not Henry. He could run, the letter said, and probably would consider he'd had a lucky escape.

She plunged a handkerchief into the jug of water on the table and scrubbed at her face until it glowed red all over instead of only at the rims of her eyes. The blackguard didn't name a price or spell out his conditions, but surely there must be something she could do. Head bent, she looked over the page once more, the cloth in her hands dripping all over it.

Where can you turn for help?

It was hardly a real question. The monster meant to grab her by the neck, forcing her head down, pressing her face into the truth. There was nowhere left to turn. *Where can you turn for help?* It was supposed to make her feel trapped, like some wild animal in a snare, and she loathed that it was working. She put a hand to her breast where her heart beat with a furious pulse.

He'd been clever, she thought, her mouth dry with ill-suppressed panic. There was no one left to give her confidences to. Henry would want nothing to do with her if he knew. Deborah and Penny were too vulnerable, Mama terrified of scandal. Papa. By rights, she should go to Papa.

She leaned over the words again. How quick they dismissed her father, his wealth and station, as though they were nothing. Even the question about his strength seemed to whisper menace.

The Beatrice that had been, the one that sat quietly, hands folded in her lap, as her mother planned how her life would be ordered, would have been helpless. But that Beatrice didn't exist anymore. She had died in these last weeks as Beatrice fought to win her future with Henry. Again came the bitter laugh. It was too late to claim that prize, but the grit she had acquired might yet save something from this disaster.

Beatrice's eyes flicked back and forth until she came to the sentences she wanted: *He has no title, no status to hide behind. His money won't protect you from being dragged like a demon into the light.*

She forced herself to read the vicious insult. No title. No status. The phrases seemed more than a nasty-minded dig at her father. They might be her way out.

She spent the next hour kneeling over the basin once more, weeping and scrubbing herself raw, but finally she gathered herself together enough to leave her room and sit in the shadows at the top of the stairs. Little wonder she was hesitant to meet her future. It was dark enough.

The front door swung open on its well-oiled hinges and Papa entered, pulling pamphlets from his coat pockets, scattering them onto the ornate side table. "Charles?" Mama called, her voice hesitant. She came from the library but paused while she was still in the hall, five wide steps from him, the air heavy with last night's angry words.

Beatrice had done that too, driven a rift between Mama and Papa. Had they ever marched out of step before?

At last, Mama wrung her hands and stepped forward, turning her face up to receive his salute. Beatrice slowed her breath to hear. "You were gone before I could—"

"The club," he murmured.

Mama put her hands behind her back where she continued to knead them, out of his sight. "You never came to bed." Beatrice's face flamed. She oughtn't be overhearing this. But it was too late to move or cough.

He shifted. "I've one of my own."

"You've never used it," she answered, injured.

"It was terribly dusty," he noted, soft mischief lighting his face. "Sneezed half the night." He reached around her, lacing his fingers in a light embrace.

"Nonsense, it's aired and dusted as often as my own," Mama retorted, but then her shoulders dropped with a deep breath. "I'm trying to apologise."

"For last night."

She shook her head. "For everything. It was a long night. My heart almost broke to see our girl so lovely. Her eyes looked as mine did all those years ago. Full of hope. Have I the right to snuff that out? Have I the right to decide everything about a life that isn't mine?" Papa leaned over and kissed the top of her head, and her voice, muffled as it was in his waistcoat, carried up the stairs. "Have I been too stubborn to listen? No matter how much I wish she had chosen Lord Fox. Gracechurch is too interested in her to ease my mind, but her plan is sound."

Beatrice shrank back, holding the letter screwed up in her fist. Not in her wildest dreams had she thought Mama would say such words. Her jailor had come into the prison, throwing the doors wide. But it was as much pain as joy that mingled in Beatrice's veins. Mama would repent those words as soon as Papa told her that Beatrice had risen, in public, and that Mama's caution and control had been justified. Beatrice braced herself for it. The opportunity was there. Papa had only to take it.

"Do you think you have been wrong?" he asked, pressing Mama to answer her own questions.

"I think I might," she answered, still unsure. They were silent for a long while, oblivious to Beatrice sitting high above them, breath held. Then Mama said, "The captain could be the answer. Do you think he is?"

Papa made no answer but kissed her again. "Let's save that worry for another day. Has she been down?" he asked, dropping his hands to gently rub her forearms.

"She has not. I meant to go up, but Cook wants me—"

"Go ahead," he urged, giving her a pat and watching her go. He stood for a minute in the hall and then looked up at Beatrice, his gaze piercing. How long had he known she was there? She climbed to her feet, feeling like a small child again, caught hanging over the bannisters, hoping the redness of her eyes might go unremarked.

"Did you sleep at all?" he asked, climbing the steps to where she stood.

"A little." The silence stretched on.

"You heard your mother."

"You didn't tell her I rose."

He had the grace to look discomfited. "It's your business what you do with that."

She nodded. "I've... I've come to a decision."

The question, when he asked it, was gentle, tinged with pity. "Thorndene?"

She shook her head and chewed at her lip, "No. But anything I imagined with Captain Gracechurch is...." Here, her mouth shook the smallest bit. "Concluded. I particularly do not wish to see him."

Papa nodded. Surely, it was only what he expected.

Beatrice closed her eyes and stepped into the darkness. "However, if he should call, I am home to Lord Fox."

Chapter Twenty-Two

The footman's rigorous training slipped and he let out a quiet sigh that seemed to express how dearly he wished Henry to Jericho.

"Good day again, sir. Miss Thornton is not at home to callers," the footman stated, glaring at the flowers Henry held, very much on his dignity. "If you wish to leave a note…"

"I didn't come to see Miss Thornton," Henry improvised. "Though I am sorry she continues to be so indisposed…" He trailed off.

Footman George did *not* take the bait. No dispatches from the sickroom would be forthcoming from that quarter. "I've an appointment with Mr Thornton."

The footman lowered sceptical brows. Henry dug around in his pockets for every bit of blunt he had, his fingers fumbling for loose change.

When he had produced it, the man stared down at the wrinkled pound note, four shillings and a few pence Henry held in his hand. "Sir," he said, in a tone that implied such things were beneath them both.

"Let me through, George," Henry asked, his voice low, coaxing. And he hoped to heaven he didn't sound like what he was doing— begging.

"I've had my orders."

Orders. That word worried him. "Please."

George looked over his shoulder at the stairs, but Henry could already see him preparing to be polite but firm. Henry couldn't let him speak, or close the door with finality.

"Mr Thornton expects me." Henry stepped forward, brushing past the massive footman as he'd never done to a servant in his life. The surprise of it gave him five or six steps head start over the man, who was already scrambling after him.

"I'll see myself in. Library?" he asked over his shoulder, not caring about anything but getting deeper into the house. George would have to drag him out bodily if he wanted him gone.

Henry reached the library door a bare second before his pursuer, giving it an urgent rap.

"Not at all well done, sir," reproached George in a whisper.

"Enter," came a voice from within.

Henry would be generous in victory. He thrust the money at the footman as George reached an annoyed arm across the door and pushed it open. "Captain Gracechurch, sir. Says he's expected. Would you like me to throw him out?" Henry turned a disgruntled look on him. That's what sort of loyalty a wrinkled pound note bought.

Mr Thornton was sitting behind his desk. He got to his feet, nudging his chair back and waving a dismissive hand at his footman. "I *was* expecting to see Captain Gracechurch."

Henry watched as the footman, deprived of the treat of turning him out neck and crop, took himself off in high dudgeon. Henry turned to Thornton. "That was a lie."

"Not at all. I was expecting you. I know what I would have done in your place," Mr Thornton told him, nodding at Henry's hand. "I don't suppose those are for me?"

Henry looked at the bouquet of overblown roses dropping dusky pink petals on the carpet. Did a man ever look more foolish than when he carried a posy?

"For your daughter," he stated, avoiding her names. While he wandered in this no-man's-land, *Miss Thornton* was too hopeless and *Beatrice* too presuming.

"If I could have a few moments with her."

The man gave a light smile. "She's not receiving visitors," Mr Thornton said, classing him with any casual acquaintance that might take it into his head to pop in today. "You may leave them with me." Mr Thornton indicated the top of his desk and Henry set them down, careful not to let the damp handkerchief wrapped around the stems drip onto the stacks of paper.

"Is she well?" Henry asked without preamble.

Mr Thornton sat heavily into his chair, crossing his arms over his chest. He nodded. "She is perfectly well."

Henry breathed out a ragged breath. Thank heavens she was well. That was the foremost feeling. Whatever else had happened, it could be borne.

But along with relief came other questions, lined up in formation and awaiting close inspection. *What else could it be? Why can't I see her? What has changed? What has happened?*

The older man stroked his beard with an absent hand. "I thought you deserved to know that much, lad."

"Won't she tell me herself?"

Mr Thornton looked away, his eyes resting on shards of sunlight, and cleared his throat.

Henry's pulse thudded in his neck, beating in his ears. Mr Thornton, who had been his champion yesterday, seemed on the point of calling back the footman and throwing him out now. Henry would have no recourse. Perhaps he should have been more sociable, led up to the subject of Beatrice gently, should have asked about... Henry's mind was blank of comfortable topics.

The older man cleared his throat and Henry knew he was about to be lied to. "There's nothing to tell." Henry was expected to take his light voice and forced smile as evidence supporting that claim.

He changed tactics. "Is it the money?" he asked, brushing aside the pretence. He would get nowhere with niceties and, anyway, he was already losing ground. He was being pushed back. He could feel it. Peeling off his gloves, he held them in a loose grip, twisting at one of the dull gold buttons on his coat.

"I am not at liberty to say."

Henry should have minded his own business and received any answer the Thorntons were prepared to hand out. Now he was stepping far outside the acceptable mark, charging on. "Is that what it is, sir? Money? Has she decided I am too much of a risk, after all?"

Mr Thornton swept his arm in a sharp line and said, his voice gruff, "You refine too much on that point, Captain. Every person under my roof knows your worth, honours your service."

"Homesickness?" Henry asked, sending another volley. He didn't believe it even as he asked. It would have to be sudden, violent homesickness to cause the reaction he'd seen Beatrice have.

Mr Thornton stood, stuffing his hands in his pockets, and walked to the door. "My daughter is perfectly capable of speaking for herself."

"Then invite her down." Henry's voice rose. "Let her do so. I wish to know what I am up against, sir."

Mr Thornton sighed. "The very devil of a mess."

"Might I have a chance to sort it out?" He was running out of fire, he could feel it.

The older man swung the door open. "I have done all I can. If Beatrice wishes to see you, she won't be kept from it by me, or her mother. That I promise."

Henry was being tossed out on his ear. Not roughly, though it might have been worse for that, but definitely. He might as well go all the way past the line. "Has she forbidden all visitors, sir? Or particular ones?"

Mr Thornton gave a light exhale, looking much older. "I don't expect you want to hear the answer to that."

Henry bit down on the words that wanted release. Soldier's words. Hot words. A string of them.

Mount a strategic retreat, Wellington might have told him. *Find a way.*

He nodded once and swallowed, walking out of the room and down the hall, doubling back when he reached a potted fern, thinking better of saying anything, pivoting on his heel, continuing on.

George stood, ready at the door, with his hat.

Henry collected it under the watchful eye of both the servant and the master of the house who stood poised, he felt sure, to tackle him. Did they think he was mad enough to dash up those stairs, shouting her name?

Even in this mood he could not be so foolish. But he looked up them for a long moment before taking his leave.

He walked up the sidewalk, trying to sort out the coil his life had become since he came back to England. Spain had been simple. Kill a French bastard before a French bastard killed you. Now, nothing was simple at all.

The clap and rumble of a carriage turned him back. And he watched as a midnight black carriage with the distinctive Fox crest stopped before Number Six.

Henry's breath sounded loud as he stood still. His cousin, holding a large bouquet of flowers, knocked. The door opened. Henry waited for Fox to be turned off. Instead, Fox waved the carriage away and turned back to the house.

He was admitted.

Chapter Twenty-Three

Beatrice did not need to be told who had come. She knew the heavy-booted tread that walked up the hall and back again. From the room at the top of the stairs she had heard the low tones of his voice, though she hadn't been able to pick out the words, no matter how she strained her ears.

It was not too late, she thought, tensing at the need to get up, run after Henry. There was nothing set in stone.

"Beatrice." She started and straightened, turning only after a furtive scrub of her eyes. Mama stood in the doorway. "We left things so awkwardly last night." Mama cleared her throat and rubbed a fingerprint off the moulding, spending time over it.

Left things so awkwardly. Is that what she called almost smashing the door off its hinges? Beatrice smiled at the understatement.

Mama, seeing that smile, tilted her head and gave a quick exhale. "I meant to say how lovely your dress was," Mama told her, walking several steps into the room and stopping there on the carpet to twist her hands. "I meant to say…."

Beatrice's eyes widened. This was heaping coals of fire on her head. She could not deserve this apology, not when she knew she had made the most dreadful botch of everything—exposure, blackmail, and danger for them all. In no particular was she innocent.

"I meant to say," Mama began again, crossing to a chair in a ruffle of skirts, "how very much I look forward to meeting your Captain Gracechurch again."

Beatrice pinched the flesh on the back of her hand, the pain pulling her away from fresh tears. She must say something. She must give Mama some warning.

"He isn't—that is, I don't…," Beatrice stumbled. She was silent for a moment. The temptation was there to lay it all before Mama and give overall responsibility for her own decisions. She'd done it before.

Beatrice's voice was brisk. "Lord Fox was particular in his attentions yesterday."

Mama's smile became uncertain. "I thought..."

"Lord Fox is everything that is agreeable and amiable. I shouldn't be surprised if—"

A soft rap on the door pushed the words back into her throat.

"You have a caller, miss," announced the footman. "Lord Fox."

There was no ominous clang of a bell when his lordship entered. Rather, the hand on the tall clock shivered and clicked forward, as it would do in another minute, and in the minute after that, and in all the long minutes to come. No doubt she would be full of plucky things to tell herself sometime. The sort of tired encouragement she'd give Penny when she tripped over her skirts. *Pick yourself up, girl. No use crying over spilt milk. Brush off.* But the enormity of those minutes, stacked one after another like a run of dominoes waiting to be knocked over, made her want to bolt.

As Lord Fox bent over Mama's hand, Beatrice was pricked anew by how little she liked how he wore his hair—long and combed over his crown in a slick cap.

"The flowers, I regret to say, are for your daughter, ma'am. For the memorable evening she gave me." He made a polished bow and proffered the large bouquet of snow-white roses in tight, perfect buds to Beatrice.

She touched a waxy petal and dropped her nose to the bouquet, nervous now that she was on the point of it. They gave off a faint scent.

"I had to be sure you were quite well," Lord Fox stated as they sat and a puzzled line creased along Mama's brow.

"I slept the whole morning away," Beatrice answered, adding a little laugh with the same calculation that Cook might use to garnish a dish. Mama's line eased away. "I'm afraid the late hours are beginning to demand repayment."

"I cannot believe that." Lord Fox's voice was oil smooth, his eyes wandering over her. "Not while you sit before me looking as lovely as ever."

Again Beatrice dipped her face to the cultivated blooms. The man was blind. Or lying. Or wholly uninterested in her.

"You are gallant, my lord," Mama offered, finding a less sour reason for his words. The tea table was brought out and conversation flowed between Mama and his lordship in a way that Beatrice envied. It would be well if she could be easy with him.

Was it Lord Fox or Mama that brought the topic around to long-dead family?

"The Purefoys don't even have a family crypt," Mama shared, delicately chewing on a biscuit. "It's no more than a score of headstones in a tumbledown churchyard. I've often told my dear husband that we should act as patrons of that little church, commission a monument or window, but hardly any of the rogues are illustrious enough to warrant it." Mama smiled, and his lordship smiled, and Beatrice, feeling unhappy and dull, smiled too.

"You are quite fortunate it is so, ma'am. One delightful country church to pay one's respects at." He gave a wistful sigh.

Beatrice didn't believe it. Lord Fox might be many charming and amiable things, but modesty was not his strong point. "Is that so impossible for you?" she asked.

"For the Foxbrough side, I am afraid it is, Miss Thornton. They rest beside kings and princes the whole length and breadth of England." She smiled into her teacup. "I suppose the country has first claim on them, though I've read enough plaques and commemorations to make me faint."

Her look was guileless. "Have you discovered which of them was responsible for the Creation?"

"Beatrice." Mama tsked.

Lord Fox smiled his appreciation. "So, you've met my great-grandfather."

Beatrice laughed and breathed more easily. All the monuments, crypts, and statues had reminded her, as nothing else could, that they would be a sort of marble breastwork for her, holding firm against attacks that would pierce one of shabby stone markers tilting over a country churchyard. And he could laugh at himself. These would be enough to see her through.

Mama, who looked as though she suspected Beatrice of rudeness, turned to another topic.

"My husband and I are delighted to be gaining a neighbour so well-known to us, so amiable. Oak Lodge has wanted as master for some time," Mama said. She added with an arch smile, "And the young ladies of the district will be pleased as well."

Lord Fox rubbed a hand along the back of his neck. Beatrice might have supposed him to be embarrassed, but had learned to be gently suspicious of his simpler shows of emotion. He replied with, "I hate to disappoint them, ma'am."

"Disappoint?" asked Mama, taking a sip of tea.

"The house will want a mistress and I hope…" He looked squarely at Beatrice, lingering over her face in a way that made her want to shrink into the shadows.

"Well, it is too soon. I will travel down to Dorset at the end of summer. I invite you to come and look it over and tell me what improvements you might recommend."

The end of summer. Beatrice turned her head and cast her eyes to the window, framing the full blue of the sky. How much would be changed for her by the end of summer?

Her lips went dry at the thought.

"I need to take some fresh air. If I may be excused," she asked politely.

"Beatrice." Mama turned, placing her cup and saucer on the table at her side. Beatrice shot a quick look at Lord Fox, tipping her head ever so slightly toward the window. "His lordship will think we are rag-mannered."

Lord Fox cleared his throat. "Not at all, ma'am. I hope Miss Thornton will allow me to escort her. I had been working up the courage to ask these last ten minutes."

Nicely done, she thought, and told him so when they were on the street.

"But I did want to come," he insisted.

"Shall I continue to bury you beneath a mountain of hereditary peerages?"

He held his hands up and laughed. "In truth, I find it excruciating," he confessed. A soft smile crossed her lips. His acting had been superb, but she had hidden her thoughts from Mama long enough to feel a quick burst of sympathy for him.

"Then why endure it?" she asked and coloured when he made no answer but to take her hand and tuck it into the crook of his arm.

"Don't you know?" he asked and looked at her until she wanted to retrace her steps and run. "Shall we go to the park?"

"No," she responded more sharply than intended. That ground was Henry's. "Taking a few turns about the square will do."

They completed a half revolution before he asked, "The square will do for what? Or I can go back to pretending you didn't lure me out of doors?"

It's not too late, Beatrice. The voice was Henry's and she closed her ears to it.

"I have... spells sometimes," she blurted out. "I'm not ill exactly, but there are times when I need rest and... and privacy." She looked up to find a curious expression on his face. But not pitying or withdrawing. "When we danced, last evening"—Beatrice wound a bonnet ribbon up and down—"you said things that..."

"You must forgive me. I had no right to speak to you."

She stopped and turned her face up to his. "Why not?"

Did she imagine it or did his face, so often hard and world-weary, soften? "Young women dream of romance. Is that not so? I wish I could offer you that and more," he explained and she went rigid. She didn't want that *ever* from him. "I cannot offer it and said so too bluntly. But, what I'm trying to tell you now, in my clumsy way, is that I find that I like you, Miss Thornton. I wondered whether you might entertain the thought of..." He didn't finish but shrugged as though words were beyond him.

She shrank away from the rest of the thought. *Not yet. Not yet.* "Why are you unable to offer something more..." she paused, searching for the correct word. "Conventional?" Every syllable carried a weight she had to measure out before she used it.

"Will you think me foolish?" He smiled a brave smile, she thought. "My heart is a stubborn organ, meant to be given only once." He lifted his shoulders in a simple, eloquent gesture.

"You love someone." She was surprised, moved to pity. A new idea of this man opened up before her.

"And lost," he admitted, looking away. "She was lost to me some time ago."

This unknown woman, standing as a ghost between them, seemed to offer her own recommendation of his character. How worthwhile, how steadfast he might be. One question more and her conscience would be satisfied. "There is no way?"

His jaw flinched and grew firm. "Not one of honour," he stated, and she had the sudden thought that Lady Ainsley, Meg's sister, was married now. "Miss Thornton... Beatrice, if I may?" he asked, holding her lightly by the elbows. She managed not to recoil at his touch, at the sound of her name on his lips. "I told you before that I had no right to speak of these things, and I will not if you do not wish me to." He stood, feet braced against rejection, silent, waiting.

Sunlight created moving mosaics against the stones of the street and dryness moved from her lips, down her throat until she felt she would wither away inside. Now was the time. "I wish you to."

He seemed to give a great sigh though her eyes were fixed on his boots. "Sweet girl, I cannot offer you my heart. I am not sure you would want it, in any case. But I offer you my name, the protection of my rank and my sincere esteem, and the promise always that you will be my friend if you would consent to be my wife." He smiled, gently forcing down her defences. "If you wished it, I would even take my seat in Parliament, voting with the interests of a certain boiled shrimp."

Beatrice gave a ghost of a smile and thought hard about what she would gain. Safety. The thought came at once and she clung to it. It was Lord Fox's primary attraction. The filthy letter, dripping with blackmail and condescension for her family's rank, had seemed to slam every door shut except one. An alliance with someone titled and well connected would make them, her sisters, her parents, and herself, beyond reproach. God bless the injustice of the peerage. Lord Fox would guard what was his. Of that she had little doubt.

The other things she would gain were small, in comparison. A home of her own. She thought of his Dorset property, not so far from her family when Lord Fox tired of her company and went back to his London dissipations. Yes. She was clear-eyed about the likelihood of that. Of a chance to do some good. Of the bluebell wood. Of privacy to live as she chose. And, in time, a child.

She choked. He wouldn't be the sturdy fair-haired lad who would be part of Henry too. No. Her child now would be tall, too elegant for chipped knees. Still, she would do her duty.

"Yes." It was a whisper carried away too quickly to catch it back.

Chapter Twenty-Four

"You had quite the day." Papa tipped way back in his chair, looking every minute of his fifty-three years and a few more besides. "Care to warn me of anything else in case the shock sends me into apoplexy?"

"His lordship spoke with you?" Beatrice didn't care for Papa's attitude at all. He was her only ally and currently didn't sound it.

"He did. Scuttled in half an hour ago."

Good. If his lordship didn't delay, she wouldn't have time to regret it. Maybe it would happen so fast that this mass of ice in her chest would not have time to melt out of her in hot, unending tears.

Papa's chair landed with a solid thunk, and he reached across the desk. "In all the delirious excitement, I quite forgot. I was supposed to give you these."

She glanced to a posy of soft pink roses. Lovely and unpretentious, Lord Fox's second offering of the day was much more to her taste than his first. She scooped them up only to have several petals drift to the carpet as she sat. It was a mercy that, as she scrounged around for things to say about her future husband, she could be plainly admiring. "They smell heavenly."

Papa frowned. "I expect that's why Captain Gracechurch brought them for you."

Blood drained from Beatrice's face and she dropped the posy to her side, wrinkling her nose against the scent, full and sweet. She could not have said precisely why, but it was impossible to sit here, filling her lungs with the perfume, letting the fragrance seep into her clothes and skin, when she was promised to someone else. "That was kind of him."

Papa grunted. What more did he want her to say? He must see that this madness with Henry was finished. Lord Fox had offered for her. He was a respectable gentleman of good family. Not a single matchmaking mother in all of London would hesitate if given a choice between a retired soldier and a titled peer. She was making an astonishingly good match. Papa's blessing was a formality.

"Yesterday"—he seemed to force his voice to be mild—"you sat in that very chair and made a brave bid for your future with a man I can admire. Stood against your mother, though it must have gone hard against the grain."

Yesterday. Yesterday felt like a thousand years ago.

"Beatrice."

"I can't," she choked out, not sure how to finish that sentence. Can't marry him? Can't bear it?

"I take no joy in this," he stated, working his jaw. "I had two visitors today."

"I don't want to hear it," she cut him off, her voice rising in panic. *Don't.*

"You're going to." The rebuke hung there for a moment as they stared, wide-eyed, at one another. Then he sat back in the chair, yanking his waistcoat into order.

"I had two visitors," he continued, still breathing himself into a more moderate frame of mind. "Lord Fox gave little of himself away. He has a good valet. I'll give him full marks for that. Never a hair out of place. And he took great care to gauge the approach that might offer the greatest success. The man hardly wasted his time trying to convince me that he is swept away with love of you." Papa picked up a pen and rolled it between his fingers. "He's a watchful man."

Beatrice pursed her lips. "He wants you to like him."

"I fear his hopes on that head will be dashed."

"Papa." She took a deep breath and her nose filled with the smell of Henry's roses. A mistake.

"He finally settled on bribery as the likeliest avenue to get what he wanted, which was somewhat honest. But so elegantly done. How preciously he dropped hints about the jewels you are to wear, the title you will hold, and the servants you will order about. Pin money, horses, the lot." Papa crossed his arms.

"I'm sure he wished to assure you I would be well taken care of."

"You have never been anything else," Papa snapped. "Nor will you ever be." He gazed across his desk for a long, uncomfortable moment, but he was gentle when he spoke. "Why are you anxious to tie yourself to a man who neither knows nor loves you?"

Beatrice's cheeks burned crimson and she clamped her lips together. She could never give the real reason. *I have ruined us. You are not enough.*

When she didn't speak, Papa breathed out in a short, aggravated burst. "My other visitor—"

"Please, Papa." She crushed the flowers, bracing herself.

"—was rude and mannerless, even pushing his way past George. The captain asked after your health even after we used him so ill." He gave a short mirthless laugh. "He begged." Papa looked at her as her teeth bit down on a shaking lip. He cleared his throat. "I did as you asked. I showed him the door, though I hated myself for it. How do you think he left? Stoic? Noble? Taking his defeat like a man of honour?"

Yes. Henry was all those things.

She nodded, her voice thick with tears, "I do not doubt those qualities will help him to reconcile—"

Plop.

A single glove landed in her lap, lobbed from her father. She picked it up, turning it over. Leather, worn about the thumb and palm, too plain for fashion. A man's glove. Then she turned the cuff and traced her fingers over the initials worked in heavy black thread. H.R.S.G.

Papa spared her nothing. "There's your Stoic, taking his rejection on the chin." *R for Robin.* He had told her that once. "He dropped it on purpose."

"Anyone might mislay a glove," she told Papa came around the desk. He dug into his waistcoat pocket.

Plop.

Another article landed in her lap. A brass button, obviously new but dented in the middle.

"Found that on the floor where he stood."

Her eyes went with awful fascination to the swirling greens and blues of the library carpet.

"It might belong to anybody. Perhaps his lordship," she offered, a little desperate to believe herself.

"His lordship wears silver. It was the captain who was strangling the life from his coat buttons."

"There you go. It was an accident."

Plop.

How she longed to do some violence. Had Henry tipped out the contents of his pockets? Beatrice's nerves were paper thin and stretched to breaking. But she only wanted a little more courage. Once Papa was convinced she truly meant to wed Lord Fox, her family would be safe.

It was a letter, creased and worn around the edges. She half expected it to be addressed to her, but the writing on the outside was visible. *Henry* in an unfamiliar feminine hand.

"That one," Papa told her, "George fished it out of the potted plant in the hall. Hid the dashed thing while we were tossing him out. Did it while we were both looking, somehow. Are you going to tell me that was an accident, too?"

Tears slid down her cheeks.

Papa gave a great sigh and crouched low beside her. He put a hand to her face and rubbed the tears away with his thumb. "I don't like this, Bea. Any of it. This haste isn't like you. And Lord Fox—"

"Am I supposed to change my mind? Pretend I don't rise at all?" she asked. She waved an arm, still holding the flowers, across her lap. "These things change nothing. Henry..." She sucked in a lip. That name belonged to her. "I am utterly convinced that Captain Gracechurch will discover my secret."

"You think his lordship won't? He has eyes like a hawk."

She answered carefully but honestly. "He doesn't watch me. Not like the captain does. And I know that my future with Lord Fox will be secure."

"Secure." Papa spat the word.

She held his gaze, head erect. "You were fortunate. You discovered you had a secret to hide after you'd been married for years and years. My aunt was not so lucky, was she?" she asked and his look wavered before her own immovable one. "So, don't scorn that word. It is not a little thing to carve out some security and a little bit of happiness and independence besides."

"Happiness?" Papa still doubted. But she had pricked his conscience. She gave a tiny nod and he sat back on his heels. She had won. Whatever happened now, Papa would back her up. She prayed to heaven he wouldn't ever have to know about the blackmail. Beatrice gathered the glove, button, and letter together and held them out to him. "These must be returned at once." But Papa didn't take them.

"I don't have anything to do with that," he informed her.

She looked down at her lap, a jumble of flowers and paper, metal and leather. "Then I'll send a footman around to his lodgings with a parcel and a note."

Papa shook his head. "I think you know how to put a proper end to the sorry business."

Dash it, she did. This is what came of Papa not having any boys. He'd passed on the rules of good sportsmanship to his daughters. Henry would have to be told she didn't want him anymore, and she'd have to do it herself. It was the only honest thing.

Papa rested a hand on her shoulder and dropped a kiss on her forehead. "I won't tell your mother until tomorrow. But I will send a note to Lord Fox and tell him he can come put his suit to you." She reached for his hand and he held hers. His words were in the nature of a pledge. "I want you to be happy."

She crimped her lips and nodded as Papa strode from the room.

Dash the man, she thought, staring at the items in her lap. Dash Henry for making it so hard to give him up. She picked up the glove and pushed her hand inside, threading her fingers into each channel. She was behaving like a goose. The glove wasn't Henry. It didn't even fit her properly. But it had been his, and his presence hovered around her as the glove's cuff kissed the soft inside of her wrist.

She ripped it off and dropped it into her lap. He'd been inventive. With no notice at all, he'd managed to secret three items around the house under her father's nose. Surrendering them back again would be a nightmare.

Standing, she gathered the items up, but the posy of flowers tumbled to the floor, scattering petals and stems and heady scent across the carpet.

And a handkerchief. Not plain lawn but embroidered along the edge with blue forget-me-nots.

Her mouth dropped open.

That was another blasted thing he had left.

Chapter Twenty-Five

Beatrice yanked the ribbons apart and sat up, swinging her legs over the side of the bed. Her hair fell forward around her face and she sat there for a minute with her hands balled into fists, sinking into the mattress.

Two days. She struck the bed with her clenched hand. Two wasn't much of a pattern, not really, not when she used to go weeks without rising at night. Still, she wouldn't fool herself into not knowing what it meant. Henry was lost to her and her heavy limbs had finally accepted it.

Her heart should too, she thought, pushing her feet into slippers.

Today, Lord Fox was coming to ask her to marry him. "Anthony," she said aloud, and wrinkled her nose. She cleared her throat and said, enunciating each word, "Anthony is coming today." Maybe she could call him by his family name. Lots of women did. "Foxbrough." Less objectionable, though it sounded like she was summoning the butler to take away the tea things.

As she pulled a silver-handled brush through her hair in slow, methodical strokes, she eyed the items lined up under the mirror. She hated Henry for his cleverness.

She tossed the brush down with a rattle. Let the anger carry her forward. Spreading a square of paper on the vanity, she set the glove down first. Henry wouldn't have many pairs to spare. A couple months more and the cool days would begin. She tucked the button inside the glove, ensuring it wouldn't be lost if he unwrapped it in haste. The letter was next. She twirled it on the pointed corners between two fingers. It hadn't been dropped by accident.

If it had been an accident, then the remedy would be clear: the owner should be found, and it should be returned, unopened. Instead, Henry had stuffed the letter into a shrubbery. He'd given it to them.

She turned the letter over and ran a finger under the fold. It was hers now. If the dashed man had left it, she wouldn't balk at reading it.

'My son...'

Her eyes darted across the page and her lips moved along with the words.

It was only a few days old. His mother wrote in a light, amusing way, sketching out news of his sisters and brother, told him "Father" was mending from his illness. Beatrice wrinkled her forehead at that. Henry had said nothing.

And then there were these lines: *'Your godmother tells me that the business keeping you in Town is a* who, *not a* what. *And, for her part, she is approving. Dearest... dearest and best... I cannot say what is in my heart, only, when your sister married, my heart was in my throat at sending her from all that was familiar and loved, worrying over her new home and family, for it is so uncomfortable to be a woman. Be assured that my arms are open for your who...'*

Beatrice's laugh was a half-cry. These were to have been her people.

And now she had to face him, tell him it was finished. The thought left Beatrice feeling hollow and heavy at once, but she folded the letter and placed it atop the glove. It was better that they should meet after she was safely engaged. Better that it happen in public.

Her mind shied away from what might happen if they weren't.

She folded the parcel, tying it up with a bow, tugging savagely at the strings.

It was time to be getting on with the day. When she was finally dressed, she descended the staircase, her eyes scouring the entry table and salver. "Has anything come for me?" she asked George.

"Not unless this is yours, miss," he said, unfolding a plain sheet with a thick, black X struck across it. "It was on the floor when I came down this morning. I can't account for it."

She shook her head and smiled though her lips leached of colour. She took the paper. "Papa is always dropping things." It could be no one else but her correspondent, he who had scraped a broken pen tip harshly across the page. How easily he could remind her he was here, watching. She crushed the paper in her fist and handed the footman one short letter with clear directions, bound for Berkeley Square. "I want this delivered today. There isn't any rush about it."

The short note represented nearly an hour of effort. Beatrice had tried to compose a message to Henry, stripping it of any hint of hope or familiarity, but had given it up as a hopeless cause. Her feelings were too raw. So she composed a letter to Meg, involving a good deal of scratching and blotting, ending in a woeful "please."

"The captain, miss," George called after her as she turned to go. "He was here too. Early. Asked after you. I did as your Pa—Mr Thornton—said. I didn't tell him nothing, didn't let him in." Beatrice ducked her head, working the blackmailer's note into her pocket. Even a beggar at the gate would be received with more welcome.

Still, Henry came. The thought was a weight dragging behind her.

She found Mama in the salon, sitting with a pencil and stack of newspapers, which she laid down with great care. For the first time, Mama's questions weren't pushed at Beatrice, shoved into her ears with all the sensitivity of a ramrod.

Beatrice gathered her courage. "Papa told you that Lord Fox is coming."

"With plans to pay his addresses." Mama nodded. Then her voice became hesitant. "Your father has rehearsed, again and again, the ways in which it is a simpler solution, but—"

"And that's why I've chosen it." Beatrice cut in.

"But what of yesterday? How can you replace—"

"As you said," Beatrice bit out. Heaven save her if Mama brought up Henry. "It's simpler."

Emotions chased one after the other across Mama's face—surprise, irritation, humility, helplessness—but she gave Beatrice a long look before she gave way.

"How will you keep your secret?" The question contained no hint of challenge and Beatrice let out a silent breath.

"Nights are my only problem." The Almighty would have to forgive her the small lie. But with Lord Fox, it was true. "I've tightened the ribbons and will add several more sets to my linens in the coming weeks, going down the limbs and across the bust. In this way, I won't rise above a quarter inch." That sounded like a comfortably scientific number.

Mama nodded, but her brow puckered. "Bed sheets won't wash themselves. It's all I can do to keep our maids from gossiping about those two ribbons you have now."

Beatrice adopted a soft, rustic burr as she said, "'Poor Lady Fox, prone to sleepwalking. Doesn't like disturbances. No harm in her, though.'" She reverted back to her own well-trained accent. "The maids may tell tales, but I will be settled far from London. The news won't have a chance to mar my Penny's chances."

There was a long silence and then Mama ventured, "Married folk do not carry on as chance-met acquaintances."

Mama and Papa certainly didn't. But London had taught Beatrice other ways. She reached over to pluck *The Times* from the side table and began to read aloud, her cheeks burning all the while.

T.D. is rumoured to be keeping R.A. warm this season. One hopes her husband doesn't catch a chill. F. becomes a bawdy lad in Town. The Editors spare you the details in order not to wound the delicate sensibilities of the Fair Sex. Something we assure you F. has done on numerous occasions, abroad, as he is, at the most shocking times of night and seen in the most shocking company.

Mama snatched the paper away, but Beatrice's voice was level. "As far as Society is concerned, I may come to any arrangement that suits me."

Mama's face filled with detestable pity. "Beatrice, that's no way—"

"It's not your way," Beatrice replied. "But it will suit me to have a husband who does not dance attendance on me."

That was enough to silence Mama on the subject and she began to spend her time more productively by offering advice on how to run a household that breathed secrets. And by the time Lord Fox walked through the doors, Mama could say, with the right mix of scolding and delight, "My lord, Mr Thornton tells me you have come to carry off our dear girl."

"I hope she will make me the happiest of men, Mrs Thornton." Lord Fox gave her a courtly bow. Papa, following Lord Fox into the room, cast his eyes to the ceiling.

His willingness to play along would only go so far. Mama, however, was giving a creditable performance of a pleased and slightly awed country gentlewoman, astonished at her daughter's good fortune. Lord Fox acted as though he was an impatient and ardent lover.

"It has long been my dearest wish to secure your daughter's regard." Eyes were turned to Beatrice and she tried to work up a maiden's blush. Not one of them of them believed her to have any regard for Lord Fox. But they must go through the pretence. "And I will endeavour to grant her smallest desire. Forgive me for coming to an understanding with her before I had a chance to speak with you both. I was quite carried away."

Mr Thornton's breath came in an incredulous short burst. "Quite," he said, his voice bland. "You look it." He shoved his hands into his pockets, but Mama hurried into the breach.

"Prettily said, sir. I can breathe easily knowing she will be safe in your hands. Of course, this has come as quite a surprise. All these weeks of courtship and Beatrice has said nothing to us."

Fox tried hard to look guilty and chagrined of being capable of conducting a clandestine romance.

"She has told you a little of her condition, I think?" Mama asked.

"Naturally, my lady. I understand that she will want for peace and seclusion. *That* I can offer her."

"I really must insist," Mama continued, sounding like a crotchety, over-anxious mother, "on hiring her a lady's maid. I would rest easier knowing that she would have someone, right at hand, to care for her."

In the most unobjectionable way, Mama negotiated terms, backing Lord Fox into small corners, making him promise things Beatrice would never have thought to ask for, making sure her daughter would have all the privacy she might need.

"I rely on you, ma'am, to help me secure Miss Thornton's comfort and safety," Lord Fox replied, leaning fashionably against the pillows. "I'm afraid she'll have to get used to being spoiled."

"What woman of sense wants to be spoiled?" Papa grumped. Beatrice felt a rush of warmth for him. Dear Papa, who still wanted her to back out and throw her lot in with a penniless captain who might make her rise several times a day and whose position wouldn't protect her sisters from a blackmailer's poison.

"We should be leaving it up to both of you," Mama responded, clapping her hands and standing, tugging Papa along with her. "We'll have a small engagement party tomorrow evening. In the meantime, we'll allow you to have Beatrice to yourself for"—she looked as though she were bestowing a great treat—"a quarter of an hour?"

How would they fill it, Beatrice wondered as she watched them go. The door closed, and she heard the minute hand on the mantel clock shiver and click.

"Miss Thornton. Beatrice," Lord Fox called, an amused smile playing along his mouth. Perhaps he thought the formalities were ridiculous. "I want to ask you to be my wife."

"I accept," she replied. The blackmailer stood over her, every moment, spurring her on. "That is, if you are satisfied that you will get what you want out of this arrangement? I'm sorry that—"

"No." He jumped in quickly. "Don't apologize. You've made me a happy man, Beatrice," She dared not raise her eyes to see what a happy Lord Fox looked like. "I hope we may always be so forthright with one another."

She nodded, ignoring the whisper of discomfort she felt and determined to be as honest with him as she could. "I am happy, as well." Blast. Her first lie. She glanced at the clock. Four minutes. Henry would have been kissing her by now.

"We have not discussed it, but I would like an early wedding date, if that suits?" he asked.

"Yes. As soon as may be." Why wait if it would put a stop to hateful notes pushed under her door.

"Then I ought to write the announcement for *The Times*. It can go in tomorrow's—"

"No," she heard herself exclaim. She added, moderating her tone, "No. I would like to wait until after the party to send the notice into the papers." She cast about for an excuse. "I want to do some trousseau shopping. You know what gossip is like. I should prefer to go without the questions and talk."

"It will be as you wish." He stood and drew her to her feet. She steeled herself and closed her eyes as he leaned forward. Then, holding her hands in his gloved grasp, he deposited a chaste kiss, square on her forehead. "Until tomorrow, my dear." And he was gone.

Eight minutes.

Chapter Twenty-Six

Henry leaned down to pat the side of the stallion's neck and coo lowly. "Easy, boy. Easy." Ceph danced on skittish hooves. The beast wanted to run, to dissipate some of the energy held in reserve.

Straightening, Henry looked down the broad, tree-lined avenue of Rotten Row. Carriages and riders bustled along, but the numbers would soon swell until the way was dammed up.

Where is she?

The note from Meg begged him to meet her, interrupting his strict daily routine of pushing breakfast around his plate, rustling the pages of *The Times,* and preparing to be turned away by Thornton's footman once again.

Ceph snorted and pawed at the ground. It was foolish to come to the Row at five o'clock, in the middle of a cursed social hour, but Meg had promised him it would be worth his while. He stood up high on his stirrups, the brim of his hat shading his eyes.

"Henry." He wheeled around, seeing Meg mounted on horseback. Her hands were held high and too wide on the reins as she steered her roan with clumsy directness through the press of carriages. Then his eyes fastened on the woman who followed in her wake. Beatrice.

He gripped his reins and his mount shied. She had come—escaped from that gorgon of a mother—moving through the noisome crowd more masterfully than Meg had done. Meg clicked her tongue to prod her horse along, but Beatrice trailed behind.

"I've brought you a gift, Henry," Meg whispered as she yanked on the reins. The plumes on her hat tossed back over her shoulder.

"Bless you, Meg."

"Captain," Beatrice acknowledged, when she joined them, her eyes brushing around him, everywhere and all at once, but never fixing themselves to one place.

"If we don't move, we're liable to get run over," he told them, anxious to be ordinary. They turned up the path, walking their horses with the flow of the crowd as Meg dawdled artfully behind.

"You visited my father, I think," Beatrice said, having the courage to speak first.

"Yes." He felt a coward, stammering out the words. "Several days ago."

She nodded, her brow as smooth and serene as a Madonna. "He charged me to return some things he believes you mislaid." She lifted a parcel, plain-wrapped with paper and string, and handed it over, her gloved hands retreating before his fingers could hope to brush against them. He knew the inventory without having to open it. A glove, a button, a letter, and a handkerchief.

He swallowed past a lump in his throat. "How thoughtless of me. I was meaning to come and collect them." Did she know he had been there every day? Sometimes twice?

"No bother," she answered, her face looking as cool and flat as a millpond.

No bother. He looked down at the package. Day after day he'd been desperate for word of her and now, here she was, close enough to touch. The thick folds of her riding habit brushed his stirrup, but he could not shake the feeling that he was botching it.

Turning in his saddle, he beckoned Meg. "Can you lose us?" he asked when she drew close. She darted a look to Beatrice who sat, white-faced but composed, in the rush of carriages.

"Please, Meg. A quarter of an hour," he asked.

Beatrice reached up to tuck a curl into her bonnet, giving a slight nod.

"Well then," Meg said, flashing a little of her gamine grin as she gave her horse a kick. "Lady Percy—" they heard her say as she moved off.

He didn't think but reached quickly, taking the reins from Beatrice's hands and pulling them over the chestnut's head in one fluid motion. Swift fingers loosed a cheek strap on the bridle and let it dangle. "Your tack has come undone, Miss Thornton," he said, loud enough to carry. Beatrice's teeth fretted along her lip. "Shall we sort ourselves out?"

His eyes scanned the park. They'd passed a copse of trees... *there*. It was a little overgrown and not populated with carriages or riders or ladies on foot, and he made for it now, guiding her horse toward the relative quiet of the wood.

The light was different here and as he dismounted, his footfalls muffled against the deep grass and heavy boughs. He reached to help her down and she hesitated for a moment, then slid neatly into his arms, her hands coming to rest against his chest. Breath fled. They should soon move clear of one another, to ask and answer the questions that lay between them.

Step away, Henry. But he couldn't. It was too natural to stay, to have her in his arms again. It was the sensation of standing on a cliff moments before jumping that gripped him now. *It's dangerous*, one voice whispered, listing off the reasons. Broad daylight. Hyde Park. He had not seen her for days. But there were Beatrice's eyes on him with a look that he could only interpret as longing whispering, *Jump. Jump.*

He tightened his arms and bent his head to meet her lips, feeling his heart beating like a rammer as it shoved powder and ball deep into a cannon. Fifteen minutes. It was nothing. The time was slipping from him. He closed his eyes against it.

Her lips were soft and warm, and he felt her reach up on her tiptoes, holding his coat, pressing into him. She was losing her head too. As their kiss deepened, he slid a glove from his hand and laid his palm against her cheek, gently pressing it under the silken ribbon of her bonnet, resting his thumb in the hollow behind her ear.

The taste of salt brushed his tongue and he lifted his head a fraction to see Beatrice crying. Her face contorted and she pulled away from him, the suddenness of the action sending her mare into a skittish dance, the ribbon fluttering loose.

He blinked and drew a ragged breath. Broad daylight. Hyde Park. What in the name of heaven had he been thinking? He could not regret it. Still, it hadn't been quite the thing. Beatrice had used her sleeve to wipe the tears away and she stood with her arms wrapped about her waist, eyes fastened on her toes.

"Forgive me, Beatrice," he murmured, doffing his hat and pushing a hand through his hair, his breath still shallow. "I never meant—"

"Captain," she said, in a tone that set him back. Her eyes had come up to his cravat and she took a large breath, darting an anxious tongue along her lips. "I ought to have told you at once. I hardly know how to… I am to be married."

The words would not arrange themselves into an order he could understand. He could not have been more bewildered than if a comet had struck the ground at his feet. "What did you say?" he managed.

"Ye—Yes," she stammered. "I am firmly engaged. So you see, I felt I should return…." Her head swivelled around until she spotted the parcel where he had flung it into the grass. She swallowed, perhaps recalling his urgent need to have both hands free, at the time. "Your solicitous inquiries about my health are no longer—"

"No, no." This wasn't some fever dream brought back from the war, but a nightmare of another sort. He shook his head. He couldn't stop shaking his head. "No."

"Yes."

"Who?" he asked, his voice controlled—barely. An old beau from Dorset? He hated him already.

Fingers twisted. She rubbed a hand up her arm. But she answered him. "Lord Fox."

Fox, he thought, trying to sort out a picture in his mind of the man who stood at Beatrice's side. But she didn't love him. "I don't understand." He groped back to the last place he had understood—a blazing bright ballroom and Beatrice's face alight. How had that moment, as solid under his feet as a granite mountain, become sand?

Her smile was a guttering flame. "He asked, and I accepted. Mama is pleased."

"She would be," he replied, feeling acrid bitterness fill his mouth. The thought of Fox and Beatrice. It turned his stomach. "*Lord* Fox has always had her approval. I was unaware he had yours."

Her smile extinguished as her chin lifted. "He does."

Scepticism traced across every line of his brow. An engagement meant nothing. It wasn't too late. "If this is about your mother—"

"No. Sir. And, please, I must ask that you call me Miss Thornton."

His eyebrows rose. "Until I am to call you Lady Fox. Is that it?" he asked, his confusion giving way to fury. "Or will you prefer Cousin?"

She flinched, turning on her heel and reaching for her horse. "I came to tell you in person."

"Yes, Cousin."

She raised her voice. "Because it was only fair. It's best if I go. Now, if you will lend me your hand," she requested, plainly furious. "There's no mounting block and I don't believe you are a man who would leave a woman stranded."

"I wish that I was," he replied, lacing his fingers together and waiting while she placed her booted foot within to boost her up. Then he began setting her horse's bridle to rights, working the leather strap through the buckle and running two fingers underneath, careful even in his anger not to cinch it too tightly.

There must be a way out, he thought. But fury extinguished all reason. Henry scooped up the parcel and with her reins still in his hands he mounted his own horse.

"I haven't seen the announcement in *The Times*."

"No. Not yet, but Lord Fox will send the note around to the publisher tomorrow," she said, her voice almost soothing.

He wouldn't be soothed. He wasn't a horse. "Are you going to ask me to wish you happy?" he growled.

"No," she whispered.

Though quietly, he raged. "Isn't it the done thing? Shouldn't I do it? Tell you that your future happiness is secure. That you make a handsome pair. That Fox is the luckiest of men." His voice became ragged. "I would wager all I have that you don't love him. How can you do this?"

Again her eyes welled over and, pulling off her gloves, she put trembling hands to her cheeks, stemming the tide of tears like a child, with indelicate smears.

A branch snapped and he jerked toward the sound. "Can I offer you any aid, Gracechurch?" came a voice from beyond the trees. An acquaintance from Whitehall. Beatrice, her back to the stranger, stiffened and dropped her hands to the horse's mane in some semblance of a normal posture but continued to weep.

Henry moved his horse to shelter her from prying eyes. "Quite all right. My companion became overheated, but it's quite shady here. I will escort her home presently." The man nodded and moved along.

Henry looked at Beatrice with her eyes screwed tightly shut. Her teeth caught her lower lip and tears coursed down her cheeks. He'd done that. The blame lay at his door.

Pulling a square of white linen from his pocket, he tucked it into her hands. "You ought to carry a handkerchief, you know," he told her, trying to let the plain fabric do his apologizing for him.

She dabbed and blotted until it was a crumpled mess, repairing everything but her blotchy cheeks and red-rimmed eyes. She held it out to him again. "I should have it laundered."

He took it and smiled, but the smile was failing him. "Then you would have to return it and I, boor that I am, might make you cry, and we would have it all to do again." He folded the linen in a careful square and placed it in his waistcoat against his heart. He was a fool.

All those years in Spain, throwing himself against city walls. What else had it taught him but that there had always been a way in? Always. He understood how to fight for something. He understood that sometimes the battle shifted unaccountably. But he didn't understand this.

She hiccupped and inhaled, her own smile wobbly. His heart overcame him.

"Marry me instead." The words could not be withheld. The proposal hovered between them for a breathless moment. *Please.*

An engagement meant nothing. It wasn't too late.

Her eyes closed for a long moment and when they opened her voice was level and her chin was firm. "Nothing could induce me to change my mind, Captain."

Lord, how he wished that his love had been bestowed on a pliable, easily swayed girl who would listen to him and do what he asked. "If your mother forced you to choose a title over—"

"Sir. You must believe that my mother had nothing to do with it." Again, her eyes closed for a moment and she took a long breath. "If I led you to believe I would consent to an uneven match, I am sorry for it."

He went white under his weathered face. She had known what he was from the outset. "That kiss, Beatrice. I know you felt as I did. Explain that away."

She didn't answer him but occupied herself with the silken bonnet ribbons, tying them up in a tight, miserly bow.

He brandished the parcel. "This, then, is meant to be goodbye?"

"It *is* goodbye. I can't have you coming to the door anymore." She looked down at her hands, gripping the chestnut mane. "It upsets the servants."

His nostrils flared. "You are determined, ma'am, to send me on my way, a whip at my heels."

He hardly recognized the hardness in her face. She did not retreat one inch. "You will recover."

"Like an old libertine? You think my love is a shallow thing? That it will it pass as quickly as a summer storm and leave nothing worse than a good soaking? Maybe it will ease your conscience to think so." He felt like he'd been handed a draught of poison and asked to drink it down every day for the rest of his life.

From the corner of his eye he saw a rider pause on the path. Meg. "Here's our friend again. Our time is up," he snapped, taking a steadying breath as Beatrice tugged her gloves on. He could tell himself he wasn't finished, that a betrothal was breakable, but once it was in the papers the scandal would not leave them untouched.

He sidled his mount along hers, waiting until she met his eyes. "I will love you until I die, Beatrice. I don't believe you're the sort of woman to be careless with a thing like that." Outside of an estate she considered worthless, it was all he had, and he would lay it at her feet whether she picked it up or not.

He tucked the reins in her hands and when she would have spoken, slapped the chestnut's flank. She was off. Not looking back but joining Meg, holding onto her saddle and looking nothing like the skilful rider she was. Soon the crowd swallowed her up.

He stared after her even when there was nothing left to see. He would pack his things. Say his farewells to Godmama. Fox. No, he didn't want to think about encountering Fox. Take the Sussex road and ride away. Tomorrow.

Still, he was rooted to the spot.

Ceph snorted and shook his head while Henry gathered the reins. He looked down to see the parcel in his lap. Maybe there would be a note. Something. His fingers tore away the paper and string. No. There was nothing more than the things he had left, the remnants of an attempt to get another moment with Beatrice. Glove, button, letter…

He turned the wrapping over.

Where was the handkerchief?

Chapter Twenty-Seven

"Don't run away from me, Beatrice," Meg called as Beatrice scurried up the steps of Number Six.

"It's nothing," Beatrice muttered, pulling off her gloves and catching a glimpse of herself in the hall mirror. A haggard, blotchy face stared back at her.

Meg took heavy breaths as she leaned against the wall, arms crossed over her chest. "I thought you wanted to see him. That's why I consented to ride a horse in the first place. But you've been crying, and Henry looked like thunder. What did he say to you?"

"Nothing. I don't want to talk about it."

Meg made a noise at the back of her throat. "Do you have a handkerchief?" Meg pushed away from the wall and held out her hand, snapping her fingers and giving them a little wave.

Beatrice reddened, right up to her ears. She did have a handkerchief but not one that she planned to share. Oh, damnation. Meg's hand was still extended, and Beatrice went hunting through the drawers of the hall table, finding a fresh folded square.

Meg didn't even glance at it but wrapped it around her index finger. "Spit," she said, and Beatrice leaned forward, depositing some saliva on the cloth. Meg rubbed at the grimy tracks on her face, harder than she needed to.

"You should have a lie down before dinner. Do you have the time?"

Yes. She had time. Far more than the scant fifteen minutes Henry had been given. Her pulse galloped in her throat. It had taken them less than a minute to forget themselves.

The heavy sound of silver being laid out in the dining room gave her a start. Meg would have to be told sometime. "We've guests coming." Beatrice's fingers picked across the table top playing a silent tune. "For my engagement dinner."

"Engagement?" Meg clapped a hand over her mouth. "Oh Beatrice, that's what the tears are for. I suppose pulling it off must have meant an awful row with your mama, but I'm so proud of you. Henry—" she trailed away as Beatrice shook her head. Meg narrowed her eyes. "What?"

"I have promised to wed Lord Fox."

Meg's dainty rosebud mouth dropped open and she slapped the table hard enough to shake the pictures on the wall. "You have not."

"Yesterday."

"Have you gone stark, staring mad? What have you done?" Meg was shouting, drowning out the clatter down in the kitchens. Her words fell on Beatrice like a shower of arrows. She deserved each one after that performance in the park, which had shattered Henry's faith in her. "You love him," Meg accused, and Beatrice could only shake her head. "You do."

Beatrice cleared her throat and laid soft fingers on Meg's arm. "Lord Fox and I would welcome—"

Meg jerked away. "Stop it, Beatrice Thornton, or so help me I will scream this house down. This"—she waved a hand, encompassing Beatrice's set smile and polite hands—"is not my friend."

"Are we not still friends?" Beatrice asked, a choke in her voice. "You would not fault me for choosing to wed one of your oldest friends, instead of the other."

"You think they are interchangeable? Tell me, how many times has Fox stood up with me at a ball?" Meg asked. "This whole season? How many?"

Beatrice's brow wrinkled. "You often sat out."

"Not once," Meg supplied. "Ever. Nearly every other man in London kept me at arm's distance, tarring me with the same brush as Isabelle. Do you know how much the support of a wealthy, personable peer might have mattered? Though he knew me in my pram, Lord Fox offered me little of it. Now," she asked, her voice tight, "how often did Henry dance with me?"

Beatrice shook her head. "I won't play this game."

"Twice. Twice at every ball and party we attended. He couldn't stop the gossip—he doesn't have the position for that, but he ignored it. Fox and Henry are nothing alike." Meg gave a bitter smile. "Still,

Society will applaud your choice as wise. Do not expect me to do so. I have known for too many years that we live in a stupid world."

"Am I stupid too?" Beatrice tried for lightness, but Meg was not taken in.

"For making him love you when you don't love him back? Yes."

Beatrice's fingers stopped their nervous drumming, becoming unnaturally still.

"I'm sure it hasn't gone as deep as that." The words dropped from her mouth, bent and twisted from the effort. "You will be dancing at his wedding next year or the year after."

"Stop making me want to throw things. For all our differences, I thought we were the sort of women who would not settle for just anybody."

Beatrice didn't respond. She couldn't. Meg's own life had been turned upside down by the reckless actions of her sister. Surely, if the words could be spoken, she would understand Beatrice's actions, if not approve them.

Finally, Meg sank onto the stairs, arms resting on her knees. "I cannot grasp this. Did Henry not make a good case for himself? He's so terribly proper where women are concerned. I can make a better one. His family isn't so poor—"

Beatrice put a hand to her cheek, touching the spot just behind her ear. Proper? No. She knew otherwise. As he had held her, her limbs had longed to rise. Only her misery had kept her moored to the earth. "Don't, Meg," she begged, her voice breaking. "This is hard for me."

Meg touched Beatrice by the hand, her eyes widening. Meg's eyes searched everywhere and something of Beatrice's grief must have communicated itself to her friend, because sweet, warm-hearted Meg jumped to her feet and folded her into an embrace.

"I am so sorry," Beatrice sobbed, her voice thick with tears.

Meg leaned back and looked her square in the face. "Don't be sorry. Be wise."

"I haven't any choice, Meg."

Meg snorted.

***

Everyone was going to have indigestion, thought Beatrice, looking down the table. Only Penny, sitting too still and ladylike, seemed unconscious of any currents flowing around the guests. Mama, Lady Sherbourne, and Beatrice sat on the ladies' side, and only Papa and his lordship represented the men.

Papa pushed his chair back and stood, glass in hand, and the room settled into quiet expectation. "Now that we are all here tonight, I wish…" He cleared his throat. "I am going to announce the engagement of Beatrice to Lord Fox here." Penny's squeal was chased at once by Mama's shush.

Lord Fox laid his hand atop Beatrice's and gave it a light press. Her reply was to smile vaguely in the direction of the stewed endive, and though she wanted to snatch her hand away, she forced herself to leave it there. This would be a part of marriage that she must accustom herself to.

"And…" Papa closed his eyes for a tense moment. "Let's drink to that."

"When is it to be?" Penny asked, bouncing in her seat.

"Penelope," Mama chided, giving her head a sharp shake.

"Why wasn't I told?" Lady Sherbourne asked, throwing her hands up. "No one told me anything."

Lord Fox leaned over. "It's been bubbling beneath the surface for quite some time now."

Lady Sherbourne rolled her eyes.

"We hope to be married quite soon," Beatrice added, rushing on. Godmama would only behave for so long, even on the most benign of topics.

"Soon?" shot Lady Sherbourne. "Why ever for?"

"Who wouldn't be anxious to make Miss Thornton his wife?" Lord Fox questioned, surprising Beatrice with an expression that looked like love. She freed her hand from his and reached for her napkin.

"Well, it's cracking good news," Penny said, taking an over-large swallow of champagne, draining her prudent half-glass and giving a tiny burp.

"Penelope," Mama scolded. "Nursery manners belong in the nursery."

Papa gave a heavy tap on the rim of his glass with two fingers, and George hastened over with the bottle of champagne, refilling the flute. The man turned, only to have Lady Sherbourne give her own glass a thump.

And somehow they all survived until the disastrous evening crashed to a close, all getting a little tight.

***

"I must send my maid 'round the shops to buy seven yards of the blackest bombazine she can find," Godmama said, standing in the entry hall and flourishing her cloak over her shoulders. "When I celebrate this marriage, I want to be swathed as befits the occasion."

Mama glared, but Penny's face lit, her emotions as liable to burst as the bubbles in a prudent half-glass of champagne. "What colour for me? Blue? Yellow?" She made a disgusted sound, too loud for the space. "Yellow is difficult. Mama says I have a pallor," she said in a roaring whisper to the footman, not precisely drunk, but quite uninhibited. Red flakes stained her cheeks and she giggled.

The party had needed someone to be bright and to be talkative, and Mama's inattention to Penny's wine glass had seemed too convenient to be chance. Penny had carried them all through the ordeal of dinner on an ocean of chatter, but, if Penny cast up her accounts into the potted plants, it would hardly be a surprise.

Lord Fox bent down at Beatrice's feet. "Your footman must have missed this," he said, watching her face as she took the simple page of folded parchment from his hand.

She flipped it open and made her face reflect a calmness she was far from feeling. Another note. Another heavy black mark through another day. Time was running out.

"Shopping list." She forced tranquillity into her smile. "Will you be writing *The Times* soon?"

"So anxious for the announcement?" he teased. But she could not share his laughter. He was her protection, and the sooner the world knew about it, the better.

"Tomorrow, please," she asked.

He nodded and leaned down, kissing her lightly on the forehead.

Lady Sherbourne, seeing them, opened her mouth then clamped it shut again. Her eyes narrowed. "I shall be calling tomorrow, Sarah. Depend on it. Now, young person," she directed herself to Lord Fox, "you will assist me to my carriage."

As soon as the front door closed with a bright click, Mama gathered her skirts, turning to the stairs. "I will murder the first person who tries to wake me."

Papa, bleary-eyed and walking with too much care, pulled Beatrice into a great hug. Then he kissed her temple and followed Mama, his step heavy on the treads of the stairs.

But Penny's feelings were not complicated by darker shades of sorrow or dashed expectations. She threw an arm around Beatrice as they made their way up to their bedrooms. "He is astonishingly good looking, Bea. Your children have a good chance—"

"Of not being wall-eyed and hump-backed?" Beatrice questioned.

"You beat me to it." Penny let out a breath that buzzed her lips and leaned heavily against her sister. Her head would be aching in the morning. "You lost me a shilling."

"Have you been gambling?"

"Only a shilling," she hiccupped. "George knows I'm good for it. I was sure you would end an old maid. That was my bet."

"Gambling with the footman? Well, what did George bet?"

"Told me it wasn't at all proper to bet, but, in any case, his money was on the captain. Said it would be fitting." She giggled.

"What?"

"Winning the bet with the captain's own coin. George says the captain's favourite coins are shillings. Apparently, he hands out loads of them. George'll have one more and I'll have one less." She wrinkled her brow as though the sum was difficult to work out. "If his lordship is half so nice as Captain Gracechurch, it's good."

Beatrice dropped an arm across her sister's shoulders and kissed her hair. *If.* The enormity of her own gamble yawned before her. "Thank you, Penny."

"Can I come sleep with you tonight?" Penny asked.

She shouldn't. Mama would forbid it if she knew. But it would be good to remember what she still had: Meg's friendship, and this sweet, slightly sotted little sister. Much better than to be reminded of what Beatrice had lost.

It would be more restful to stay up all night talking to Penny than to lie there and think. Anyway, Beatrice had never felt less like rising in her life. She gave only the smallest hesitation.

"Just this once."

Chapter Twenty-Eight

Today could not be the hell of yesterday.

The worst was behind her and nothing, surely, could be worse than that. Soft morning sun made an amber light against the inside of her closed eyes and she took a long breath, building a wall between herself and thoughts of Henry. It would become easier to bear. It had to.

Today her future husband would be writing to the papers, a step hardly less binding than the blessing of a bishop and a shower of rice. She tried to imagine him dashing off the note: *Miss Beatrice Thornton to be wed to The Right Honourable Lord Fox.* What would he think when he scratched her name across the paper, pairing it with his own? Would it make his belly feel pitted and sour?

Beatrice pushed a hand over her own unsettled stomach and pulled the goose down pillow across her face, blocking out the light. With every breath, hot air spread against the linen. Maybe she would suffocate.

"Beatrice."

Panic tensed her limbs. *Penny.* She had completely forgotten. She felt the soft mattress pressing against her back and relaxed.

"Beatrice." Penny's voice was strange and Beatrice cast the pillow off, sweeping her eyes around the room. Then she looked up and shrieked, clapping a hand over her mouth. Her sister was floating.

Penny's eyes were wide with terror as her fingers pressed like church steeples against the ceiling. "How is this happening?" Her voice shook. "I can't feel any ropes."

Beatrice ripped away her ribbons and scrambled to her feet. The mattress seemed to sink with every step as she crooned all the while, "Easy... shhhh... I'll have you down."

Beatrice stretched up and grabbed a handful of hanging night-rail, tugging at it. Every jostle sent Penny into whimpers, the kind a scared puppy would make, but her body did not drop an inch. Of course it wouldn't, thought Beatrice, finally letting her go. She knew that Penny must come down herself.

"Help," Penny whispered, crying now. "Help me."

At least Beatrice could go to Penny. *Meringues, seafoam...* Beatrice stepped into position.

Come on. *Linens lifting in the breeze. Come on.* It had never failed her.

But no gathering lightness travelled her limbs. She hunted for it, prodding every corner of her mind for some trace of it, but found she had been drained dry.

Possibly, she could have told herself, she was simply fatigued. Perhaps shock had driven it away. But she knew at once where it had gone. With Henry.

"Listen, Penny, don't move," Beatrice ordered, running her tongue along her lips. "And don't make another noise. We'll get you down." Her eyes darted frantically around the room and she jumped from the bed and bolted the door. That would have to do. Then she ran to the bureau, unearthing a wad of shawls.

"Beatrice." Penny's breath was fast and shallow. She would make herself sick.

"I know, Penny. But you have to be quiet," Beatrice insisted, ignoring how cruel she sounded. "It's going to be all right. It will. I want you to settle yourself down. Breathe."

Penny's fumbling hands pressed flat against the ceiling. "I'm st—stuck." Penny's voice was hardly more than a whisper. It had been the excitement of the party, Beatrice reasoned, and staying up with the grown-ups, and drinking more than was prudent that had cast her up there.

"You won't be able to climb down. That's not how it works."

Memories of her own first rising clawed across her mind. The screaming. Mama shouting at Papa to bolt the door. The terror. The lies that followed.

"I want you to close your eyes. Do it." Her voice was harsher than she wished, and she gentled her tone. "Now, think of something heavy."

"Like... like a cannonball?"

Beatrice let out a quavering breath. "Good girl. Yes. Don't think of anything else but a cannonball. Close your eyes and think about how hard it would be to lift one, how it would drag on your shoulders. Think of the weight sitting in your hands. That's it, that's it." Inch by painstaking inch, Penny dropped lower.

Beatrice pushed aside the covers with her feet and guided Penny until she rested where Beatrice had been. Penny's body fitted into the depression Beatrice had left.

"You're doing beautifully. Cannonball, cannonball," Beatrice whispered as she pulled the ribbons—the loathsome ribbons—around her sister's waist. She cinched the bow tight and looked away as tears stung the back of her eyes and bile rose in her throat.

Beatrice bit the inside of her lip and grabbed the pile of shawls, tying the fringed ends together in a knot. "I'm going to secure your legs now to hold you," she explained, expelling long, clean breaths.

Penny's head bobbed, but her face crumpled. Then she reached a hand to touch the ribbons at her waist. "You lied."

"What?" Beatrice asked, bending low and stuffing a length of Indian muslin around the bed rail.

"You always said these were for sleepwalking, but it's not that. Is it?"

Beatrice's hand stilled, but she looked up. "I should go get Mama," she muttered, but made no move to do so.

"Does she know?" Penny burst out, looking haunted. "Has she ever…?"

Look at her.

Penny wanted to run screaming from her own body. She was too young for this. Beatrice looked at the limp ends of fabric she held in her hands, which had been moving with brisk efficiency. In truth, Beatrice had been even younger.

She shut her eyes, pulled the shawl tightly into a knot, and clasped Penny by the hand. "Yes, Mama knows about me… rising. I expect you have lots of questions."

"You expect?" Penny asked, showing a little of her natural spirit.

Beatrice gave a sigh and lay down on the bed next to her sister, staring up at the ceiling. Mama's first impulse, even now, would be to frighten Penny.

"It's a gift," Beatrice began. She picked her words with care, each one meant to avoid any suggestion that Penny was damaged or broken.

Penny's breath, as fast as the beat of a wing, calmed.

"It took Mama and Papa three hours to get me down the first time," Beatrice told her sister, and Penny gave a watery laugh. "And then they stacked heavy books on my lap to keep me there. Can you imagine? Piled high with Chaucer and Milton and Shakespeare and estate ledgers until Papa could fetch rope from the stables. Getting you down so easily puts you miles ahead of where I was. That's good news, dearest."

Beatrice turned her head and they looked at one another, appraising.

Penny inhaled, her lower lip sucking inward. She was thinking. "It's going to be all right. That's what you want me to believe." Her forehead wrinkled. "I don't know if I should." Penny's shoulders shifted. "Can you tell me it hasn't ruined your life?"

Beatrice opened her mouth to say, "Of course I can." To lie.

Penny went on, her voice spilling like water down a hill. "Because if you say it hasn't, I'll believe you. And it'll be all right then, you see. It means this feeling"—Penny's face twisted away and tears coursed from her eyes—"it means that it will go away."

That feeling. Beatrice knew it. She had felt it yesterday in the little wood in the park. She had felt it again and again this Season. Again and again and again these seven years. The panic of feeling like this thing—rising—had her by the throat and would never let her go.

Penny's tears travelled in a track down to her ear. Poor child. Beatrice scrubbed at them with her sleeve and pushed her arm under Penny's back, rolling her sister's head onto her shoulder. Mama must know sometime.

Unfortunately, Beatrice knew how it would be. She would call Mama and Mama would begin, almost at once, to teach Penny about making compromises and being content with doing as she was told. Mama would drill her in secrecy, control, and the sort of reserve that would keep people at arm's length. And she would mean it for the best. Beatrice bit on her lip and looked up, blinking back the tears. Heaven knew she would mean it for the best.

It wasn't anger that welled up in her now, but grief, flowing like a wide river, permeating every part of her until the pressure threatened to rip her apart. *Poor little girl,* she repeated to herself. *Poor little girl.* And she did not know if she meant Penny or herself. The young child lying at Beatrice's side, confused and weeping, or the one that had done so all those years ago without even the consolation of someone telling her that it was all going to be all right.

And it wasn't all right. Not for her or for the child she had been. *Poor little girl.*

Why hadn't she looked after that child? Beatrice took a deep, clean breath. What if she had taken as much care for herself as she was taking now for Penny? What if she began to do so now?

Answers rushed in and around her, spilling at her feet.

For one thing, she would not allow Penny to be ruled by fear. The fear of discovery was a dragon she must be prepared to battle her whole life long, but there was no need to feed the monster.

For another thing, Beatrice wouldn't let her sister be shoved into a rubbishy, second-rate marriage at the bidding of some nameless blackmailer without a fight.

***

It was still early when Beatrice crept down to the kitchens, spinning a story about a foolish girl who drank too freely of the wine last night. The scullery could not hide her laughter, but their butler Harrison agreed to leave Penny in peace, not rousing the missus by telling tales.

"Also," Beatrice instructed, turning to go up the stairs. "I should like George to make several deliveries in a quarter of an hour."

Then she went, with steps that sounded certain and sound, to the drawing room. Taking three pieces of foolscap from a drawer, she dipped her pen and wrote on the first one, *Dear Captain Gracechurch...* That was wrong. She struck a black mark through it and began again, *Dearest Henry...*

Chapter Twenty-Nine

Beatrice flicked the grimy curtain back as the hackney carriage bounced over each cobblestone. The smell of none-too-fresh hay and sour beer pressed in on her, but the conveyance, hailed on the street and hired for a few coins, allowed her to move about the city with anonymity.

"I thought it would be me," Meg whispered from the opposite bench, her face alight with gleeful intrigue. Though the interior was dim, Beatrice cast her a puzzled look. "When we met, I was sure it would be me getting *you* into trouble."

From almost the moment they set off, Meg hadn't stopped talking, and thank goodness she hadn't. It was an effective distraction from the perils ahead. Beatrice wondered which would be more ruinous: Visiting a bachelor's establishment unchaperoned or floating in full view of a shocked public above a ballroom floor. And Meg hadn't hesitated a second to come with her.

"I am sorry to involve you."

"No," Meg replied. "The cold shoulders turned on me this Season could hardly grow more frigid. If we are caught, at least I will begin to feel I've earned it." Meg sobered. "I'm proud of you."

Was Meg proud to see her break a second engagement in as many days? Beatrice twitched the curtain again and felt the hollow emptiness of her stomach. Penny's future and Beatrice's stood in the balance. In less than an hour, she would be free.

It was a comfort to think that Lord Fox must know what was coming. The signs were all there in the terse little note she had composed. *Sir, I must beg you to hold the notice of our engagement from delivery and shall call upon you within the hour. Please wait upon me. Yours respectfully...*

Perhaps she should have been more obvious. She shook her head. Even if she hadn't said it straight out, he would know she meant to break it off. She took a steady breath as the carriage rocked to a stop.

Yes. He had been kind and there was no reason he wouldn't make it easy for her.

Feeling like enemy spies, they waited until the street was clear of carriages and foot traffic and dashed across the sidewalk to stand at the door in the bright glare of the morning sun. It was Meg who rapped the knocker and then reached to take Beatrice's hand. "For all his sins, Fox has never eaten anyone," she said, and Beatrice nodded, almost sure this was so.

The door swung back to reveal a butler whose mouth hung slightly open at the sight of two genteel young ladies on his doorstep. "We are expected," Beatrice stated and thrust a calling card into his hands with more confidence than she felt.

There was a moment of hesitation and then he pulled the door a fraction wider. "This way." He checked the card. "Miss."

She swept in and stopped almost at once. Her note to Henry lay on the salver in the hall. "Captain Gracechurch?" she questioned.

"Away at the moment, miss," he answered, punctuating each word with disapproval. Young ladies did not belong here.

Beatrice persisted. "He's not left for Sussex."

"Later this morning, I expect," the butler replied with an air that said that this would be his last crumb of information.

They found Lord Fox in the drawing room bending over the hearth. "Ah, Beatrice," he called easily, and then his gaze shifted past her. With notably less welcome, he added, "and Margaret too."

He continued in his task, holding a paper as it smoked and caught fire, the flames blackening and curling the edges as it burned. When the blaze consumed it, he dropped it into the hearth, waited a moment, then ground out the charred remains with his booted foot.

"Destroying the evidence," he said with a smile. "I don't imagine you want your visit broadcast."

She gave a shaky sigh. "No, not at all. My parents don't even know I came."

Lord Fox raised his brows and swung his gaze to Meg. "And you, Margaret? Does your aunt know?"

"She is still asleep, I'd wager."

He clicked his tongue and focused back on Beatrice. "How wicked you've both been." His look was warm, and a mottled flush climbed her cheeks.

"Meg." Beatrice touched her friend's arm, and Meg nodded, taking herself off to the other side of the room to pretend an interest in the portrait of a woman.

"How obedient you've made her, Beatrice," he drawled, taking her hand and guiding her to the sofa. "Margaret doesn't jump to anybody's tune."

Beatrice lifted her chin. What a pricking thing to say, making Meg sound like a half-trained puppy. She had never admired that part of him. Then she blew out a quick breath and gave the smile she reserved for children. She had come to put an end to his hopes. He deserved nothing but patience.

"I am sorry to come like this," she said, wishing he'd let go of her hand. The pressure was nothing—enough to press a bruise into the soft flesh of a peach—but withdrawing would call his attention to it. She struggled on. "You must be wondering what brought me to your home in such a strange way, my lord."

"Anthony," he stated. "You should call me Anthony." His face was as clear and honest as it had been the day he proposed. Could he possibly not know why she had come? "After all, we are to be married."

Her expression faltered. "Anthony. That's the problem. My lord—"

"Anthony," he corrected, like a patient schoolmaster to his dull-witted student. "You must try, Beatrice."

Forgetting about politeness, she yanked her hand from his. She did not speak again until she told herself that breaking their engagement would be a more severe rebuke than a ringing set-down could ever hope to be. But it was suddenly much more imperative to be clear rather than kind.

"I have come because I wish to be released from our engagement," she told him and, all at once, a mountain seemed to lift from her shoulders.

He looked surprised, but he couldn't have been. The Lord Fox she had known all Season could not be so naive. There was no time to consider it, but it rested there in the back of her mind, the sense that his character was blurry around the edges. Not like a real person at all, but a smudged imitation of one.

"Only two days. What could have changed your mind, I wonder."

Henry, Penny, her—Beatrice had a hundred reasons.

"It is not anything you have done."

"Oh dear," he muttered, sitting back with a smile. "I am to be placated with soothing platitudes. No, Miss Thornton—I suppose I've lost the privilege of your Christian name—do not exert yourself. There is no need. I had hoped we might make a good match, but if your feelings revolt, you are released at once. Will that do?"

"Thank you, yes. I owe you a great debt for your understanding, and hope I have not injured you in any way."

"That's not the way to go about it at all, Miss Thornton. These lines must be as tiresome to say as they are to hear." He reached over and rang a bell. "But you may clear your debt by taking tea with me."

Penny was waiting for her to return. And, later, she prayed, Henry.

"The hackney—"

"The hackney is long gone, and I think you would not wish to stand on the street hailing another. Moreover," he gave her a blinding smile, bright enough to burn off all those lingering doubts, "your debt to me remains. My coach will be harnessed and ready almost as soon as the tea is consumed." His smile became teasing and confidential. "You cannot tell me you don't feel the need for some restorative."

She laughed, the tension falling from her like a dog shaking off a soaking. There had been no raised voices or impassioned speeches. She was free again and it had not been so terrible, after all.

When the refreshments arrived, the servant departed and Meg joined them on the sofa.

"Shall I?" Beatrice asked, reaching for the teapot.

"No, let me pour out." Fox waved away any help. "Bachelors are adept at these sorts of things."

Beatrice exchanged a guilty look with Meg as his lordship took some time manipulating the sugar spoon. "In the event no lady ever accepts me, I'll never starve if I can pour out the tea."

She felt like a heel. Was he doing it deliberately? As he passed around the teacups, Meg gave her a heartening look, turning the subject. "What's your mama doing squirreled away in a dark corner, Fox? She ought to be hanging over the mantel." Beatrice glanced up to see a large gilt mirror mounted over the fireplace, reflecting the elegant room and its elegant master.

"I am content to leave her where she is," Lord Fox replied, his face growing hard. "Moreover, only one person will have the right to make changes to the arrangements of my home, Margaret. Now that there's a vacancy, I should be amused to hear your qualifications."

Beatrice sucked in her breath. If it was a joke, it was in poor taste. But Meg answered him calmly enough. "If you cannot appreciate the painting, at least give it to Henry to take back to Sussex. Lady Fox was his aunt and I would imagine your Gracechurch connections would like it."

Lord Fox's smile was tight, and Beatrice thought she saw a sneer in it. "I have had quite enough of Henry poaching on my preserves. That's one woman he *cannot* have."

Dead silence dropped like night in the room, bathing it in unease. Beatrice focused her energies on draining the last drops from the teacup as quickly as possible. The worries of the morning piled up in her mind, giving her the beginnings of a splitting headache. But at last, she heard the distinctive rumble of the heavy travelling coach on the street outside.

"Why, you've four horses," Beatrice noted, looking toward the window and blinking from the brightness of the sun. "St. James's Square is less than a mile away."

"Well, I never was much good at geography." He chuckled, a sound he had not quite mastered. "The coach is enclosed to secure your privacy, and the horses need exercising." He looked at them closely. "But it will stand at the door until you are ready. We can have the two of you dash out when no one is there to notice." He smiled again, his face empty of reproach or other complicated feelings, but this time she felt no ease from it.

She lifted her chin to look out the window again. "We should not keep him waiting."

"No, we should not," Lord Fox agreed, speaking slowly.

Meg, who had been so quiet, stood, her fingers pressing the back of her chair, her face clammy and grey. She swayed ever so slightly back, her hand lifting for a brief moment, and stumbled forward.

"I do not feel at all well," she said as her eyes rolled up in her head. Fox caught her at the moment she slumped forward.

"Meg," Beatrice cried, as Fox carried Meg to the sofa. Beatrice flung off her gloves and untied the ribbons of Meg's bonnet. She began fanning her with it and then thrust it into Lord Fox's hands. "Keep the air moving," she commanded as she loosened the buttons on Meg's spencer, the rush of activity making her heart race and her brow grow damp with sweat. "She was well enough when we set out. Perhaps we should call a doctor."

Lord Fox lifted one of Meg's eyelids with a lazy finger. "A mere swoon. If we call a doctor, it will be sure to get out that you visited my home with no fit chaperone."

Beatrice had been gently patting Meg's cheeks in an effort to awaken her, but now she frowned at his half-hearted attempts to wave the crushed bonnet. She grabbed it back and bent over her friend, fanning Meg herself, though her arms moved like she was swimming through sand.

"She will rouse in another moment, though I am sadly without a vinaigrette." He looked at Beatrice closely, triumph lighting his eyes. She would have felt more confused, but the cold and hot wind that seemed to swirl in every joint and muscle claimed all thought. "Are you quite sure you are feeling yourself, Miss Thornton?"

The bonnet slipped from her fingers and her legs buckled out from under her. She collapsed into an untidy pile on the carpet and pushed her own bonnet off her head as her breathing became heavy and laboured.

"You... you..." she accused weakly, distrust coming too late.

She fell back.

Chapter Thirty

Henry stood in the silent front hall. He was finished with packing, finished with errands and leave-taking. The last grains of sand were sliding down the narrow neck of the hourglass. There was nothing left to keep him in London.

Fox's butler wandered from the door of the dining room. "Can I help you, sir?"

Henry nodded to the cases in the hall. "I'm leaving, Noakes. The boxes are labelled. If you could see to it."

"Of course. Any message you wish me to relay to his lordship?"

Henry shook his head. Fox would not want any of his messages. "Is he from home?"

"Oh, yes. Went tearing off for the coast not more than an hour ago. Left without hardly a word." Noakes pointed a bony finger. "You'll want to collect your mail. That came while you were out." He sniffed.

Not another request from Whitehall. They could whistle into the wind for once. If he didn't get out of London today before he saw the papers he would begin having drunken brawls.

"That young miss is a bold one." Noakes sniffed once more and took himself off.

Henry's body rooted where it was, and he took a breath. Young miss. He swiped the letter off the salver, hands fumbling to open it.

'*Dearest Henry,*' she had written in a hand that raced across the page, spitting flicks and blots of ink. His heart stopped in his chest. '*I pray this letter finds you. I beg you will call on me at your earliest convenience after the hour of eleven. I will watch for your coming. I hope...*' Here she had struck out several words, marking the page in heavy strokes. '*Please come. Yours, Beatrice.*'

Yours.

His.

"Noakes," he shouted, checking the clock and hastily folding the letter again. Noon. He'd wasted an hour already. "I'm going out."

He dashed from the house and threw himself into the saddle, surprising the hired horse enough that the mare put on a burst of speed. He raced through the streets, the sound of hooves clattering and echoing behind him.

When he arrived, he beat his fist on the door and he stepped back, putting his clothing to rights. He reached for his hat only to find he had forgotten it. No matter. Nervous fingers raked his hair into order.

"Sir," the Thornton butler admonished when he opened the door.

Henry reached into his coat, feeling for the letter, and tried not to blurt out his news. "Miss Thornton asked that I call."

"Impossible." The answer was a brick in a wall full of bricks. "The family is not home to visitors today. I will take your card—"

Henry's jaw flexed. "You've enough of my cards to paper a whole room with them. I have this letter," he insisted.

"I tell you the family is not receiving."

"And I tell you Miss Thornton is."

"Harrison," a weary voice came from the stairs. Mr Thornton stood there in his dressing robe, holding an ewer by the handle. "Let the man in." He handed the pitcher to the servant. "Fill this and send me something to eat."

"You released most of the staff for the day, sir."

"Anything will do," Thornton said. "I'll be in the library." Beatrice's father waved Henry forward and shuffled in slippered feet down the hall.

"Penny's not feeling well and we're at sixes and sevens," Mr Thornton advised, digging into his pocket and taking out a pipe.

"Nothing serious, I hope."

"Mmmm...," Mr Thornton replied, lighting his tobacco.

Henry bounced on his heels. "When Miss Thornton wrote me this morning—"

"This morning?" Mr Thornton asked, raising his eyebrows and gesturing for the letter. As he read the words, he dragged the stem of his pipe across the page and looked up, nodding, the faintest twinkle in his eye. "You're forgiven for beating the door down. If it were me—"

A tap heralded the arrival of the water and refreshments. "Ah. George. Would you fetch Miss Thornton? She isn't upstairs, so don't look for her there."

"Your pardon sir, she hasn't returned."

"What do you mean 'returned'?" Mr Thornton asked, surprised.

George's eyes darted between the two men. "She asked me to call her a hackney." He looked to the clock on the mantel. "Going on two hours ago."

"The letter says eleven." Henry pointed to the paper. "She expected to be here."

Mr Thornton muttered, then looked up at George. "Do a quick search: the garden and square. I'll check upstairs."

Henry waited as noises from the hurried search creaked and carried from around the massive house. His hair, passed through with nervous fingers, was past redemption. Where was she? Beatrice would not have dared those words without intending to give him hope.

George returned first and Mr Thornton broke in a moment later, carrying his boots under one arm and stuffing his shirt tails into the waist of his breeches. "No?" he asked, and George shook his head. "Well, then she's not home. George, did she say where she was going?"

The footman shifted on his feet. "Not exactly, sir. She had me deliver three notes this morning. Miss Summers got one—"

"She's with Meg," Henry stated. He could be at her door in ten minutes.

"The note said, ah—" George looked to the ceiling and closed his eyes, reaching into his memory. "'*You're right, Meg. I cannot settle,*' and then she said she needed her help."

"You are a terrible footman," Mr Thornton scolded with a heavy frown.

"There was no seal on them," George explained.

"Lord Fox got the third letter?" Henry asked, impatient.

"His lordship would not have been best pleased to get that one. She meant to break it off."

Henry didn't even bother hiding his smile.

"So they're with him, then," Mr Thornton speculated, buttoning his waistcoat. "As long as they're back soon—"

"Not possible." Henry felt his heart race. Lord, how he wished the simple answer were the right one. "He's gone. He left for the coast this morning." Henry could hardly blame his cousin for tearing off to the country in the wake of a personal defeat. Hadn't Henry been doing just that?

"Something's wrong," Thornton whispered, looking blindly at the carpet. His cravat hung untied about his neck.

"I'm sure she was only delayed," Henry tried to assure him. "Perhaps she met someone she knew."

Mr Thornton shook his head and his voice was certain. "She would not choose today, of all days, to stay away from home a minute more than she must. I don't like it."

At those words, Henry felt the hairs on the back of his neck stand on end exactly as they had done in the last, breathless moment before a battle as two armies faced off, no shots yet splitting the air.

He shouldered the feeling back. The truth was bound to be simpler than that. "She was last seen at Fox's on Uppercross Street. I'm starting there."

***

When they arrived at Fox's townhouse, Henry's boxes were still stacked by the front door. Everything was as he had left it.

"See if you can find out anything from the servants," Henry told George, who had seemed to trail along without invitation. He gestured to Mr Thornton. "And you take the ground floor." Henry raced up the stairs, calling out for Beatrice.

Any moment, she would step from behind the curtains or out of a doorway. She would say "Here" and laugh at him for looking so Friday-faced. Other worries jostled for attention. Had she been struck by a vehicle? Had she been spirited off by a dishonest hackney driver? It could be anything. It could be nothing.

"Beatrice," he called.

When he came to the drawing room, he pushed against the door, bumping into a barrier. The light was dim here, but he put his head around the corner to find a pile of crumpled cloth, and rope trailing away. His brain worked to make sense of it. Then he heard a soft groan.

Meg.

His heart lodged in his throat as he pushed the door, rolling her body back as gently as he could and squeezing himself around it. He bent and ran deft hands over her limbs, feeling for her pulse. It beat strong under his fingers. "In here," he shouted, ducking his head into the hall again. "Meg is insensible. Bring me some water," he commanded, scooping up the untidy bundle and rushing her onto the sofa.

Where was Beatrice? He turned in a tight circle, but there was no sign of her. He set his burden down. "Meg," he repeated over and over as he tugged at her bonds. Filthy rope threaded around her wrists, travelled to her knees and ankles. A wrinkled napkin, knotted at the back of her hair, gagged her mouth. He worked it loose first.

Mr Thornton was soon at his elbow. "The housekeeper had smelling salts," he said, waving them under Meg's nose as Henry tipped back her lolling head. He worked at her ropes, rage igniting in him at the sight of the raw welts crossing her wrists. Whoever had done this was going to pay.

"Beatrice," Meg slurred, and Henry held her face as her gaze rolled in and out of focus. "Henry?"

"Yes, Meg. Where's Beatrice?"

Meg shook her head and winced, pressing her palms against each temple. Lifting a glass of water from Mr Thornton's hands, Henry held it to her mouth. Meg gulped, sloshing it down her dress.

"Tea," she ground out. "He drugged our tea."

"Who?"

Her breathing was laboured and she gritted her teeth between each word. "Villain. Fox. Smiled as he watched me fall."

"Where's Beatrice?"

Meg shook her head, again. Henry felt cold fear and flaming rage. "She... she broke the engagement." Meg took several deep breaths, her chest rising and falling in great gusts. "Find her, Henry."

"Rest a while," he ordered, and she nodded, her eyelids falling closed.

Knuckles rapped on the drawing room door as it swung open. "I've got something, maybe," George said, his words sliding to a stop as he took in the scene. At Henry's look he went on. "A stable boy says he just came up from the coast, near Pevensey, but south along the cliffs. His master, Lord Fox, had a crew working on setting mooring rings well inland and right down to the waterline. The boy says his lordship scared him half out of his wits."

The men exchanged looks.

"There's something else," Mr Thornton added. "Downstairs, the whole library's torn apart. It looks like your cousin packed up in a damned hurry, and he wasn't careful," he said, placing a packet of letters on the table.

Henry flicked open one of them and scrolled down the page. Even with his rough school-boy French, he could pick out the evil in it. Money, information, promises. Enough evidence to get Fox hanged. Henry closed his eyes as he tried to absorb the facts, each odd exchange with Fox fitting into this new mould as cleanly as tumblers in a lock. Fox's unceasing interest in Whitehall, his preference for parties where military men would be found drinking and talking. The rough characters walking to and from his home, and the way the wax seals on Henry's letters had seemed to disintegrate before he got to them. Henry felt his stomach roil, the sharp bile settling under his heart.

Traitor. Spy. Did that blackguard have Beatrice?

Mr Thornton's voice was stern. "He didn't try to hide Miss Summers or those papers. Your cousin is headed for France and he doesn't mean to come back."

Henry leafed through the other messages, looking for clues. Fox didn't matter now. But, by God, if he had Beatrice then Henry would tear him from limb to limb.

His eyes arrested in their frantic race and he began to translate aloud. "'*Napoleon will not thank you for your threats. I am bringing him a girl. Her secrets are....*'" He wrinkled his brow. "'*Precious and will aid the effort of the war.*' Do you think he means Beatrice?"

Henry looked up to Mr Thornton and watched as the blood drained from his face. He looked like a fresh recruit at his first battle.

Finally, the older man nodded. "Yes. She will never be safe while he lives. You should know...." He wrung hands that shook. "She's—"

"She's coming back." It was the only thing that mattered. Henry's voice was flint hard. "The mooring rings. That'll be on Fox land. If France is his aim, he'll leave from there. They have a couple of hours on us, but he's in a coach." Henry made for the door and Mr Thornton rushed behind him down the stairs.

Henry shouted to Fox's staff as they stood hovering by the baize door. "Saddle Bucephalus and bring him around. Be quick about it." Then to Mr Thornton: "The pace I keep will be punishing," he advised. This was no time for deference, not when every second counted.

Mr Thornton nodded. "I'll slow you down."

In that he was quite wrong. Henry would let nothing check his flight. He bent to a case on the floor and threw the lid open. His hands waded through books and shirts, searching for what he wanted.

"I'll follow as fast as I can," Mr Thornton told him. "God help you."

Henry stood, pistol in hand.

Chapter Thirty-One

Beatrice's hands tingled. The thought found her cloth-headed and half asleep. Why did her hands tingle? She swam to the surface of consciousness.

Sensations poked, jabbing at her until she took a breath. She flinched, wrinkling her nose against the stale air and feeling the familiar rocking of a coach. Bad roads. The motion was making her stomach soft and sick. Probably she would have to open her eyes. A great, stretching sigh shook her and she curled back into a ball. Later. She would wake up later.

"You look like hell."

The voice stabbed, penetrating the fog. She furrowed her brow and put a name to it. Lord Fox. She must open her eyes.

By the dim light, she could see her wrists bound together in knots. A sharp intake of breath filled her lungs as she struggled to make sense of it. She looked up to find Lord Fox seated opposite her, waiting. His stare was flat, and she saw a pistol resting on the seat beside him. The barrel of it was pointed at her and she shivered. It was improper to be alone in a coach with a man, but impropriety seemed the last of her worries now.

Lord Fox crossed his legs and his hands rose and settled on his knee. Her eyes fastened on the stout rope he gripped in his fingers. It threaded through a heavy ring, bolted with brutal disregard into the rich wood of the panelling. He held her fast.

"Oh, Lord—" she choked and bent forward, retching over his boots. The heaving shook her, and she heard him curse as bile spattered the coach floor. She made no effort to stop it. A rope and a closed carriage, and some sort of sedative, desperately forcing the last of the vomit up her throat in a bid to get it clear of her body.

"Meg," she gasped, when she was done at last, weak and sweating. She rubbed her mouth across her short sleeve. Lord Fox wasn't listening, but was wadding up the once-rich carpet and giving his boots and the interior of the coach a cursory scrub. Still, he never set the rope aside. She gave her tired hands a feeble yank and he dragged the rope taut, jerking her bound hands against the metal ring and sending pins and needles up her arm.

She gasped, crying out and hating herself for giving him the satisfaction.

Lord Fox turned the door handle, kicking the carpet out onto the rugged country road. For a moment she saw the tall summer grass and a tired, orange sky and felt the wind and the speed. It would be dark soon. How long had she been sitting here, vulnerable and helpless? Her flesh crawled. The door snapped closed.

"Meg," she repeated, though her mouth felt thick and sour.

Lord Fox ignored her, busy with a large handkerchief, wiping away at his boots. He pushed the cloth down the top of the boot and wiped this way and that trying to mop up the sick, driving the handkerchief deeper. It was her turn to be satisfied. Her aim had been good even in the middle of a bilious attack.

"Where is my friend?" she asked.

He crumpled the linen into a ball and tossed it aside. Then he sat back and crossed his arms over his chest, never letting the rope drop from his fingers. They stared at one another across the dimness, and, though Beatrice kept her chin up, fear spread and bloomed inside her.

She prayed to heaven, biting on her lip all the while. She had been so full of hope this morning, so sure that it would all turn out right. She trembled.

Then the breath of a smile passed over his lips and she felt rage fill the deep hole scoured clean by fear. She longed to follow the lure of unconsciousness, curling into herself, but she made herself sit up, shoving steel into her spine.

"My father would never put my fortune into the hands of such an ugly, desperate stain of a man."

Lord Fox raised his eyebrows gently.

"He will know that you forced me to Scotland."

"Scotland?" Lord Fox chuckled, fingers running lightly over the pistol grip. "Is that what you think? That this is an elopement? For your money? I'm not my poor, tatty cousin, Miss Thornton."

She kept her chin up, but her mind raced for explanations.

"France," he corrected, and she fought to keep the shock from showing on her face. France. The word was a knife at her throat. There was no safety for an Englishwoman in France.

"How will you manage that?" she asked. If he wanted to gloat, she would let him. Beatrice allowed more fear to seep around her voice, pitching it higher, more quavering. "The coast guard will catch you."

"They can't be everywhere. Smugglers will take us over."

Beatrice could picture it, being tossed into the bottom of some foul-smelling longboat and rowed across the channel with empty casks and crude oarsmen. Suddenly the coach felt less like a prison and more like a last refuge.

"Hostage," she whispered to herself. And then louder, more outraged, "Am I some petticoat for you to hide behind while you scuttle off for—" She halted. "For what?

Lord Fox leaned forward. "The usual, Miss Thornton," he answered, his hot breath washing over her. "The weapon I deliver to France—to Napoleon—will bring glory. Power. I will rise to a station more suited to my—"

"You're a traitor," she ground out, understanding at last. "A filthy, loathsome, monstrous traitor. How many men have you already betrayed to their deaths?"

"A gentleman never tells," he replied with a hateful smirk. Her fingers curled into claws. *Henry.* Lord Fox would have sent him to his death without a second thought.

She spit in his face.

For a brief moment she had the pleasure of seeing his sneering expression drip with spittle before his hand reared back. He belted her across the cheek, causing pain to ring through her teeth and ears.

Darting her tongue across her lip, she tasted blood. It had been worth it. He gripped her upper arm, digging hard fingers into her flesh, and wiped his face with her bare skin. "I'm fresh out of handkerchiefs," he growled, flinging her back against the seat.

The sound of trundling wheels met her ears and she took a deep breath. Lord Fox picked up the pistol and pointed it at her heart, his face wearing a look of boredom that told her more clearly than the slap had that he would shoot her if she screamed.

"What are you going to do to me?" she asked as the carter moved along, an involuntary tremor racing through her shoulders.

He didn't answer at once, but pushed the window curtain aside with the muzzle of his gun. She could see that the sun had set now, pulling the last of the light after it.

She was in his power now, but Lord Fox would have to be vigilant every second. She only needed one of those seconds to get free.

"I would prefer not to kill you," he drawled, turning his gaze back to her.

Hope lifted a feathered wing. "Then you'll let me go?" He would be safe in France from whatever dangers pursued them on English soil, and if she could find a way to pay the boatmen to carry her back....

"I didn't say that." His lip curled.

"Then?"

He leaned forward once more and gripped her jaw with a large hand, fingers digging into the bones. He looked at her for a long moment and went on. "I know your secret," he said, watching her eyes as she fumbled and found her answers in the darkest corner. Lord Fox was her blackmailer. "I saw you that night. In the fog."

Oh, God. This was her nightmare come alive. Hollowness rolled through her, leaving her sweating and shaking, hot and cold. There was nothing left inside to absorb this feeling. Nothing left to gag up and choke out.

He knew.

She had lowered her guard once. The unfairness of it made her lash out. "You'll never get what you want," she stated, deadly serious. "You'll have to be prepared to kill me."

"Must I?" he asked with blank unconcern. "Maybe. Eventually. It would be much simpler to kill your family. Pick them off one by one until you are in a more willing frame of mind. Father, mother, little sister...."

"No."

"You're so much more cooperative already," he said, doubling the rope around his fist. "When you adjust your mind to the idea, you will see I am right. Power like yours was never made to rust on the shelf."

She was silent, letting him talk. Looking, probing for a weakness somewhere, like a mouse bumping along a wall. "I am sorry we had to fly to the coast in such a manner," he explained. "I was sure we had things well in hand when you accepted my proposal. But you tipped my hand by calling off the wedding. What prompted that, I wonder?"

She sat in stony silence.

"My poor cousin, perhaps?" She stiffened. He wasn't fit to say Henry's name. Beatrice wished more than anything in the world to have the means to wipe that smug look from Fox's mouth.

"In any case, I meant to wrest the secret of your strange ability from you after we were married."

Secret.

The word dropped into the black pool of her consciousness. Secret.

He didn't know how she worked. He didn't know what she could do. Not fully. There was opportunity there.

She felt the coach and horses turn from the road onto rougher ground and she pressed into the corner to steady herself. With the change Lord Fox became quiet. Time passed and she tried to reckon it. *Twenty minutes? Thirty?* By and by the coach came to a halt. Her ears pricked. Wind. It was stronger now, and was blowing in fits and gusts. Water. The tang of sea filled her nostrils. She didn't have to see it to know the vast channel rolling toward France under a cloudless sky was outside the carriage.

Lord Fox threw the door open to see the coachman. He was young. Hardly older than herself, though the bright moonlight turned his hair to white.

"Please, for the love of mercy—" Beatrice begged before Lord Fox's smooth hand gripped her around the neck and shoved her back to her seat.

The pad of his thumb pressed on the vein that pulsed beneath her skin and black fog began to creep in from the edges of her vision. "The horses are the reward for your silence," he said evenly to the coachman.

Lord Fox waited until they heard the sound of four horses galloping off, and then he began his work, letting go of the rope that held her. This was her chance. She cannoned into his shoulder, knocking him off balance, and jumped from the door hoping to make a getaway.

A hard blow knocked her to the ground, leaving her on her knees and gasping in the dirt.

"Do you think I didn't make precautions, Miss Thornton?" he asked, pointing to where the rope was secured, knotted in the corner of the coach. She'd been tied down all along. "That moment you're looking for? It's not coming." Then he bent to his task, pulling her over to where a long, thick rope snaked through the grass. Two shorter ropes were grappled onto it with padlocks and these were secured to the rope binding her wrist.

"A lot of effort for one small woman," she noted, pricking at his pride.

He made no answer but went on with his ruthless work, taking every care.

As she knelt on the ground her eyes followed the rope down toward the cliff's edge. It was anchored to the ground at intervals. These short ropes—she looked at her wrists, working it out—they would leapfrog over the mooring rings. She would never be untied. It was never going to be him and her and the great sky above them.

"We're going to take all the time we need, Miss Thornton," he said, taking out a pocketknife. She shrank back, crouching on her heels, and he grinned, sawing through the rope that tethered her to the coach. "I would never rush a lady."

Then he got to it, dragging her over the rough ground until she was filthy and bleeding. Beatrice bit back a moan as a sharp rock scraped the length of her leg through the thin material of her gown. She might have saved herself by walking sedately behind him, but now she was a bonfire of rage. She would not help him do a blasted thing.

As they approached the top of the cliff path, wind blew in from every direction, tossing her hair around her face. A long line of moonlight stretched over the water. There was her future laid out before her. France or death.

"Almost there," Lord Fox muttered, unlocking one padlock and attaching it to the rope below the rim of the cliff. He turned to work on the other. "The boat will meet us."

The roar of the ocean beat up from below, meeting them on the bluff. It almost masked the sounds of hooves. She had a thought that it might be the young coachman. She knew better than to expect a rescue there.

She turned to look a moment before Lord Fox, and saw Henry slide off his horse. With steady hands gripping his pistol he took deadly aim at his cousin. Fury marked every line on his face and Beatrice choked. He'd come for her, at the edge of England, and must have ridden like an angel across open country to do it.

Fox dropped the padlock and Beatrice dug in her heels, lunging for the heavy rope as her captor grappled her to him. Cold steel touched her temple and she froze.

"I'll shoot her, Harry," Fox shouted over the rush of the wind. He yanked her and inched toward the cliff. They were almost to the edge now, where the steep trail fell away to the right, travelling down the face in sharp switchbacks. Henry, not twenty feet away, had nothing to give him cover. Ropes bit into her wrists and Beatrice's eyes widened.

She threw her weight forward—a hysterical woman running from danger—and Lord Fox grabbed at her, hauling her back. When he caught her again, she shifted her weight, leaning hard into him and knocking him off his footing. She heard the roar of her name as she sent them both flying over the edge of the cliff.

She missed the lip of the cliff path and stopped short with a painful jolt, her hands catching on the rope that bound her to the larger cable. She'd counted on that. Lord Fox tumbled down past her in the dark, falling hard against the switchbacks and tumbling still farther. Relief lit her insides. It had worked. No matter that her body was in agony. Henry was here. It would soon be over.

"Beatrice." Henry's voice came again as he scrambled to the cliff's edge. She could not see his face with the moon at his back, but his voice was ragged, broken. "I thought I lost you." He dropped to his knees, his hands reaching for hers.

"My arms," she called in a small voice. They were in danger of being torn from her body.

She could hear his laboured breath. "I'll have you up in—"

A shot rang out from below, cracking through the air.

And Henry crumpled to the ground.

Chapter Thirty-Two

Beatrice opened her mouth but could not scream. Instead, the pain bore inward, gutting and wrecking. It hadn't happened. It *couldn't* have happened. She was desperate to rise, to see him. With a feral swipe she dashed aside all thought and focused. *Soft clouds, swift birds, gleaming light.*

Nothing.

She tried again, frantic to marshal her thoughts. When the lightness refused to be gathered and gleaned, she gave in to the panic. *Oh, God, Henry.*

She forced herself into silence and dangled from the ledge, listening for any sign that Henry still lived, raging against the noise of the water below. She heard a kind of scrambling sound, like a rat scratching over a rubbish heap. It was Lord Fox clambering up the narrow switchbacks, his gait uneven.

"No," Beatrice screamed as he reached her. This was no answer to her prayers.

He grabbed her ropes with filthy hands and hauled her onto the cliff path, putting his face inches from hers. A gash seamed along his hairline and his forehead was slick with blood. "Shut your mouth. I need you alive but not much more."

He vented his fury as he dragged her down the path and she let him storm at her all he liked—calling her vile names, pushing her to the ground until she felt bruised and broken—so long as he ignored Henry lying in the grass.

Finally, she stumbled onto the beach—a small sliver of loose shingle ringing a cramped bay—and looked up to the clifftop. Her throat was stiff and aching with unshed tears. Lord Fox jumped down after her, yanking her to her feet.

"Any more rebellions and I'll snap your arm." He waited for her response, but Beatrice only gave a hard look at the rock face behind him. Henry might be dead. Was a threat supposed to frighten her?

"Nothing to say for yourself? Such manners," he taunted, once more the London lord.

He checked her restraints and she held her hands close, taking the weight off shoulders burning with pain. No one else was coming. It was a simple terrifying fact. Lord Fox, satisfied that she could not hope to escape, stalked down the beach.

The cliff top loomed over her and she gave it an intense look. Henry had once told her that fear would make its reckoning. He'd said it on a sparkling bright day when the first gossamer threads began to bind them together. Not so long ago. Fear would come to collect its price, he'd said with hands that shook, but a soldier hoped to push off the settlement until the battle was over.

She took a long breath and dragged her eyes to the beach. There was the ocean with its long undulations. If Lord Fox got her out there, she was as good as dead. Her hands were useless. If she tried to jump into the water, the current would push her out to sea. If she somehow managed to rise, the wind would push her even faster.

She saw a small, flimsy boat nearly overturning as each rolling wave broke against the beach. Far too tiny for open water, she thought. Likely they would row out and meet a smuggling crew. The wheels in her mind spun, looking for anything to put to use.

Lord Fox stalked the few feet down the beach and she watched him, inventorying his clothes, buckles, buttons, coat, hair, trying to find something to grab onto, something to bite.

"There." He turned from the sea, sending a cascade of chipped rocks to the water, and ran to a bag stuffed in the hull of the tiny craft. He worked over it for a few minutes and finally raised a lantern, holding it aloft and waving it slowly back and forth. A small light, a pinprick really, winked from the distant waves.

"France awaits, Miss Thornton," he hissed, fingers biting into her flesh as he carried her down the beach and dumped her onto the rough wooden seat of the boat. He threaded her rope through a simple hinge that turned over and clamped, then pulled out his knife once again to cut away the tie that bound her to the path.

As his attention was caught elsewhere for a moment, she tugged on her restraints. The hinge tightened. Such a simple mechanism would make it easier to move her on the open sea, she supposed. But it was only a hinge.

Lord Fox gave a heavy grunt and pushed off the beach, the rocks scraping the bottom of the small boat. He clambered past her to sit at the oars, and when the rasp of rock and wood fell away, so did England.

Beatrice gripped the gunwale as he bent his body to the oars, rowing them out to sea. She looked back to the lantern light glowing from the sand as the wind-met waves threw plumes of spray across her face. Soon they were a hundred yards out, their progress slow but steady. Then her heart stopped and banged double time. A bright figure tore down the dark cliffs over the narrow track.

Henry.

She choked out a sob. She could barely make him out as he jumped the last several feet, pulling off his boots and running into the waves.

"I'll kill him," Fox shouted, digging hard into the waves, pulling them around the headland with all his strength.

A promontory of jutting rock hid Henry from sight and Beatrice looked into the hard face of Lord Fox. She watched as his lean muscles worked the water-soaked oars forward and back, scooping at the ocean and dragging it with ease. How effortless it would be for him to strike at a swimmer from the boat, to crack Henry across the skull before he even reached the craft.

If he caught them.

Though his wound would slow him, Henry would throw his life away trying to save her.

They were passing another curving bay, narrower and deeper than the last, striking away from the coastline across the mouth of it. The waves were rough and it would take precious minutes for him to get out of the first inlet if he wasn't injured. She might yet save him.

Beatrice stared at her wrists. There was no time for the perfect plan. She closed her eyes and ruthlessly cleared her mind to think. She thought of Penny's hunger for adventure, of her mama's hand resting with proud possession on the lapel of Papa's evening clothes, his swooping kiss on Mama's mouth. Of Deborah's little family, and of Henry, and his thumb pressing the crumbs of a spice cake, nibbling them off his finger. He was alive and racing down the cliff. Lightness, like horses nosing for carrots, gathered around her.

She choked up on her rope and threw her bound hands forward against the hinge, pushing it open. The rope slackened. Lord Fox flailed at the oars, knocking them loose, and shoved her back with rough hands. The rope followed after her, running nimbly through the slot.

Freedom.

"Sit," he snarled, pushing her shoulders down. But they would not go. Faster and faster she gathered lightness until she felt it, the stirrings of weightlessness. It came back to her in a rush and she lifted from her seat. Lord Fox's eyes bulged but soon she was as high as his head. His surprise didn't last long as he leapt at her legs, catching her, wrapping his arms around her knees and pinning them tight while the boat slipped out from under them.

"I knew it," he shouted, twisting his hands into her skirts to gain some purchase. "I knew you could fly. Sit down."

But he might as well have been raging against a storm. Her rising had never been about her strength, how fast she could move, or how much weight her arms would bear. Some internal mechanism was at work, more mental than physical, and though Lord Fox could slow her down, he could not stop her.

Twenty feet.

Forty.

"Jump and you might yet live," she shouted above the wind, using all her concentration to hold herself in place.

His furious gaze met hers and he redoubled his hold.

Beatrice pushed upward, stoking her power, up and up until she could see over the rim of the cliffs. Two hundred feet? She had never been so high. The wind buffeted her, but she would never return to that little boat to be dragged off to France, no matter what. Lord Fox had made his choice.

He swung his legs and leapt, vaulting to her waist and clamping her hands against her body. Beatrice gasped and twisted.

His hand fumbled for his coat.

The knife. She shouldered his arm back and pushed her hands as deep as they would go into his pocket. Her fingers brushed the handle and there was a desperate struggle before she clasped it.

Could she stab a man? Her stomach clenched against the thought. Instead, she pushed against him with all her strength and Lord Fox slipped down to her feet, his eyes promising murder. She pointed her toes and he slipped again—enough for her to drag one foot free. Fighting and frantic, he struggled to hold her and grasp her other limb.

She landed her foot against his throat and she saw his eyes widen in surprise before she gave one hard shove. He plummeted then, jerking to a short stop. He'd caught her dangling rope and twisted on the end of it like a bird caught in string. She cried out as her arms took the punishment.

"You're worthless," he snarled.

He was flagging. She could see it in his deep, ragged breathing. But he would come at her and keep coming.

"You stupid cow," he bellowed, beginning to make his way up the rope. She inched the knife from between her hands and bent the blade open. He saw it glinting in the moonlight and howled in rage.

The heaviness of Lord Fox kept the rope taut, and it began to twist and fray where she sawed, popping from his weight. He made a desperate, flying leap for her skirts. She felt the brush of his fingertips against her ripped hem and then nothing.

He fell.

Down to hell, for all she knew.

Or cared.

Beatrice watched the splash and knew it was enough to kill him. On a sob the strength went out of her. She shook as she steadily dropped, weakness stealing over her limbs, her own weight an unbearable burden.

She crashed into the water, plunging into freezing silence and darkness before she reignited the fire of her rising and surfaced, gasping. *Don't think of it. Don't think of it.* But she looked anyway. Lord Fox's body floated face down, following the current out to sea. The cut of his coat still exquisitely framed his shoulders.

Convulsions wracked her chest and her teeth chattered, taking hold of her jaw. It wasn't only the frigid water, but the broken body out there in the darkness, riding the waves. The thought made her sick, but the current dragged on her skirts. She must see to her own safety.

She could not rise into the air again. Though the shock of cold water chilled her to the bone, the current would move her far more slowly from the cliffs than the wind that buffeted above her. The ropes kept her from stroking against the water. She'd lost the knife in the fall. As it was, she was barely rising enough to keep her head above the waves. And even this store of energy would be exhausted sometime soon. It was running low now. Her mind shrank from the thought of the deepness below her.

Something hard banged her between the shoulder blades and she turned to fish it back, clinging to the oar as if to a lifeline.

***

Henry's arm dragged behind him as he struggled around the headland and he stopped to tread water. He pressed a hand against the wound in his shoulder and felt the banging in his veins and head subside.

"Beatrice," he shouted above the cursed wind. "Bea—" He took a mouthful of seawater and choked it out. His legs churned beneath him as he scanned the open ocean. He saw a light.

He breathed deeply, nostrils pinching, fighting off the pain. He wouldn't catch them—not with a bullet hole in his arm. He could only hope Fox would abandon Beatrice in his final flight to France.

Abandon. That might mean anything.

"Beatrice."

He let go of his arm and grunted, cutting through the water toward the light, his progress slow.

"Henry."

He stopped, his neck turning to find the source of the call.

"Beatrice," he shouted once more, praying for a miracle.

"I'm here."

His eyes scoured the waterline and… *there.* Her call was a thread of sound carried on the wind, but he thought he could see her. A bobbing shape catching a little moonlight. Henry made an inarticulate sound, changing his angle and pulling for the far side of the inlet.

It took too long and she wept as he got to her, ducking under the oar she held and clamping an arm around her waist. He pulled her against him and felt her shaking body. "I thought that snake had killed you," she called, sounding fierce.

He could not answer but leaned his head against hers as the ocean rose and fell.

Beatrice lifted her hands and he saw the knots. He sucked in his breath. "Can you kick at all?" Rough hemp rope, water, grit, and salt. The bastard had treated her worse than an animal.

She nodded, gulping air now.

"Did you jump from the boat?" he asked, beginning to kick his feet. "Where is Fox?"

"Gone," she answered and slipped more heavily against him.

He hitched her up, lifting and dropping with each wave. Thank heaven for that oar. "We haven't far to go. I can see the waves break against that beach there. Can you make it?"

She nodded, her body shaking with cold.

"Hold fast, my love. We have an appointment to keep. Hold fast."

Urging her on, keeping her head above water, kicking for her and for himself. These were the sum of his tasks now. She was alive. It was miracle enough. If the path to safety was arduous, he would take it.

They came near to the beach, only to find it wasn't a beach at all but little more than a rock ledge to heave themselves onto. "I can't," she gasped, her hands useless.

"You can," he urged, panting. "We wait for a wave and then..." Henry put a hand about her legs and heaved her up, feeling a ragged bolt of pain stab his shoulder.

She clung to the rocks. "Home," she breathed as she lay on her side. She sent him a weak smile. He waited for his own wave and gritted his teeth, hoisting himself up beside her with muscles that shook. The wave was perilously high, washing thinly over the rock shelf and he pulled the oar up after him, perching it against the cliff face.

"Are you hurt?" he asked.

"No." Her answer was short, breathless.

"Dearest, we can't stay here. We have to make a plan," he said, dripping water and holding her elbows as he pulled them to their feet.

Moonlight shone on her up-tilted face, but her eyes went in and out of focus. "I sent for you this morning. I was going to tell you I'd been a fool."

"Any other time, my love." He looked up at the cliff, feeling it with his hand. *Blast.* Being tossed about in the waves, he had thought it made sense to reach the nearest shore. But this was no refuge. "Beatrice," he began.

"You're bleeding," she cried, her voice a mixture of childish confusion and womanly anguish. That look of hers—Beatrice was on the verge of delirium. It didn't matter now if it was caused from exhaustion or illness. She'd be useless to help herself if it took her. Yet one more complication to factor in. One more problem to think through.

"A flesh wound. Fox always was a terrible shot," he lied. "We need to get off this rock before the water rises," he told, rubbing her arms.

"He shot you," she stated, doggedly unable to focus on anything else.

"Beatrice, listen." He crouched low to look her right in the eyes as the wind whipped her wet hair between them. His brows furrowed at what he saw. "We have to get around that headland and we have to do it soon. The tide has turned. We'll be swimming against it, but we'll run out of room if we stay. We can't go up."

"But we can," she insisted, which made him feel her forehead. She wasn't hot, but it was madness to say such a thing. Couldn't she see it?

"No. We can't climb. I wouldn't get ten feet. Swimming is hardly better, but you'll have to help me."

Beatrice looked at his shoulder again and gave it an intense stare.

"Untie the ropes," she whispered, bringing the sodden mess up between them. His heart sank. It would take too long.

He clamped his lips then nodded and bent his head, beginning to work at them. The ocean pulled and pushed against their legs, testing their balance, each cycle offering only the briefest reprieve, each wave climbing higher than the last.

Water swirled and sucked midway up his calves and a wave picked up the oar, knocking it into the water. He hardly heard the clatter. Another surge swept it toward the open water, beyond his reach. His jaw tensed and he worked faster, finally feeling the loops of the rope come apart.

Beatrice whimpered as they fell away and he saw her wrists, lacerated and bloody. The veins in her hands would be pounding. He kissed them. That monster.

"Come," he started.

Her hand pulled his sleeve and he glanced into her face, tight with anguish. "I need you to trust me. You won't understand." Her fingers wrung together. "We'll go straight up, but you'll have to hold us close to the cliff," she explained, shaking her head when he looked deep into her eyes. "I am perfectly lucid." But he could see her struggling. "Now."

"Beatrice, we have to swim." A wave knocked against him and he stumbled into her. How much longer could they stay here, perched on this sliver of England? Ten more waves? Twenty?

"I'm not swimming." She stared, commanding him. "Look at me."

Look at me. When had he ever needed to be told to do that? His eyes had wanted to do nothing else, almost from the first. And he had never seen her like this, as though holding her head on her neck was a burden. She would need to be carried on his back the whole way.

Henry calculated. No oar. A half-lamed arm. Incoming tide. He balled his fist, wishing he could knock it through Fox's teeth.

He didn't care much for heroics. Years of war had cured him of needing to be a saviour. But how much time had he spent fighting for inches of barren Spanish soil? Bleeding for villages so insignificant that there was nothing left to salvage after the battle?

Now he wanted something for himself. And he would die for it, gladly a thousand times over. *Let me keep her safe*, he prayed. There had to be a way. There had to be a way to save one woman when it really mattered to him.

How could he accept her answer that she would not swim when it meant accepting her death? Maybe he should toss her into the water and hope.

But he looked at the pounding waves and the spray whirling near the headland. It was deadly. They would be dashed against the rocks before making it out of the bay. Death lay in every direction.

"Swimming will kill you. I won't do it." Beatrice pleaded with him. But she didn't need to convince him. Not anymore.

He looked back to her face and gave her a smile. His fingers came up to her cheek. "All right, love," he relented, sealing his fate with hers. He had done that in any case. Where she was, he would stay.

"Don't look like that," she said, blinking once more.

"Like what?" he asked, pulling her close so that her hands had nowhere to go but against his chest, warming his skin through his sodden shirt.

"Like this is the end."

Resting his cheek against her hair, he hid his expression. She was delirious. Maybe that was a mercy. Beatrice wouldn't know what was coming. It would be fast, he prayed, and he would not let her out of his arms. Never again.

She touched his face and lifted his head, looking at him with a grave expression. Had she finally realized how dire things were?

Her first words dispelled that idea. "When we are back in London, I don't expect—I won't hold you to anything." Her words tumbled over each other, not making sense. "You aren't bound in honour. But, before you see what I am, I must do this."

She kissed him. Leaned right up on her tiptoes and pressed cold lips to his. He stilled as her fingers rested on his unshaven jaw, as he felt the gentle pressure of her weight curving against his. It lasted no more than a moment before she drew her head back.

"That will do. We can climb now," she said, her eyes blinking open.

Hell. "That will *not* do." It couldn't even begin to satisfy.

He forgot the rising tide and the pain radiating from his shoulder. Forgot that death hovered nearby. Remembered only the simple fact of loving her.

"We can do better." He pulled her to him, wrapping his arms about her, pressing a hand to the curve of her back and lifting her close. He felt her arms steal around his chest and bent his head. She met him halfway with a smile playing on her lips. *Impudent woman.* This is what he wanted at the end.

"I'd like to see you try," she whispered before he stopped her mouth with a kiss.

Henry held nothing back. No reserve to salvage his pride if she drew away. His hands crossed her back and his lips fitted over hers, asking her to believe that heaven was here, trapped between cliff and sea. It is, he told himself, as she offered her sweet response. It is.

She made a restless sound and shifted her hands around him, nuzzling closer. They would die here, swept away by a wave that might come any minute. *Don't think of that.*

Henry deepened the kiss, putting a whole lifetime of loving into it, willing her to forget the danger. Warmth spiralled through his blood as she followed his lead, matching his passion with her own.

Small wonder that he seemed to lose all feeling in his toes.

He couldn't feel the ocean breaking against his legs. Had some phenomenon made it still? Henry raised his head from Beatrice with great reluctance. If there was even a chance of escape he must look.

He gave a shout and pulled Beatrice close to him, reaching for the cliff and crushing her between it and him. "Don't look down," he commanded to her as he scrambled for any hold. "Keep your eyes shut," he ordered and then encountered her level gaze meeting his with a calmness that was in stark contrast to his own.

***

Beatrice's smile faltered and her lips, rosy and freshly kissed, trembled. "You won't find a rope holding us. I know it's impossible," she said, risking a look into his eyes where she read panic and confusion. She poured a portion of her lightness into him. Would he feel it? His eyes widened as hers skittered away. "You must trust me, Henry. As we go, you've got to hold onto the rocks. Not climbing them, but guiding. We'll be blown off course, otherwise. I'll hold you tight and I'll lift us up." She tried to sound matter-of-fact.

"What?"

"Not now," she answered, her voice uncompromising.

He gave her one short nod, clamping his jaw, and gripped the cliff. There was fear in his eyes. She could sense it.

The rising though, that was easy. Her body was spent, but her whole being was crowded with love for him, and the power of making him safe, of saving his life. Her curse was a gift. She felt her frame begin the long journey up and he held her close as he guided them past the rocks.

Beatrice looked at his shoulder, the sleeve dark with blood. Damn him. He'd lied about that. It was no flesh wound. A sensible man would never have dragged himself through the water to find her. She placed her lips against his neck, the only spot she could reach, and kissed him. His chin rested on the top of her head.

She could feel how rigidly he held himself, how he was hardly breathing, how his heart was racing. It was enough to hold him, she told herself. It was enough. Thinking of other things would slow her down. Thinking of how things would change now that he knew—she felt her momentum check and beat the thought back, resuming her steady pace.

She was saving his life.

Nothing else mattered.

"Wait," he called, his voice sounding tight in her ear as he steered them away from the cliff and a small overhang of rock. He cupped the back of her head with one hand as they came around the jutting mass. It was like him to protect her.

"Are we nearing the top?" she asked, looking at his chin. There was nothing to see there. No expression to be upset and heartbroken by.

He gave a short, careful nod, as though he was afraid of overturning a boat. The wind began rolling and gusting and he pressed her more firmly against the wall of the cliff, his breath mixing with hers. But finally his grip met sturdy, coast grass and he yanked them over the lip of the precipice to safety. He fell against her and rolled away.

A shaking weakness met her at once. Her vision went black along the edges, closing in as a wave of fatigue unleashed.

"Beatrice," he cried. It seemed to come from a long way and it was too difficult to tell if he was pleased or angry. His hands were on her face, but she couldn't think.

The darkness crashed in on her, pulling her down once more.

Chapter Thirty-Three

"Should we move them?" Beatrice's ears pricked at the sound of the voice. George? Though what her father's footman should be doing here was beyond her present powers of reason. "They're not at all decent."

"No. It's not long now." Papa. A wave of consciousness rose to meet him, but she could not quite stir. The steady rocking of the coach was putting her to sleep, but one word popped through to the surface of her thoughts. *Coach.* She was in a coach. How silly it was to be waking like this for a second time. "If we take her from him he'll fight us again."

Beatrice cracked her eyes. A lantern set into the wall threw strange shadows, illuminating the figures on the seat opposite her. She was stiff and sore, and her damp clothes clung to her, but she wasn't cold. Her fingers found the rough wool blanket tucked around her reclining form. A heavy arm clasped her loosely around her waist.

"I wish he would wake. We'll have a devil of a time finding the place if his directions were no good."

Henry. Beatrice turned, feeling the gentle rise and fall of his chest under her head. She ran her fingers down his arm and rested them over the rough hand encircling her. Sea drenched though she was, she would not wish herself at her journey's end. She matched her breath to his.

Papa gave a weary sigh. "I am getting too old for this." Papa's hand waved toward her seat. "Let him take over."

Beatrice felt the sharp prod of wakefulness again.

"It's a sure thing," George said, slipping into informality. That was always his problem. "They were alone. The captain bleedin' to death, half out of his mind, and he still wouldn't let go of her. He'll have to wed her now. No choice."

The veil of exhaustion disappeared. *No choice.* Dreadful words. If the issue was one of honour, he would be duty-bound to marry her. Papa would call him on the carpet and tell him what he'd seen. Beatrice blushed hot to imagine it spoken aloud as a magistrate might read charges from the bench. Henry would step to the mark, a condemned man, to make his proposals.

He would be kind. She couldn't imagine him any other way. It wasn't in him to reprove and shame her, and nothing would change that. But the ugly thought persisted, waiting. Would his stomach turn at the thought of passing this "thing" on to his children? Would he find her unnatural?

At last the coach rumbled to a stop, swinging gently as her father and George stepped out. The wool blanket picked and tugged along her scratched wrists, but she lifted Henry's hand, her heart wrenching as he moaned and hauled her against him. She brushed a damp lock of hair from his forehead and touched his skin as he had done to her on those rocks. No fever.

"My girl." Papa swung the door back and Beatrice jerked her hand from Henry. "I wondered if—" He pulled her from the coach and wrapped her in a fierce embrace, pushing back her hair from her face over and over as he struggled to keep his composure.

For a moment he lost his words. When they returned, they came in a rush. "I spoke with the housekeeper. She is making up beds for us." He touched her hair again.

She looked past him to the house, a grey shadow in the darkness. The air smelled fresh off the ocean. "Where are we?" she asked but did not wait to hear his reply. It hardly mattered. Nothing mattered if Henry would not wake. She scrambled to the coach but Papa caught her back.

"Servants are coming to carry Captain Gracechurch. The surgeon has been called. He lost a deal of blood." He tugged her toward the heavy front door.

The dark yard began to fill with five or six soft-footed servants, men and women in their night things bleary-eyed and staring at the sight of her. The coach lanterns shone on her, barefoot in her crumpled muslin dress, damp hair snarling down her back, blood staining her hands. Like a wild thing Beatrice turned, gravel digging into her feet as she rushed back to the coach.

"Careful," she told the men lifting Henry. They eased him from his seat and slung his body between two manservants. Beatrice reached to hold the hand that hung limp. His skin glowed white in the moonlight.

At the entry hall, where the servants hovered indecisively, she told them. "A table." Several girls scurried forward into the dining room, streaming around Henry and his procession, dragging heavy chairs back against the wall.

"Gently," Beatrice coaxed as they set him down, though it seemed unnecessary. These men treated Henry as carefully as they would a newborn babe. "We'll need clean linen and hot water," she said, directing a plump middle-aged woman who was standing nearby, the housekeeper of the small domestic staff.

"They're coming, miss. Won't be five minutes 'afore everything is laid out ready for the surgeon." The woman was obliging, but her eyes were riveted to Beatrice. She probably had never seen anyone so dishevelled. "I sent a girl to wake the mistress. The master is laid up with his injury still."

Beatrice had no patience to absorb the information. "Have you extra candles and candlesticks? The fire here should be stoked."

"Come now," Papa urged, standing at her side. "This good woman will see to the captain. You need some rest."

Beatrice looked down at Henry, his body stretched the length of the table, his shirt hanging off him in limp folds, his feet as bare as her own. She was avoiding looking at the wound, and, when she forced herself to glance at his shoulder, she sucked her lip in her mouth, biting down on the flesh. Papa, she supposed, had tied a wad of linen around it, but it was soaked with blood.

"I'm not leaving him," she whispered, her eyes taking in the lips stretched taut against the pain, his skin pallid.

Papa gave her a hard stare and when she did not give way, he nodded. He rubbed a hand over bleary eyes. "I'm all in, honeybee."

"You go. I'll come up when he's been seen to," she said. She gave him a brief smile, calculated to ease his worries, and watched his heavy tread as he went on his way. *Goodnight, Papa.*

The room became a frenzy of activity as servants rushed to ready the room. The housekeeper set out an armful of supplies. "Best clean him up before the surgeon comes."

"I'll do it if you have some shears," Beatrice offered before she could regret it. She would have to look at the wound now.

A woman with a quilted dressing gown cinched around a comfortable waist, her long brown hair threaded with grey, rushed into the room. "Mrs Abbot. Nell says that—" She approached the table, her lips opening and closing in tiny gasps as she took in the sight. She clasped a hand to her mouth, letting out a small wail. The housekeeper gathered her into a close embrace.

"Hold his hand," Beatrice told her, sparing the woman some pity. Henry was restless, moaning out in his delirium, and the woman would feel better if she had something to do. It was shocking to have strangers decamp on your doorstep, bloodied and broken, in the middle of the night. "You don't have to look."

The woman's head jerked up and she sniffed, letting go of Mrs Abbot. Then she did as she was bid, cradling Henry's rough hand between her own.

Beatrice breathed through her nose, willing her hand to stop shaking. It wasn't Henry here. It was a dress that needed sewing, a piece of linen that needed hemming. She cut through the blood-soaked cloth binding his shoulder and lifted the wad of material—Papa's cravat—setting it aside.

The shirt was next. From neck to cuff she made long, jagged cuts, and the woman at her side gently tugged the pieces away. Beatrice took up a clean cloth, dipping it into a basin of water again and again to remove the worst of the crimson stain. She worked her way to the centre as Henry moved restlessly on the table, her voice crooning to him.

When she had finished, the heart of the injury itself was black, deep, and continued to seep bright blood. Beatrice gave it one long look and felt her knees go soft, leaning on the table with both hands as her hot tears splashed against his skin.

She stayed like that, fighting off the fright and the heavy lassitude that seemed to charge at her from the dark corners of the room, until she heard the surgeon's voice carrying from the head of the table.

"Ma'am, he's almost thrashing."

Beatrice raised her head, dashing the tears from her cheeks. "I'll hold him." She found the housekeeper. "You can hold his legs," Beatrice directed. Mrs Abbot had done quick work. Hot water and clean linen were ready. The room was ablaze with light and cleared of onlookers.

These brisk, dispassionate observations crashed into the brick wall of Henry lying on the hard table, a light sheet folded at his stomach. Beads of sweat dotted his brow, and his head strained from side to side, pulling the cords of his neck into high relief. His was a soldier's body, well muscled and fit, but her eyes traced over the maze of criss-crossing scars marking his skin. So many of them. She might have lost him a dozen times before tonight.

The woman at her side hovered fingers over a long purple mark across his ribs. She could not seem to look away.

"If you'll take his other hand," Beatrice suggested gently, ignoring the sharp sting of tears that prickled her nose.

"Has he woken?" the surgeon asked, sorting his instruments.

"No."

"Better if he's out for this," he answered, turning and giving her a startled look. Maybe he didn't want women in his surgery. "Will you look at that?" he asked the older woman, nodding at Henry's form, no longer restive.

"Ready?" prodded Beatrice, and the surgeon bent to examine the wound. A sharp intake of breath drew her attention. The poor woman seemed to be feeling it keenly.

"Have him bite on this," the surgeon said, nudging Beatrice's hand with a stick. "No knowing how long it'll take."

Beatrice fitted it between Henry's clenched teeth and gripped his free hand as the surgeon bent over his work. The sounds of it, wet scraping, and blood sucking in and out of the wound, made her shake. Henry's back arched tightly above the table as he crushed her hand in his. Short, snuffing breaths came from his nose. She heard herself cry out.

Finally, she heard the ping of metal on metal. A pistol ball rolled in a basin. The surgeon grunted. It was done.

He sewed the wound shut with the swiftness of long practice, and the older woman handed him a fresh towel. "Tell me it's good news, Mr Fletcher?" She looked with intense, red-rimmed eyes at his unconscious patient.

"Promising, ma'am," he answered. "The ball came out in one piece and I found no bits of cloth in the hole. It hit no bone. He's young and healthy. Though I should like to know how he got shot in Sussex." He looked at Henry's form, still now. "He'll do."

Beatrice closed her eyes, offering up a silent prayer as the woman spoke, "When I saw him looking like that..." Her lips trembled into a smile as her eyes rested on Henry's form. "Bless you."

"I will call again tomorrow." Mr Fletcher donned his coat and picked up his bag. Good night, miss," he said to Beatrice. "Your assistance was excellent. And good night, Mrs Gracechurch."

Mrs Gracechurch. Beatrice grew sensible of her own hand clutching Henry's, of the way she had taken it as her right to manage and direct the servants in their care of him, of the sad, sweet-faced woman standing at the hearth of the long, dark-panelled dining room that looked exactly as Henry's home should look.

Beatrice was near Pevensey in the strong stone house set back from the sea. Past the time for daffodils.

Henry's mother walked over to the table and bent over her son's face, planting a kiss against his temple, wearing a look she had seen Mama wear, joy mixed up with pain. Beatrice stepped back at once, though Mrs Gracechurch hardly seemed to notice her.

"Mrs Abbot," Mrs Gracechurch called. "Find a board long enough for our boy to sleep on tonight. Have Jem and Frank carry Master Henry up..." She paused, choking on the words. "To his old room. I will sit with him tonight. What a surprise Mr Gracechurch and the others will have when they wake."

"That they will, mistress," Mrs Abbot replied, seeming happier to be taking orders from her mistress than from some bedraggled chit of a girl she'd never seen before. "He should have come straight home from those nasty foreign parts instead of dawdling in London, getting himself shot. But we will have him fighting fit in no time."

Servants moved through the room as before and Beatrice stood by feeling as though she was in the rush of an outgoing tide. She was the outsider here. Their young soldier had come home from the wars.

The last of them went through the doorway, but Henry's mother turned to Beatrice. "Perhaps you will let me see to your wrists?"

Beatrice turned her palms over as a child would, waiting for fingernails to be inspected. "Yes, ma'am." Now that Henry was settled, throbbing pain burned across the lacerations and up her arms.

Mrs. Gracechurch was gentle as she cleaned the scrapes and applied a salve. As she wound the bandages around the cuts on Beatrice's wrists, Mrs Gracechurch told her, "You kept your head better than I did. I understand it was you and your father who found my son and brought him here. I want to thank you."

"No," Beatrice exclaimed. And then explained, "No, ma'am. Henry, Captain Gracechurch, would not be injured if not for me. He acted with great honour."

"Then he has not changed so very much since I sent him off," his mother replied, her voice betraying that worry. She took a long, clean breath, beginning to douse the candle flames. "You called him by his Christian name. I did not understand before that you are acquainted with him. May I know your name?"

"Name? Yes, ma'am, of course. Thornton." Beatrice almost missed the flick of her hostess's eyebrow. "My father is Mr Charles Thornton of Dorset. I am his second daughter."

"Beatrice." Mrs Gracechurch said her name and her eyes seemed to size Beatrice up in one go, looking for a long, quiet moment into her face.

At last she nodded. "His letters are full of you."

***

Within her room, Beatrice kept her vigil by the fire until the deep black of night turned into a heavy grey. No one would be abroad for more than an hour yet. And even then, the servants would be stepping, soft-footed, around the kitchens.

Her muscles rebelled as she unfolded herself from the depths of the chair and felt along the drying rack. The chemise and petticoat were wholly dry, and the dress was only damp along the thickest seams.

She dressed quickly and edged her way to Papa's room in her bare feet, shaking him awake. He roused at her whisper. "We've got to go," she said, helping him upright.

He rubbed a heavy hand over his face and sat up. "What are you talking about?"

Beatrice tiptoed around the room, plucking up his clothes and piling them on the counterpane. "It's impossible for me to stay here in his family home," she explained and squirmed a little at the way Papa's brow rose at "his." "You know what it looks like."

"Like you belong here," he declared, shaking off sleep and cutting through to the heart of it. "It's what I wish."

"It looks like he got to choose. He didn't."

"No? I found you less than a hundred yards from the coach, passed out on the ground. The captain was doing his best to bleed to death while holding onto you in what, I must say, was a compromising position," Papa stated, sounding only sort of disapproving and more than half hopeful. How could she allow it? Papa playing the concerned father, satisfied by an engagement without knowing Henry's mind?

"He knows about me," she admitted, sinking onto the edge of the bed next to her father. "He knows."

Papa's hand covered hers and they stared for a long moment into the dying fire.

"Your mother accepted things well enough."

Beatrice nodded and wiped her cheeks with the back of her hand. "What choice did she have? Henry is not yet tied to me, and what do you suppose is going to happen, Papa, now that he has seen what I can do?" She made a noise in the back of her throat.

"He loves you," Papa told her, his voice low and ferocious. "And you love him. It is the ordinary course of events."

"Nothing is ordinary. Because of me he has been shot, and his cousin is dead," she stuttered. The image of Henry laid out on that table pushed away the uglier one of Lord Fox face down in the ocean. But it was all ugly.

"How will he sort himself out if I stay here, making myself at home while he is yet so weak, expecting a proposal he isn't sure he wants to make?"

"He's sure enough. He'll have to."

"I don't want him to *have* to."

Papa allowed her to have her way then. He left to see to the carriage, but Beatrice had one more tryst to keep.

Making her way to Henry's room, she kept close to the walls where the floorboards could not signal her passage and swung back his door on noiseless hinges.

He wouldn't have to know about this visit. It wouldn't be one more burden for him to carry, to shrug off when and if he found her power too much to accept.

The fire's glow was brighter here, but Beatrice was halfway across the room before she noticed the slumbering form of Henry's mother curled into a chair as though her mere presence would make him well. Maybe it would. Mrs Gracechurch would watch over Henry when Beatrice took her leave in the chilly, Sussex fog. His mother would be there to make sure he was not careless or incautious, and that he was getting the care he needed.

Beatrice crept closer to the bed where she noted a cup of water near at hand, the soft pillows removed. Henry lay still but for the even rise and fall of his chest as he slept, and the bandage wrapping his shoulder was clean and white. She longed to slip her hand in his and breathe with him until his eyes blinked open. Instead, she leaned over him, placing a cool hand on his forehead.

She dared a kiss and went.

Chapter Thirty-Four

Penny's laughter echoed across the empty ballroom of Number Six, jerking Beatrice from her thoughts. Beatrice gathered the lightness. She had only to think of Henry, alive, and it rushed upon her. She shot from the floor to the ceiling, cupping the flame dancing on the end of a reedy taper, willing the candles on the chandelier to take.

Penny was beating her in this game, though she overshot the marks, climbed too fast so that her flame blew out, and she landed hard, but she was improving fast.

"Done," Penny exclaimed, her chandelier ablaze, sending light bouncing off the mirrors and around the room. Beatrice's hand arrested, straining for the last candle. *Blast.*

"I surrender," Beatrice called out, winded. "Blow them out. Carefully. Bottom to top."

She extinguished her own candles, trying to focus on the guttering as each flame died, the curl of smoke that wound in the air, and the light that faded as they went about their task. But it wasn't enough to distract her from other thoughts that crowded back like noisome birds at her feet.

She rubbed the back of her neck.

Fourteen days, and neither sight nor sound of Henry. He didn't deserve her concern, she thought, feeding a sort of indignation. But the thought petered out. No amount of pretended anger could turn him into a callous, unfeeling brute. He was surely still as he had always been, honourable, kind, steady. Knowing what he knew, he simply couldn't bring himself to court her again.

Beatrice bit her lip. The sound of Penny working at her task intruded and she shook her head bracingly. Better to know how things stood now than after they were bound together inextricably.

"Duck." Penny laughed, and Beatrice dropped fast, feeling a dull stinging through the balls of her feet as she landed.

"You'll take my head off if you keep doing that." Beatrice watched as her sister flew past her, gradually slowing to a stop as she ran out of momentum. Penny had taken to crouching against a wall and pushing off, discovering she could travel horizontally for considerable distances.

The smile Beatrice turned on her sister was real. Why had she never thought of that? But her own rough apprenticeship had been about forcing her power into a strongbox. Flying would have been beyond the question. Penny, however, was determined to do it properly. It was, she'd explained with extreme patience, simply a matter of thinking the right thoughts.

"Are you quite finished?" she asked as Penny descended. "Mama wants you this afternoon. There's packing to be done."

Penny's eyes shone and she squealed. "Packing? Are we finally going home?"

Beatrice nodded and this time the smile did not quite reach her eyes. The journey would take them west. Away from London, and further from the sturdy country house set near the sea. "Mama thought that doing it all in one day—no staying overnight at an inn—could be managed."

"You did it. It was you who persuaded her."

She had. "Only a little."

Penny snorted. "Only a little."

"Mama soon saw the sense of it. Thorndene will protect you far better than a townhouse in the heart of London." There was a part of this journey Penny would not care for at all. Beatrice broke the news. "You'll have to travel as an invalid."

"Stupid," Penny muttered. "Never felt better in my life."

"I know you're upset, cooped up inside the house while the sun is shining, but you must allow Mama these precautions. Exposure is dangerous." Penny's expression was mulish and Beatrice brushed a shaking hand against her leaf-green skirts, trying to hide what no one could see. The long black bruises running up her legs and over her body had turned to sickly yellow, ugly but fading.

Beatrice prayed that Penny would never fully understand how dangerous their secret was.

She blinked the image away and began to remove the chairs and curtains that ensured their privacy from the door. "You must admit that Mama has unbent a good deal."

Penny's laugh was rueful. "You've got Mama wrapped around your thumb. She's ransacked Madame Durand's shop for you. It is an improvement," she noted, nodding at the dress. Beatrice tugged at the cuffs of the long, tight sleeves.

Penny went on. "And she agreed to let you train me. If there's anything you really want from Mama, now is the time to ask."

Beatrice murmured nothings. What she really wanted was not in Mama's power to grant.

"Off you go," Beatrice told her, scooting Penny toward the stairs as she peeled away to the drawing room. She scooped up a book she'd not been reading for days and tucked her feet up under her on the sofa. Here was an empty hour. She might safely sit by herself and let her face wear the same expression as her heart without worrying that anyone would want to ask her what the matter was. She didn't have to reassure anxious parents that she was fine or that she was going to be fine.

She rubbed a hand over her face, pinching the bridge of her nose. The nearest thing she'd had from Henry was a letter Papa had brought her last week. It was from his mother, assuring the Thorntons that Henry was on the mend, sitting up and taking soup. No fever or infection.

From his *mother*.

Beatrice stared out the window for a long while then withdrew the note that she had tucked between the pages of the book. *'You are to call for me the moment you can bear a visit. Meg.'* Her concern at such a time had been precious. Beatrice unfolded and refolded the paper, now as soft as fabric. She should call on Meg today. The soreness and fatigue were no longer an excuse. Nor was the worry that she would spend the whole of the visit howling into Meg's shoulder. Of course she would. But Meg would simply stuff a handkerchief at her.

The mantel clock chimed the hour and Beatrice stood in a flurry of skirts. It wasn't good to be sitting so long in her own company. Not now.

Before she could decide on a direction, Mama walked in, her face a little flushed and her hands pleating a light shawl. "There you are. You're wanted in the library."

Beatrice made her expression pleasantly neutral—an expression she had practiced in the mirror this week—and followed Mama from the room. She was to have a whispered conference with her parents around the library fire. It would be a fitting end to her disastrous Season.

Papa stepped into the hall, closing the library door behind him, crowding them against the dark panelling. "Now, Beatrice..." he said, glancing over his shoulder and tenting his hands. Beatrice's eyes got big. Did Papa mean to begin the discussion out here where anyone might pass?

"Charles," Mama cautioned, taking him by the arm and pulling him away from the door. Strange. "This is not yours to manage." She lifted her chin and nodded Beatrice toward the library. "Go on in."

Curious, Beatrice did as she was bid and walked in, only to have her heart leap into her throat.

Henry.

Her slippers were rooted to one end of the Aubusson carpet and, across the room, his Hessians rested on the other. He was standing upright, wearing his military bearing like an invisible uniform, waiting for her.

Mama's hand covered hers and peeled it from the door handle. Beatrice turned to watch her mother draw the door closed behind her. The latch clicked shut and the quietness stretched thin. Beatrice turned back to Henry to encounter an expression that told her nothing.

When he spoke, his voice was tight. "My mother informed me that you hardly stayed the night before you left. I was sorry I was not in any condition to see you off properly."

Beatrice coloured. "I wrote to your mother expressing thanks for her hospitality."

"A perfect bread and butter letter. She read it out, and even I, who read it fifty times, could not find any trace of you."

"It was correct."

"As correct as a clerk adding up his sums." He stood near the fire, a little tired around the eyes, she thought, his mouth drawn. Was he eating as he ought? "It was obvious to me you were running away. That letter was a correct little snub."

"At least I wrote one," she said, stung.

A gleam of something leaped in his eyes and his head cocked. "What was I supposed to write, Beatrice? Polite nothings? My feelings could hardly be characterized as polite. Can you imagine what they were?" he asked, and a frisson of warmth went up her neck. "I'll tell you. Desperate to follow after you, laid up in a sickbed, surrounded by a loving family I wished to Jericho. All of them only too willing to take a dictated letter I had no intention of giving. You called me brave once," he said, crossing his arms. "But I am not brave enough to say aloud, as my mother sat at my bedside, *'Dearest, I am longing for you.'*"

He hadn't moved an inch, but all at once she felt the hot flush of intimacy, wishing such a letter had been written in his own hand. Her fingers tugged again on the cuff of her dress.

"Am I so frightening? You won't come any closer?" he asked, flicking her pride. She stepped forward, behind a chair, resting anxious hands on the curved wooden back. Now she was ten steps nearer to him and she felt it as she might feel the warmth of a fire.

"Why did you leave my home?"

His home. How could she explain? She couldn't sleep under his roof and eat bread at his table until he made up his mind.

So she said, "Mama would have worried."

"Ours is only a modest estate, but we could surely have run the cost of sending a letter. You and your father were exhausted, and our post service is good. I daresay it would even have arrived before you did."

"I had no wish to put your family to any trouble."

"My mother credits you with saving the life of her child, Beatrice. Nothing would be too much trouble. You could ask for her firstborn and she would give him to you." The ghost of a smile crossed his face and then he looked up, eyes bright. "But she could make no sense of your departure, particularly when, as she told me, you looked half dead on your feet when they brought me in. She was worried for you." His look took her in and she withstood the scrutiny, already knowing what he would see. Scrapes, bruises, eyes smudged by sleeplessness, scars. "I was more than worried."

She put a hand up to her hair, tucking in the strays. "I am recovered, as you see."

"Recovered?" he asked, crossing the carpet and hefting the chair, moving it aside with a thump. It would be silly to run from him and she wasn't sure he wouldn't chase her down.

Henry picked up her hand and turned it over so that her wrist was exposed—the deep red slashes showing up brightly against the unforgiving white muslin ruffle. Her heart beat loudly in her ears and she fought to keep her hand steady. He could see that she would never be recovered.

"When you were on that table," she murmured, too intent to be embarrassed. "I saw your scars." There was a long pause. "Do you forget you have them?"

He raised his eyes, lingering over the gash that split her eyebrow. "No," he answered.

Good. Though her heart sank. She hadn't wanted platitudes. None of Mama's "good as new in no time."

He continued. "I am reminded every time I look in a mirror."

Every time. She would see Lord Fox in these disfigurations every time. "That's a shame."

"Shame? Not that. A reminder. I think how I healed once. They give me hope I can heal again, from wounds that are harder to see. So, you know, these scars are useful."

Remembrance and resiliency. These weren't what she wanted. She wanted her scars to disappear. Beatrice bent her free wrist back and forth, feeling a sharp tug on new skin, feeling the weight of the ropes that had been there. When the angry redness faded, leaving white lines criss-crossing her wrists, she might have reason to be glad of such a lesson.

A gentle finger traced over the marks. "Your father says Fox is dead."

She flinched from his grasp and hugged her arms about her waist. It was her fault. "He was your cousin and friend."

His expression was grim. "Not if he could do that to you. He was never my friend. He let me see what he wanted me to see and hid the rest." He lifted her hand away from her waist and held it lightly, examining her scars once more. His eyes missed nothing.

She held her breath.

"Why did you really run away from me?" he asked, cupping her hand in his and resting both around the curve of his neck where she felt the close-cropped hair meet his collar.

She wanted to deny it, to make up another of her excuses. She even began to shake her head. And then she remembered the bitterness in his voice. *He let me see what he wanted me to see and hid the rest.* Beatrice glanced to where Aunt Martha looked down from her portrait. No more lies. "Yes. I was frantic to get away. I dreaded meeting your family."

"My family? They stand ready to love you."

"What choice would you have had if I stayed?" She raised her free hand quickly and pressed fingers to his lips, stopping the words that would have flowed between them. "None. They all thought you had no choice but to offer for me."

He pulled her hand from his mouth and pressed it to his chest. It had lain there once before. "No choice but the one I already made weeks ago, Beatrice."

"That was before you knew what I was," she insisted.

His brows knit together. "What you are? You saved our lives on that rock. You rose up in thin air and lifted me with you." How long had she thought to keep her power a secret from him, and he stood there saying it out loud like it wasn't a weight that crushed her. "What you are is enormously brave. I *love* what you are."

"And I remember telling you I held you to nothing, expected nothing." Her voice was firm. She made sure it was.

"Desired nothing?" he added, watching her face as she tried to wash it clean of wanting him. "Tell me that's so."

She closed her eyes for a moment. Her chin tightened and she blinked her eyes open again. "I cannot."

"I spoke with your father," he began, his voice rough, threaded through with hope.

He had to know the whole of it. "Did he tell you how they found me, the day I first rose? The three of us, frightened out of our wits. Frightened enough to bury ourselves in the country for seven years. Frightened enough to confine me to one room for almost a whole year. Did he tell you how my mother has dreaded discovery, becoming less herself each day? Did he tell you that our—my—children might inherit this curse? Society is cruel, Henry. *Lord Fox* was cruel. If it was found out, there is little hope we would find others merciful. That is your life, if we wed," she stated, sparing him nothing.

His hand slipped down and she felt his arm encircle her waist. He put another hand to her face, rubbing her cheek with his thumb, and gave her such a look as she had never hoped to have again— tender and solemn, full of promises.

"Peace," he whispered, leaning his forehead against hers, breathing in the same air that left her body. "You think I haven't had chances to consider? Two weeks of wondering, Beatrice. And today your parents spent hours offering me every opportunity to run back to Sussex, to stalk about muddy cow pastures, cursing God and taking your secret to my grave." His cheek lifted with a lopsided smile. "At one point in their recitation, I feared that I would be forced to run off and marry you out of hand." He shook his head. "How can you think knowing about your gift would change how I feel?"

She caught her lower lip between her teeth. *Gift*.

Still. "What if I have children and they—?" she asked, unable to articulate the whole of it.

His eyes blazed and he embraced her so tightly that her toes lifted from the ground. "*We*, Beatrice Thornton. *Our* children. And I pray they have a fraction of their mother's magic." He looked quite fierce about it, the small scar on his chin white against his ruddy skin, daring her to believe him. She searched her heart for any lingering fog of doubt, only to find it had receded.

Henry loved her.

He would always love her.

Rising had not changed that.

Joy cast loose from its tether and this time she didn't fight it. Instead, she leaned up to plant a warm kiss against his chin.

"Don't distract me during my proposals," he scolded, rubbing his rough cheek against hers, his mouth above her ear. "I want you to promise to marry me."

"I will," she nodded, tugging a handkerchief free from her bodice. Tears pooled in her eyes.

"Soon." It wasn't a question.

She nodded again, catching the tears before they fell. Henry's eyes narrowed, capturing her hand. Her fingers held the white scrap of fabric bordered by an uneven row of forget-me-nots.

"You little thief. You had it all along."

She began to laugh, and this time there was no hint of a shadow colouring the sound. "Aren't you going to kiss me?"

His head bent over hers and he gave her a grin that curled her fingers into her palms. But he waited, teasing out the moment, giving her time to imagine the future stretching beyond the horizon.

When she resolved to close the gap herself, he whispered against her lips, "Hold onto something."

ABOUT THE AUTHOR

Keira graduated from BYU with a B.A. in Humanities, and lives in Portland, Oregon with her husband and five children.

Over the last decade, she has co-authored *The Uncrushable Jersey Dress*, a blog and Facebook page dedicated to mid-century author, Betty Neels. Cultivating this corner of fandom confirmed the suspicion that people who like sweet romances are as smart, funny, and are as interesting as readers of any other genre.

When Keira is not busy avoiding volunteerism at her kids' schools like it is the literal plague, she enjoys scoring a deal at Goodwill, repainting her rooms an unnecessary amount of times, and being seized by sudden enthusiasms.

Take Tea with Keira at:
keiradominguez.com
facebook.com/keiradominguez8/
twitter.com/keira_dominguez
instagram.com/keiradominguezwrites

www.BOROUGHSPUBLISHINGGROUP.COM

If you enjoyed this book, please write a review. Our authors appreciate the feedback, and it helps future readers find books they love. We welcome your comments and invite you to send them to info@boroughspublishinggroup.com. Follow us on Facebook, Twitter and Instagram, and be sure to sign up for our newsletter for surprises and new releases from your favorite authors.

Are you an aspiring writer? Check out www.boroughspublishinggroup.com/submit and see if we can help you make your dreams come true.

CPSIA information can be obtained
at www.ICGtesting.com
Printed in the USA
FSHW011952300421
81022FS